The Sword of Elilah

Genesis

C.F. Rose

THE SWORD OF ELILAH: GENESIS

Published by Redwood Moon Publishing

Cover art by J. Caleb Design

This book is a work of fiction. Names, characters, places, and incidents are products of the author's imagination, and any resemblance to actual events or locales or persons, living or dead, is entirely coincidental.

Copyright © 2025 by Chelsea Fryer

https://swordofelilah.wixsite.com/rose

ISBN 979-8-9926820-0-7 (pbk)

ISBN979-8-9926820-1-4 (hc)

ISBN 979-8-9926820-2-1 (eBook)

While the Sword of Elilah takes place in a fantastical land, much of it is rooted in our own world. The elven culture is largely based off of Indigenous American cultures, including the Wampanoag, the Navajo/Diné, the Keetoowah, and the Ojibwe, among others. The violence, including rape, sexual abuse, and slavery featured in the Sword of Elilah is a call to fight against such injustices that occur in our world every day. Please consider donating to a charity that supports Indigenous Peoples or victims of violence and slavery, such as Stronghearts Native Helpline, Not Our Native Daughters, or Free the Slaves.

The Sword of Elilah Trilogy:

Genesis

Legacy

Restoration

Additional books set in this universe
follow the other divine weapons:

The War Hammer of Karthais

The Bow of Lillian

The Shield of Ziad

The Lance of Justar

The Gauntlet of Carve

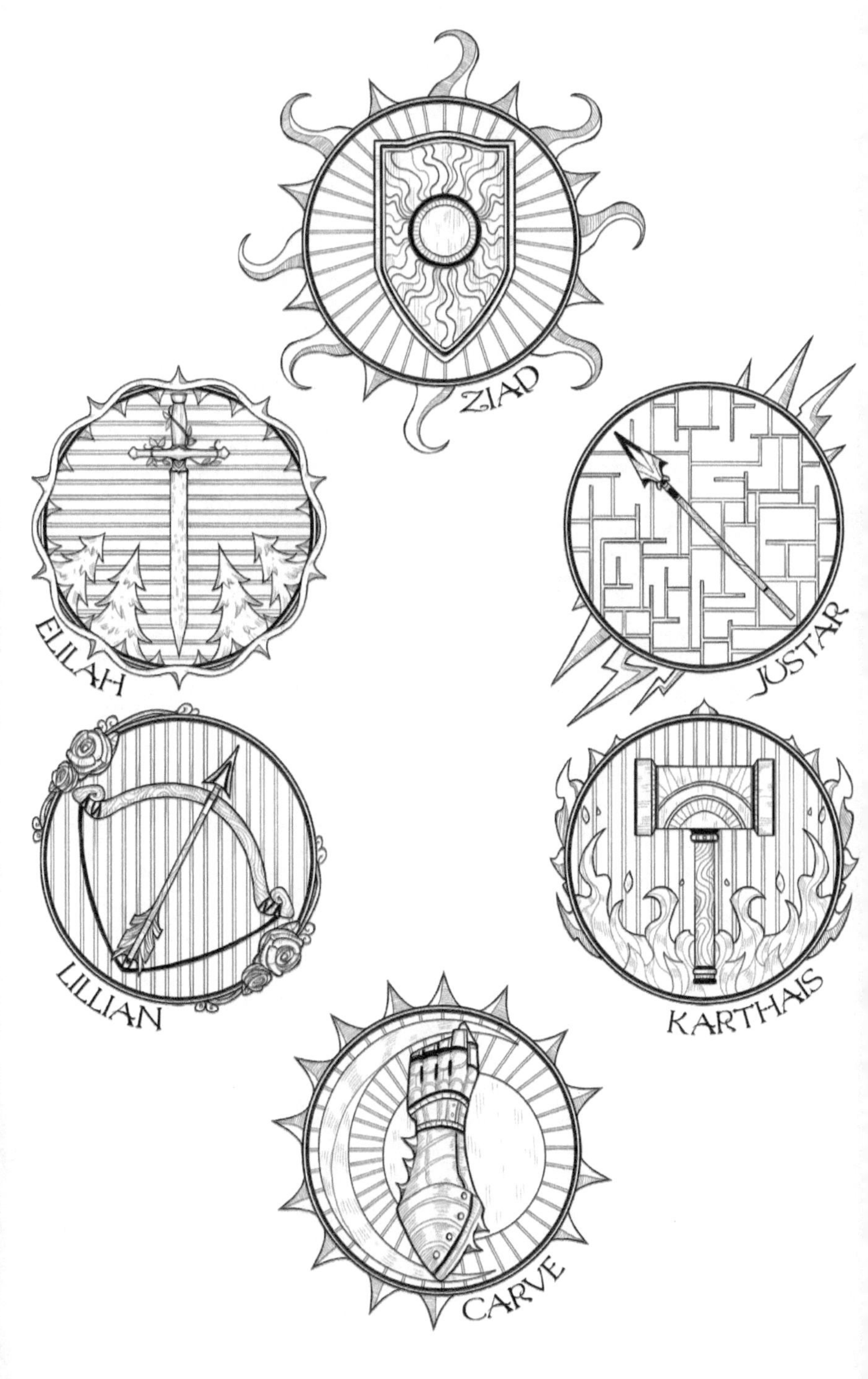

ZIAD
ELILAH
JUSTAR
LILLIAN
KARTHAIS
CARVE

NORTH
LANDS
THE WILDS
ELVEN TERRITORY
ELENA SWAMP
NORTHERN PLAINS
TASVRAN
THE GREAT RIVER
ETMOS
THE CANAEN RIVER
MASIL
TASVRAN MOUNTAINS
VESDAR
OMRIS

PROLOGUE

"Dear Elilah," Coral whispered. He set the book down atop a pile of coins and looked up at the beautiful statue. "I pray my brother's dreams are truly your voice. Watch over us."

He crept away as quietly as he could, trying not to cry at the thought of what was happening. Abandoning his castle, his home. It felt like his whole world. Was this truly what Elilah wanted? But he supposed it was the only way they could survive.

A hand clamped over his mouth. "What in the abyss are you doing here, Coral?"

He recognized the voice and was instantly relieved. It was just his older brother, Lotus. Not one of General Grathios' soldiers. "I was just leaving." He turned to face his brother, the elf's eyes a stern glare.

"You're supposed to be evacuating the civilians!" His voice was strict and harsh despite being no louder than a whisper.

"Calm down," Coral retorted. "I've already evacuated them. They're marching south as we speak. I came back to—"

"Please don't say to assassinate General Grathios."

Coral rolled his eyes. "Even I'm not that stupid."

"Sometimes I wonder," Lotus said with a smirk. Coral was about to give him a soft punch on the shoulder, but Lotus' countenance changed. "He has one of the weapons."

Coral's jaw dropped ever so slightly. "You're lying."

The weapons were gifts from the gods. There were six, each given by a different god to a different kingdom of ancient times. They were meant to protect the kingdoms, wielded once upon a time when a great war arose. Millions died and the kingdoms disintegrated. The lands decided the weapons were no gift, but rather a curse. They could not be destroyed, and so they were locked away, never to be seen by mortals again.

Yet somehow this general had retrieved one?

Lotus opened his mouth to say more, but the sound of shattering rock disrupted their conversation. Without a word, they ducked down and began to scramble away. Marching echoed throughout the caverns. Coral led the way down one hallway but halted at the sight of torch light. Signaling his brother, they turned back the way they had come. The marching was closing in around them and, with an exchange of glances, the brothers knew to hide instead of run.

Hiding was simple enough in the dark, underground cave. They crouched down in a dip in the floor, hidden behind a wall of stalagmites. Lotus' emerald green hair blended in with the moss that grew plentifully in the damp cave. Coral's aqua blue hair was much too bright to camouflage in with their surroundings, so he pulled his hooded cloak tight around his face.

The brothers held their breath as they watched the soldiers pass.

Coral now cursed himself for coming back. If one of them died it would be a tragedy. But if they both died? Their people would be left leaderless. No King Lotus. No Prince Coral.

"Nothing over here," one soldier announced. "The elves couldn't have gone this way." Coral smirked, knowing the humans hadn't searched hard enough. But that was why their castle had been built on top of the large caves in the first place. You could easily get lost if you didn't know where you were going. It was perfect for an evacuation like this.

A red light radiated and bounced off the slick black walls, growing closer with each clank of his footsteps. A large man stepped into view and, without a doubt, Coral knew this man was General Grathios.

His height and build were impressive enough. His onyx armor would have made him impossible to see if not for the eerie red light emanating from the weapon hanging to his side.

The War Hammer of Karthais.

So Lotus was right. This General Grathios did indeed have one of the holy weapons. Nothing else could cause a light like that. Though it was seemingly crafted of rusted iron, the hammer glowed throughout the caves.

"No elves, hmm?" General Grathios asked aloud. His soldiers replied, but he hardly seemed to take notice of them. He stared up at the statue where Coral had left the book. "Pathetic."

The general bent down and Coral's heart began to pound, wondering if he would pick up the book. But instead he grabbed one of the many offering coins. He turned it over in his hand and the human soldiers went as quiet as Coral and Lotus. In unison they sucked in their breath as Grathios threw the coin with all his might against the beautiful statue.

It stuck into the polished black graphite. As if that wasn't enough, the general then raised his leg to kick the coin in further. The crackle echoed throughout the cave.

Lotus gripped Coral around the bicep, as if instructing him to stay still. His brother knew him well. After watching the blasphemous act, it was true that Coral wanted to jump from their hiding place. To run out at the general, to scream, to curse, to cut him down then and there.

But he didn't dare move.

The cave was silent for another moment, and then it burst with General Grathios' laughter. "How pathetic!" His soldiers laughed with him. Who knew what they were laughing at. Coral's body tensed. How he wanted to kill this man. This man who had driven them from their home. This man who had now defiled the statue of their goddess.

"So you didn't find a single elf?" the general finally asked one of the men next to him.

"No sign of them."

"Pathetic indeed. The cowards simply fled and left us their castle." After a pause, he turned back the way he had come and gave a simple order: "Seal it up. If there are any elves down here, they'll die of starvation."

The soldiers followed after him, and he continued to bark out orders. "We can let the frightened little devils keep their sword. For now, anyway. There are plenty of other weapons for me to hunt, and my search shall not end." His voice bounced off the cavern walls as he returned towards the main flight of stairs. Once again, Coral and Lotus were alone.

They breathed a sigh of relief. "Thank Elilah. I thought we were dead for sure," Lotus whispered. Coral inspected the statue for a moment, running his finger along the freshly made cracks. "Come on, Coral. It's time to go."

He glanced towards his brother. "Are you sure? Shouldn't we—?"

"Leave it," Lotus said firmly. "I am telling you. Elilah sent me a prophecy in that dream. We must do as she says."

Coral nodded and said a silent prayer before leaving the chamber and following Lotus further into the caves. Though Grathios assumed any remaining elves would be trapped, Coral and Lotus knew the way out and exactly where it emerged. "So why did you come back again?"

"I wanted to leave the book," Coral explained. "I thought we should leave a copy here."

"Here?" Lotus asked, surprised. "You know the book is only for us. As long as you have a copy and I have a copy," he began.

"I know, I know. But who knows what will happen. I just thought to be safe. In any case, I can copy your book any time and then we both have a copy. Right?"

Lotus shrugged and gave a nod. "I suppose so." They walked through the halls in silence, looking for the tiny signs and landmarks to find the exit. "You'll want to do it sooner rather than later," he began again. "I have a task for you."

"Oh?" Coral asked curiously.

"When we've migrated south, rebuilt and settled in," Lotus explained, "I want you to come back here with a troop of soldiers. Not here here, just close enough to keep an eye on Grathios." Even in the dark Coral could sense fear in his brother's eyes. "He's already found one weapon. Who knows how powerful he will become if he finds more."

Chapter 1

The world was bathed in light. Perhaps there were trees and grass, a mountain in the distance. But none of that mattered. The only thing in focus was herself: a lone elven woman. She tried to take in her surroundings and get her bearings, but the light was too strong. "Hello?"

A figure stepped into her vision. A beautiful woman, towering above her. Ivory skin, long hair, and an enchanting smile. "Hello. I am here to give you something." Her outstretched hand held a sword.

"This is for me?" the elven woman asked curiously, reaching out. Her hand hovered just over the hilt. It was a beautiful sword: silver, with ancient runes across the blade and a light green vine budding around the hilt. It seemed mysteriously familiar.

The beautiful woman smiled again. "For you. It is freedom."

When her hand finally rested upon the hilt, the sensation crashed into her like lightning.

The woman jolted awake. The dream scattered, yet she could still feel the pain. It ached inside her. Sore muscles, deep bruises, possibly fractures in her bones.

She slowly counted to ten before sitting up, making sure her body had adjusted. Her senses were coming back and her eyes focused on her surroundings. She reminded herself of where she was. "I am in a tree," she said to herself, her voice hoarse and weak. "I am in a village. I was saved by a man." No, not just a man. A sachem; a king. She paused for a moment trying to remember his name, but skipped over it. "My name is Sheik. He named me Sheik."

Sheik wasn't really her name, at least not her birth name. But the elven man—Atarius, she remembered suddenly—had named her Sheik when she couldn't remember her real name. It was after she had told him about the dream.

She had been having the same dream for over a week now. Every night the beautiful woman presented her with the beautiful sword. And every night she touched it, and it caused her tremendous pain. At first she had assumed the dream had incorporated pain because of her injuries. But after so many nights of the same dream, she wondered if the pain was truly from touching the sword. Sometimes she wondered if she was on the verge of death itself and the dream was calling her towards the abyss.

But Atarius assured her that she was recovering. He had been healing her for over a week now. Her village had been attacked, and he had found her among the wreckage. He had rescued several people, but unfortunately their injuries had been worse than Sheik's. They died within two days.

Sheik took a deep breath and pulled herself out of bed. Her legs had grown weak from underuse and so she forced herself to take a few steps around the room. If you could call it a room, anyway. It was just the interior of a carved-out redwood tree. Admittedly it was large for a tree, nearly twice her height in diameter. But she still didn't consider it a typical room.

A cup of water rested on the table to her left and she helped herself to a sip. "I am in a tree," she repeated, whispering. "I am in a village. I was saved by Atarius. He named me Sheik."

Her first conversation with Atarius had been a panicked one. Sheik had just woken up and realized that not only was she physically injured, but she also had no memory. She understood concepts, she could still speak, she knew all her numbers and how to read and write, but she couldn't remember a thing about her life. Not even her own name.

Atarius at first had assured her that her memories would come back and she'd have a name soon enough. But when several days passed, and still she could not remember her name, she decided she needed a new one. She had just told Atarius about her recurring dream, with the beautiful woman and the sword. Though she thought it was only a silly dream, he had listened intently and asked questions. Then, with sudden decisiveness, he had declared, "Your name should be Sheik."

"Sheik." It wasn't a bad name. It was odd-sounding, though she couldn't put her finger on why. It was simple and unique and sounded quite regal. "Sheik," she had repeated, and accepted it.

A quiet knock on the outside of the bark door disrupted her thoughts. "Yeah?" she called out, as loud as she could manage. Her voice still hadn't returned to normal. It was likely she had damaged her vocal cords screaming for help when her village was attacked. She tried not to think about it.

Atarius scrambled up the ladder etched into the bark and lifted his head into her room. "You're up!" he said with a bit of surprise. Atarius frequently had to help her out of bed. But she was indeed recovering.

She nodded. "I think I might even climb down myself today." Because the rooms were not carved at ground level, she typically needed help out of the tree in order to relieve herself.

"Just be careful," Atarius cautioned, getting out of her way.

But she climbed down without much difficulty. Pain echoed through her body when she hit the ground, and she tried to hide her wince from Atarius. He was always worrying about her. She gave him a proud smile and he gave her a solemn nod. "Not bad," he admitted. "You really are getting better. You wouldn't feel up to a walk, would you?"

He was impossible to read. Did he want her walking because it would help prevent her muscles from growing too stiff? Or did he want her company? In either case, a walk would do her good and so she agreed. They chatted and he led her to a cave where several docile wolves lived. One particularly friendly wolf ventured toward them and allowed Sheik to scratch her behind the ear.

She caught Atarius smiling down at her, though he tried to hide it when she looked his way. He broke the silence and asked, "Have you had any more of those dreams?"

Sheik nodded, a frown forming on her face. "Unfortunately."

Atarius stared back at her. "Unfortunately? Why do you say that?"

"Because I hate it," she laughed. "The same dream night after night? Not to mention I always wake up in pain."

He waved the second statement away. "That's only because of your injuries. The dream is important." She gave him a curious glance and he continued, "The sword. It's the Sword of Elilah."

A memory shot through her. She had forgotten nearly everything about her past, but now there was a series of pictures playing through her mind. A sketch of the sword drawn in charcoal and an older man whispering, "The Sword of Elilah."

Atarius continued, "Elilah, the woodland goddess." That much, Sheik already knew. Elilah, goddess of freedom. She was one of six gods, specifically goddess to the elves. Her memory fragments filled in the rest: each god had crafted a single weapon. Elilah, the goddess of freedom, gave her sword. "It is told that all of the holy weapons were given to a bloodline," Atarius continued. "Only people of those bloodlines can dream of them." He paused. "Such dreams are prophecies."

At this, Sheik laughed. "Prophecy? I'm not so sure about that." Atarius raised an eyebrow but said nothing. "It's only a dream," Sheik explained. "Nothing special about it." Though of course there was indeed something special about it. She did not know how to describe it. The dream never seemed real, per se. But it did seem... significant. And, after all, she recognized both the sword and its name. It was somehow tangled up in her lost memories.

But Sheik wasn't one to believe in superstitious, silly things like prophecy. Apparently Atarius was. He gave her a serious look. "The sword is seeking you out."

"Don't be ridiculous," she said with a flick of her wrist, dismissing the thought.

Before Atarius could argue any more on the matter, a figure jumped between them both, startling Sheik half to death. "Farin!" she shouted, causing her throat a twinge of pain.

The elven man grinned. "Got you both!" Farin was Atarius' closest friend, and the village prankster. He prided himself on his ability to sneak up on others and scare them out of their wits.

"Farin!" Atarius glared. "You should know better. Sheik is still recovering."

Farin's face bunched up with worry. "Oh no, I'm sorry!" he apologized immediately. "I hadn't thought anything of—"

"Of course not, because you never think," Atarius said with a hint of annoyance.

Farin glanced at Sheik and she gave him a soft smile, letting him know she was perfectly fine. He seized the opportunity. "I'm sorry to have scared you, Atarius," he began, and Sheik watched his movements carefully as he reached around and gave Atarius' shoulder a squeeze. "I shouldn't have startled you both, but I needed to let you know..." He let the silence linger. Atarius knew he was up to something but couldn't quite place it. Sheik held in her giggle when she realized what Farin was doing. "I had to let you know that there is something in your hair."

Atarius ran his fingers through his long green hair. Farin had nimbly snuck two daisies behind Atarius' ears. When he discovered Farin's trick he pulled them out and threw them at him. "How you manage to do things like that without magic I'll never know." And his stern face finally spread into a smile.

Farin revealed several more daisies from behind his back and began placing them into Sheik's hair. He started singing—loudly and offkey—that Sheik was "Queen of the Daisies." She took her bows and Atarius laughed at them both.

Sheik was grateful for Farin's sudden distraction and silliness. Atarius was beginning to take her dream about the sword far too seriously. After all, it was only a dream.

⁕

Sheik sprinted as fast as she could. Her heart pounded. She wanted to gasp and take in deep breaths of air, but she forced herself to breathe through her nose. She could not risk making too much noise.

A bush rustled. Another one on her side. She continued to keep up the run, but she knew they had located her. They were closing in on her. She forced herself to go faster no matter how badly her lungs burned. Sweat dripped into her eyes as the rustling grew closer. They would have her in seconds.

Then she saw her chance. A tree up ahead, only a good twenty paces away, had a low enough branch she knew she could reach with a running jump. Just as they burst out of the bushes, she leapt, clutching the branch for dear life and hoping it would withstand her weight. She propelled off it, thrusting her body forwards towards another tree and forcing herself to climb higher.

They were below her, and continued to pursue her, branch by branch. How was she to escape? Her body ached and it seemed as if gravity had somehow managed to grow stronger. She swallowed what liquid she had left in her dry mouth and balanced carefully on a thick branch. They were only a short distance beneath her. She jumped to another tree, barely managing to grab hold of a branch and pull herself up.

She had taken too much time. They only had to make that same leap and they would have her. She had one last option. Concentrating with all her mind, the branches around her began bending towards and interlocking with each other. Though it was hard to focus on her magic while balancing, she had created a nearly perfect bridge.

Taking off at a full sprint, she ran across the bridge and readied herself to make another dangerous leap.

But as she was midair, vines burst forth and entangled her.

Despite her struggles, they forced her down. She could hardly breathe. Her pursuers approached slowly.

Atarius released the vines.

"That's no fair, you cheated," Farin whined, helping her to her feet. "We specifically declared no magic."

"That's true," Atarius piped in. "Though I'm impressed you were able to bend those branches so well."

Sheik brushed the dirt off herself and wiped the sweat from her forehead. "Hey there aren't any rules in a real fight, I can use whatever I want!" she laughed. The three continued to bicker as they walked back to the village. The entire village trained for combat, in case of human attacks. But Sheik had noticed that Atarius and Farin trained quite a bit more than the others. And now that she had made a full recovery, they urged her to join them. She enjoyed the pastime and, despite their current debate over rules, she had grown quite good at most combat related things.

It was impossible to outrun Farin. His wiry frame didn't appear athletic, but he was by far the fastest, sneakiest elf in the village. And boy did he let her know it. He reminded her at every opportunity that he could run circles around her. But she could never stay mad at him long. He was easy to joke with and easy to talk to. She had come to love him like a brother. And he was about as annoying as a brother, she began to think, as he made fun of her poor climbing.

She gave him a shove and moved next to Atarius. Like herself, he was still out of breath. He was not as good at running as Farin, but he was much better with a bow. And, of course, he was legendary for his abilities in magic.

"How did I do?" she asked him.

"Good, until you cheated," he teased.

She rolled her eyes and smiled. She had done well. "I'm going to the stream." She left the men alone as she turned towards the nearby creek, located about a league east of the village.

Sheik glanced around the forest before stripping off her heavy garments. Normally the stream was unbearable this late in the season, but she had been sweating so hard it was refreshing. She dunked her head under, washing her emerald hair thoroughly.

For some reason, even though she could remember nothing of her past, she knew her hair had once been long. Atarius had to cut it short because of how much the fire had damaged it during the attack on her village. It had finally grown out past her shoulders. But even though it had now been months, when she reached to wash her hair, she still sometimes felt around her waist as if she had forgotten how long it was.

Most of the time not being able to remember things did not bother her. She was too occupied with fitting into the new village and all the training with Atarius and Farin to worry about her past. But it still lurked in the back of her mind. It was more than her old life, friends, and family. She did not know who *she* was.

She splashed her face with water, trying not to think about it. It seemed whenever she was alone the thoughts crept into her mind. To distract herself, she focused on the beautiful scenery of the forest.

There were both deciduous and evergreen trees. The trees towered far above the eye could see, but they never made Sheik feel trapped. Though the ground was constantly covered in several layers of needles, leaves, or moss, there was always enough room between the overwhelming trees to run through the forest.

The redwood trees were extremely large. This was what allowed the elves to carve homes inside of them. But Sheik preferred the skinny, colorful trees, especially the ones that blossomed and shed their leaves in autumn.

Suddenly Atarius burst through the nearby bushes. He almost collapsed into the stream as he scanned it up and down. Spotting Sheik's body, he instantly snapped his eyes shut.

"Atarius!" she yelled, ducking under the water.

"Sorry," he called back, his eyes still closed. "Get dressed, Alta's giving birth!" He stumbled around for a moment, not daring to peek. Finally, pointed away from Sheik, he opened his eyes and took off at a full sprint back towards the village.

Once she was sure he was far enough away, Sheik climbed out of the water and began to throw on her clothes even though she was still soaking. She caught up with Atarius at the cave.

Crouching inside, they could hear whining. "It's okay, Alta," Sheik whispered, inching closer. Her hand reached out slowly, searching the air.

She smiled when she felt the rough tongue lick her hand. She scratched behind the wolf's ear and crawled next to her. Atarius crowded behind her. "How is she doing?"

Sheik felt the wolf's stomach. "They'll be coming out any minute." Atarius was holding his breath. It almost made her laugh seeing how nervous he was. For some reason she was not nervous at all. Perhaps, before the fire, she had been used to this kind of thing.

Alta began panting harder. The puppies were coming out. Sheik went to ask Atarius for help, but his queasy expression made her turn back around. She could do this on her own.

The first puppy was an easy delivery. It hardly seemed to hurt the mother. Sheik was quite proud until she went to hand it back to Atarius. Her heart sank. It was stillborn. Alta whimpered, trying to reach her baby. "No Alta," Sheik whispered. She didn't know if the wolf would understand.

She whined for another moment, and then the second puppy was ready. Sheik prayed this one would go better. With a final push it came free, along with a flow of blood. Sheik checked to make sure the puppy was alive, and then passed it back to Atarius.

There was a lot of blood. Too much blood.

She felt the wolf's stomach. There was still one more in there, maybe two. "Come on, Alta," she whispered, petting her. But her stomach was turning in knots. As much as she didn't want to admit it, she knew. Alta was dying.

"Atarius." She turned around. "She needs to be healed. Can you take over?" He nodded. "I'll take that one until she's all done." Sheik carefully took the tiny wolf, covered in mucus, and climbed out of the cave.

"It's gonna be okay," she insisted, sitting in a sunny spot and cleaning what fluids she could from the small puppy. It was a boy. She talked to him, trying to ease her own nervousness. Alta should not have been bleeding that bad. But it would be okay. Atarius was a healer. He could fix this. Everything would be okay.

But Atarius' face painted a different story. He didn't look her in the eye as he climbed out of the cave.

"Is she alright?" Sheik asked. Her heart was thumping out of her chest. Atarius was a healer—how could she not be alright?

He shook his head. "She didn't make it. The puppies, either."

No.

Sheik refused to accept it. "No. Go back in, keep healing her!"

He gave her a slight shake of the head. "It's too late. There was nothing I could do. I couldn't—"

"I don't understand!" Sheik shouted back at him. "You're a healer! Heal her!" She was crying now and yelling even though he didn't deserve it. She knew he didn't deserve it. She knew Atarius would have done anything in his power. Yet she couldn't help but yell as the tears welled in her eyes. "Why can't you? You're Atarius, dammit! You're the sachem! Why couldn't you heal her? Why didn't your magic work?"

He said nothing. Ever calm, ever patient. It almost made her madder. "Magic doesn't solve everything," he finally said. "I'm sorry."

They sat in the silence.

"Can you keep watching after that one? I don't feel well." His face was pale, and Sheik did not object. She bit down on the inside of her lip to not say anything more out of anger and gave him a solitary nod. In her arms, the puppy whined.

Poor Alta. Alta had been Sheik's favorite. But the wolf was too old to be delivering puppies. Sheik had known that it might be too hard on her aged body.

Sheik knew little about healing magic. It felt good in the moment to blame someone, to say Atarius hadn't done enough. But the truth was, it didn't matter how hard Atarius had tried; no magic could heal old age.

<hr>

The seasons passed steadily, and her wolf pup grew. She kept him close for the first few weeks and then, once she deemed him old enough, introduced him to his pack. The other wolves neither accepted nor rejected him. They didn't attack him, but he also wasn't quite one of them. So he traded his time between the two worlds. He ran with the pack at night and tagged along with Sheik during the day. She eventually named him; Fang, for the one tooth that came in before all the others.

Sheik was happy to have Fang trotting alongside her. They had a special bond and in a strange way he reminded her of herself. Disconnected. Not quite belonging to the pack.

Once upon a time Sheik had thought of leaving. She had hated being a burden on everyone during her recovery, having people wait on her, bringing her food, helping her in and out of the medic tree.

Someday, she had told herself, when she was better, she'd go off on her own.

But before she knew it, Sheik had made a full recovery. She pushed back the thoughts of leaving, finding excuses to stay. She was in no hurry to leave and, as the months went by, she found herself growing fonder and fonder of the peculiar redwood town.

Yet she wasn't exactly a member of the village. At least she didn't quite feel like one. Everyone here had known each other for generations. And Sheik still was learning the foreign rules of the village. Informal rules—hardly any of it was written down in a village code. It was like everyone had this unspoken understanding of village norms that Sheik was still trying to figure out.

The forest was sacred to them, and there was an understanding that no one should take from nature while it was still living. So one couldn't pull an apple off a tree, only pick it up after it had fallen to the ground. Yet the bark they stripped from trees to make cloth wasn't viewed as living and was therefore okay to take. Similarly, they could carve their homes into redwood trees so long as they left the roots intact. It was all rather arbitrary, but Sheik did her best to follow the rules despite how odd they were to her.

Besides, it seemed only the older elves followed the rules religiously. Elves like Hael, an old healer who was about to turn 92 years old. Unfortunately, Atarius also took the rules seriously, even though he was only a few years older than Sheik. She supposed, as village sachem, he felt pressured to set a good example.

Ultimately, it was for Atarius that Sheik stayed.

The year anniversary of her arrival at the village was approaching. And it was then that she suggested that she should have a coming-of-age ceremony. Such ceremonies marked an elf's twentieth birthday, the year of adulthood.

Atarius lit up at the suggestion.

When elves came of age, they selected their own tree. A permanent home. It meant Sheik had no plans to leave.

"What a brilliant idea, of course!" Atarius beamed. He didn't say anything of what it implied, that it meant Sheik was indeed intending to become a permanent member of their village. But she could tell that this was the reason behind his enthusiasm. After all, she had never seen him so excited by a ceremony before.

"Well, if you agree, then I'll announce it," Sheik smiled, happy for his reaction. "We'll have to start planning and see who all is available to help with the carving of the tree." Even with magic, it took several strong elves to carve out the inside of a redwood.

Farin crinkled his forehead and gave a curious look. "Do you even know your age?" he asked with a laugh.

Sheik rolled her eyes. "No, but I feel like I'm twenty," she said insistently. And it was the truth. Even when she couldn't remember details about her past, she still had vague feelings.

"I don't know," he said skeptically, "I think you're only eighteen. Are you sure you can approve this, Atarius?"

Atarius also rolled his eyes. "She looks twenty, Farin," he said, a hint of annoyance in his voice.

"Well if she's twenty, then she's already passed!" he bickered back.

Sheik went along with his banter. "Well then, where's my home tree? Are you telling me I've been cooped up in the medic tree for the past eleven months when I've been twenty this whole time?"

"What if you aren't even twenty!" Farin fake gasped, "Why you could be thirty or forty and have had us tricked all along!"

She laughed out loud, knowing she couldn't possibly be older than twenty-two. "Wait, then that makes me your elder! You've got to start doing what I say!"

Farin made a look of exaggerated fear. "Good point. I dub you eighteen!"

Atarius rolled his eyes. "If she says she is twenty, then she's twenty. We'll celebrate next month. For your one-year mark?"

Sheik nodded. One year had passed and she was about to become an official part of the village.

There wasn't much to plan besides preparing her home tree. Sheik picked out a large redwood within the vicinity. One of the older women, Aiyla, inspected it to ensure it was healthy and free of fungi and insects. They prayed over it, that Elilah would bless the tree with sturdiness to keep Sheik safe. Then Sheik and Aiyla used their magic to soften the inside of the tree, make it a clay-like consistency, while four strong men carved out the inside.

Atarius planned the coming-of-age ceremony. The ceremonies were typically simple and short, consisting of a few words shared by Sachem Atarius, the parents, and sometimes one of the elder elves. Sheik had seen two coming-of-age ceremonies since her arrival, Lamir's and Ilisa's. Ilisa had married not long after, and Sheik had learned that wedding ceremonies were far more extravagant and drawn out.

Sheik cared very little about what the ceremony consisted of and was far more invested in what it signified. Being twenty meant being an adult and therefore a contributing member of the village. This would make it official. She would have a home tree. She would take up more village responsibilities. She would belong.

Currently, she really only felt like she belonged with Atarius and Farin. They trained relentlessly for combat and always encouraged Sheik to join them. She spent more time fletching and shooting arrows than she did making cloth or gathering fallen foods.

And, for the most part, she didn't mind. For one, she was good at it. She loved being praised by Atarius and she relished in bragging to Farin whenever she could beat him at something. She enjoyed the exercise from all the practice. But none of the other elves seemed to train as much as them and Sheik always felt a little different because of it. It was this unmentioned thing, that she was training with Atarius and Farin. And sometimes it felt like it set her apart and created some unspoken gap between her and the rest of the village.

Sheik wondered if, perhaps, it was simply because she had grown so attached to Atarius. It was hard to see him as sachem since they had become so close. They were more than friends, at least in Sheik's mind. Ever since the kiss.

He had only kissed her once, but that was enough for Sheik to know how he felt about her. And perhaps the rest of the village had picked up on their lingering eyes and smiles for each other, and now treated Sheik with some sort of distant reverence.

This coming-of-age ceremony wouldn't just make her an official member of the village. By declaring her an adult, it would also mean she was of the age to be married. She didn't know how long he would wait, but eventually she could only assume that Atarius would propose. She had been thinking about it since the kiss. And after much thought, Sheik decided that, when he proposed, she would say yes. She had begun to like this new village, this new life. And she had begun to love Atarius.

Sheik held her breath as she waited just beyond the line of trees. All the elves were gathered, seated in the meadow. She hadn't been anxious until now, seeing them all at once. It was a tiny village, but with everyone together it suddenly felt very large.

And they were all there for her. All gathered to celebrate her becoming one of them.

"Nervous?" Farin asked, standing to her right.

She shook her head and lied, "No."

Farin gave her a skeptical look and she knew he could see right through her. "I was nervous for mine," he admitted after a pause. "What was it, four years ago? Now I hardly even remember it. It'll be over quick."

Atarius stood to her left. Normally the adult-to-be was led in by her parents, but of course Sheik had no parents. So Atarius and Farin, being her closest friends, decided to take their place. Atarius had done something similar when he came of age because of his parents' untimely death. They had died when he was only twelve, trying to stop a human raid on a nearby town. A raid similar to the one in which all of Sheik's family had been slaughtered.

Farin kept talking but she hardly heard his words. She focused on Atarius' serious countenance. He had an angular face with piercing features, particularly his silver eyes. She had never seen eyes like his before. His hair was similar in both color and length to Sheik's, emerald green, hanging to his shoulders. He was surveying the crowd, looking for something, some sort of cue to start.

He stepped forward and Sheik moved to follow him, but Farin caught her by the shoulder. "Hold on, he'll wave you in," he explained. Sheik didn't understand at first. The adult-to-be always entered with a parent on their left and a parent on their right. But then she realized Atarius was entering first because he was sachem. He had to make a formal announcement.

"Thank you everyone for gathering for Sheik's coming-of-age ceremony." The crowd of villagers gave a light applause. Then Atarius lifted his hand and the light tapping of drums began. A row of elves in the back held small leaf wrapped drums that made a faint sound, but together created a steady beat.

"That's our cue," Farin urged, and Sheik walked to Atarius' side. His serious face broke just a little into a small smile.

The drumming stopped and Farin stepped forward. "As Sheik's elder, I would like to say a few quick words," he began, a grin forming on his mischievous face. The crowd held back giggles, preparing for whatever joke he might make. Sheik gave him a cynical look, wondering how he might tease her.

He pulled a small parchment from his pocket and glanced between it and the crowd several times before finally starting. "I'm sorry, I've got this note written down here," he explained. "Sheik wanted me to only say good things," he moved up next to her and held out the note, "but Sheik, I'm afraid I can't read your handwriting." The villagers laughed and even Sheik cracked a smile, giving Farin a light push.

"I joke, I joke," he reassured her. "I have plenty of wonderful things to say about Sheik. She's a great friend. She's very honest, mature, independent. And incredibly driven. If she has a goal, she follows through. After all, she arranged this whole ceremony. Just decided one day, you know what? I'd like to be twenty by the end of the month. Who else could pull that off but Sheik?" His audience laughed again. "But Sheik, I am happy for you to be twenty. You have no idea what a relief it will be to finally have a proper drinking buddy," he winked.

At this Sheik laughed. Atarius never drank wine. Farin glanced his way and Atarius frowned as he stepped forward. "I'm supposed to follow that?" Farin grinned and Atarius shrugged. "Sheik, now that you have come of age, you'll have more responsibilities. To take some of the weight off my shoulders, one of those responsibilities shall be babysitting Farin." The villagers laughed and several even burst into applause, both because it was so uncommon for Atarius to joke and only fair that Farin should be the subject of it.

Farin feigned offense and Atarius tossed him a grin. Then he turned his attention back to Sheik. "Truly, Sheik, I am privileged to speak on your behalf as you come of age. You have been a blessing to this village and I thank Elilah every day that she put you in my life." Sheik smiled back at him and felt her heart flutter. The rest of the village melted away as she looked into his silver eyes. "Your future holds great things, and I am honored to stand by your side and witness you accomplish them."

They lingered for a moment, Sheik lost in his eyes, until an elbow from Farin brought her back into reality. "Alright, love birds, end the ceremony already," he whispered.

Atarius nodded frantically and Sheik blushed. "As sachem, I am proud to announce Sheik as the latest adult resident of the village," Atarius rushed through his words. The village clapped and the light drums began again as everyone stood to resume their day.

As the villagers dispersed, a few stopped to congratulate Sheik. She wanted to say more to Atarius, but he left in a hurry, either embarrassed by Farin's 'love birds' comment or simply trying to avoid being social.

There was no avoiding it for Sheik though. That evening there was a feast. Sheik didn't really consider it a feast, but that was what it was called. Really it was more of a gathering. Normally meals were done individually, or with friends or families. Not as a community.

But for coming-of-ages, weddings, and funerals, the village gathered and ate together.

The food itself was no different. Fallen foods were rare in winter. Those who didn't have the gift of magic might have broken the village rules by picking some fruits or wild mushrooms. But with Atarius and the elders present, everyone was proper. There were some fallen pears that weren't too far gone and their most frequent staple, bread made of acorn flour. Anything else one desired had to be created with magic.

For most people this was no trouble. Nearly two thirds of the village could use magic at least well enough to form food. The remaining third had to rely on another if they wanted something beyond acorn bread or bruised fruits. Every magic user was generous enough to lend their abilities to their friends and families. Of course, Sheik did like to lord it over Farin occasionally when he was being particularly insufferable.

But at the moment he was on his best behavior. He sat with her at the feast, breaking a piece of bread. "So was the ceremony short enough you weren't terribly embarrassed?"

"Only during your speech," she teased, before adding, "no it was just fine."

"You think my speech was embarrassing? You should have heard my mother's speech at my coming-of-age ceremony."

"I thought you didn't remember your ceremony?" she asked, creating some grapes with her magic and handing him a few.

He gobbled them down quickly, like she might let her magic go at any moment. "I don't remember what she said," he admitted. "Just that she went on for over ten minutes." Sheik laughed, knowing it was very likely true. Farin's mother was a sweet lady, but she sure could talk. She supposed that was where Farin got it from.

"Well," Sheik changed subjects. "I couldn't care less about the ceremony. I'm excited to move into my new tree." She was excited, too, to begin helping more. With adulthood came added responsibilities. She'd walk with those who searched for fallen food. She'd help those who pulled bark from trees. She'd chat with those who stripped, dried, and wove the bark into cloth, and gossip with those who soaked acorns to make flour and baked bread.

Farin interrupted her thoughts. "That was my favorite part, too. Independence. Not that you don't really have independence already. Well anyway, you'll enjoy what's waiting for you in your new tree." She gave him an inquisitive look and he smiled. "Why do you think Atarius ran off after the ceremony? He's got a surprise waiting for you."

Sheik tried to hide her grin. "Oh, I didn't realize."

He chuckled at her inability to mask her feelings. "Mm," he motioned with his chin between bites. "Even Fang came to celebrate."

Sheik spied the wolf behind several trees and whistled for him to come. He approached nervously. She supposed he hadn't ever seen the whole village gathered before, and while one or two elves didn't frighten him, a group of several hundred clearly did. After a few scratches behind the ear, he relaxed and lay by her side as she finished eating with Farin.

"Well, I guess I'll go see what Atarius has waiting for me," Sheik finally declared, eager to find out. Farin gave Fang the core of his pear, though the wolf was hardly interested. He moved to follow Sheik, but she motioned for him to stay. "Stay with Farin, boy. I'll see you tomorrow." Fang lay back down and Farin waved goodbye.

Sheik wound through the woods to find her new tree. It was easy to get lost in the village, as the homes were spread apart and carved several body lengths high. You had to be looking up to spot them, and even then they had bark doors that pulled tight and made the rooms nearly invisible. If travelers wandered through the forest, they wouldn't even notice that they were in a village at all.

When she finally reached her new tree, her heart began to pound. "Atarius?" she called out.

"Sheik?" His head peered out at her. "Oh, you're back early. I thought you'd stay at the feast a little longer."

"I was told you have a surprise for me," she smiled. "Can I come up?"

"Oh, that Farin," he mumbled, knowing perfectly well who gave away his secret. "Yes of course, come up, it's your home after all!"

She climbed up the ladder that was etched into the side of the tree and pulled herself into her new room. To one side was a small chest of drawers to store the few clothes and tools she had. To the other side was her bed. And in the center of the bed lay a newly made bow.

Sheik stared at it for a moment.

A bow?

"Do you like it?" Atarius asked nervously.

She stepped forward and ran her fingers along the grip. It was very well made and looked to be designed with her height and strength in mind. It was beautiful, really, but completely caught her off guard. "You made it?" He nodded. "It's nice." She had to say something more than that. He had spent days on this bow. He might have spent weeks making it. Yet here she was with nothing to say. What was wrong with her? "It's very pretty," she finally managed.

He seemed to sense the awkwardness and added, "I promise it shoots well. Better than my old bow you've been using. But uh, we can go practicing tomorrow and you can see for yourself?"

"Tomorrow?" She hesitated, wondering if she should tell him that she wanted to cut back on the archery in place of helping more around the village. But realizing how rude she was already sounding, she decided at least to humor him for the time being. She forced a smile and said, "Yes, tomorrow. That sounds great."

He smiled back. "Great. Tomorrow." Heading towards the door, he climbed down the etched ladder. "Enjoy your new tree. Goodnight."

"Goodnight," she nodded back at him as he descended. When she felt the light thud of him landing and knew he had completely gone, she sank into the bed, staring at the bow. Why was she so annoyed? She enjoyed archery, and the bow she had been using certainly needed replacing. This bow was clearly well made. Even now, admiring its beauty, she noticed where he had carved her name into the grip, declaring it hers.

Yet it meant only more training. More of this thing that set her apart, that kept her from being like all the other villagers.

And it was no proposal.

Chapter 2

Sheik trained with Atarius the next day, as promised. She practiced with the new bow and found it released much smoother than Atarius' old one. It was a bit bigger than she was used to and took quite a bit of force to pull back on. With time, Atarius assured her, her strength would build and she'd be able to use it naturally.

She tried to keep any bitterness to herself and act natural, but it only prompted Atarius to ask to practice again with her the next day. She reluctantly agreed and another day of training with Atarius and Farin passed by. Target practice with the new bow, racing Farin at top speed, honing her magic. If she was lucky, Farin would let her try out his prized throwing knives.

Perhaps the most frustrating part was how much fun she had. When she finally forgot that she was supposed to be upset, she enjoyed every second with them. Farin teased her and she teased him back. Atarius challenged her to be better at everything and then heaped praise upon her when she succeeded. But ultimately nothing had changed. Here they were, still out playing in the forest just the three of them while Sheik continued to feel disconnected from the rest of the village.

By the end of the third day, Sheik finally resolved to confront Atarius.

"I'm going to get some sleep," Atarius said as he stretched out his muscles. "See you tomorrow after breakfast. We can start with some more archery?"

"I want to take tomorrow off," Sheik suggested instead. She'd let him down easy.

His forehead crinkled with worry. "Oh, are you not feeling well?" It was very like him to become instantly worried over her wellbeing.

"I'm fine," she assured him. "But I'm an adult now. I need to be helping. I thought I'd help Ralin and Faer pull some bark tomorrow."

Atarius looked surprised. "What? What for?"

She gave him an equally surprised look. "What do you mean what for? To help. I've got six outfits and I didn't make a single one of them. It's time I pulled my own weight. Gather food. Make clothes." Atarius rarely did anything of the sort. As sachem, he had different, equally important duties. But Sheik wasn't anyone special. To never be helping was odd. Even Farin, who perhaps goofed off more than anyone, helped with gathering fallen foods.

Yet Atarius waved the thought away. "Nonsense. Ralin and Faer can manage on their own just fine. It's more important that you train."

"I *want* to help," she insisted. He gave her an odd look, an expression she couldn't quite interpret. For fear of hurting his feelings, she added, "Look, it's not like I don't enjoy archery. We can keep practicing together, just not every day. I don't want to be a burden on anyone—"

"You aren't a burden on anyone," he interrupted.

"Yes, I am. If I don't ever help gather food or make tools or cloth, then yes, I am a burden." She didn't know what else to call it. And she didn't understand why Atarius was so blind to her lack of contributing. Surely all the other villagers had noticed by now. Why didn't he?

He stared at her for a moment, those silver eyes piercing through her. "Okay," he finally relented. "Do what you want." She could tell he was annoyed, though she didn't understand why. But she let him leave without pushing it any further. He'd see soon enough that it was only reasonable for her to help out in the village and that they'd still get plenty of time together.

⸎

Sheik worked with Ralin and Faer the first day, learning to strip bark from birch trees. It was still winter and a bit early to be pulling bark, but they managed to get a few good strips off which she then took to Aiyla, Mame, Naiton, and two sisters, Lia and Tayra, who Sheik still couldn't quite tell apart.

Aiyla was once an expert at cutting the bark and forming it into string and then weaving with it. But with her old age, her fingers had grown bony and ached when she did too much work with her hands. Now she supervised the others as they did the manual work. The group of women were all welcoming when Sheik asked to join them.

Sheik wasn't particularly good at weaving. She was good at plenty of small work with her hands, like whittling and fletching. Yet she found the string difficult and after only two days of work she was ready for a break.

Knocking at Atarius' throne room he welcomed her in. The laws, books, and maps that were normally stored so orderly on the shelves were scattered on the floor. Atarius sat in the middle of the mess, reading a book. She didn't know what he was reading. Normally when he had 'sachem duties' it mostly consisted of listening to villagers complain and seeing what he could do about their problems.

"I'm taking today off," she explained, holding her bow up. "Want to practice?"

He glanced up at her and then back down at the book. He hesitated for a moment before saying, "Why don't you go ahead and get started with Farin? I'll join you this afternoon."

"Are you sure?" Sheik asked. He simply nodded. She climbed back down the tree and furrowed her brow. What was wrong with him? Was he avoiding her now? She didn't know what he wanted or expected and why he was being so difficult. But she went ahead and did as he suggested, finding Farin.

Finding Farin was both impossible and quite easy. Farin took absolute delight in catching someone alone, striking a ridiculous pose, and then waiting for them to notice him. He prided himself on his ability to stay absolutely silent. So all Sheik had to do was shout his name a few times and then have a seat. She would spot him eventually.

And sure enough, after about ten minutes had passed, she noticed him in a tree just outside her peripheral. He was draped across a branch, one leg crossed over the other, his arms behind his neck.

"Oh, hey there," he said casually, when he could tell she had finally spotted him.

Sheik couldn't help but chuckle, knowing the position he was in had to have been extremely painful on his abdominals. Yet he managed to make it look so effortless. "Alright, you've had your fun. Come on down from there. Did you want to practice with me?"

He made an inquisitive expression as he dropped down next to her. "I thought you'd put practicing on hold? Atarius said you didn't want to train anymore."

She sighed and led him away from the village, so their conversation wouldn't be overheard. Not that anyone could sneak up on Farin. He had the best hearing around. "It's not that I don't want to train anymore. Just... I'm an adult now, right? So I should be helping around the village. I mean isn't all this archery and sparring just a little childish?"

Farin took it all in for a moment. Sheik thought he'd laugh at her or make a joke like he always did, but instead he said, "Well I suppose it just depends on your perspective. I mean sure, we've never had an attack here on our village. But obviously there's been attacks elsewhere. You're living proof of that, aren't you?"

Sheik sighed again. "I guess."

"Keep in mind how Atarius' parents died. They saw smoke. Went to help. Then next thing you know they're dead. It was all so sudden. The village they saved, their leader brought their bodies back to us. He told us how bravely they fought, how Tarian and Ilia saved their village. But," Farin shrugged, "if they'd only been a little faster. A little stronger. A better shot with their bow. Who knows, maybe they'd have lived."

Sheik looked towards the ground, not sure what to say. "I think Atarius thinks that way and wants to do better," Farin continued. "So he takes the training seriously. And," he hesitated a moment, like he wasn't sure if he should continue, "and Atarius cares a lot about you. If there's anyone he wants to be prepared, to be safe, it's you."

At this, Sheik let out a dry, sarcastic chuckle.

Farin shot her a look of disbelief. "What, you don't think he likes you?"

"Can you keep a secret?"

He grinned. "With how often I eavesdrop on people? I'm keeping more secrets than you can count!"

Despite his joke, Sheik remained serious. She couldn't believe she was saying it out loud. "I thought," she began slowly, "you know that surprise, for my coming-of-age ceremony? I thought that Atarius was going to propose to me."

"Propose, like marriage?" Farin asked, a hint of shock in his voice.

"Ha, see, you said he cares about me and even you think it's ridiculous!" Sheik laughed.

"No, no," he quickly corrected. "Not ridiculous. Just," he hesitated again, "just it's more complicated than that."

She made a face. "What do you mean? What's complicated? If he likes me, then he'd propose. Or at least announce publicly that we're seeing each other!"

Again, Farin seemed to take his time choosing his words. "He's the leader of the village," he explained carefully. "He has certain responsibilities. Responsibilities that come before things like marriage."

"It's not like sachems can't marry. Atarius' mom married Tarian, right?"

Farin gave a sideways turn of his head. "Well yes, but that's different. Tarian was just a normal guy."

Sheik shot him a contemptuous look. "And what is that supposed to mean? I'm not normal?" Farin attempted to take back his words, but Sheik continued, "What, because I'm not from the village?"

"No, it's nothing to do with that," he explained. Sheik continued to stare at him expectantly. He sighed and mumbled, "Elilah, what have I gotten myself into?" He collected himself and then said calmly, "Look it's just that you're special, Sheik."

"Special?" she said skeptically, raising an eyebrow.

He nodded. "Special."

"Farin, what in the abyss are you talking about?"

"Atarius is going to kill me," he muttered. "But I suppose he couldn't keep it from you forever. You might as well just hear it from him."

Sheik hadn't a clue what he was talking about. But he led the way back towards Atarius' throne room, where Sheik had left him reading a book. They climbed the tree and knocked.

"Come on up!" Seeing it was them, Atarius smiled. "I thought you two were practicing?" he asked, closing his book.

"We were going to, but Sheik decided it would be more fun to pester me," Farin explained as he pulled himself into the room. He moved aside so Sheik could enter as well. "You need to tell her."

Atarius raised an eyebrow and gave Farin a long gaze. "Tell her what?" he finally asked.

"Who she is. About the sword."

An old conversation crept back into Sheik's mind. When she had first been recovering, when she had been having the bizarre dreams. Atarius had told her something about the Sword of Elilah. "What are you two talking about?" she whispered. Her dreams had gone away many months ago. Why was this still something they were discussing?

Atarius sighed and started thumbing through his book. When he reached the page he was searching for, he held it open for her.

Sheik stared at it for a moment. It was exactly as it had been in her dream. The ancient runes that she couldn't read carved into the blade. The vine budding around the hilt. It was the sword from her dream. "How did you draw that?"

He chuckled and handed the book over to her. Sheik studied it closer, trying to tell if it was indeed as she remembered. It was. "I didn't draw it. The drawing has been passed down from hundreds of years ago. It's the Sword of Elilah. That's the sword from your dream, right?"

She set the book down. "Okay, so what? So I had a dream about this sword. Big deal. Am I missing something?"

"The holy weapons each belong to a bloodline. Only those in the bloodline can dream of them. If you've dreamed of this Sword of Elilah," he tapped the image in the page, "then it means you're of the bloodline."

Sheik rolled her eyes and took a seat. This was ridiculous. "Okay, sure, say you're right. So I'm part of this—"

Farin cut her off and explained, "There's more." He looked expectantly towards Atarius.

Atarius picked up the book and flipped through its pages once more. "There was an oracle, about," he pondered, "maybe sixty years ago? He passed through our village. Ah, here," he handed the book over to Sheik. "He gave us this prophecy."

Sheik read the quote aloud. "The son of Hellod will save the Speaker of Secret Tongues, the one who shall recover the lost Sword of Elilah." She glanced between Atarius and Farin and gave a shrug. "I don't even know what this means. Who is Hellod?"

"My great grandfather," Atarius replied. "For the longest time they thought the prophecy was about my grandfather. When he passed away and nothing happened, my mother assumed the oracle was a fake. I did too, until, well, until you. Even after I saved you, I didn't really think anything of it. Then you told me about your dream."

"So because of a dream and something someone said half a century ago," Sheik questioned as she closed the book, "you think I'm going to miraculously find the Sword of Elilah?" Atarius gave her a sober nod. "This is ridiculous. The Sword of Elilah isn't even real. Those weapons are just children's stories. And you weren't alive when this 'oracle' showed up, you don't even know if this is true," she finished, waving the book around.

Farin and Atarius stared at her without reply. Their expressions were blank and she began to grow angry at their superstitious beliefs. What did they want from her? They wanted her to accomplish some impossible task because of some silly stories and dreams? Then, with sudden realization, she blurted out, "This is why you've had me training, isn't it? The archery, the magic, the combat practice? It's all for this stupid sword, isn't it?"

"I wanted you to be prepared," Atarius began quietly. "I don't know what's going to—"

Sheik slammed the book down. "Nothing is going to happen. I had that ceremony so I could be a part of this village. So I could finally fit in. And now I find out the only reason I'm not fitting in is because you two think I'm some sort of," she stumbled for words, "some story-book legend!" Still they said nothing. She continued, "Well I'm not. I don't want to find some holy sword. I want to make clothes and trinkets and gather water and just be normal." With that, she climbed out of the tree and stormed away.

Sheik nocked an arrow to the bow, held her arm steady, and took aim. It was just her and the tree, a target drawn on it with holly berries. She took in a breath. The world around her grew dim, almost black. It was just her and her target.

The arrow slammed into the tree, a perfect shot.

As much as she hated the idea of training for Atarius' purposes, archery was still one of her favorite activities. With each arrow, she released a little more anger.

She removed the arrow from her mark and took another pace back from her original starting place. Another arrow, raised, aimed. The world became black.

"Sheik."

Startled, she released the arrow and it struck just high of her mark. "Atarius! You scared me!" Then, remembering she was mad at him, she added bitterly, "What do you want?"

"I wanted to apologize." She said nothing, knowing she should accept it but feeling particularly stubborn. "I should have told you. I should have told you that first day you told me about the dream. I should have told you why I wanted you to train. I shouldn't have kept you in the dark. I should have been honest. And I really am sorry."

"Yes," she replied, "you should have. Thank you." She retrieved her arrow, took a step back, and shot once again. "I still don't believe all this nonsense."

Atarius sighed. "I don't see how."

"Because the weapons aren't real," Sheik reiterated. "And even if they are, so what? What am I supposed to do with a magic sword? What's the point of me finding it?"

"You're part of the bloodline. You're descended from the one who first received the sword from Elilah herself," Atarius explained, his voice full of passion. "The bloodline is meant to protect the sword."

Sheik loosed another arrow. "Protect it from what?"

He rolled his eyes. "You've been chosen by Elilah herself, and that's what you have to say?"

"That has yet to be seen," she retorted. "And I think it's a valid question. I have absolutely no use for a sword. So why is it my job to find it?"

Atarius crossed his arms. "Perhaps someday you'll need it." Sheik shrugged before firing once again. With a sigh, he pleaded, "I've said my piece. Please just consider it seriously." Sheik didn't know exactly what he was expecting her to consider, but she tried her best to give him a sincere nod so he would leave her be.

⎯⎯◈⎯⎯

Light enveloped her. Sheik tried to get a look around, to discern where she was, but the light was too strong. "Hello?"

A figure stepped into her vision. A beautiful woman. Ivory skin, long hair. And an enchanting smile. "Hello. I am here to give you something." Her outstretched hand held a sword.

Sheik stared at the woman. She had been here before. She had seen this woman before. She had touched this sword. Despite wanting to recoil, she found herself reaching for the sword. "This is for me?" she asked. Her hand hovered over the green vine, wrapped around the hilt.

The beautiful woman smiled again. "For you. It is freedom."

When her hand finally rested upon the hilt, the sensation crashed into her like lightning.

Sheik awoke in a sweat.

"No," she whispered. The pain had subsided, but it was replaced by dread. "No, no, no!" She pounded her fist against the wooden wall of her tree home. How could this be happening? She was all better. She had fully recovered. How could she be having this dream again?

It was all the talk about Elilah and the stupid sword and destiny. Maybe even seeing the image of the sword drawn in Atarius' old book. Something must have triggered her memory and now the dream was back.

Things had started to go back to normal with Atarius. It had been over a week since the confrontation. She had gone back to working with Ralin and Faer and a few others, stripping bark from trees, but still made time for archery. Atarius went back to praising her. She went back to trying to impress him. Farin went back to trying to sneak up on her and she went back to teasing him. Though there was this looming, unspoken silence around the sword, things had become like they once used to be.

But now this dream shattered the façade. She was suddenly very aware of the rift between her and Atarius once again.

Sheik left her tree, bow in hand, despite that it was still dark out. The moonlight guided her as she looked for a spot to practice her archery. Fang managed to find her, whining happily, as if excited that she was awake during his normal hours. She scratched him behind the ear, but even the comfort of her loyal companion was not enough to distract her from her frustration at the returning dream. She needed to release her anger with arrows.

She started at her usual thirty paces away to warm up. Once she had sunk a few arrows into the tree, she began stepping back. She made it easily to forty paces before finding there were too many trees in the way for her to step back any farther.

With a sigh of frustration, she went to find a new spot to practice. Normally she and Atarius practiced in the same designated spot because there was a clear line of sight for nearly seventy paces. But right now, she didn't feel like going to the regular spot, where surely Atarius would find her. Right now, she didn't feel like seeing Atarius. For the first time in the year she had been here, she felt like she couldn't tell Atarius the truth.

Normally she told him everything. What she liked to do, whose company she enjoyed most, and so on. She always shared with him when she was able to do something new with her magic or whittled a new piece of wood. He always listened attentively, even when she felt she was boring herself. He sat with her when she was sad or frustrated, and made her feel safe, comforted, and not alone in the world.

But this was different.

If Atarius knew her dream had come back, he would only lecture her more. So as much as it bothered her, she had to keep the dream a secret.

Upon finding a new spot to target practice, she let loose several more rounds, trying to regain her accuracy. Her arms grew tired with each and every pull to the point where she had to massage her muscles in order to loose another arrow. One more try, she thought to herself, trying to hold the bow straight as her arm burned in pain.

"Having trouble?"

She nearly screamed. Farin was hanging upside down on a tree branch behind her. By how red his face was, she knew he had been there a long time.

Sheik was about to grow defensive, but she couldn't help but laugh as he dropped to the ground. It was like watching a fish flop down from a tree. "How long have you been there?"

"You have no idea," he laughed, trying to stretch out his legs.

"You're a tomato."

"I thought you'd notice me sooner! Help me up," he extended his hand. She pulled him to his feet and he took a couple of shaky steps. "I finally had to speak up. I could've died up there!"

She laughed again. "How'd you find me anyway?" She had specifically gone to a different spot so she wouldn't be found.

"Oh please. You should know by now that no one can hide from me." It was true, he was an incredible tracker. "You're normally an observant person, Sheik, but when you're holding that," he motioned to her weapon, "well it's like you're blind to the whole world. There could be an earthquake and you wouldn't notice anything but your target."

She gave him an exasperated glance. "So what? As long as I hit my target, right?"

"I guess," Farin laughed. "But in real combat, it isn't just target practice. If you zone out, you could get hurt."

Sheik went from annoyed to angry. "A real combat? And why would I ever be in a real combat?" Though she knew she was getting needlessly defensive, she couldn't help it. Even Fang, who had grown bored of her archery, now raised his head to glance their way.

Farin raised his hands as if to calm her down. "Whoa, whoa, relax," he muttered. "I didn't say a thing about the sword."

That damned sword.

Her forehead bunched up and her eyebrows furrowed. She wanted to scream, to curse. But all she managed was to bury her face in her hands and begin to cry.

"Whoa, Sheik, what's going on?" Farin asked, moving next to her and placing a hand on her back. Fang, too, wiggled close to her and began to whine, trying to stop her crying. But she couldn't stop. And when she finally managed to unbury her face, she confessed the secret she had sworn she wouldn't share.

"I had that dream last night." She wiped her eyes and nose with her sleeve and let the thoughts flow. "And I can't tell Atarius because he'll just give me some shit about destiny and the sword calling to me. And it's just a dream and he doesn't understand. And it isn't even about that, the sword doesn't even matter, what matters is Atarius. I thought he loved me, Farin," and at this she began crying harder. "I thought he was going to propose and now there's this thing between us and here I am lying to him and avoiding him and I can't even tell him!"

Farin's hand continued to make small circles on her back, but he said nothing as she ranted and wept. When he could sense that she was finished, he whispered, "I'm so sorry. I can talk to him if you—"

"No," Sheik cut off the idea before he could finish it. "Please, don't tell him any of this."

He hesitated, like he might argue with her. But instead, he sighed, gave her hand a squeeze, and said, "I won't. Not a word."

<hr>

Atarius hummed a quiet tune to himself as he walked through the forest. Searching the ground as he stepped, he gathered up pieces of whittling wood, hoping to gift them to Sheik once he'd gathered a good amount. Things had been tense between them, but they were beginning to mend.

He had sensed that something was wrong the moment he'd given her the bow on the night of her coming-of-age ceremony. At the time, he couldn't have guessed what the matter was. But after she had blurted out that she felt isolated from the rest of the village because of the rigorous training he had put her through, he suddenly understood.

And so over the past week, he hadn't pushed her towards training at all. She worked with Ralin and Faer and some of the women, and while he missed her company, he was glad to let her relish in the mundane and mingle with the other villagers. Even though it meant more space between them, Atarius was willing to adjust to her new schedule and routine so long as it made her happy.

And it wasn't as if she was absent from his life. Even after their disagreement about the sword, she continued to practice archery with him occasionally. With time and a little effort, things would return to normal.

As he turned around the next tree, he spotted Farin in a suggestive pose.

Atarius dropped what was in his hands and clutched his chest in surprise. Farin whistled at him before breaking his pose and bursting into laughter.

"Farin, I swear!" Atarius yelled, and then let his frustration dissolve into a chuckle. "What's wrong with you?"

"Too many things to count, I'm sure," Farin quipped back. "What's this?" he asked, helping Atarius recollect the wood chips.

"For Sheik," he explained. "Thought it would make a nice present."

"What's the occasion?"

"Just trying to fix things," he admitted. Farin was the only one he confessed such troubles to. "Things are getting better, but still, I know I've got some making up to do. I shouldn't have ever kept the prophecy from her." Farin listened attentively, and so Atarius continued, "I guess I partially didn't want to admit it to myself. Not after I got to know her and we grew so close. I'm just me and she's chosen by Elilah herself."

Farin laughed. "You're just you? You're sachem!"

Atarius couldn't help but smirk. "Of a three-hundred-person village. Yes, I'm someone important indeed. And Sheik is," he trailed off, wondering if there were words to describe how special she was. "Well anyway, she doesn't seem to realize what it all means. I've been trying not to bring up the sword and the bloodline and all, I know it annoys her. But she's got to realize it eventually."

"She'll start believing it soon enough," Farin assured him. Atarius glanced his way and noticed him tense up.

"What do you mean?" he asked delicately.

Farin remained stiff. "Just give it time, that's all."

"Come on." Atarius crossed his arms. "We've been friends for some time, Farin. I know when there's something you aren't telling me."

"I'm just saying, she'll believe it in time, that's all!" Farin retorted with a huff. Now Atarius knew for certain something was awry. He gave Farin a look. "Just leave it be."

Atarius frowned. "Farin, tell me what's going on. What did she say?"

"Fine, but you'd better not tell her I said anything," Farin finally relented. "Her dream has come back." He didn't need to elaborate. Atarius knew plenty well what dream he was talking about.

"Why didn't she tell me?" he asked quietly. Sheik came to him with practically everything. Had this really changed their relationship so much? Had she really lost so much trust in him? He began to walk back towards the village.

"Where are you going?" his friend called out after him.

"To find her."

"What?" Farin exclaimed. He ran in front of him, blocking his movement. "What did I just say? You can't tell her I told you! She'll be furious!"

He took in a deep breath. "This is more important than that." Farin began to argue but Atarius cut him off. "I know it'll hurt her, and don't you think I'm hurt too? That she wouldn't tell me? But this is bigger than us. Elilah is sending her a message and she's ignoring it. This is more important than a few hurt feelings."

Farin's eyebrows furrowed. "Fine, but I'm getting to her first!" he announced and took off at top speed.

Atarius lurched after him but decided to return to a walk. Farin was faster. He couldn't outrun him. And he didn't mind dragging his feet. After all, this was a conversation he wasn't looking forward to. If Sheik was annoyed with him now, he couldn't imagine how she'd feel after this confrontation. He wondered if, after this was all said and done, she'd ever forgive him. He wondered if things would ever go back to the way they once were.

He didn't see how.

<hr>

"Sheik!" She glanced around to see which direction Farin was coming from. Here she was, by the edge of the river, gathering water, perfectly alone. The fact that he didn't take this opportunity to sneak into one of his silly poses meant something was wrong. "Sheik!" he screamed again before coming into view.

She was on her feet in an instant. "Farin, what is it?"

His eyes were watering. "Sheik, I'm so sorry."

"What? What's going on?"

"I told Atarius. I didn't mean to, it just slipped out." He didn't need to say what he was talking about; Sheik knew very well. The secret she had asked him to keep only two days ago. Her stomach dropped.

"Farin, how could you?" She believed that it was an accident. But still, how could he have messed up so badly? She bit her lip and rubbed her temple. "Let me guess, he's on his way now?"

Farin nodded. "I'm sorry, Sheik. I really am."

She took a seat on a nearby log. "I know." She glanced up at him and gave him a half smile. "Don't worry about it, Farin. He would have found out eventually." The dream had come to her again last night. If the dreams kept up, Atarius would have figured it out sooner or later.

"Still," Farin mumbled, "I can't tell you how—"

Sheik was about to wave it away, but Atarius entered her field of view. "And here he is," she muttered under her breath. "We'll see how this goes."

When Atarius approached, he turned towards Farin. "Will you leave us alone?" Farin nodded and skulked away, though Sheik knew quite well that he would stay within hearing range and eavesdrop. It was for the better that he listened in. In fact, part of her wished that it would be an open conversation to be heard by the entire village. Then maybe someone else could talk some sense into Atarius.

"Farin told me you know," Sheik began.

"That you've started having that dream again?" Atarius clarified. She nodded. "So you believe it now?"

Sheik laughed. "No, not really."

His eyebrows bounced up in surprise. "Really?"

"Really. It's just a dream."

"So what would it take? A beam of light? The skies to open up and Elilah's voice to proclaim it?" Sheik could sense a frustration in his voice she hadn't heard before. She simply couldn't understand it. How could he believe in such a silly thing? And even if it were true, why did it matter so much?

"Fine, Atarius. Let's say it's true," she decided suddenly, switching strategies. "You've convinced me. I'm the 'chosen one,' destined to find Elilah's magic sword. Where shall I begin looking? Do you want me to start with your throne room? Or how about the meadow, should I search there?" She did a fake scan of the riverbed. "Hmm, it's not here by the river. Maybe in Farin's tree?" Atarius' face began to grow red, and in that instant she knew she had him. "See how ridiculous it sounds? Even if I did believe in all this nonsense, the sword would have to be right here in this village for me to find it."

He stared back at her in silence, and she crossed her arms, awaiting his response. "You're right," he admittedly weakly. She tried to hide her grin at having finally put a stop to this foolishness. But then Atarius looked into her with those piercing silver eyes and said with sudden sternness, "You need to leave."

"What?" She couldn't have heard him right. Could she?

"If you're to find the Sword of Elilah, you cannot stay here. You need to leave."

Her heart pounded. It was like the moment after her dream, when she would awake in a panic, in pain, out of breath. Atarius wanted her to leave? "Fine!" she said with sudden defiance. She had only chosen to stay because of him. And now he wanted her gone. She wouldn't stay where she wasn't wanted. "If you don't want me here—"

Farin dropped down from where he had hidden nearby and ran into their conversation. "Stop it you two," he shouted. "Atarius, take it back, you know you don't—"

"Quiet, Farin!" Atarius shouted. "She cannot stay here."

Sheik's eyebrows furrowed. "I don't *want* to stay here." Again, Farin tried to calm them, but Sheik didn't bother listening. "I'll be gone by tomorrow." With that, she stormed off towards her home tree, holding in her breath, holding in her emotions, refusing to give Atarius the satisfaction of knowing how he had hurt her.

When she reached the privacy of her home, she allowed herself to sob.

Atarius had never been clear about how much he cared for Sheik. He rarely spoke about his feelings. But despite his shyness and modesty, she had always believed he loved her. He spent countless hours with her, listening to her, giving her advice, helping her. At every chance he could, he tried to please her. He constantly was doing whatever small thing that he could to express his care for her.

But now Sheik realized how much he really cared about her: enough to ask her to leave the village.

How could he do this to her? After her ceremony, after finally becoming a part of the village? How could he rip it all away from her?

After nearly an hour of weeping, she began to pack her things. She had said she would be gone by tomorrow and she meant to keep her word. Pulling out a backpack she had hardly ever used, she threw all her clothes inside. What else would she need?

Sheik hadn't been away from the village for longer than two days. Perhaps medical wrap, in case she was somehow wounded? Flint and steel, she thought to herself, for if the weather was unusually cold. She had never been very good with fire magic and thought it would be smart to have a backup plan. A blanket, of course. When she could think of nothing more, she closed both her backpack and tear-stained eyes.

⁘

Sheik was not sure if it was technically morning yet. It was cold, the stars barely illuminating the sky. She reminded herself to stop by the medic tree for supplies before leaving. Seeing the bed where she had first awoken to Atarius' silver eyes brought forth a flood of memories and emotions. Shrugging them aside, she dug through a cabinet helping herself to whatever she felt she might need.

Normally anyone was welcome to anything in the medic tree. But was she even a part of the village anymore? Atarius had essentially banished her. Still, she took what she needed. Bow, arrows, cloak, backpack, she thought, checking each item off in her mind. Was she missing anything?

"Sheik?" a voice whispered.

She jumped, trying not to scream. It was obviously Farin. He was the only one ever quiet enough to sneak up on her. She sighed, knowing she would miss his immature antics. "Yes?" she asked, facing him.

59

"Are you really leaving?" She feared crying and so all she could do was nod. "Sheik, you don't need to do this."

"Yes, I do," she insisted, wiping a couple of tears as they managed to well up in her eyes. "If he would cast me out so easily, how can I stay?"

"Just talk to him, please," he urged.

She stepped past him towards the door, shaking her head. "I'm sorry, Farin."

"Wait," he grabbed her by the shoulder. "Before you leave." He untied his belt of throwing knives and held it out for her. "I don't know where you're headed. You probably won't ever need them," he shrugged. "But it's something to remember me by." His perfectly weighted throwing knives. He had always bragged about them. He had gotten them from traders a couple of years before Sheik came to the village. They had always been his favorite, most prized possession. It made more tears well up in her eyes.

Sheik tightened the belt around her waist and gave him a hug. She thought she had woken up early enough to avoid saying goodbyes. "I'm going to miss you," she said softly.

"You too," he smiled, letting her go. He stayed behind in the medic room as she climbed down the tree and left the village behind.

The wolf cave would be her last familiar stop. She couldn't imagine leaving without saying goodbye to Fang. As she walked, she removed one of the knives. It came out easier than expected and she twirled it in her hands. She almost chuckled, remembering how protective Farin had been of his favorite set, rarely letting anyone touch them. Now, he had given them away altogether. She placed it back in its sheath.

It was still dark out, only the moon and sparse stars lighting the path. She whistled as she grew close to the cave and Fang trotted out to see her. Tears sprang forward once again. "Oh Fang, I'm going to miss you." She gave him a hug and scratches until the sun began to rise.

When her goodbye was finally complete, she wiped her tears and began her trek eastward. Fang followed. "No, boy. You aren't coming with me." But he ignored her orders. "You don't understand," she explained, dropping to one knee so she could look him in the eye. "I'm leaving for good."

He looked back into her eyes and gave her a single whine as if to say he knew.

Still he followed after her. She thought to argue and try to force him to sit and stay, but decided that if he wanted to come she couldn't object to the company. At least she wouldn't be entirely alone. He faithfully followed behind her as she led them eastward.

As the morning sun began to light up the woods, she made out a figure in the distance. She knew who it would be.

"Atarius," she said calmly, trying to hide any tears she had cried over the past few hours.

"Sheik," he replied, and for once the emotion in his voice was obvious. Sorrow.

She wouldn't give him any sympathy. This was his doing. He wanted her gone. He had told her to leave. "I told you I would be gone by morning."

He sighed and looked at her for a long while, like he wanted desperately to say something. His silence lingered. "This is bigger than both of us, Sheik."

There was nothing more to be said. This imaginary sword meant more to him than she ever had. "Goodbye, Atarius." She waved for Fang to follow her and walked past him.

"Good luck," he called out after her.

Those words, meant to be reassuring, pained her. He meant good luck finding the sword, not good luck being on her own.

She did not look back.

CHAPTER 3

Auni had struggled at first to pull away from their grasp. But once one of the men had gotten a firm grip on his arm, he knew it was hopeless. He did not stand a chance. The four men were adults. Auni was only a boy. And these men were burly and well fed. Auni had no such luxuries.

Auni was a slave. He was small and malnourished. And if he fought back now, they would only beat him more.

He let his body go limp. It was all he could do to protest. But even that was in vain; the four men had no problems dragging him to the barn. And in only moments they had him chained, his arms held up above him, pointing to the ceiling. He had to stand on his toes to not be hung by the wrists.

As his head dropped in defeat, he noticed the ground. It was stained by a dark brown color he knew instantly to be blood. Soon that stain would become a pool of his own blood.

One of the men slapped his tired face and spat in it. He was unable to wipe it away, and simply closed his eyes, hoping it would be over soon. The sound of a cracking whip startled him. Two of the men laughed as he flinched, preparing to lash him. The other two men began heating up a metal rod. That metal rod scared the boy much more than the whip.

The whip cracked against his back once. Then twice. Three times. He soon lost count, the pain all blurring together. He guessed it was maybe twenty lashes. Then he was done. The whips stopped.

But it wasn't really done.

He heard the sizzling of the metal rod. It was ready. He was too frightened to open his eyes. One man unchained his left arm and let it dangle. The hissing of the hot rod came closer and closer.

It burned into his left shoulder. In an instant his skin had blistered and bubbled.

It was over. The boy was fully unchained, the men still laughing as they kicked at him, scrambling away. He was picked up, carried, and thrown out into the fields he was so familiar with. When he finally managed to open his eyes, he could hardly see anything in the dark of the night. He fell asleep quickly, hoping he would be dead by morning.

⬥

He awoke in a bed. Not the bundle of straw he normally slept on, but a real bed. He was still in terrible pain. The lacerations on his back were throbbing, bloody. His hand had a small wound that he couldn't quite remember acquiring. It wasn't deep, yet somehow it managed to sting the most.

He was face down and his vision was blurry from the pain pulsing through his body, yet he recognized where he was with only a glance. The walls were made of fine wood and the ceiling was tall. There was art around the room and fur fringe on the sheets draped across the bed. The things in that room alone would make him rich beyond his wildest dreams.

A girl entered his field of view. He knew her. Shit. Horrible realization flooded through his mind. He had to get out of there. What if he was unable to walk? He would force himself to crawl then. It did not matter how he got out of that room; he simply knew he needed out.

"You're awake." Her words were soft and friendly, but her Mainlander accent sent shivers down his spine. His eyes darted about wildly, looking for an exit, an escape. How did he even get in here? Why wasn't she screaming for guards, for workers, for her father? "Please, try not to be frightened. Do you know who I am?"

He nodded the best he could, given that his head was still sideways against the pillow, his body crumpled on the bed. Was he supposed to speak? He risked it. "Miss Tara, daughter of Master Dubose."

She let out a breath, either a chuckle or a sigh. "Perhaps I should ask you a different question, then. Do you know who you are?"

His stomach flipped. Was she implying what he thought she was? How did she know? He held his breath. He couldn't say the truth. He did not know what would happen to him if he admitted to knowing. "Auni, Master Dubose's servant." Servant was the euphemism. It really meant slave. But Mainlanders didn't like the word. They liked to pretend that the Islanders were just subservient. Happy to work for nothing. Auni wanted to say more. He wanted to scream out in pain. He wanted to ask why he was there, what she was doing, what was going to happen to him.

He remained silent.

Tara nodded. "A pleasure to make your acquaintance, Auni. I'm grateful to finally know your name." She looked him over. "Do you need another pillow? There's some water here," she offered. "I can find some pain relief herbs?"

He was in too much pain to sit up. Not that he could have accepted her offer anyway. Surely it was a trap. She set the cup on a table just beside him. It was meant to taunt him.

Moving aside the curtain she glanced out the window. Daylight entered the room. The manse was on a hill, overlooking the many fields owned by Tara's father. "I watch you sometimes, working out there." Her voice became monotone, like she did not really care if he was listening to her. "My mother told me about you once when she was angry at my father. I wondered how it was fair that you sweat and bled out there while I sat in here."

She turned back to him. "How is it fair? That you were born an Islander, so you must be a slave. And I am born a Mainlander, so I am allowed freedom. I know the Islanders attacked us so many years ago, but surely we are more than the sins of our fathers, right?" She gave him a pleading look. "Right?"

He didn't know what she wanted him to say, so he merely nodded.

"And the truth of the matter is," she added, regaining her composure, "is you aren't an Islander."

Auni's heart thumped. She knew.

Auni had all the outward signs of being an Islander. Islanders had jet black, curly hair. Their skin ranged from bronze to ebony, their eyes golden in the sun. But she was right: Auni's blood was just as much Mainlander as it was Islander.

"Your mother was an Islander, as you know. But your father..." she hesitated to say the words out loud. "I am your sister, Auni."

Why was she telling him this? What did she want? His eyes danced between her and the door. How would he get out of here?

"We have the same father," she spoke solemnly. "He had relations with—no, raped," she corrected herself. And she paused on that word deliberately, like she was letting it sink into her own mind. "He raped your mother. And then he treated you no different than any other slave."

Tara stared at him for a long time.

At first he was still churning out ways to escape. To make it out of the room, out of the house, down the hill. Then he wondered why Tara remained silent. Why had she told him all this? If she was setting him up to be found in her room so he might be tortured, why hadn't she called over guards yet?

"I want to help you run away," she finally whispered. "I have wanted to help you for so long now." When Auni still said nothing, she pointed at his shoulder and where it had been branded. "You cannot do it on your own. But I can get you out of here."

He couldn't bend his body in a way where he could see it. And he certainly couldn't touch it. But it was there all the same. And it would be for the rest of his life.

Though Auni didn't know how to read, there was one letter that every slave was familiar with: the letter R.

Runaway.

It probably didn't even look like a letter yet. It was probably just a yellow lumpy mass. He'd seen them fresh before.

And he'd seen them after years had passed. After they'd faded into a slick, shiny scar. All the guards now would look at him with wrath. They would spit at him when they passed him. He had to run away. He couldn't live like this any longer.

He didn't want to put his fate in Tara's hands, but he also didn't have a lot of other options. He hadn't been the only slave to run away last night, so the guards would be extra alert for months. Having Tara to help him would be his best option.

Auni studied her for a moment. She looked like his exact opposite. It was hard to believe they were siblings. How did helping him escape benefit her? Was she really doing this out of some notion of kinship? Probably just guilt.

But that guilt could be exploited. So despite all of his hesitations, all of his fears, he decided to agree to her plan.

⸺◦⬦◦⸺

The straw poked at his open wounds. It hurt. The gashes were likely infected. Despite the pain, he kept quiet, knowing even a small cry could give them away. He could hear a guard's voice. "Miss Tara? Where are you going?"

She was the plantation owner's daughter. Surely the guards wouldn't pose a problem. "To town."

"Miss, I don't know if I can permit you to pass at this hour. It's dangerous, there may be thugs or some of those runaways still lurking around. I don't think your father would approve if he were here."

The young woman interrupted him. "My father sent a worker back from town saying he needed me to take the wagon to him immediately. He sold more than expected and wanted me to drive it so I could meet a young businessman. My father would not be very happy if I did not arrive by morning to meet a client of his. A suitor."

He stuttered an okay and opened the small gate for her. "Good luck," he added after a moment. She nodded, pushing the horses onwards.

Auni gave a sigh of relief. They had made it! It concerned him how good Tara was at lying. What if she was lying to him? When they were out of hearing range of the guard, he turned a little, though it hurt no matter how he was positioned.

There was a small metallic clank.

He did not open his eyes; it was impossible to see in the darkness anyway. He felt around, wincing when the straw rubbed against his wounds. Buried beneath it was a small coin.

He pushed his arm further into the straw. Sure enough, there was more cool metal. Tara was a thief! It was strange, running his hands through all the coins. He had never felt so much money, even if it was only copper or bronze. But considering she had stolen it from her own mansion, he had a feeling it was gold.

His head banged against the cart as it slammed to a stop. "Who goes there?" Tara called out.

"Miss Tara?" a voice whispered back. "Little Miss Tara, all by herself. Even better." Auni recognized the voice.

Kanja.

He was one of the several others who had run away with Auni. Apparently, the diversion Auni had given the others had worked. Though it had led to Auni's capture, it had allowed Kanja and the others to escape.

Kanja had always been angry. He had good reason to be. They all did. But the others tried to stay positive. Kanja never did. Someday, he used to tell them, we'll have our rightful revenge.

Tonight, Kanja would seek his revenge.

"Where you going all alone?" the man asked, hiding in the darkness. "Come down from up there. Pretty girls like you shouldn't be driving horses." There was a quiet clink of steel as Kanja drew a knife. Auni shuffled around in the cart despite the searing pain that ran through his body. He was not sure what he would do. Kanja was older and much larger than he was. But he crawled quietly, inching towards them, watching them from within the pile of straw.

Kanja hopped up next to Tara and smiled at the frightened girl. "Does your dear old dad know you're out here all alone?" Tara reached around, clearly looking for something she could defend herself with. There was nothing.

"Yes," she lied, "there are workers bringing a second wagon just behind. They should be along any minute."

Either he knew she was lying or he didn't care. "What a shame. I'd have preferred to leave your body for your father to find. I'd like to see his face, the Mighty Mr. Dubose."

"Look, I know my father is horrible. I do not condone his actions," Tara sputtered. But Kanja showed no signs of being talked down. He pressed the knife against her skin. She sucked in her breath and went silent.

Auni was afraid the knife would cut Tara if he tried to intervene. But she was going to be hurt either way. It was now or never.

He screamed, leaping out of the loose straw and tackling Kanja. With a thud, the two crashed against the horses and landed on the hard ground. The horses were instantly startled and began to kick frantically. Auni ducked and crawled out of the way.

With a crack, a hoof crushed Kanja's skull and their combat ended abruptly.

Then the horses took off.

It took Auni a second to regain himself. Did Kanja just die? He had hoped to knock him off the wagon and just talk some sense into him. But he was dead now. It had all happened so fast, and he stared at the half of his head that was crushed and unrecognizable.

He snapped out of it and glanced towards the wagon. Tara was clutching her chest while struggling to pull on the reins, yelling for them to slow. Then suddenly her screaming stopped.

"Tara!" Auni shouted, watching her faint and fall backwards into the straw. He sprinted, ignoring the searing pain that burned through his body. The horses began to pick up speed again. Auni sped up. Just a little further. With a leap, he barely managed to make it onto the cart before the horses took off at a full gallop.

Scrambling around Tara's body he grabbed the reins and yanked as hard as he could. He felt his wounds tear open with the force. The horses instantly came to a stop.

"Miss Tara?" he asked. She was still breathing, but unconscious. There was a cut across her chest. Spotting Kanja's knife in the wagon, he cut off his pant legs from the knee down, and quickly fashioned a bandage, pressing it against her wound.

A thought flickered in the back of his mind.

She was injured, but she probably wouldn't die. If he left her by the side of the road, someone would come across her by morning. She would be fine. He glanced at the wagon, topped with straw but full of gold and swallowed hard.

No, he couldn't do it.

He could, in the sense that he was past the hardest part. They were outside the plantation gates. They were far enough away he wasn't in imminent danger of being caught. He no longer needed Tara.

But he couldn't abandon her. He had no one anymore. Not since his mother had been taken from him. No family. He was lost and alone in this world.

He had originally seen Tara as merely an escape route, but now he realized that deep down he wanted more. He wanted a friend. He wanted a sister. Had he lost his mind?

Her eyes flickered. "Tara!" He gave her a gentle squeeze as she awoke. "You're alright, thank Ziad!"

"Auni? What happened?"

He motioned for her not to talk. "Let me finish with the bandage. I'll lift you into the straw and keep driving until we reach town, okay? It's going to be alright."

As he finished tying the cloth, Tara reached up and grabbed his hand. There was a twinge of pain from the cut on his palm, but he ignored it, mostly out of shock. A Mainlander touching an Islander in this way? It was unheard of. Tara smiled, but only for a second. Then she let out a cry and fainted once again.

"Tara?" What in the abyss had happened? He studied her to see what might have caused her to faint. She had no other wounds, only the one he had bandaged. He lifted his hand to her neck to check her pulse but found himself staring at his palm in shock. As if by magic, the cut on his hand was now gone.

———◆———

Tara jolted awake as the cart thudded over a particularly large tree root. "Where are we?" she asked, overwhelmed with pain and confusion.

Auni was to her side in an instant. "Tara? Are you alright?"

She shook her head. No, she was not alright. Her chest hurt, her head ached, and her mouth was dry. "Where are we?" she asked again.

"Just east of town. I didn't know where we were headed, but I was too scared to go into town by myself." He motioned to his shoulder.

Right. Because of the brand, everyone would know he was a runaway. And it would not look good that he had an unconscious Mainlander woman and a mound of gold hidden in a cart.

But now she was awake. Surely it was safe to go into town. She sat up, or rather she tried to sit up and found herself lightheaded again. "Whoa, are you okay?" Auni asked, his arm ready to catch her. "You look like you're going to pass out again."

It took a moment of concentration to keep herself from doing just that. Then another long pause before she concocted an idea. "East of town? There's an inn. Northeast. Can we make it there?" She glanced around but because of the dark of the night had no idea which way was north.

Auni seemed to know and oriented the wagon accordingly. "Northeast. Got it. Go back to sleep."

She tried to go back to sleep but could not. Now that she was awake there were too many bumps to sleep in a wagon. Especially since they were not on any main road. The main road would have taken them straight to town, but she had no idea what path Auni had gotten onto or even where they were. She just had to trust that he knew which way was up. Otherwise they would have to camp out in the middle of the woods. And with the cut on her chest and all of Auni's terrible wounds, she knew what an absolute disaster that would be. Not to mention that she had never camped out a day in her life.

But thankfully Auni knew exactly what he was doing and in another hour or so they pulled up to the inn that she had remembered. Far on the outskirts of town, so she would not attract too much attention.

"Help me up." He did as told and she clutched the wound on her chest. Then she looked at her hand. Something had happened to it, but she could not quite remember what. Had it gotten hurt in the scuffle with that other runaway? It didn't look injured, so she shrugged off the odd feeling.

She knocked extra loud on the door of the inn. It was too late for them to expect guests. She knocked again. "Cover your shoulder," Tara whispered before knocking a third time. Auni nodded and placed his right hand just in front of the brand on his left shoulder. After her forth knock, a man finally came to the door.

"Oh, help us, please," she burst into tears, ready to be as convincing as need be. "Bandits attacked us. We were supposed to deliver supplies into town, but they drove us off the road, we barely escaped. Do you have a room? And space in the stable to store our wagon? I can pay, I promise!" She dug through her dress pocket and pulled out a few silver coins. "Please, for the love of Ziad!"

The inn keeper immediately took pity on her and placed a warm hand on her shoulder. "Of course, poor thing, come in, come in. The stable is just there," he pointed, "you can sleep there, and Miss let me take you inside."

"No, I insist he stay inside with me," Tara interrupted. "He nearly died saving me from the bandits. He needs a proper bath and bed or else he might get infection. He's my best servant, I cannot have him dying on me."

The man made a face. "We've only one room left, I'm afraid."

"Well, he can sleep on the floor. At least he should be less likely to get infection. I insist, please, my father will be so disappointed if his best servant were to die." She increased her blubbering. "Oh, and it would be all my fault!"

If only to put out her tears, the man consented. "Very well, here is the key. It's up the stairs, last door on the right. Come in, come in, I'll take your wagon to the stable."

Tara's tears faded as quickly as they had arrived once they had made it into the room and closed the door. "Whew!" With a sigh of relief, she flopped onto the bed. "We did it. Listen, if you want to take a bath now, feel free, but I'm too tired to wait for the water to heat."

"Me too. I just want to sleep."

She patted the bed next to her. "Well squeeze in, we can both fit." He looked shocked at the suggestion, but she insisted. She knew how bizarre it was. The fact that an Islander and a Mainlander were sharing a room was scandalous enough. If anyone knew Auni was sleeping in bed next to her, he would likely be killed. But she could not imagine leaving him to sleep on the floor.

He was snoring in a matter of minutes.

Tara began to think it might keep her up, but before she could finish the thought, she too was asleep.

When she awoke, Auni had already started the fire and began heating some water for the bathtub. She yawned and felt the cut across her chest. It was only a thin scab. "I am surprised I healed so fast. I thought I was going to die," she chuckled. "I thought you had died! Oh, when I saw you go down with that man. And the horses started rearing, I thought for certain. And then I fainted and there you were. How are you doing?"

He shrugged. "I don't think sleeping indoors kept my cuts from getting infected." He showed her a few that had ripped open and were now covered with a layer of yellowish white. While Tara's cut had grown better during the night, Auni's wounds had grown worse.

"Before you passed out, you grabbed my hand," Auni added. "Do you know what you did?"

Tara shook her head. "No, you squeezed my hand."

"Huh?"

She thought about it for a moment, trying to remember it clearly. It all came back to her. She had not hurt her hand in the scuffle—Auni had simply squeezed it so hard it felt like it had split open.

"Yes, you squeezed my hand, and it hurt so bad I fainted. Why did you do that?"

"I didn't," he argued. "When you let go, the cut on my hand was healed. Do you know how you did it?"

"Really?" She had gone unconscious a moment later. When she had awoken, she had forgotten all about it and simply focused on getting safely to the inn.

"You don't think you could do it again, huh?" Auni muttered.

Tara looked at him for a moment. "I can certainly try." She placed her hand on his shoulder, where the R had been branded into him. He screamed out unlike any cry she had ever heard before.

Instantly, she felt searing pain rising from his arm. She screamed and clutched her hand. She shook it, hoping to shake out the pain. It departed as instantly as it came, and she looked it up and down. There was no mark. Despite the blinding ache, the feeling that blisters were bubbling up on her palm, there was nothing.

Then she looked at Auni. His wound had healed before her eyes. The blisters had melted away, leaving nothing but the small, imprinted R, as if it had been branded many years ago.

"Are you okay?" he asked, his voice laden with terror. "You did it, it's all better, what's wrong?" She was unable to speak, still in too much shock. He grabbed her hand, peering at it to see what she was staring at.

Tears welled in the corner of her eyes, and it took her a moment to gather the ability to speak. When she did, all she could say was, "It was so painful."

He put an arm around her. "I'm sorry. I won't make you do it again. I'm sorry. It's okay," he repeated over and over until she had calmed down.

"No." She wiped away her tears. "No, when I dragged you into my room, I promised myself I would help you." She looked at her hand. "I will not break that promise." She reached out her hand again, pressing it against one of the many lacerations across his back.

It had taken Tara the rest of the day to finish healing his wounds. She had needed to rest many times so the pain would not overwhelm her. Auni shared in the pain as she scrubbed his wounds with soap and water, unsure if her healing would cure the infections that had begun to set in. At first it took her nearly an hour between healings to recover from whatever intense pain she was feeling. But as the day passed, she built up a resistance to the previously unbearable pain and was able to heal several wounds within an hour.

By the time his final cut was healed, it was dark, and they stayed in the inn another night. When they left the next morning, the fresh air was glorious. Auni was healthy, all his wounds completely healed. Back in the fields he had never been in such good condition. He usually had at least a cut or two and felt the sting of hunger or thirst.

But now he would have all the food he wanted. His pockets were filled with coins. He had never dreamed of such wealth. Ten gold coins would have been astonishing to him a week ago. Perhaps even stranger to him than the wealth was the love he felt from Tara. Islanders always stuck together, but this was different. Tara was family.

And Auni hadn't had family in years. His mother had been sold away when he was still a young boy. He could hardly recall her face. His only other family was his slave-owning father and half-sister, whom he had always hated and resented.

But everything was different now. He no longer was suspicious of Tara. She had meant everything she had said from moment one. She had helped him escape, just as she had promised. But more than that, she stayed by his side. He had thought she would return to the manse on the hill, happy to have done her one good deed and return to her old life of luxury while Auni settled elsewhere. But apparently that had never been her plan.

Tara had run away too. She had no intention of going back. Together they would start a new life.

They didn't stop traveling until they had put two towns between them and the Dubose plantation. They left their horses and wagon at a stable for a silver and strolled through the town, pockets full of coin. Auni had never been into town before and gawked at the many stores, full of tools, supplies, and food. Eventually they paraded into a small clothing shop. "Could we try on some clothes?" Tara asked the clerk.

"We?" he chuckled. "You're dressing up your slave?" Not all Islanders were slaves. Many had been freed. But if an Islander and a Mainlander were traveling together, it was the most likely assumption that the Islander belonged to the Mainlander.

Auni thought Tara might correct the man, but she gave a cheery, "Yes, sir."

The shop keeper shrugged as he brought them out a pile of clothing that was roughly their size. Auni stayed quiet as he tried on different pants. He didn't care for the way Tara so readily called him her slave, but he trusted that it was simply to not draw attention. He oriented his left side away from the clerk, hoping the man wouldn't spot the R branded into his shoulder. The last thing they needed was trouble.

Tara picked out several dresses, skirts, and blouses. Auni handed her several pairs of pants he had tried on. Tara fussed about the coloring and chose different ones for him. He didn't really care either way. "Now shirts," she motioned to a rack.

Auni had never worn a proper shirt with buttons before. Just his one scrappy shirt for particularly cold winters. Now that he tried on a button up shirt, it felt foreign and constricting. He glanced at himself in the mirror. He looked like a Mainlander. He hated it.

"No," Auni mumbled, taking it off. "I don't want a shirt."

"You must have a shirt!" she retorted. "How do you expect to look civilized without a shirt?"

He grabbed her sleeve and pulled her away from the clerk. "Civilized?" he asked in a tense whisper. "I dress like an Islander. Is that not civilized? I have to look like a Mainlander to be civilized?"

She swallowed. "I'm sorry." She looked at the clothes around her, flustered. "You are absolutely right. I'm sorry. But here," she picked out a single, plain jacket. "Just to cover your shoulder?" As he put it on, she added, "Maybe someday you can get a tattoo to cover it." Tattoos were common among Islanders, but they were earned when one came of age or accomplished various life achievements. They weren't to cover up degrading scars or brands.

But rather than correct her, Auni gave a simple shrug. "Maybe." At least she was trying.

Tara gathered up the rest of the clothes they had tried on and presented them to the shop keeper. "This is all we want, plus the jacket."

As she paid and the clerk folded and stuffed the clothes into their backpack, Auni glanced outside the window, back at the foreign town. It was all he had imagined a town to be. Other slaves who had served as wheat haulers for Mr. Dubose had passed through many towns as they delivered to the plantation's many clients. Auni had always wanted to go on a hauling trip, but it only happened twice a year and you had to be much bigger and stronger than Auni ever was.

His smile turned into an inquisitive frown. A group of men caught his eye. They were looking at a poster, nailed onto a fence. He squinted. It looked like a portrait but he couldn't make out any details beyond that. The men then collectively glanced towards Tara.

Casually exiting the store, Auni managed to get a better look. The poster was the spitting image of Tara. Her porcelain skin, her straight hair, her thin eyebrows, her dimples. And though he was unable to read, he had a feeling it was a reward sign. He ran to her side as she left the store. "Walk quickly."

"Why?" she asked, increasing her pace. "What is it? Is something wrong?"

He glanced back. Sure enough, the men were following them. Three men. "We need to get back to the wagon. Now." He remembered the tool shop they had passed on their way to the clothing store. There had been a display in front of the shop.

He looked back again. They had begun to fan out. "Run." The men also began to run. Upon reaching the tool shop, Auni spotted exactly what he needed. "Keep going!" he shouted at Tara while he grabbed a hammer from the display. He spun back around to face the men.

They stopped. "You let us pass, Islander. We aren't here for you," one spoke up. "We just want the girl." Auni did not reply but continued to hold out the hammer. "Go on and get her," the same man muttered, motioning to one of his friends. "We'll take care of this runt." He drew a sword and stepped towards Auni.

Auni leapt forward at the third man, who had not yet drawn his sword. With all his might he smashed the hammer into the man's chest. He spun back just in time to block the first man's attack, and then gave him a forceful kick to the groin. As the man doubled over in pain, Auni crashed the hammer into the man's knee. Neither of them would be able to follow him now.

He sprinted after the man who was pursuing Tara. As he finally caught up to them, she was already coming back with the wagon, riding one of the horses. The man smiled, seeing his chance. He drew his sword and, as the wagon began to slow, slammed it into the leg of the horse Tara was riding.

Auni dropped his hammer and quickly shoved the man out of the way so he could catch Tara as she fell off the stumbling horse. He set her down quickly as the man picked himself up and raised his sword to attack. "She can heal me afterwards," Auni whispered to himself. The damage would not be permanent. It was only pain. He could do this.

Auni dodged the man's strike and then grabbed the blade with his left hand. Though it sliced open his palm, he used the sword to pull the man off his balance. Blood sprayed everywhere. He ignored it, delivering a quick punch to the man's face. Then he angled himself to elbow the man in the gut. Auni pressed his back against the man's chest with all his might, holding him in place against the wagon.

The man brought his sword up to slit Auni's throat, but Auni blocked the blade with his left forearm. The sword sliced easily through his skin but couldn't cut the muscle and bone. They struggled for a moment, the man's blade and Auni's forearm locked in a contest of strength.

This was the opportunity Auni needed.

When he felt his arm about to give, he quickly slid out of the way and ducked. The man was unable to stop the sword's momentum as it cut into his own throat.

Auni kneeled next to Tara. "Please, you need to heal me quick," he explained. "I'm losing too much blood. My arm first."

She nodded. After having healed him so many times in the inn, she was easily able to command the power. She gave a quick scream of pain and the skin on Auni's arm replenished itself.

"I will need to wait a moment," she caught her breath, "for your hand." Auni tore apart what remained of his tattered pants. Gold spilled out of his pockets as he began to wrap his palm.

"I'll be fine for a while, don't rush yourself. We need to get out of here though."

She gathered the fallen coins and placed them in the backpack, full of their recently purchased clothes and the rest of their gold. Tossing a pair of pants at Auni, he quickly dressed himself in the middle of the street. "Grab the sword," she motioned to the bloody weapon lying on the road. "The sheriff's soldiers will be after us soon." She unhitched the healthy horse, Nutmeg, leaving behind the wounded one. "Sorry, Willow," she whispered as he continued to buck and whine. They would have to leave him and the wagon if they wanted to escape quickly.

"Where are we going?" Auni asked, helping her mount Nutmeg the best he could with one hand. "East?"

She shook her head. "North."

He hopped on in front of her and kicked his heels against the horse's side. "Why north? Why not east to the islands?" With the gold they had, Tara could easily buy his freedom. And Auni had heard the islands had sanctuaries, where freed or runaway slaves could seek refuge.

"No, we need to get out of Omris," Tara insisted. "Even if I buy your freedom, you'll never really be *free*." The horse was galloping now as they put distance between them and the town. "You'll never be given the proper respect you deserve. But once we're far enough north, it'll be different."

"How so?" he asked.

"Vesdar has no slavery. It doesn't have the history Omris does between Mainlanders and Islanders. No one is going to look at you and just assume," she trailed off awkwardly. "Just assume you're nothing more than a slave."

"Really?"

"Not once we get out of Omris."

It was hard to believe. He pushed his heels in again and rode faster. He would soon be free.

Chapter 4

Sheik and Fang had been traveling for just over a week. She wished she had a map. The further she trekked, the more unfamiliar the forest became. Having been unsuccessful in finding an elven town to stay in, she merely continued to travel east. Sooner or later, she knew she would reach the end of the forest.

Despite the circumstances, it was exciting. She did not know what to expect. Atarius had left the forest once with his father, before he had died. He had told Sheik about the fields of grass, stretching as far as the eye could see. And the Great River that went from sea to sea.

Most of all she was eager to see human cities, populating as many as a million people. She couldn't fathom such a number. Crowded, condensed spaces of people coming and going. And she wanted so desperately to see what a human city looked like. She had grown accustomed to homes being inside of trees.

She was happy, really, that she had not come across any elven villages. Her curiosity made her eager to get out of the forest. Discover the world. She hardly knew what existed beyond elven territory. All she really knew was that the human lands were divided into five nations; Etmos to the north, Vesdar in the west next to the elven forest, Masil in the east alongside the Tasvran Mountain territory, and a peninsula to the south, Omris.

Sheik talked to Fang more and more. It was lonely by herself, and she felt a strange connection with the young wolf. Perhaps because she had helped birth him. Sometimes she felt like he really could understand her and was trying to talk to her. Other times she thought she must be crazy.

It did not stop her though. The solitude was overwhelming. It did not matter if she had to talk to animals to protect herself against complete loneliness. Would she ever see another person again? It seemed like she was stuck in this never-ending forest with only her faithful wolf to follow her. Those trees, which had once seemed so free and alive were now restricting walls, always surrounding her. She had to escape the forest and discover who and what lay beyond.

Despite being free of Atarius' law, she still did not pluck growing fruits and vegetables. Something about it felt wrong. For people without magic, there was need for such food. But she could sustain herself without meat or plants. And it was the rule she had been obediently following for over a year.

Of course she did not keep Fang from hunting. Wolves were made by Elilah to eat other creatures. It was only natural. So, whenever he chased after a critter, she simply tried to turn away from the poor prey and the subsequent bloodshed.

Sheik generally walked through the woods at a calm, easy pace. There were always interesting, unique plants and animals to spot, especially the further east she traveled. The terrain was not difficult to travel through. Sometimes she was able to travel a good twenty leagues a day, while still watching squirrels chatter and birds chirp.

During the day, she felt no need to be cautious. The forest was not highly populated. Few beings besides elves lived in it, and elves were known for their peaceful nature. If she did stumble upon humans or some other unfriendly people, Atarius had always told her she was better than most with both magic and bow.

She wondered if she actually was. She had never been in a real fight, only sparring matches with Atarius, Farin, and some of the other village elves. Sure, she was better than most of them, but perhaps the outside world was still hundreds of times better than her. There was no way of knowing, really. That was the danger of living in an isolated village. Who knew what lurked beyond?

At night, those fears nipped at her. It was often chilly, and so she would always create a small fire, whether with flint and steel or her magic, before going to sleep. She asked Fang to keep watch when she was feeling uneasy. He was always completely alert and ready, as if he fully understood the concept of staying on guard.

Other times, haunting thoughts prevented her from sleeping. The dream had gone away once she had left the village. Likely because she was no longer being constantly reminded of it by Atarius and Farin. She refused to reflect on it and would pull out a dagger and fletch some arrows from fallen wood. Using broad, aggressive strokes, she channeled the anger of the thoughts into her arrows until she felt at peace.

Sometimes the thoughts that called to her were pleasant. She thought of Atarius. His stunning eyes that seemed to enchant her. His long, emerald hair that hung just past his shoulders. He had dark features, yet soft lips. His arms were muscular from constantly practicing with his bow and climbing into the difficult to reach village rooms. The long tunics he wore as sachem hid his body, but she had caught sight of him without them before. His abs were well defined along with his chest, all of which was hard with muscle.

The more Sheik thought about him, the more attractive he was. Sometimes she would think about him for what felt like hours. The way he used to brush her hair behind her ear or touch her shoulder when he was helping her train. When she thought about him, she did not angrily fletch arrows. She would whittle small figurines. She was not particularly good at whittling, but she could usually at least make the wood look generally like what she was intending to carve.

But after carving the small figurines she would remember how Atarius had banished her. How he had cast her out, abandoned her. The feelings she was feeling for him—no, the feelings she *had once* felt for him—he clearly did not feel for her. And quickly she would toss the carving into the fire and begin fletching again.

⚯

Sheik scrambled up the tree as rapidly as she could. Her breath quickened and her heart began to race. She leaped from branch to branch, magically moving any obstacles that stood in her way. Her strength began to give in. Her arms shook with pain. Finally she could not take anymore and dropped to the ground, tumbling onto her feet. "How was that, Fang?"

He glanced up at her emotionlessly, as if telling her he was bored and unimpressed. She rolled her eyes at him. "Well, I thought it was pretty good. I'm probably better than Farin at this point." She chuckled. "I'd like to challenge him again. He sure wouldn't make fun of me about climbing trees." Her hair, damp with sweat, clung to her face. She had been practicing her climbing, remembering how Farin had teased her for it. Unfortunately, she feared she may never see him again and might not have the chance to show him how much better she had become.

She also trained with the knives Farin had given her. She was unable to throw them well at first, but after the week of traveling and constant practicing she could now hit a target with vague accuracy from about four paces away.

Sheik, still sweaty, bent down to pet Fang. He accepted the attention graciously. Then he froze. His hair pricked up and he growled lightly. "What is it? You hear something?"

He trotted forward through the thinning trees. Giving off a single bark, Sheik ran to his side. They had reached the edge of the forest. There were still trees, but they were sparse, scattered across the grass.

She pushed past the final bush of the forest, now standing fully in the world beyond. The world she had desired to visit for so long.

She could now hear the sound that had caused Fang to growl. There was a rushing river, much larger than any creeks or streams she had ever seen before. From the slight hill Sheik stood on, she was able to see it winding across the land, perhaps three leagues away.

The Great River.

As much as she wanted to continue towards it, night would set in shortly. She started a fire and pulled out her kenaf woven blanket. "Will you keep watch for a while?" she asked Fang. He sat up perfectly still, scanning the hill, as if he understood. She chuckled at the strange wolf, but she was glad he could understand what she was requesting. Who knew what dangerous creatures might exist in this new world.

<hr>

It was still dark when Sheik awoke. Fang had been up most of the night and it was only fair she traded places with him. Upon seeing her rise, he curled up on the ground and laid his head down.

Sheik was not entirely sure how to cross the river. The Great River stretched all the way north and south until it reached both seas. There were only two bridges across it. It was far too wide to swim across safely, she imagined. And she doubted her magic was strong enough to control the waters.

Several more uneventful hours went by in darkness as she pondered the problem. Finding no immediate solution, she built up a fire and managed to whittle a small figurine of Fang. She smiled as she glanced at him, sleeping quietly. He was a good companion. He was her friend. And she had no doubt that he would fiercely protect her to the death.

The sky began to glow and Sheik watched the sun rise above the river. It was the most beautiful sight she had ever seen. It lit up the entire world with pink and gold. The reflection of brilliant colors in the water made the heavens blend in with the world. In that instant, they were one.

Sunrises and sunsets had never seemed so glorious in the forest. They were difficult to see with all the trees, their true beauty always obscured. But here, the sun's light and colors stretched as far as the eye could see. It was magnificent. This alone, Sheik thought for a moment, was worth leaving the village for.

The sky remained a light pink for some time, but then slowly faded into its natural blue. Sheik and Fang began hiking down the hill towards the river. Though Sheik was eager to cross the river and explore the unfamiliar lands, their pace was slow. Animals, which Sheik nicknamed "soil-rats," burrowed under the ground and proceeded to occasionally pop out to examine the strange elf and wolf.

The birds were different, too. They were not grand, like eagles, nor delicate like larks. She tried cooing to them once in a while, but they stayed clear. She also spotted a fox, though besides its coloring, it was nothing new or exciting.

When she reached the river, she realized just how large it was. The sound of the rapids was deafening and the opposite bank seemed impossibly far away.

"What are we gonna do, boy?" she asked Fang, as if he had a solution. He looked directly into her eyes. She glanced at him, chuckling. She swore he was trying to talk to her sometimes. He whined, and she gave him another glance. "What is it?" It was insane. He was a wolf. What made her think he was trying to speak to her? Hesitantly, she knelt down and asked, "Can you understand me?"

He gave a single bark, neither loud nor intimidating.

"You can, can't you?" Was it just wishful thinking? It was bizarre to even consider the notion. Yet he always seemed to follow her commands, and the way he stared at her was unsettling. Like he wanted so desperately for her to hear him. And so, she listened. "Do you have an idea? How to cross the river?" Sheik glanced across it. The other side was hardly visible. They would simply have to hike southward until they reached the southern bridge.

Fang interrupted her thoughts. He didn't make a noise, yet something in her head felt his presence, guiding her attention towards him. He tentatively placed a paw on the surface of the water. It floated there. He kept it steady, not raising it nor letting it splash.

And if he was able to understand her, then certainly she would be able to understand him.

"What are you trying to tell me?" His paw hardly glazed the top of the water. "You want us to cross on top. Not through, on top."

Understanding washed over her. "With my magic, I solidify the river, and we cross over it?" He barked in affirmation.

"It's too big, I can't make the river solid all the way across." She thought back to winter, when the village stream had frozen. The parts with rapids never froze. They were moving too quickly. While parts of this river might be safe enough to cross, other parts were fast. She wasn't sure how she might keep the water still enough to cross, even with magic.

But perhaps they could do it one section at a time.

She used the magic inside of her to solidify a small section of the water, just large enough for her to walk on. Yet another area of the water became solid as she moved her other foot on top of it. It was difficult to maneuver and balance on her magical stepping stones, as water spilled over the top and pulled on them. And she had to concentrate hard to allow them to exist at all.

Fang whined, wanting to follow her. She sighed. It was difficult enough to travel across the river by herself, let alone trying to focus on creating a pathway for him as well. But she kept her stepping stones alive even after she passed over them to allow Fang to catch up.

He struggled across slowly while Sheik proceeded forward. The balancing was not difficult, but the concentration and sheer fortitude required to keep the stone real was wearing on her. By the halfway point, she felt her magic wavering. Her mind was growing weary, her vision blurry.

Only eight paces or so away was a stuck log. If she could balance herself on it, she could allow her mind to rest. With a few quick strides she made the leap and clung to it with relief. "Come on, Fang!"

Despite how difficult it was for Fang to balance on the magical blocks, he made it to the log and rested next to Sheik for a moment. "Alright, if you can really understand me, then I want you to cross to the other side before me. It will be easier for me to focus."

She created several patches of solid land and he followed her orders. At first it was easy, with slow and steady water bubbling just over the surface of her magical stones. Then it grew fast, the rapids churning, and she had to focus hard to keep the stone real, to keep the stone level, to keep the stone from sinking or sailing down the river with the rest of the driftwood. Then finally it was shallow, and Fang no longer needed her magical assistance, trotting through the current that swirled around his legs.

He was across. And now it would be a much easier travel, with Sheik only having to worry about herself. Step by step, she moved across the magical chunks of earth.

Fang barked frantically and his warning echoed in her mind.

Danger.

But it was too late.

Between concentrating on her magic and balancing on the stones, she had not noticed a log being carried by the rapids. It smashed into her leg and sent her flying into the river. Fang leapt into the water as it splashed over her.

Then everything disappeared.

The rapids pulled her under. She had never experienced such a river and hardly knew how to fight it. All she could do was hold her breath and swing her arms about wildly. Her lungs burned, desperately wanting to gasp for air. She refrained, trying to calm her body. But just as solutions to escape the river began to come to mind, she felt a sharp pain against the back of her head. She had hit something, whether a log or rock she did not know. Patches of black began to cloud her vision. She struggled for another second, trying not to give in to the temptation to breathe.

In one moment, she fought frantically for her life. In the next moment, she was unconscious.

Chapter 5

"Where did you find this?" his father screamed. Asroth was not sure the last time Father had yelled.

"It was in the city library, towards the back," Asroth whispered. He was not afraid of his father. He was certainly embarrassed though.

"You must burn it." His father gave him an impatient look. "Now!"

Asroth tucked the book close to him, protecting it. "I knew you would do this. Listen to me!" he yelled back. "Education is everything: strength, wisdom, wealth, happiness."

His father scoffed. "Faith is everything son, do you hear nothing I preach?"

"This book is a book of wisdom!" Asroth quickly retorted. "It teaches everything of magic. Magic, which is quickly dwindling from this world. You use magic, you regard it as important, do you not?"

"That is not magic!"

"It is! And it is dying much faster than the magic of your clergy. To burn this book is to destroy history." His tone calmed. "Father, please. I understand you fear it. But there is nothing to fear," he smiled, waving the book around as if to prove it was harmless. "It is not evil. The magic it teaches is stronger than yours. You should embrace it to help protect the church. You know I am right."

His father shook his head slowly. "The first page is the Oath of Evil."

"The Oath of Power," Asroth quickly corrected. "Power is only a weapon. It can be used by evil, yes. But it can also be used by good to fight evil. I want to be strong enough to fight evil."

A look of realization washed over his father. Reaching out a hand, he felt his son's hair. Several strands easily came out. "Dear Ziad," he whispered, referring to the god he so devoutly served. "You have taken the oath." He hastily put on his robes. In only a few moments he was to give his daily service. "Take the book and leave," he muttered, almost crying. "Your soul no longer belongs to Ziad. You are servant only to Carve, god of all things evil. Leave my sight now."

Pushing past his son, he exited his preparation room and entered the main hall of the cathedral. "Bishop," a priest spoke up as he entered. "Lead us in prayer." The large community that attended every service of the bishop's kneeled.

"I beg forgiveness of all of you. There will be no service today, for I am in sorrow. My son, Asroth, today, has welcomed his soul into the land of demons. He no longer basks in the light of Ziad but has retreated into the darkness of Carve. From this day forth he is excommunicated from the church and banished from Darinshire. Though it pains me to push away my son, Ziad asks us to sever all ties with evil.

"Asroth has taken the Oath of Evil. His hair has begun to shed. He is not just a sinner, like all of us, but a true creature of wickedness."

Asroth supposed his father continued to speak, but he was sick of it. He held the book close to him as he marched home. After he packed his bags, he would leave Darinshire for good. He never had cared much for it, anyway.

He ran his fingers through his hair. He did not notice any hairs fall out. "I am not shedding," he mumbled to himself. The loss of hair was believed to be the sign of Carve's followers; a curse supposedly given to them by Ziad so his worshipers could detect those who had taken "The Oath." So they could detect who had allowed darkness into their soul for the power of ancient magic.

Asroth rolled his eyes as he threw open the door to his home. He was twenty-six; he could make his own decisions. He was not even losing any hair. And the oath was of power, not evil. It didn't even mention Carve. All it did was allow you to use moon magic. That did not make it evil. Magic was simply a weapon, just like a sword. Just because he was now wielding a bigger sword did not mean he was evil.

He gathered all the robes his father had forced him to wear his whole life. He had always been the son of a holy man. His mother had died in a fire when he was only two, and since that day his father decided to lean on Ziad for everything. He had become a priest quickly and several years ago had been given the honor to serve Ziad as a bishop. There were very few bishops throughout Etmos. It was a position of authority.

But Asroth only felt bitterness towards his father's position.

The more he thought about it, the more he hated his father. His father always put the church first. Anytime Asroth had been troubled, all his father would say is, "Ziad has a reason for all things." Asroth rolled his eyes, thinking about the old man. He was happy to be free of him.

He threw the last of his things in a satchel. He did not have much. His father never allowed them to be wealthy, so all he really owned were his books. He had far too many books to bring, but he had read all of them multiple times. The only one he currently cared about was the one he had gotten from the library last week. The book which had caused his father to cast him out: the book of moon magic.

Flipping through the pages, he did not understand why his father hated it so much. It was just another form of magic. It made him angry.

Asroth had hoped to leave the city before his father had dismissed the church service. He was not quick enough. People stared at him on the streets as he left. He could hear their whispers, mumbling about him being some evil, twisted freak. They had most likely begun creating far-fetched rumors. He would forever be known as the outcast of the city, having sworn his allegiance to the corrupt god, Carve. It sickened him, watching those people stare at him.

It made him want to burn them alive.

He tried to ignore their comments and stares. The high steeples of the city walls were nearby. He would soon be free of the wretched city. Upon reaching the gates, he took in a deep breath. The entire world was out there for him to discover. He could go anywhere, do anything.

As he left the horrid city behind, he considered what he would do. He no longer had to be a clergyman, like his father was training him to be. He could do whatever he wanted; no one could force him to do anything ever again.

He remembered when he was a little boy. He had wanted to be nothing more than a stone carver. Perhaps he could open up a shop somewhere selling carvings he made.

While such a simple life was partially appealing, something inside him told him no. He was destined for greater things. It was not by chance that he had seen that book buried behind the many shelves. Covered in spider webs and dust, it had clearly not been touched in many years. It was fate that he was the one to find it.

It was fate that he was to learn this magic. Very few people knew the ancient magic. Normally, if one found a book with the Oath printed in it, they would have it burned. Taking the Oath was necessary to use the magic, and with fewer copies of the Oath there were fewer wizards capable of using moon magic. It was unfortunate, but it also made Asroth feel special. He was one of maybe only thirty people west of the Tasvran Mountains able to use such magic.

He hated that people feared the magic. He supposed they called it evil because they did not fully understand it. People always feared the unknown. People also feared what was stronger than them, and moon magic was the most powerful magic to exist.

They made up rumors and stories about it. The Oath was believed to be a direct prayer to Carve, offering a small section of the oath taker's soul. As they used the magic, the rumors claimed, Carve consumed more and more of the oath taker's soul. Until finally they were nothing more than an empty vessel, fully under the evil god's control.

Such stories made Asroth laugh. It was ridiculous to believe one could sacrifice their soul by memorizing several sentences. He had the power to use the magic now, but he had not given up any of his soul and Carve certainly was not going to steal his life's essence from him.

He was now eager to use this new found magic. To master it. He had not yet had the time to practice. Now, he had all the time in the world. Already being able to use standard magic and healing magic, the addition of moon magic would make him powerful beyond belief. He had never before heard of someone conquering all three types of magic.

Contrary to his father's beliefs, he would not use his power for evil. Sometimes, Asroth admitted, he rejected Ziad's ways. The church seemed corrupt in many of their beliefs. But not conforming to their customs did not make him evil. He was a good man, and he wanted to help people. Once he had dominated the magic, he would be able to fight off evil and help those who needed his assistance.

In order to do so, he needed a study. Somewhere he could practice his magic and read more on it. He had always thrived on knowledge. He loved to learn. Magic required much patience, concentration, and often intelligence. It was always a challenge to Asroth. He had to have a study so he could refine his magic and help the world.

He was not sure how to go about obtaining a study. Or what exactly he would need in it. However, he knew it would require money; money he didn't have. He would have to save up for it.

In the meantime, even without a study, he could still practice using this new magic. Tomorrow, he resolved. He would start tomorrow, when he was a far enough distance from his old city, which he hated so deeply.

Asroth held a tiny flower in his hand. First, he tried to meditate, closing his eyes and forcing his body to relax. Meditation was often difficult for him. But finally he felt calm.

Even with his eyes closed, he sensed the light of the stars and moon. The magic was easiest in the presence of the moon. It was nearly full, and there were no clouds in the sky.

He could feel the power building up in his eyes. It was a strange feeling; almost tingling with pleasure and almost sickening with pain. The book had instructed him to lower the energy into his heart. It began to sink down his throat. The feeling grew stronger. It was as if it was wriggling. The sensation was terrifying. He couldn't breathe, and he felt like he was swallowing maggots.

Vomiting, he dropped the small flower. It was the second time he had thrown up. The puke was black and bubbled with heat. He knew it meant he had the dark magic in him, but he still had made very little progress and it drove him mad. An entire week had passed by since he had left his home and, no matter how hard he tried, he had been unable to use the moon magic.

He moved away from the pool of bile and opened up his book once again. "Chapter twelve, how to control dark magic," he read out loud. He had read through the entire book twice already and read chapter twelve at least seven times. "Meditate to allow the power to come to your eyes," he read, skimming the text. "Best done under light of the moon, yes, yes. Swallow the power and force it into your chest." He was having difficulty swallowing the power. It made him gag every time.

"What next?" he muttered. "Your heart will absorb the magic once in the chest," he continued skimming paragraph by paragraph. "Finally, once in the heart, the power will run through your veins. It will be painful, but only then can it be commanded."

He understood all the steps. He simply had to deal with the sickness and the pain. That was all. He sighed, knowing these steps would have to be repeated every time he wanted to use the magic. It did not even seem practical. It took him sometimes as much as an hour when he tried. How was he ever to use such magic in combat?

However, the book claimed that upon practice the ritual would become instinct and would only take seconds. He simply needed to try again.

Asroth plucked another flower. The meditation had already grown quicker. In only a minute he felt the power rising in his eyes. His face grew pale and his veins bulged as it sunk down his jaw and dripped into his throat. It danced about in his throat, squirming and tempting him to vomit. He tried not to imagine all the disgusting things it felt like. Maggots, worms, slugs. Asroth held his breath and forced the twisting, writhing feeling down his throat.

He could feel it slide down into his chest. Asroth was not sure if his heart was drawing in the power or if the power was forcing its way towards his heart. There was a small pain that slowly grew worse. Then suddenly he felt all the power snap in at once. His heart pounded.

The pain was unbearable.

The book had told Asroth he could release the power out of his heart at any moment if the pain became too overbearing. But if he was able to stand it and focus the power, as it pumped through his veins and arteries, he could use it to decay any form of life, whether plant or creature.

He cried out in pain, trying to hold out long enough to focus the energy out of his arm and into the tiny flower. The pain was like nothing he had ever felt before. It was like an intense fire burning inside of his heart, ripping and tearing at it. An increasing pressure grew inside his chest. The power was too painful; he could not stand it any longer.

It released from his heart and fizzled away into nothingness. Asroth curled up, vomiting black, boiling bile. Whenever the power was too intense, he would end up bent over, throwing up the painful sickness. Nearly ten minutes went by before he was finished puking. He was practically surrounded in bubbling bile. Pulling himself away, he gathered up his possessions and collapsed, instantly falling asleep.

———— ✤ ————

It was three weeks since Asroth had first managed to summon the power. He practiced for hours every night. It was becoming easier and quicker, and he was vomiting less and less from the magic.

During the past month, magic was all he thought of. As he hiked, he would think about performing magic. He sustained himself with magic. He read his books on magic. He practiced magic. It was his life.

He had grown so obsessed with magic that it had replaced any lonely thoughts. He didn't miss being around people. But he still continued to travel. There were two large cities within a couple month's travel from Darinshire. The larger was Isandas, the capital of Etmos. As much as he wanted to go there, he had heard rumors of turmoil and conflict, which would pull attention and fame away from himself. No, it would be better to head to a more stable city where his talent would be properly appreciated and respected.

And so he marched southward to the other city, Calert.

Calert was a quickly growing city in the country of Vesdar. Assuming his sense of direction was accurate, it was only a month's more travel. His goal was to be able to use the moon magic, if even only to wither a flower, by the time he reached the city.

Though it was broad daylight, Asroth sat down in a field of grass to practice his moon magic once again. It was a new moon, so sitting in the darkness of night would hardly help him. Besides, that suggestion was only to help aid meditation and bring the power to one's eyes. That part had become easy to Asroth now. It was swallowing and withstanding the pain of the magic that was difficult for him.

He took a deep breath and the power quickly rose to his eyes. It drained easily into his throat and he forced it down, stomaching the disgusting, slimy feeling. From his chest it began to absorb into his heart.

Asroth screamed, the pain burning inside him. He doubled over but refused to let go of the power. "Control it," he whispered to himself. "Own it. It belongs to you now." He clenched until his jaw, too, began to hurt. It was a slow process at first, focusing the power from his heart to his veins. Then, suddenly, the power burst from his shoulder out to his palm.

He gave out a final cry before collapsing. The pain disappeared and his body began to relax. He did not even vomit. Asroth smiled. He had controlled the power. Moving his hand, he stared at the grass. In a distinct palm print shape, the grass was browned and dying, sapped of life.

He had succeeded.

<hr>

Asroth reached the city he had been looking for. It was larger than the city he had grown up in—the cursed city he had been banished from. But it was also much poorer. There was no elegant architecture. No fancy cathedrals with towering steeples.

It was mostly all shoddy stone buildings, no more than two or three stories high. The marketplace took up most of the inner city. If he did not want someone pushing past him or shoving up against him, he would have to retreat to the outskirts.

Moments later he realized why the marketplace seemed so large. It bled into a fighting arena, just east of the main circle of bartering. The entry was crowded with people paying the arena workers the fee to watch the fights.

Asroth had never seen a fighting arena before. They were banned in Etmos because of the influence of the clergy. His father would have never condoned the bloodshed of an arena.

Curious, Asroth headed towards it to examine the talent of the men fighting. Asroth was a large man, standing taller and weighing more than most his age, but here some of the men towered over him. There were multiple divisions, broken down by both skill levels and styles: hand-to-hand, jousting, and sword duels.

Asroth had never trained with a weapon before. His father would be appalled at the thought. But Asroth had always wanted to wield a sword. So he stepped up to a booth containing a list of names and wrote his down under the entry level sword division.

"Asroth versus Balthak!" a man called out nearly an hour after Asroth had signed his name. He entered the arena in awe of the giant crowd watching. It was then that he became nervous. The announcer stepped up to him and handed him a dulled short sword and simple shield. Balthak had brought his own sword, something Asroth didn't know was allowed. The announcer inspected it to ensure it was dulled and then offered him a shield, but the burly man waved it away.

"Let the fight begin!" the announcer shouted over the noisy crowd. Asroth crouched, holding his shield and sword close to him. Balthak chuckled. Asroth wondered for a moment if he was holding his weapon incorrectly.

His enemy charged at him. Asroth dodged the first attack, barely escaping the blunt tip of the man's sword. Before he had enough time to even lower his own, his opponent spun around quickly and used his momentum to thrust the sword towards him.

Asroth realized then that this man was physically faster and in better shape than him. In a fair fight, he might have knocked the wind out of him right then and there. However, Asroth's mind was quicker than the man's sword. Underneath his clergy robes, so no one could see, a chunk of steel formed, blocking the sword's strike.

The impact still pushed Asroth back a pace, but it did not hurt like it could have.

Balthak must have felt the collision of his sword with something metal because surprise registered on his face. Still, the fight continued and he advanced once again.

Asroth withdrew the magic and the piece of steel disappeared into the air. Pleased with how well his magic had served him, he decided to use it in other ways.

The arena's sword was purposefully dull, built with the intention of bludgeoning rather than lacerating. Though certainly people still died fighting in the arena, the goal was to keep death as preventable as possible. A contender won when the opponent forfeited. With a little help from his magic, Asroth could make his opponent forfeit much easier.

The edges of his blade grew sharp. Taking a large step, he thrust it forwards and, again with magic, lengthened the sword just a bit.

His opponent practically ran into it without realizing it. It pierced into his side. Asroth read his expression like a book—had he really miscalculated something so simple? The sword had seemed so far away only a split second ago. And now he was bleeding.

Asroth struck again while Balthak was still surprised, cutting across his chest.

Balthak's hands went up in submission as he forfeited and the crowd surrounding the arena cheered. Balthak glared at Asroth. He knew something was amiss. But the crowd was clueless and continued to applaud. Not being in the battle, they had not noticed the magic Asroth had used. It was all so quick to them; there was no time to realize Asroth had cheated. To them, he was simply the victor. He raised his bloody sword into the air and listened to the applause grow louder.

This would be so much easier than he had first anticipated.

Chapter 6

Sheik awoke to the repulsive sensation of coughing up water. She dropped to the ground, and it was only upon the impact that she realized someone had been carrying her. But, still retching, she didn't have the strength to sit up and look at who it was. They stood over her awkwardly, shouting something though she wasn't sure what. Maybe she still had water in her ears?

Fang was to her side in an instant, licking at her face and whining how happy he was that she was alright. She coughed up a bit more and then collapsed into a heap. She wasn't sure if she could stand even if she tried. The person beside her lifted her up once again. Sheik could only assume by how effortlessly he tossed her over his shoulder that it must have been a man carrying her. To her surprise, Fang did not growl at him.

From her angle, Sheik couldn't properly see her surroundings. She didn't particularly care. She was focused much harder on breathing and staying conscious. But the man readjusted her as he carried her into a worn-down house, something like the homes that Sheik could only faintly remember.

He placed her on a mattress. It was comfortable but smelled of moldy straw. "Where am I?"

He spoke back at her but again his words made no sense. She smacked the side of her head, hoping to clear water from her ears. Again his speech was jarring and impossible to interpret. A word here and there sounded familiar, like they were on the tip of her tongue. But then, without warning, he sprinted away, leaving her alone.

Alone in this strange house.

The walls were made of stone and brick. It was only one room, as far as she could tell. There was loose wood and cobwebs scattered about, like no one had been there in years. But in the center, there was the remnants of a campfire, a few coals still glowing.

It was then that she shivered. Perhaps just the sight of warmth was all it took to snap her into remembering that she was still soaked through from the river. She had been numb before, likely numb from shock. But now her teeth chattered.

She stripped off her clothes, though she left her undergarments on in case the man came back. The fire had a wooden stick propped above it which she draped her clothes over in hopes that they might dry. Then she inched closer and built the fire up just a little with some of the loose wood lying about. As if sensing her temperature, Fang curled up next to her.

Sheik wasn't sure how much time had passed, but her clothes were still wet when the man sprinted back into the house, which she just now realized had no door.

Now that she was able to focus on him, she realized he was much different looking than anyone Sheik had ever seen. It was like all his features were just not quite right.

The most obvious peculiarity was his hair. It was reddish brown, like the bark of a tree. Sheik had seen sage hair and chartreuse hair, even aqua hair, but she'd never seen anything so brown. It was shoulder length, pulled back with a head band, and was accompanied by strange hair growing on his chin.

Something was wrong with his skin, too. Sheik couldn't quite place it. It was a different hue and pale. His eyes were grey, which wasn't odd, but his eyelids somehow had an extra crease in them. She stared in silence and took in the sight of him. Then she remembered that she had crossed the river.

This man wasn't an elf. He was a human.

He froze and said about a million words Sheik could still not understand. She inched back against Fang, but the wolf did not bother lifting his head. This man was not a threat.

She focused on him, staring blankly as he continued to talk. It was just gibberish. He must have been speaking another language. Human tongue, she figured, if he was indeed a human.

He squatted next to her. "Can't you understand me?"

Sheik vaguely recognized what he said. How did she understand him? She had never spoken human before. She racked her brain for words. "Slowly."

He repeated everything he had said before. She generally understood that he had found her by the river. He introduced himself as Kazzak, and he mentioned he had sent for help.

"I am Sheik," she replied in the foreign language. How, exactly, she was able to speak human tongue, she couldn't say. But here she was, communicating in it. The only thing she could think of was that she must have learned it before she lost her memory, and she simply never recalled it because everyone in Atarius' village had always spoken elven tongue. As the language rushed back to her, she realized she must have once been fluent. "I thought I drowned."

"I was going fishing and got there just in time to see the wolf here dragging you out of the water."

She smiled at Fang, giving him a hug. "You saved me, boy?"

"Are your, uh, clothes dry?" Kazzak asked awkwardly.

Sheik felt them, and although they were still a bit damp, she pulled them on anyway out of embarrassment. "Where are we?"

"Gibrald. Well, it's Calert now. The western expansion." She stared without understanding. "They vacated the old town to expand Calert to the Great River. But well, they haven't actually started construction and so some of us live out here. It's free shelter, you see, but we have to lay low," he trailed off. "Well anyway, we're on the outskirts of Calert. I ran into the city and some of my friends are coming. One of them is a healer. I'm not sure if you need it. You seem fine now, but at first you were unconscious so I thought it'd be best," he continued rambling on. Sheik only caught about half of what he said, but she was still amazed that she was able to understand anything. All this time she had known human tongue and never even realized it.

"So what were you doing trying to swim across the river?" he asked.

Sheik was now sitting up, warming her hands by the fire. "I wasn't planning on swimming," she chuckled. "I was using magic to cross, but a log hit me. I'm just glad I had Fang." She scratched behind his ear. She could tell he was tired. He had probably had a difficult struggle in the rapids trying to pull her out.

"You can use magic?" Kazzak asked, astonished.

It was not that surprising to her. Most of the elves in the village could use magic. "You can't?"

"Are you kidding?" he exclaimed. "Hardly anyone uses magic. There's probably less than fifty people in all of Calert who can." Fifty seemed like a decent number to Sheik, and so she realized this Calert City must have been much larger than Atarius' village. "Maybe it's different for you elves, but around here it's definitely a rarity. So why did you want to cross the river? You are an elf, right? Didn't you live back in the forest?"

She looked down, shamefully. "I was banished."

"Oh." His forehead wrinkled with concern. "I'm sorry."

As strange as the entire situation was to Sheik, the man who had helped her seemed friendly. She never would have guessed that her first encounter with humans would be speaking with a man in her undergarments. The thought almost made her laugh.

"Well, you can stay here as long as you'd like," he offered kindly, trying to break the silence as he dug through some drawers to reveal a pan flute, which seemed particularly small in his large hands. The man was large in general, larger than any elves in the village at least, built with muscle. He seemed older than her by a few years, maybe twenty-five years old? But it was hard to tell because of his strange features. Rough, light skin, facial hair, and reddish-brown hair. She studied him hard as he played the pan flute.

Several of the elves in the village had played similar instruments. Sheik had never had much musical talent. It seemed Kazzak did not either, as he played notes at random with little rhythm. She smiled a bit, though she was polite enough not to laugh.

Interrupting the man's music, two people barged into the house. One of them was a boy who couldn't have been older than sixteen. His skin was like the bark of a walnut tree. Sheik had never known people could have such dark skin. If Kazzak's hair was strange, this boy's hair was stranger. It was jet black and curled in tight ringlets behind his ears. He wore only tattered pants, his abdomen shirtless and well-toned. Slung across his back was a hefty backpack and a sword.

The other person was a girl, perhaps a year or two older than the boy. Her skin was lighter than Kazzak's and her hair a golden brown, cut short in a bob style. Both she and the boy had the same unfamiliar creases to their eyelids. "Must you be playing that thing again?" the girl winced at the sound of it. She then spotted Sheik. "Wow! I have never seen an elf before. What's your name?" she asked. "Are you okay?" She glanced at Kazzak, who tucked the instrument away. "Does she need to be healed?"

"My name is Sheik," she replied, standing up. "I think I'm fine, really."

The girl stuck out her hand and Sheik flinched. "Do you not shake hands where you come from?" She laughed and pulled it back. "My name is Tara. This is my brother, Auni."

"Hello," the shirtless boy gave her a nod.

"How did you do in the arena?" Kazzak asked. "That's how we met," he explained. "I actually fought the boy. He's good. If he was my size, I doubt I'd stand a chance. But I got him pinned. Then this girl," he smiled, slapping Tara on the back, "ran up and just healed the kid. Crowd went wild! I think they liked her magic more than me winning," he chuckled. "I told you it was rare. Even more so with healing magic." He turned to Auni, "And I'm glad your sister was blessed with such a gift. I'd left him pretty bloody," he added, facing Sheik again.

Sheik had a feeling Kazzak and Tara got along well. They both never seemed to stop talking. Auni never did answer Kazzak's original question. "Arena?" Sheik asked.

Kazzak nodded. "Yeah, you know, you pay to see fights? Well, we're the fighters. Sometimes I wrestle, sometimes I sword fight. Tried jousting once, but I'm no good."

Tara added, "Auni used to only wrestle, but Kazzak has gotten him into swords now. I don't care for it. I find it more dangerous. But you make more money doing sword duels, so I permit it for now," she said with an air of authority.

Their entire conversation was going over Sheik's head. "Slow down." It was hard enough to understand the language. She thought she understood the fighting. It was like sparring or competing, like what she and Atarius and Farin did, only with swords. "What's money?"

Kazzak and Tara started laughing, but Auni remained quiet. "What world are you from?" Tara joked. But as they explained the concept of purchasing food, clothes, and other items with coins, it came rushing back to her.

Of course. Money. Gold, silver. Other metals and jewelry and polished shells. It was so basic, so intrinsic and yet Sheik had forgotten it. Atarius' village didn't use money. Everything belonged to everyone. But outside of Atarius' village, the memories of currency came back to her.

Tara explained that she had once been the daughter of a wealthy plantation owner. But she had run away and left her old life behind because of how her family mistreated Auni. She had stolen a mound of gold from her father, but they had spent through it quickly. Tara hadn't expected that they might land themselves in poverty. By the time they had reached Calert, they had to sell their horse just to afford food.

"I had such grand dreams of living off that gold," Tara explained wistfully. "But we really did not know what we were doing. At least Auni has real skills, like fighting in the arena."

"Healing isn't a real skill?" Sheik asked. In a place that used money, she could only assume healing would be a valuable service.

Kazzak chimed in to explain. "Just like any kind of magic, healing is risky. In Etmos, anyone with the ability to heal is forced to join the clergy. It's not quite the same in Vesdar, but if a nobleman gets word?"

"It's almost guaranteed I would be pressured into his service."

"She'd basically be a slave," Kazzak finished for her.

Auni's eyes snapped shut at the word. Sheik hadn't been paying attention to him at all, but now she glanced him over. Sheik could hardly imagine that he and Tara really were brother and sister. They looked and acted like absolute opposites. Tara eventually mentioned that Auni was only her half-brother; the two of them had different mothers. Sheik didn't completely understand how or why such a relationship would occur, but Auni looked uncomfortable talking about it and so she changed the subject to Kazzak.

Kazzak had grown up an orphan in Calert, surviving mostly off thievery. He claimed it was really easy—you just reached into people's pockets and they rarely noticed. But he tried not to do it anymore, not since he started earning money at the arena.

He described how the three of them had become like family after they first met half a season ago. After beating Auni in the arena, Kazzak had offered to buy him a meal. "Mostly," Kazzak admitted, "I thought it might be good to get to know Tara. Befriending a healer's not a bad idea for someone who fights in the arena," he winked. But they had all gotten along so well, and they all had no one else to call family. They pooled their money together and camped out in vacated areas on the west side of Calert, moving every so often as construction took place.

Sheik supposed it was time to tell her tale.

"Well, I guess my story starts the day my village was attacked." Tara and Auni leaned in close, hanging on her every word. "I lost my memory, so I don't remember anything from before that day. But I remember the attack. Bits and pieces anyway. It was humans." She paused, wondering if saying so might be offensive. But they listened on.

"They had started a fire." It was all fuzzy. She remembered they had swords and axes and were chopping people down left and right. "Some of the elves were fighting back, some were trying to hide, some were trying to escape. It was complete chaos." The humans were killing everyone, women and children too. They were seeking them out, bursting into homes.

"I was trying to escape," she recalled. Someone was trying to help her escape, but she couldn't quite remember who. Maybe her father or her mother? "But somehow I got hit in the head. Then boom, out. Nothing."

The room was silent, her captive audience of three waiting for her to continue.

"Next thing I knew I woke up in Atarius' village. I was sick for a while, kept waking up and falling back asleep. I kept having this recurring dream." She didn't want to tell them this part of the story, but she knew she had to in order to explain the banishment.

"The dream went on for months." She had been grateful that it had finally gone away. "Well, Atarius, he thought it was some ridiculous prophecy." She half sighed, half laughed. It was so stupid. "He thought it meant I was destined to find the Sword of Elilah. So he trains me for over a year," she let out a miserable chuckle, "and then, when I'm finally fitting in, finally feeling like it's my home, he tells me to leave. He banishes me. Trying to get me to fulfill this stupid prophecy."

Kazzak frowned. "How's he allowed to banish you?"

"Atarius is sachem," Sheik said simply.

Tara gave her a confused look. "What's a sachem?"

"You know, a king."

Their mouths hung open. "Wait, you knew the king? Like, personally?"

Sheik chuckled and shrugged. "There's only a few hundred people. Everyone knows everyone."

"Oh," Tara interjected with understanding. "So, he is not really a king then."

"Huh?" Sheik raised an eyebrow. "Of course he is. He's descended from royal blood; he's a king."

Kazzak interceded, "Well here, kings rule over millions of people."

"And if they only ruled over thousands, then they wouldn't be a king?" Sheik asked, a hint of annoyance in her voice. As much as she didn't want to defend Atarius, who she still felt so bitterly towards, she also didn't appreciate how dismissive they were being.

"No, no, you're right," Kazzak conceded, "just not what we were expecting. King or no king, it doesn't sound like he was very kind to you."

Sheik wanted to interject again. To explain that, no, actually Atarius had been incredibly kind. She had been in love with him. But then she realized she was defending him again for no good reason. "It's just so silly," she settled on. "Banishing me thinking I'm going to randomly stumble upon the Sword of Elilah?"

"The Sword of Elilah? Elilah like the goddess, yes?" Tara asked.

Sheik raised her eyebrows, astonished that Tara would have to ask. "Of course! The goddess of freedom, of nature."

Kazzak explained simply, "Most humans worship Ziad or Justar."

"I hardly know much about any of them," Tara admitted. "I never liked studying the gods."

"But in the myths, they each have a holy weapon," Kazzak filled in for Tara. "Elilah's is the sword."

Tara nodded with understanding. "Right, right. Okay, so the goddess has this sword, and you are looking for it?"

Sheik shook her head and laughed. "No. I'm not looking for anything. I traveled across that river to see human lands. Explore the world a bit."

"I wouldn't mind exploring the world," Tara and Kazzak said at the same time. They began laughing and the subject quickly changed. Sheik was glad it did. The more she spoke about Atarius the more she was defending him, and that only made her angrier.

But it was a relief that none of the group seemed to believe in his prophecy. These people simply wanted to live their life. They just existed. It was all Sheik had wanted back in Atarius' village. And perhaps now that she had stumbled upon these people, she could have a perfectly ordinary, simple life. She wondered how long they might let her stay. Was this an invitation to join their makeshift family? Or would they ask her to leave after a time?

As it grew late, the group spread out several blankets and curled together in the small one room house. They promised they would take her into the city and show her around the next day when she was fully rested. Sheik tried to sleep but the day had been so eventful it was difficult. She couldn't help but think about what the human city and her new future held.

⋅⋅⋅❖⋅⋅⋅

Sheik awoke bright and early, while the morning was still dark. She blinked several times and took in her surroundings. "I am in human lands," she whispered to herself. "I am in a house with," she looked over each sleeping person, "Kazzak, Tara, and Auni."

Fang's head perked up at her whispering. She continued to run her mind through everything that had happened. "I crossed the river. I am okay. I speak human tongue," she added with a chuckle. With a stretch, she rose to her feet and Fang joined her as she left the tiny shack.

It was disorienting, almost scary, looking at the abandoned homes. It was nothing but an empty shell, a framework of a town. Broken wood, crumbling stone. A brief image flashed in her mind of what it reminded her of.

Her own village.

She had visited the raided, burned down village only once. Atarius had thought it might be helpful, that it might rebuild her memories. Plenty of time had passed, she had physically recovered, and all the corpses had been long since cleared out and given a proper pyre. Greenery had started to touch the area, but the village had still been in shambles and the death and destruction that had taken place there was obvious.

It had not brought back Sheik's memories, at least not any pleasant ones. It had only triggered the memories of the attack: people dying, fire burning, trying to escape, the smell of smoke. The images rushing back to her had caused a panic attack and Atarius had needed to carry her away from the sight as she sobbed and struggled to breathe.

She focused on her breathing now, hoping she would not have a similar episode. Placing her leg in the empty window of the abandoned house, she propelled up and reached the beam along the roof. Pulling herself up, she climbed on top of the old shack and faced east. It wasn't long before the sun began to rise and the beautiful sky distracted her from the sight of abandoned homes.

"What are you doing up there?"

The voice startled her. She glanced down to find Auni peering up at her. "I'm just watching the sunrise. Want to join me?" He stared at her skeptically. "Come on," she added, outstretching her hand, "I'll help you up."

Auni didn't take her hand but climbed easily on top of the roof in the same fashion she had. "Isn't it beautiful?" she asked. He nodded but said nothing. She glanced over at him and noticed he had an R branded into his left shoulder. Apparently, she realized, in addition to speaking human tongue she could read it as well. "What is it?" she asked, pointing.

The boy flinched and placed his right hand over the brand. "Nothing," he said sharply.

She sighed. Kazzak and Tara had both warmed up to her right away, but Auni seemed on edge. She couldn't tell if he was just quiet or actually upset by her being with them. Finally, after a long silence, she decided to just ask. "You've hardly said a word to me," she began. "Is it just because the other two talk so much? Or did I do something wrong?"

"No, no," he replied apologetically. Sheik could read the sincerity in his voice. "I'm just quiet, that's all."

Sheik sighed again, this time with relief. "Okay. I understand. I was just worried that you didn't really want me here. You seemed so guarded."

He gave her a faint smile and admitted, "I guess so." Then, after a pause, he added, "You said you use magic. You can't like, read minds or anything can you?"

"Read minds?" she laughed. "Of course not. Have you really never met someone who can use magic before?"

Auni shook his head. "Just Tara, but she only just figured it out this year. Maybe," he said with a little excitement, "you could help her learn?"

She gave him a hesitant look. "I'm afraid I can't use healing magic." When he gave her a blank expression, she explained, "Standard magic, all it's used for is objects. Moving things, creating things. Healing magic is something separate. So I wouldn't know the first step to teaching Tara."

"Oh," he said simply.

"Sorry." In an attempt to cheer him up, she said, "I might not be able to heal and read minds, but I can at least create breakfast." She offered him her hand and blackberries appeared in it. He stared, wide-eyed. "Go on," she insisted, "they're perfectly safe."

He took one nervously and bit into it. His demeanor changed as he savored the bite and then grabbed a few more from her hand. When he was satisfied, she let the rest disappear. He looked at her suspiciously. "So you can disappear things too?"

"Well, they disappear on their own as soon as I stop concentrating on them."

His skepticism continued. "So whatever I've swallowed just disappeared then, right?"

She shook her head. "Nope. You can live on just magically conjured food, believe it or not." After all, most of the elves in Atarius' village did. Even the elves without magic, like Farin, often relied on magically created food. "You're the one using magic now," she explained. "Everyone has at least a little bit of magic in them. And so the magic in you helps keep my magic alive until your body can absorb all the nutrients." Auni didn't seem satisfied with the answer. She thought for a moment of a better way to explain. "Okay, so for example I can create a spark that starts a fire. Once the fire gets going, I can take away my spark. It doesn't stop the flames because they've already started. It's kind of like that."

He seemed to understand and nodded a few times. "But you can't disappear people, right?"

She laughed. "Nope. No disappearing people."

"Okay, okay. I guess I'll trust you then," he said with a smirk.

Sheik smiled, happy that she had won him over. The sun had risen but they watched the sky in silence for a little longer. The quiet was soon broken by Kazzak. "Hello? Auni? Sheik?"

"Up here," they both called back.

Kazzak came into vision just outside the house. "Oh. Hey! What are you two doing up there?"

"Eating breakfast," Auni replied.

"Oh? What have you got?"

"It's all gone now." He and Sheik shared a smile.

Kazzak gave them a frown, not understanding their inside joke. "Alright, well let's head to the market and buy something. Sheik, you ready to see the city?"

She climbed down from the rooftop. "Sure. We don't need to buy anything, though." An apple appeared in her hand, which she handed to Kazzak.

His eyebrows raised and he inspected it carefully before taking a bite. Sheik held in her laughter. Why were they so skeptical to try her magically created food?

"It's delicious!" he announced. "So you can create an apple whenever you want?"

"Berries, too," Auni added. Sheik went ahead and showed them, a mound of blackberries appearing in her hand.

Kazzak scarfed down the apple and Sheik whisked away the core. "Tara, you're missing out!"

The girl joined them, rubbing sleep from her eyes, her hair a mess. "What's going on?" Her eyes lit up as she watched Sheik hand out more food. "Can you create anything you want?"

She shrugged. "Sure, I guess so. What do you want?"

"Cake!" Tara exclaimed.

Sheik wasn't familiar with the word. Maybe she only knew it in elven? "What's cake?" Auni peered over at Tara like he didn't know either.

Kazzak merely chuckled. "It's a very sweet bread, with icing or chocolate. A luxury we can't typically afford."

Sheik did her best to conjure an image to mind. Acorn bread, sweetened with crushed berries, layered with honey. She whipped the food into reality and held it up for them to see. "How's that?"

Tara's face melted from excitement to disappointment. Kazzak nudged her, as if to tell her she was being rude. "Well, let me try it," she said hesitantly. Pinching off a bite, her dejected expression remained the same. "Sorry, it just... was not quite what I was expecting."

But Auni tried a bite and immediately went back for seconds. "It's amazing!"

Sheik thought so too, and Kazzak offered many compliments as he tried it. "Well, Tara," he compromised, "maybe after eating a couple of meals made from Sheik, we'll have saved enough money to buy the kind of cake you're used to."

At this, Tara lit up. "Oh, of course! With you around, Sheik, we shall save up our money in no time!" She rattled off all the wonderful things they might be able to afford now and waved for them to follow her towards the city.

Kazzak gave Sheik a grin. She smiled back, grateful to have brought so much joy to them. She couldn't remember the last time she had felt so elated. Or at peace.

Probably her coming-of-age ceremony. Back then, she had been so happy to belong. Then everything had happened with the dream and... she shook the thoughts from her mind. She was with Kazzak, and Auni, and Tara now. They liked her. Maybe she could belong with them?

"Listen, don't use your magic once we're in the city," Kazzak interrupted her thoughts. "Or at least, don't let anyone see you if you do. It's not illegal per se, but it makes people nervous. The sheriff has cracked down on it a lot." Sheik didn't know what a sheriff was, but Kazzak continued without explanation. "You know, if people were to make gold with their magic, buy out a store, then let it all disappear and the shop owner has nothing."

"Why would someone do that, though?"

He gave a small smile. "Some of us are just desperate to survive." Right. He had once been a thief. He waved away her apologetic look. "It's okay. I just don't want any of us to land in trouble."

Sheik nodded. "I won't use magic." She certainly didn't want to be in trouble, and she didn't want to endanger any of her new friends. "Anything else?"

He hesitated, like he was unsure if he should say it. "You should wear one of my cloaks. Keep your ears and hair covered."

"Because I'm an elf?" Did most humans not like elves?

"Yeah," he sighed, like he was ashamed. "People are scared of things they don't know. I've lived in Calert my whole life and I've only ever seen two or three elves. I'm not sure how people will react."

She nodded and accepted Kazzak's cloak, pulling it tight around her face. "Understood," she said in her best human accent. "Nothing to see here. I am a non-magical human."

The two laughed and caught up with Auni and Tara as they entered the city of Calert.

It was marvelous.

The streets were wide yet crowded, full of people. Full of horses! She had forgotten about horses, but now vaguely remembered the majestic beasts.

The buildings were tall. Shops were two stories high. People sold things from the windows, from the stairs, from the alleys, from tents, from everywhere. It was nothing but hustle and bustle. She could hardly take two steps without someone shoving something in her face. Whether it was food or clothes or perfumes or children's toys, someone was constantly trying to sell her things.

There was just so much *stuff*. No wonder it was so easy to run out of money. People were trying to take it from you everywhere you went.

And she also understood how magic could be used so deceptively. It would be so easy to create two coins in her palm and trade them for any number of things, then get lost in the crowd while the payment disappeared.

In only a couple of hours, Sheik was ready to retreat. The city was fun and exciting, but it made her long for her old home. The forest was quiet and still. It was freedom.

"I'm sure it is a lot to take in," Kazzak nodded when she expressed her desire to leave.

So they returned to the worn down shack of a home and huddled around the campfire. And this was their pattern for the next five days. Each day they showed Sheik a new part of Calert and each evening they talked and told stories as they feasted on Sheik's magically created food.

When Tara realized that Sheik could only create foods that she had tried before, she made sure to buy Sheik some of her favorite foods to sample. Sheik refused to try meat, which she wasn't sure could be made with magic anyway. But she agreed to try fluffy breads and new fruits and roasted vegetables so she might expand her magical, culinary dishes.

And tomorrow they would be trying cake. Kazzak promised Tara that if they didn't have enough money to buy it, he would lift a few coins from someone in the crowd. "No one poor," he assured Sheik. "Some richie-rich with flowing robes and a ring on each finger."

Sheik went to bed with a full stomach, cuddled up against Fang, listening to the crackle of the fire and wondering what cake must taste like. A pang of guilt hit her. Should she be eating non-magically created foods? Atarius would have been disappointed.

Why did she care what Atarius thought? But try as she might, she couldn't shake the feeling. She would try this cake that Tara spoke so highly of, then she would stop.

Besides, these new friends of hers liked her *because* of her ability to create food with magic. They wouldn't mind, right? She certainly hoped not. This past week had been amazing. They had been so kind to her. They had grown so close. This is what she had longed for. Family.

Auni's voice interrupted her thoughts. "Can't sleep?"

Sheik shifted her head and realized he wasn't speaking to her; he was speaking to Tara. Tara sat up and sighed. "No, not really. Between the fleas and Kazzak's snoring," she grumbled.

Auni gave a small chuckle. "Sorry."

"What's our plan, Auni?"

Now he sat up too. "What do you mean?"

"This is not what I expected. I thought once we had made it out of Omris…" she trailed off. "I don't know. Is this what you expected?" Auni said nothing and Sheik wasn't sure what that silence meant. "Well, someday the arena will grow too hard on you. We need to find another way to survive."

"Sheik can make food," he offered. "So we don't have to worry about that expense for now."

For now? What did that mean? Were they assuming that Sheik would eventually move on from them? Or were they implying that she could only stay with them temporarily? She held her breath.

"Just think on it," Tara whispered. She gave a big yawn. "I'll try going back to sleep."

Their conversation ended and Sheik listened as their breathing grew heavier and heavier. What kinds of plans would they make? And would they involve Sheik?

Her stomach flipped and she wondered if this would just be another Atarius situation. Accepted with open arms, treated like family… and then cast aside when you were no longer needed.

Chapter 7

Asroth pushed through the crowd. He held a heavy staff. A powerful wizard needed a staff. He supposed a wizard as great as himself needed a beard too, but he did not want to compromise his handsome face. Facial hair had never looked good on him.

Besides, he couldn't really be out and in the open about being a wizard. It was one thing when he was a clergy member in Etmos. The clergy could get away with many things an average citizen could not. But now that he was in Vesdar, now that he was no longer associated with the church, he had to keep his magic secret.

And people were already growing skeptical of him due to his success in the arena. Rumors had begun that he was cheating. People were refusing to fight him. But thankfully he had already had enough successes to put his mind at ease for the foreseeable future.

Right now, he scanned the many buildings in hope of finding a tucked away room he might be able to rent. Renting out a business room would be cheaper than buying an actual house.

Suddenly Asroth felt something in his pocket. He spun around quickly enough to grab a man's hand. A thief! With his staff, he struck the man in the face. Blood gushed from the thief's nose and the few coins he had stolen fell to the ground.

Several people pulled the man away, but Asroth followed after them. He would teach this thief a lesson. Though he did not always follow Ziad's ways, he still had strong moral standards. Thievery was disgusting and made him furious. He would punish this thief.

Asroth spotted them as they broke free of the crowd. It was a group of four people. They were sitting on a patch of grass on the outskirts of the marketplace, crowded around the bleeding man who had tried to steal Asroth's money. "Thief!" he yelled, coming at them with his staff.

The two men of the group stood up to face him, while the women remained seated, unsure how to respond. He pushed the two men back with his staff. One of the men, a dark-skinned boy, toppled over onto one of the girls. The bleeding thief, though, pushed back against him. Asroth raised his staff and flung it wildly. Eventually one of his swings managed to clip the thief, spraying blood.

The younger boy jumped back to his feet, wielding a sword. He chopped Asroth's staff into two. Asroth dropped one of the halves and, using his magic, extended the other half into a full-length staff once again. He was about to strike the boy in the stomach with it when it shortened back to its half-length. He swung wildly, unsure what was happening.

Then he noticed her.

One of the women was using magic on his staff. The other woman was looking at the thief Asroth had wounded.

A cry of agony stopped him in his tracks. The girl helping the thief looked like she was in terrible pain. They all turned to look at her. Something strange was going on.

The thief's face was unscathed.

Asroth dropped his weapon, fell to one knee, and ducked his head. "Please, I beg your forgiveness. In Ziad's mercy, please forgive me."

The group looked puzzled as to why he suddenly stopped attacking. "Excuse me?" the thief asked.

"That girl," Asroth spoke, raising his head. The young woman was still in pain, but managed to stand, along with the others. "Well, she healed you. She's a sister isn't she? A holy woman?" Attacking a sister was a serious crime. He was trying to stop crime, but in doing so nearly injured a holy woman. Asroth couldn't afford to be arrested. "And surely the other girl," he motioned with his head. "She too uses magic. Please, forgive me for attacking such a group. I'm sure your thievery was justified, for Ziad's will."

"Right," the thief muttered. "You're forgiven, you bastard." He rubbed the side of his head. "Thank you for healing me, Tara."

"You do not call her Sister here?" Asroth asked. Back in Etmos, holy people were always addressed by their title, whether a sister, priest, or bishop.

The healer moved towards him. "I am no holy woman, you daft man. Leave us alone."

Asroth was in shock. She was not a sister? But healers were required to join the clergy! And how dare she call him daft? Why he was probably the wisest, strongest, most intelligent man in all Vesdar! He ignored the insult. "You aren't? And you?" he asked the other woman. Suddenly, he realized what was so strange about the other girl. Behind her hood was green hair, tucked around tall, pointed ears. She was not even human—she was an elf! "What in Ziad is going on?"

"He's a nut job," the thief whispered to the healer. "Let's just go before he attacks us again."

"I'm not crazy!" Asroth shouted. "Surely it's no coincidence an elven spell caster and a healer who does not belong to the clergy are traveling together with two strong men to protect them. You must be on a secret mission. Or," he gasped, remembering the rumors of rebellion in Isandas, "are you royalty?"

The healer laughed. "In these clothes? I don't think so. Please, leave us alone."

"Well, I thought maybe nobles might be fleeing," he stuttered for a moment. "Wait!" he cried as they began to walk away. "Let me join you. I'm powerful, I can assist you in whatever it is you are doing."

"We aren't doing anything!" the thief yelled. "Now leave us alone!"

Asroth saw through his guise. It was too coincidental. They were up to something. Perhaps good, perhaps bad. Either way, they were a powerful band. He belonged beside power. Joining forces with such a team could get his name known. Once he grew famous, he could break away from their little party. "I pledge my allegiance to you!" he called, kneeling. "I promise to protect all of you, to fight for your safety and honor." He raised his head. "I am much more powerful than you understand. I'm a wizard and a healer! If you aren't a group now, perhaps together we could form one. A community of heroes!"

The others continued to walk away, but the elf stopped. "What do you mean?"

Asroth rose. He was quite a bit taller than her. "Well, I know the four of you are strong. Together we would make quite the team. A team capable of helping those in need. Like the clergy, but our own separate image."

"A community of heroes?" she repeated the phrase he had used.

His lips curled into a smile. So she wanted to be a hero, hmm? He nodded. "Exactly."

The thief rolled his eyes. "We aren't doing anything of the sort. We're just normal citizens like everyone else. Just because they can use a few magic tricks doesn't mean they have to go slay dragons," he said, annoyance in his voice.

The elf stopped him before he could turn away. "My name is Sheik. We are not royalty or anything like that, I can assure you. Like Kazzak said, we're just normal folk. But," she glanced back at the other three, "even normal people can help protect others. Excuse us for one moment."

She turned and faced the thief. "Why not?"

"Why not?" the man exclaimed. "I just had my skull bashed in, in case you hadn't noticed. I'm not helping this brute parade around the countryside pulling wagons out of the mud and chasing off bandits."

"There is something chilling about him," the healer whispered. "I'm not sure."

"Well, we do make a strong team, right?" the elf insisted. "Maybe it would be good. And we'd be helping people." The group hesitated a moment longer. She glanced towards the younger two in the group. "It could be a better way to make money. Plus he said he's a healer, maybe he could help train Tara?"

Asroth smiled, leaning into their conversation. "What do you say?"

After another exchange of glances, the thief finally gave a reluctant nod.

<hr />

Asroth had been with the group for just over two weeks. But, to Sheik, he did not really feel like one of them. He refused to stay with them in the abandoned houses. He spent his money on fine inns every night. The man often disappeared for multiple days in a row. Though all of them had shared their past with him, he would not even share the name of the town he came from.

Yet it was clear he thought of himself as the leader. He orchestrated their world-saving plans and always made sure his opinion was known. To start, he instructed that they would visit the sheriff's castle every week to gather any new wanted posters. He explained that they would begin as bounty hunters and then, once they became more well-known, people would hire them out as mercenaries. That was when their fame and wealth would really increase.

Sheik could not care less about fame and wealth. She only went along with his plan out of fear. Fear that maybe this friendship with Kazzak and Tara and Auni was temporary. And once they'd grown bored of Sheik's magical meals and showing her around Calert, they would expect her to move on. To find a new home. And the truth was, Sheik did not have a home.

But now they were banded together in this new role. Asroth had many names for it: an organization, a company, an order. To Sheik, it was a family, or at least she hoped that it would become one. In any case, it was a commitment to stick together.

And once they started their bounty hunter work, Sheik discovered that she truly cared about their cause. She wanted to help. She hadn't realized how many wanted criminals there were, nor had she anticipated the severity of their crimes. Back in Atarius' village, crime was largely unheard of. At most, some of the elves would get into disputes over personal possessions. But here in Calert, humans were wanted for horrible atrocities like assault, rape, and murder.

Kazzak had just picked up the most recent wanted posters and they were currently following a lead for a man wanted for four counts of robbery and six counts of murder. Kazzak and Asroth had asked around in different circles and followed a rumor to a potential hideout where criminals often took refuge. Taking turns, they stood watch near the house, waiting for him to show up.

After several days of lying in wait, Sheik and Kazzak were the two on watch when the man finally showed.

With a silent flick of his wrist, Kazzak pointed to the two men approaching the house. He passed the wanted paper to Sheik. She squinted, trying to compare the man on the left to the image on her paper. They were indeed the same person.

Just as she nodded, the man noticed their staring. She tried to look away but knew it was quite obvious that she and Kazzak had been watching them. The man said something to his friend and then began to walk towards them. "What do we do?" Sheik whispered, noting Kazzak's hand moving to his sword.

"Stay calm, it's—" Before he could say any more the men were there. "Can I help you gentlemen?"

The wanted man smirked and merely stuck out his hand. Despite his silence, they both knew he was asking for the wanted poster. Sheik took a step away, glancing around to see if Asroth or Auni were nearby. She hoped to flag them down so they might help if there was trouble, but they were nowhere to be seen.

She turned back to find Kazzak handing them the poster and saying quite simply, "We don't want any trouble." She wondered if he was actually worried or just waiting for an opportune moment.

"How kind," the wanted man smiled as he tore the poster up in front of them.

But the second man shook his head. "He's a bounty hunter." With a shrug, he pulled out a knife, and said, "No hard feelings."

The wanted man held out his hand to stop him. "You seem a little inexperienced. You won't go turning us in if we let you live, right?" Kazzak nodded compliantly. "How about we make a little trade then?" The man stepped forward and smoothed out Kazzak's collar, clearly trying to intimidate him. "How about you give us the girl and we'll let you live. Let us have a little fun for a few hours. What do you say?"

Sheik's left hand had already been carrying her bow, but now her right hand moved to her quiver as she held her breath and watched Kazzak.

Kazzak's response was defiant but calm. "Over my dead body." Then he slammed his forehead against the man's nose, sending him staggering backwards.

By the time Kazzak had drawn his sword the second man had stepped up with his knife and was putting up a fight. It had happened so suddenly, in only an instant, that Sheik hardly had time to gather her thoughts. She ripped an arrow from her quiver and nocked it to her bow.

Somehow in the blur of combat Kazzak had managed to stab one of the men. Sheik had trouble finding a target in the close-ranged chaos. The unwounded man had knocked Kazzak to his knees. Raising his sword, he was about to bring it crashing down on Kazzak's skull. But it only took the still of that moment for Sheik to steady her aim and release her arrow.

It sunk into his throat and ended his life in a matter of seconds.

Kazzak stabbed the other man, who had also ended up on the ground during the fray. Sheik had lost track of which one was which, but it hardly mattered. Kazzak's second stab killed the man, and Sheik was left staring at two dead bodies as Kazzak pulled himself back onto his feet.

"Sheik?"

She heard him say her name several times before she finally looked up at him. "What?"

"Are you okay?"

Was she? Everything felt quiet and distant. All her muscles were still tense, adrenaline pulsing through her system. Though the combat was over, her heart wouldn't stop pounding. She tried to relax her muscles, but the world simply wouldn't return to normal.

Kazzak left her staring at the bodies, but only for a moment as he flagged down someone and relayed what had happened so it could be reported to the sheriff. Then he took her by the hand and walked her away. She stared at his hand, wondering why it was there. Should he have been holding her hand? Considering that they had almost just died and had taken two lives, she wondered why she was even thinking about something as mundane as him holding her hand.

"Sheik?" he said again, now that they were far away from the combat, the bodies, the blood. "Sheik?"

She nodded, finally looking him in the eyes. He looked concerned. More than concerned. Frightened for her well-being. It was kind of sweet, really. "Are you okay?" she asked, trying to come to her senses.

He smiled. "Yes, I'm fine. Are you?"

Again she nodded. At least she wasn't physically wounded. And everything was finally beginning to calm.

Sensing that she wasn't fine, he asked again, "Are you sure?"

"We just killed them." Kazzak had killed people before. Sometimes the battles in the arena got rough and people didn't forfeit soon enough and they ended up dying from their wounds. But Sheik had never killed anything, not even an animal. And even though she knew those men deserved it more than anyone, it was still unfathomable.

As if knowing she was still feeling very distant, Kazzak said, "Hey, I'm here. It's going to be okay." Then he stepped forward and embraced her in a tight hug, all the while whispering, "I'm here."

She let his words wash over her and tried to focus on the feeling of his arms and his heartbeat. Her heart beat faster, too, and she wondered if it still had to do with the intensity of the combat or if it was because of the way Kazzak was holding her.

He kept holding her for a long time. And she would have let him keep holding her if it weren't for Asroth suddenly catching up to them and wanting to know the details of the fight. Kazzak let go of her and began to explain what had happened. It was suddenly very hard to stand without him. Sheik sat on the ground, trying to sort through her thoughts.

She cried that evening.

During the night, she snuck out of their worn-down shack and went for a walk with Fang. For some reason an image of the man's face came to mind and she just couldn't help but cry, just for a moment. Once she had pulled herself together, she and Fang crept quietly back to the house. To her surprise, Kazzak was up and waiting for her, having woken up and noticed that she was gone.

He stayed up with her that night and several nights after. He didn't hold her again, at least not like he had before. He would ask if she was okay. She would insist that she was fine even though she was having trouble grasping the thought of killing something. Then eventually after him sitting with her in silence she would confess that she didn't know how she was supposed to feel. He didn't usually offer much advice. Just listened and sat with her in silence and stillness. Somehow that was enough.

He told her they didn't need to do this. They could stop this vigilantism, this notion of trying to be a bounty hunter and fix the world's problems. But she didn't want to give up altogether.

She remembered how Atarius had praised her for being talented with a bow and arrow. How he had told her she was better than most. In the village it didn't matter. It was just fun and games. But here in human lands, people committed horrible crimes. If Sheik truly was stronger than most, then she couldn't sit idly by while people suffered.

But she swore to herself that she would be better. She would be more prepared, she would have better aim, she would react quicker, so that next time she could handle the situation differently. She didn't want to ever kill again. If she could help it, she would maim, disable, immobilize. She would do whatever it took to avoid having to take another life.

The others went on as normal. Asroth returned to gathering information on recent bandit raids. And though Kazzak told Auni and Tara what had happened, Sheik didn't let them see her when she was struggling. Tara had made a brief comment, telling her she could talk to her if she needed to. Auni told her once in privacy that he was sorry and asked if she was alright. And while they both were sweet, somehow, she preferred Kazzak's company best.

But in a few days, she stopped bothering him, insisting that she was fine. She wasn't sure if she was, but it wasn't fair to keep making Kazzak lose sleep over her. Besides, she still had Fang to stay up with her when she was struggling with all her thoughts and questions. And she reassured herself with the knowledge that next time she would be better.

CHAPTER 8

For the next few days, Asroth followed leads with little success. There had been some bandits raiding the farms to the south. Stealing gold, supplies, even needlessly killing horses just to prevent the farmers from pursuing them. It was a big enough case that Sheriff Varick's men were taking the lead on it. Asroth was currently scheming how to get information so they could try to track the bandits down first.

Sheik took the opportunity to spend time with Fang and fletch a mound of arrows. She was sitting peacefully by the fire in their small, abandoned house, when Auni's voice pierced the silence. "Workers are coming!"

Kazzak had warned her of this.

He had explained that they were staying illegally in Gibrald. The town had been evacuated for builders to expand Calert and make it one large metropolis. And so they had to be ready to move if workers arrived or else they'd face being arrested.

It all seemed bizarre to Sheik. That some lord in Calert could demand people to leave their homes and declare the whole region unlivable, only then to finish construction and sell the homes back to people. But Sheik didn't argue. She didn't want to get into trouble, and so she began gathering their things at the sound of Auni's voice.

The boy entered the house out of breath. "Kazzak and Tara are just behind," he explained. Sheik threw her half-finished arrows into her quiver and Auni helped scoop items into her backpack. "Workers are still a ways off, so we have time to grab everything." He stamped out the campfire. Fang began pacing, picking up on his worried tone. "We're not sure how far out they're working. Kazzak wants you and him to scout north, and Tara and I will scout south. See if we can get an idea of where they'll stop construction so we can find another home base."

"Hey," Kazzak entered only a moment later. "Auni tell you the news?"

Sheik nodded and slung her backpack over her shoulder. "Yeah, almost done here."

"Yeah, good work." He dug through the chest of drawers, pulling out clothes and some small things. Sheik glanced over, trying to see what all he had. It was mostly coins and jewelry, and of course his silly pan flute. He threw a necklace over his head, stuffed the coins in his pockets, and tied the pan flute to his pack. She wondered if any of it was sentimental, or if Kazzak only bothered with practical items that could be sold.

Sheik checked that she had her bow and Farin's knives. They were the only things of hers that could be considered sentimental. If she lost something like her flint and steel it would be an annoyance, but she didn't know what she would do without her bow. The stupid bow that Atarius had gifted her. It was one of the only things that reminded her of her old home.

"Good to go?" Kazzak asked as she ran her fingers along her name, whittled into the bow's grip.

"Yeah." She slung it over her shoulder alongside her backpack.

Tara entered as they exited. "All packed?" She was the slowest of the group but took a few things from Auni to lighten his load.

Kazzak nodded. "You two head south, we'll head north. Let's see which of us finds a better house." He tossed them a wink, like it was a game.

Tara smiled and played right along. "One perfect new home coming right up."

As the two siblings took off, Kazzak called after them, "Don't stay out too late! We're meeting at the arena before sundown, okay?" The two waved and headed south. Kazzak turned to Sheik. "Well come on, let's get a move on. Gotta beat them, right?"

"Oh of course," she said with a laugh. While she was certainly the competitive type, this hardly seemed a competition worth having. Sheik just hoped they might find a mattress without fleas. They walked at a quick pace for the first ten minutes, trying to find the workers while also keeping their distance.

"How many times have you had to move out here?" Sheik asked.

Kazzak shrugged. "Out here? Only twice. But they only started the city expansion a few years ago. Before that, I moved around all the time in Calert."

"How come? Why couldn't you find one place to stick?"

He laughed. "It's not that simple. Buying a house is expensive in a big city like Calert. I barely scraped enough together to afford food, let alone save for my own place."

"Huh. Makes Atarius' village seem nice."

"What do you mean?"

"You're given a home when you come of age," she explained. "A few people from the village come together and carve out a tree."

He stopped his walking to give her a silly look. "Carve it out? You mean cut it down? To build a house?"

She shook her head and pressed on past him. "No, I mean carve it out. They're big enough to sleep in." She could tell he didn't believe her, but she continued all the same. "I know, it's odd. It's funny, I don't remember anything about my life before Atarius' village, but I know that the idea of living in a tree is odd. Four walls and a roof like out here feels more familiar to me."

"Maybe you grew up with humans," Kazzak mused.

Admittedly, she was fluent in human tongue. Yet she doubted that she had grown up with humans because they still looked so foreign to her. And even in a city as big as Calert, she hadn't seen a single elf. It clearly wasn't common. "Well, if I did, I'm glad I've forgotten it," she joked. "It sounds like growing up in a human city is rough."

He shrugged but said nothing. Sheik wondered if she had struck a nerve, as they continued to walk in silence. Sheik hated walking through the abandoned town. It was so desolate. It felt haunted. Nothing like the bustle of Calert or even the forest, which was teeming with life.

After another few minutes, Kazzak pulled himself onto a rooftop. "Well?" Sheik called up to him.

He hopped back down. "Looks like the workers are setting up in a straight line towards the river. I don't think they'll come this far north anytime soon."

"So we can start looking?" He nodded. "Good, let me know if you find a house with a clean mattress. That's about all I care about," she laughed.

He laughed too and she was glad for the conversation to return. "I want a tile roof for when it rains." Most of the roofs had been made of straw and were now just beams with wide gaping holes. "With a chimney so we don't have to makeshift our own."

"And I suppose some glass in the windows, too?" Sheik asked with a smirk.

"Stained glass, of course," he teased.

She let out a whistle. "You just might get your wish. Look at that one!" It was still a bit away, but she could see it because of its height. The house wasn't one story, like most of the abandoned homes, but two, like the shops in Calert.

It was set apart from the other homes, too. Kazzak hesitated. "I don't know, it's a little exposed." He glanced into the window. Sure enough, the window had once had glass, though it had since been shattered. "It's totally empty, too."

"Yes, but it must have four rooms!" Sheik exclaimed, now that they were close. "We can gather things from other homes. It'll be great, come on!"

He stared at her for a long moment, and she gave him pleading eyes. "Oh fine," he finally relented, and they walked around to find the entrance.

Unlike their last house, this one still had a door. Sheik went to pull it open, but found it was bound to the wall with a lock. She lifted up the padlock and let it fall and clank against the wall. "It's locked." Again, despite that Atarius' village didn't have a single lock, she had faint memories of them. "I can melt it off with my magic," she offered.

Kazzak waved away the thought and began digging through his bag. "No don't, that will break it. I have my lockpick in here somewhere. Here we are!" He revealed a thin piece of metal. "Then we can get it open and use it in the future if need be."

Sheik glanced at him skeptically. "Lockpick?"

"Look, I'll show you. See the lock has little pins inside of it. Normally a key lifts the pins. But if you don't have a key, you can lift them with something else." He stuck in the metal and jiggled it back and forth inside the lock. Sheik crossed her arms and stared at him. She didn't know how locks worked exactly, but she had a hard time believing he knew their inner workings and could just open one without the key. But Kazzak was determined. "There's two. Must be a third," he mumbled.

And then it popped open.

Sheik's eyes widened. "How did you do that?"

He laughed. "I just explained it to you!" He pulled off the lock and swung open the door. "Wow, it is big in here."

"No, seriously," Sheik emphasized, taking the lock from him and staring into the keyhole.

"I told you. There's pins in there." He took the lock from her and placed the thin metal back inside. Giving it over to her, he cupped her hand inside his and guided her fingers until the lock clicked. "There, see?"

"Huh." She meddled with it for a moment more, but Kazzak moved on.

"Well, shall we start looking for some furniture?" he asked, setting his backpack just inside the door. He pulled out one of his shirts, wrapped up his hand, and began cleaning the broken glass from the shattered window.

Sheik finally set down the lock and inspected the house. There were two rooms, and just as Kazzak had hoped, the second one had a chimney. "Yeah, what's the plan? Just go house to house?" she called from the other room. Climbing up the set of stairs, there was a third room, long with a short ceiling.

"Sounds good to me! Anything up there?"

She came back down as Kazzak picked up the last shard and threw it out the window. "Nope, but three rooms plus an actual fireplace.

Not bad." He led the way back out and they glanced in and out of abandoned homes, looking for any luxuries they might be able to find. "So how did you learn all that about locks anyway?"

"Still on about that?" he retorted with a chuckle. "It isn't exactly surgery." She stared at him until he said more. "Alright, alright. I ran with kind of a bad crowd." He adjusted his necklace and shirt collar. For the first time since meeting him, he seemed nervous. "When I was a kid. I don't know, maybe eleven or twelve? They gave me shelter and food and taught me to steal. I didn't think it was a big deal, and it was just a couple years after my mom had disappeared."

He hadn't ever mentioned his parents before. Of course Sheik knew he had to have had them at some point. But he exuded this energy like he had taught himself everything. Raised himself. "So, they taught you to pick locks?"

He nodded. "And lift coins from people's purses. I used to be better at it than I displayed with Asroth before," he insisted, embarrassed over the incident. Sheik smirked. "Course it's easier when you're a kid."

They ducked in and out of houses together, finding the occasional dusty pillow or half melted candle. "So, whatever happened to them?" Sheik finally asked. "The people who taught you."

Kazzak gave her a shrug. "Not really sure. I stopped seeing them after I got busted."

"Busted?"

"Yeah. I got caught stealing. Thrown in jail for a couple weeks. Thankfully I was still just a kid, so they let me go without too much trouble." He paused, and then his voice became a low whisper. "But I saw stuff there." He seemed lost in thought for a moment. "Just a bunch of bad people," he finally said, his demeanor returning to normal. "It scared me. I didn't want to end up there. So, when they let me go, I never went back to the old group.

"I started training for the arena. Honest work. I still had to lift coins here and there until I started winning fights. You know," he flexed his muscles and added with a teasing tone, "really bulked up and became the masculine man you know today."

Sheik laughed and gave him a shove. He grinned back at her. That silly grin, where his eyes crinkled and his dimples appeared. The light fell on his reddish-brown hair and lit up his face, and she couldn't help but stare.

He stared back at her and she wondered if he would hold her the way he had just over a week ago. But he didn't. He looked at her for a moment longer, then glanced up at the sun. "Come on, let's run this back to the new house. We have to meet Auni and Tara back in Calert."

Sheik nodded and followed after him.

By the time they reached the arena in Calert, it was nearly evening. Auni and Tara were not yet there, and so they watched a few sword duels. Sheik knew nothing about sword fighting, but Kazzak pointed out when he saw sloppy stances or a particularly good parry.

A hand on her shoulder caught her attention. "I've been looking for you guys."

It was Asroth, several sheets of parchment in his hand. "We had some trouble with workers coming a bit too close to where we were staying," Kazzak explained.

He rolled his eyes. "Why don't you just rent a room instead of living like vagrants? Then I might actually be able to find you when I need you."

Sheik thought to argue but held her tongue. "What have you got there?" she asked instead.

He handed it over. Wanted posters. "I was finally able to convince Sheriff Varick's soldiers to get me information about that bandit group. Like ten to twelve guys. He had sketches of three of them."

She looked over each of the drawings, then handed them to Kazzak. "These are the ones that raided those farms and killed all those horses?" he asked as he studied the pictures.

"Yeah. Ready to get to work?"

⁕

Sheik nocked an arrow to her bow. Lifting her head, she motioned for the others to act. Though their movement was hardly noticeable, Sheik could sense the bushes rustling. Kazzak and Asroth were surrounding the group below: the bandits who had been attacking farms on the outskirts of Calert.

"Now?" a voice behind her asked.

She did not bother turning to face Tara and Auni but instead focused on her target. The pair had both been eager to assist in tracking

162

down and fighting the bandits, feeling guilty for being absent from the first bounty hunting skirmish. "Now," she whispered.

Auni ran down the small hill, pretending to cry the best he could. "Help! Please!"

The rugged men hardly paid attention to him. Sheik's arrow remained steady as she watched the boy, hoping his part went well. Tara sat nervously next to her, having only come along in case one of them became wounded. "Are you sure there are only ten?"

Sheik nodded. "Yes, Tara. Don't worry he will be fine. We all will." She had not actually had the opportunity to count each of the men, but she knew how many there were by their tracks, which they had been following for just over a day. "You can watch if you'd like but please stay quiet," she said as gently as possible. She worried Tara might scream and give away their position when the fight began.

The men walked over to Auni, who held up his hands to show he was unarmed. As soon as one man was in close enough range, Auni took a swing at him. His once bare fist instantaneously became covered in metal.

Asroth had done his part.

Auni continued to attack with his gauntleted fist, constructed of Asroth's magic. Sheik let loose her arrow, which hit one of the men's knees with unerring accuracy. Flawlessly, she nocked and released another. A third. A fourth.

Before Kazzak was able to jump from his hiding place among the bushes, Fang had already sprinted into action. Sheik stood up so she could check how many men were still fighting.

She had disabled four. Auni had beaten the wind out of two. Fang had dragged one to the ground and was shaking him like he was a child's toy. Asroth had joined the fray and beaten one with a staff—whether he was unconscious or dead she couldn't tell. She watched Kazzak slash the hamstring of one man and then stab the last man standing through the gut. Her stomach ached as she watched the man slide off Kazzak's sword, clearly dead.

Tara sucked in her breath. She must have seen it happen too. Sheik glanced at her to see if she was alright. It was hard to tell. "Tara?"

The girl nodded. "I'm okay. Really," she insisted. Sheik noticed the girl's palms shaking.

Sheik knew all too well what she was going through. "It's okay. I know how you feel. I think it's normal."

She was about to say more, but Kazzak interrupted her thoughts. "Sheik? Are you alright?" he called to her.

"Yeah, we're coming!" Sheik ran down the hill quickly, despite the brush. By the time she reached the bottom, Kazzak and Asroth had tied up the seven men who were still alive. The one Kazzak had stabbed was clearly dead, as was the one Fang had ripped apart. Sheik put a finger to the neck of the one Asroth had attacked. There was no pulse.

"He's dead, don't worry," Asroth said flatly.

He clearly had no idea what it was she was actually worried about. She sighed and gave Kazzak a look. If anyone knew how she felt about killing, it was Kazzak. "Sorry," he said simply. "I tried."

A scream disrupted her thoughts. Asroth was kicking one of the injured men in the gut. "What in the abyss are you doing?" Sheik yelled at him.

He gave her an odd look, like she was the crazy one. "Trying to get him to talk, to tell us which farmers he stole from."

But the robber just let out a string of curses, half of which Sheik didn't understand.

Asroth shoved a bit of cloth in the man's mouth to shut him up. Pulling out the poster he had gotten from the sheriff, he skimmed it quickly. "It doesn't say any specific tools." He sighed. "I guess we can go to the nearest farm and ask what was stolen, see if it matches," he suggested, kicking at the wagon full of farming goods.

Sheik and Kazzak nodded. If the robbers wouldn't help them, it seemed like the simplest solution. "Auni, Tara, why don't you go fetch the sheriff's soldiers?" The siblings nodded and took off back towards Calert. "Those who are still *living*," she said pointedly, "can stand trial."

Asroth paid no mind to the comment and merely offered to stay with the bandits. "I'll keep an eye on them until the sheriff's men arrive."

And so Sheik and Kazzak pulled the wagon along, Fang leading the way. He was able to find the farms quickly and let out a string of barks. The smell of the farm's horses lingered in the air. It guided him to the front door of a barn where Sheik introduced herself to the farmer.

"I'll gather up some of the other farmers that were attacked," one of the ranchers said. "We're more than grateful, really. Is there any way we can thank you?"

Sheik shook her head as she stepped away from the wagon. "Just let us know if you ever have bandit problems again," she smiled. "We'll try and help out the best we can."

"Bandits?" the rancher asked. "We weren't raided by bandits," he mumbled, thinking to himself. "You're thinking of the farms to the south. These supplies must be theirs. No, we were robbed by soldiers."

She froze. "Soldiers?"

CHAPTER 9

"I hold in my hands a blank parchment!" the man bellowed, raising up a long scroll. He stood on top of a table in the marketplace. Surrounding him were four burly soldiers, who kept the crowd at a considerable distance. "It shall soon be a conscription list. If at least one quarter of the men in this city do not sign their name on it," he paused to give the crowd a moment to think, "the entire city of Calert will be burned to the ground. Everyone shall be slaughtered, regardless of age."

The crowd gasped. The soldier waited for the whispers and cries to calm before he continued. "This fate can be avoided if enough men sign their name. Please, for the sake of your lives. The sake of your families. Your wives and daughters. For the sake of peace. For the sake of building a better tomorrow for your loved ones, I give you the honor of joining the New Prosper Army.

"This is the generation meant to make history. Together, we can achieve peace. We can join arms and unite under a single kingdom. Sign your name and live your lives in prosperity!"

Sheik and the others watched the man as he continued to speak with individuals as they approached the table. "So the rumors were true," Asroth whispered. "I had heard there was a rebellion in Isandas. I didn't think it would spread outside of Etmos. Who knew it had gotten this bad."

"What do you mean?" Sheik asked, not fully understanding what was going on. "What is the New Prosper Army? What rebellion?"

Asroth shrugged. "The nations have been stable for years. Even the standing armies have been greatly reduced in the last decade. But lately I heard there was a rebellion in Isandas."

"Isandas?"

"The capital of Etmos. The north nation."

"Obviously the rebellion succeeded. The leader must have created this New Prosper Army," Kazzak chimed in, putting two and two together.

Asroth agreed. "I thought this would just be confined to Etmos but apparently the leader wants to conquer all of the nations. Unify them all under his control. Vesdar and Masil have such weak councils, if this New Prosper has absorbed Etmos' original army, I doubt they'll stand a chance."

Kazzak nodded. "At least in Vesdar. The feudal lords will scramble and the council will get nothing done. Meanwhile the New Prosper will recruit those who fear them and overpower those who don't want to surrender. The further they go, the stronger their army will be."

Sheik nodded, as she began to understand what was going on. "Who knows what this means," Asroth continued rambling, mostly to himself. "The army could succeed without violence, uniting all the countries as one. Nothing would change besides who was sitting on the throne. But—"

"The army could also wreak havoc trying to assert their authority," Sheik finished for him. "I have a feeling it will be the latter."

"I agree," Tara spoke up. "Those soldiers were responsible for raiding the farms. That man just threatened to kill everyone in Calert. Those are not peaceful orders. Whoever is commanding them clearly does not care about the people."

Kazzak glanced to Asroth, who seemed to agree. "Sheik?" he asked next, but she was already on the move.

Jumping onto one of the market stands, Sheik pulled herself onto the rooftop. Kazzak and Asroth shouted up at her. She crouched down low and tried to block out their voices. Nocking an arrow to her bow, she took aim at the soldiers. Fang barked as the others shouted.

Sheik's mind closed to the rest of the world until she could hardly hear the voices calling her name, begging her to stop. The men were a good distance away, but they were not moving. She had hit targets even further away before. Her aim was set. Blackness began to absorb around her until she saw only her arrow and the target.

The arrow flew.

The man on the table dropped to his knee as it struck his leg.

"Sheik!" the group let out a final cry. She glanced down at them for a quick instant. They stared back at her, dumbfounded.

The soldier's companions pulled him off the table and began dragging him away. Sheik tried to aim another arrow, but they were lost in the crowd. To her surprise, no one was stopping them from getting away. Instead, they were staring in horror, shocked that someone had attacked at all. Soon, they were turning and searching for the archer.

Sheik scrambled across the many rooftops, trying to reach the crowd. "People!" she cried. "Listen!"

But before she could explain her actions, a man shouted, "What are you doing? You've doomed us all!"

"Those men were going to slaughter you!" Sheik shouted back.

"They might have been reasoned with!"

She doubted it. Men ordered to kill entire towns were not reasonable.

"We could have signed!" yelled another.

Why would they want to join an army by force? An army that would march around making the same demands of the next town.

But she didn't have a chance to defend herself. People were screaming at her, saying she had sentenced them all to death. And then some noticed she was an elf and shouted, "Why in the abyss are we listening to an elf?" and, "Go back to your woods and let us deal with our own problems!" More people joined in, yelling curses at her. "If someone is going to provoke an army at least let it be one of our own kind!"

Someone threw a stone at her, though it was small and easy enough to dodge. A chant began. "Kill the elf!" More things were thrown at her, none of them terribly dangerous. But the mob was growing. This had not been what Sheik was expecting. She was going to help the people fight off the soldiers. She had a plan but no longer tried convincing the mob. Leaping from roof to roof, she attempted to escape the pursuing crowd.

When she was finally able to slip into an alley, she quickly made her way out of the main city. Retreating to the evacuated Gibrald to the west, she found the abandoned home they had been camping in over the past two weeks. It was empty, but she assumed the others would meet her there when they got the chance.

Fang reached her within a few minutes. Together they paced back and forth, waiting for the others. What was taking them so long? It was no more than a twenty-minute walk to the market. She could easily jog it in ten. Were they not coming? Maybe the crowd had followed them. Her heart sank. Maybe the crowd had hurt them.

Finally, almost an hour later, Kazzak, Tara, and Auni entered the house. "Where have you guys been?" Sheik exclaimed. She wanted to hug them, relieved they were okay. But Kazzak's face was stern.

He took in a deep breath. "Sheik. Why did you do that? They want you dead, Sheik. Do you get that? Dead! Look, I'm a pretty reasonable guy, but what in Ziad's name were you thinking? The townspeople are right. That army is going to come in and kill every last person. How could you shoot that man?"

Sheik felt stupid. She had been trying to do something right. Something to help the people. "That army isn't uniting the lands, they're trying to conquer. They're not trying to help the people, you know that!"

"Of course they aren't, but you can't just shoot them! They're probably evil, cruel men, but they're stronger than us. And now they're going to hurt a lot of innocent people."

Fang sat next to Sheik as if defending her. Tara and Auni did not say a word.

"Where is Asroth?" Sheik asked.

Kazzak stuttered for a moment. "Who cares? Did you not hear a word I said? Asroth's so mad he doesn't even want to see you."

Sheik stared at the ground. How naïve she had been. Not for shooting down the New Prosper messenger, but for ever believing that forming this organization, making this agreement to fight to-gether, would make them a family.

Family didn't abandon each other when someone made a mistake.

These people were not her family. They did not love her uncon-ditionally. And if she misjudged a situation again, they would leave her. If she wanted them to stay, she needed to be better.

She was lost in deep thought, when Kazzak finally mumbled, "We need to get out of the city."

"Please don't leave me." Sheik tried her best not to cry. "Look, I have a plan. I won't let those soldiers harm a soul. Are you with me?"

Auni took a step towards her. "I am," he whispered. "I mean, if it's alright, Tara," he added, glancing at his half-sister. "I wanted to do the same thing when I heard that man speaking. I wanted to kill him. And if you have a plan, then I want to help kill all those bastards."

Tara nodded. "Absolutely. We stand behind you all the way, Sheik."

Sheik smiled. She hadn't lost their trust completely. She just needed to show them that she could lead them, to prove that she hadn't made a mistake. That they could trust her and that it was in their best interest to stay with her.

Kazzak sighed. "Alright, fine. What's this plan of yours?"

⋙∘⋘

The soldiers marched through the tall grass. They were all dressed differently. Some in chain mail, some in full plates, and some wearing no armor at all. They wielded different weapons, like a group of disorganized mercenaries. There were probably ten thousand men, marching forward in no particular order. It was obvious they had not been well trained, probably having just been recruited from another city. There was only one unifying element among the soldiers. Each man carried a shield with two words painted across it.

New Prosper.

It was almost dawn, the sun barely making its appearance above the hills. Sheik did not find this sunrise beautiful like that first morning she had watched it ascend over the Great River. This sunrise was an omen of bloodshed to come. She hid in the tall grass.

Kazzak sat nearby, peering down the hill. "Still a few minutes," he whispered to her, urging her to be patient.

But a sound distracted them both.

From Calert, a trumpet blared. The sheriff's soldiers. They were no group of ten thousand. Perhaps only five hundred. As Kazzak had explained, Vesdar didn't have a standing army. But each city had a sheriff with at least a small amount of troops to maintain peace. There hadn't been war between nations in decades. And the sheriff's soldiers were not prepared for the bloody battle they were charging into.

"Damn," Kazzak whispered. "Never mind, we don't have time. Light it now!"

Sheik lit her already nocked arrow with magical fire then stood up and released it. The tiny red light flew through the dark sky and hit the ground, just in front of the New Propser soldiers.

The darkness vanished as the grass burst into flames. The fire spread instantly among the soldiers, trapping nearly half the army in it.

Sheik and Kazzak had broken into Calert's largest lamp shop that night and stolen all of its oil. The gallons were dumped and soaked into various places throughout the fields. The soldiers had just entered the first and largest trap.

Even though it was Sheik's idea, she didn't love it. She knew it would kill most of the soldiers. But at this point, death was inevitable. Someone would die this day. She would rather it be the soldiers than the citizens of Calert. Besides, as Sheik and Kazzak loosed countless arrows at the surprised army, she hoped that the untrained soldiers might simply abandon post and flee.

And she had been right. Many of them immediately started to retreat. Others were trampled in the chaos. The Calert soldiers, shocked by the sudden change in dynamics, halted. "Please stay there," Sheik mumbled to herself. They had more plots drenched in oil, prepared for when the New Prosper broke through the current flames.

Fang helped them sniff out the oil, but they were not alone when they reached it. Ten of the sheriff's troops had reached them easily on horseback. "The elf!" one shouted. "You're under arrest!"

Sheik and Kazzak shared a glance. Auni was holding the torch meant to light the field and he looked to Sheik for guidance. "You need to step back," she said simply.

The soldier scoffed. "You're under arrest," he said again.

Kazzak stepped between them. "Look," he explained, "we have set up fire traps all along this field. If you arrest us, you won't know where they are. And there are still at least five thousand troops heading this way. We don't have time for this conversation!"

There was a pause. The soldiers glanced between each other. "Very well. But Sheriff Varick has orders for your arrest." Then he clicked his tongue and the horses returned towards the city walls.

"Light it," Sheik muttered. Auni followed her directions and set the ground ablaze. It trailed north for a few seconds and then another huge plot of grass burst into flames. The group started sprinting once again.

Sheik couldn't believe the sheriff would have her arrested. Their group had single handedly arrested murderers and taken out the bandit raiders. And now they were fighting off a ten-thousand-man army more successfully than his men would have.

Most of the army was decimated, having been caught in the flames, shot down by Sheik and Kazzak's arrows, or trampled by their own men. Many were fleeing. Sheik lit their final fire trap. "That's the last one!" she yelled, running back to join with everyone.

There were still at least a thousand men charging up the hill. Maybe more. "What now?" Kazzak asked. "Let the sheriff's men take care of them? Or stand and fight with them?"

Sheik certainly wanted to let the sheriff eat his own words and struggle through this battle without her. But it wasn't fair to his troops. "We'll join them."

Tara shook her head. "No, there are still too many," she protested. "Unless... send me back. I'll go back to Calert and get help."

Sheik didn't know what she meant. The small amount of help she might get was already here. But she nodded anyway and Tara sprinted back towards the city as fast as she could.

<hr>

When Tara reached the arena, it was nearly empty. There were no fights going on, simply several warriors loafing around. She supposed they might be preparing to stand up when the soldiers arrived.

Other people in the town were trying to flee. Others likely sat in their homes and prayed to Ziad for protection.

"Please!" she shouted, gasping for air. Her lungs burned but she knew there was no time to stop. She forced the words out of her mouth. "There is a group standing up against the soldiers. They need assistance. If you warriors are waiting for the army to come here, you might as well meet them at the gate. Fewer people will be harmed. Please," she pleaded.

Several men stood up upon hearing her request. "How many soldiers are left?"

Tara shook her head. She didn't know. "I'm not certain but we have killed well over half of them. There cannot be more than a couple thousand."

One of the men laughed. "There's less than fifty of us. It's suicide."

"The sheriff's men are—"

The man laughed again. "How in Ziad's name did the sheriff's men fight off thousands?"

Tara wished the man would stop laughing at her. She wanted to explain how they had made fire traps, but was afraid she would get in trouble if the man knew anything about the oil theft at the lamp shop. They were in enough trouble as it was. "Please, you must believe me. They need help, surely—"

"Tara?" The voice rose above hers, echoing across the practically empty arena.

It was Asroth! She had not seen him since Sheik had attacked the soldier in the marketplace. "Asroth," she smiled, her voice full of relief.

"So the elf is doing it after all, huh? Even after the entire city wanted her dead, she is still fighting to protect them?" Tara nodded, praying to Ziad that he would help her. "Well, I suppose such a noble act forgives her stupidity then, hmm? And I suppose you could use the assistance of a mighty warrior like myself?"

Asroth had left in such a hurry the day before. He had been furious and took his leave of them quickly before he could be associated with the elf. Now he seemed calm and relaxed. Perhaps he was no longer mad at Sheik. Or perhaps he simply knew the city needed his help. He stepped next to Tara and placed a hand on her lower back, rubbing it slightly. Maybe he was trying to be comforting, but it made her feel strange and uneasy.

He took his hand away. "Come on you cowards!" he called out. "Afraid of some soldiers? You're trained warriors! We can fight off this ragtag group of rebels!" He leaned in next to Tara. "Let's go, this dumb bunch will follow."

The soldiers were approaching. Sheik tried to count their numbers as she rained arrows upon them. Using her magic, she would bend away an inch of their armor a split second before the arrow struck. As long as her aim was direct, such protection did not matter. The smallest section, just larger than her arrowhead, would magically disappear and allow her arrows to pierce through before the armor warped back.

Soldier after soldier dropped. Though Sheik aimed for the legs so as not to kill, she knew many of the men would still end up trampled and die all the same. But she could think of no better way to both stop them and try to keep them alive.

Then the sheriff's men rode down into battle. Her arrows were running out and she knew it would be impossible to aim accurately anymore. Instead, she used her magic. She focused on their armor, locking up their knees or making their chest plates heavy. The troops on horseback cut them down easily as their armor betrayed them and made it impossible for them to move.

Kazzak and Auni drew their swords and protected Sheik, as did Fang. Anyone who got past the sheriff's line were stabbed or torn apart by the wolf. But the sheriff's numbers were dwindling too. It still wasn't an even fight.

"Charge!" a familiar voice called over the noise. She turned to find Asroth and Tara with at least fifty men behind them. Sheik smiled. Perhaps the narcissistic wizard was not so bad after all.

The sheriff's horses pulled back so they could regroup and the men formed a defensive wall. "Mud?" Asroth asked.

Sheik nodded. That would be simple enough. As the New Prosper charged forward, Sheik and Asroth concentrated their magic, turning the ground into a sloshy, watery mess. The men sank in, struggling to get their knees high enough to keep moving.

The sheriff's men and arena fighters cut down what remained of the soldiers easily.

The once impossible battle ended in a matter of minutes.

Tara and Asroth tended to several of the wounded. Sheik glanced across the battlefield until she locked eyes with the sheriff's soldier that had spoken to her earlier. He approached.

"The rest of my men will follow their trail back to wherever they make camp," he stated simply. "I advise you are not here when we return. I will report back that we lost track of you during the chaos of the battle."

She folded her arms. This man likely wouldn't be alive if not for her. But Kazzak nodded on her behalf. "Understood."

The soldier rode off and led the rest of his troops north.

Sheik rolled her eyes at Kazzak. "Understood? Really?"

He shrugged. "He gave us an out. Let's go."

Sheik didn't care if he was right or not, it was a matter of pride. "Go where?"

Again, he shrugged. "Anywhere. But you heard the man. We can't stay in Calert."

She didn't like how quickly he was accepting this. But she said nothing. She glanced across the battlefield. Tara was still healing several of the fighters from the arena. And Asroth and Auni were dragging together a pile of soldiers. She wondered if it was the living or dead. "What are they doing?"

"Not sure," Kazzak mumbled, and they jogged over to them.

"Thank you for helping us," Sheik admitted when they reached Asroth. She was embarrassed that Asroth of all people had been one of the ones to come to her aid. "You still mad at me?"

He shook his head. "Oh, no. No, I'm not mad anymore. But I still think you're an idiot and you better never do something so foolish ever again. You're a good fighter, Sheik, and you've got a good heart. But there are a lot of factors you didn't consider when you shot that first arrow." She hated that he of all people was lecturing her. "You just have to think things through a little more before you go starting wars."

She looked over the small group of soldiers he and Auni had gathered up. They were still alive, a group of twelve. "Now," Asroth turned to them. "Let's deal with them before the sheriff's men return. You are going to answer all of our questions. You will answer them as soon as they are asked, without hesitation, and with respect." Sheik, Kazzak, and Auni shared a silent glance, wondering what information he was trying to learn but not wanting to disturb his interrogation.

The soldiers spat at him or cursed. Asroth remained calm and bent down next to one. "Who do you take orders from?"

"I'll never tell you anything!" he yelled.

Sheik began to speak up, but Asroth stopped her. "No, please. Let me handle this." He reached out and touched the man, concentrating for a moment. Sheik watched Asroth as he grew pale, like he was sick. Suddenly the soldier screamed in pain.

She did not know what Asroth was doing, but her body recoiled at it.

The soldier began shaking and his skin turned black and began to wilt before her eyes. "Asroth, stop," she whispered. She thought to reach out and grab him but feared that touching him might leave her with the same fate as the soldier. Fang, who lingered a few paces away let out a low growl. "Asroth!" she screamed. "Asroth stop!"

When he finally did, the soldier was dead. Asroth fell to the ground beside him, vomiting up a black liquid. She, Kazzak, and Auni stared at him in silence and shock. Were they supposed to help him? What was wrong with him? What had he just done to the soldier?

After a moment, he rose back to his feet and faced the remaining soldiers. They, too, had been shocked into silence. "So," Asroth began again. "Tell me who you're working for."

They nodded instantly and collectively gave a name: "Spike."

Asroth chuckled and rolled his eyes. "An intimidating name meant to scare his foes. Well, who is he? Leader of the army? Is he a general? A king?"

One of the men shook his head. "That's what makes him different from the rest of the world. He has no title. He is only a man."

Asroth rolled his eyes. "Just because he has no title doesn't change a thing. He is your leader, king or not. You serve him the same." He paused. "So, he is the one who led the rebellion against Isandas and now leads the army, correct?" The soldier nodded. "How many more platoons like this one exist? Where is the base of the army?"

Sheik added in a question of her own. "Are the soldiers recruited the way your men tried to in Calert?"

The soldier who had first volunteered information continued. "I'm not sure. There are perhaps fifty other armies. Each group was ordered out of Isandas in different directions in search of reinforcements. We are trying to pacify the nations by uniting everyone under the New Prosper Army. Once that has been done, Spike wants the army to disband."

He didn't exactly answer Sheik's question, but she figured she knew the answer anyway. She stared down at him and whispered, "Fifty." She could not even imagine so many armies.

Kazzak, who had not yet said a word, finally spoke up. "We can do that," he mumbled coolly.

"Are you kidding?" Sheik could not believe his carefree attitude. "We would need soldiers of our own. Thousands."

Asroth piped in with, "No, the thief is right. You were able to take out most of this army with only four people." He thought for a moment. "Besides, we don't need to take out the entire army. Just Isandas. If we eliminate Spike and his main source of men, the army will disintegrate. The people who were recruited against their will would start rebelling. And by then maybe the councils will have pulled their heads out of their asses and gotten a conscription of their own started."

Kazzak nodded. "You wanted to know where we would go. How about Isandas?"

Sheik laughed. This was insane. They had managed to save one city, did that really mean they could take on the entirety of this New Prosper army?

"I'm serious," Kazzak reiterated. "Vesdar doesn't have a standing army. I don't think Masil does either. This," he motioned vaguely to the battlefield, "is going to keep happening all over until someone does something. Why not us?"

Asroth agreed. "We'll head back to your little shack, pack up, and make a plan. In the meantime, what do you want me to do with the soldiers?"

Sheik sighed. "I guess we can tie them up so you can heal them," she offered. "Then the sheriff could—"

Asroth interrupted with a quick, "I can't heal them."

"What?" Sheik didn't understand. He was a healer. She had seen him heal.

"Healing magic requires empathy," Asroth explained. "I don't exactly have sympathy for these brutes." He looked them over. "If it were up to me, I'd kill them."

Sheik rubbed her eyes. "Just tie them up. When the sheriff's soldiers come back, they'll handle them." Asroth left to where Tara was healing the arena fighters, looking for something he could use to tie them up.

Auni and Kazzak stayed by Sheik's side. She noticed Auni staring at the dead body, the one Asroth had touched. She took a glance but couldn't bear to look at it for more than a moment. The man's torso had split open, and the surrounding skin and internal organs were as black as charcoal. She studied Auni's face instead. "You okay?"

He glanced over at her. "I thought you said magic couldn't do this." He took a step back and finally stopped staring at the body.

"It can't," Sheik whispered, suddenly unsure of herself. "This isn't…" she trailed off. She wanted to say that it wasn't magic, but of course it was. What else could it have been? "I don't know what he did."

"Black magic."

Sheik and Auni both turned to Kazzak, who had said the words so quietly that Sheik was hardly certain she'd heard them correctly. But he said it again: "Black magic. I've only ever seen it once before."

Kazzak didn't bother making eye contact as he told his brief story. "There was a man accused of witchcraft. He was held in prison, awaiting trial." He and Sheik shared a look, and she understood. This was what he had seen during his time in prison. "He tried to escape. Used black magic on the prison guards." He glanced over at the dead body and gave a nod. "Just like this. Took out four men with just a touch. The guards killed him then and there. He was too dangerous to keep alive."

As they waited for Asroth to return, Sheik wondered how dangerous he might be.

CHAPTER 10

Tara's feet ached from the laborious marching. Her back ached from sleeping on the hard ground. When they had been in Calert working as bounty hunters, they had never walked more than a few hours a day and had a straw mattress to share, even if it was flea-ridden. But now they marched almost ten hours a day, traveling south-east across the plains to make it into the safety of the southern forest. The forest would offer them greater shelter and protection, and they could use its cover the rest of the way to Isandas.

But they had to make it to the forest first. Out on the plains, they were easy targets. After the battle at Calert, word had spread that two troops had fought: the sheriff's men and a mysterious small group who aimed to dethrone Spike.

And now Spike was sending horde after horde at them. At first the groups were small, only about sixty or seventy men at a time. With Sheik and Asroth's magic, they'd managed to survive. But the groups were getting larger and the openness of the plains left them with few available tactics. Once they got to the forest, Sheik assured them, they would be fine.

Tara could hardly wait. Perhaps when they reached the forest they could stop marching for so long. Back home in Omris, Tara had thought herself of average build. But compared to the other four, she was wildly out of shape. She hated the idea of being the weakest link, especially since she was unable to help when it came time to fight.

Auni always reminded her that she was invaluable to them as a healer. At least she had grown in that regard. She found it hard to believe that she had once fainted from healing the cut on Auni's hand so many months ago. It was laughable now. She had learned to endure great pain. And she had managed to do so without complaint. Perhaps that was her biggest growth of all.

Once upon a time, Tara had been a spoiled brat.

She had taken for granted the great wealth her family owned, all gained from the backs of slaves. And as much as she did not agree with slavery, she never truly opposed it until finding out that one of the slaves was her half-brother. Her own flesh and blood. Working in the fields, while she studied indoors.

Part of her missed the luxurious life she used to live. What she wouldn't give for a proper mattress. For a roof without leaks. For her nanny's baking. Apart from Auni, the others had no idea what kind of wealth she came from. And even then, she wasn't sure Auni knew all the indulgences she was accustomed to.

But part of her despised who she used to be and all she came from. So she thrust herself into this new life. She thrust herself into marching until she had blisters. She thrust herself into camping in the dirt, among the bugs. She thrust herself into healing every one of her friends' wounds despite the pain it caused her. How her mother and father would faint if they could see her now.

Yet as miserable as this marching was, and as terrifying as the battles were, this was the happiest she had ever been. Auni was her best friend. He listened to her attentively, even when she rambled on. Sheik and Kazzak treated her like an adult in a way that no one ever had before.

Most importantly, for the first time in her life, she was doing something that mattered. Something that helped society. She did not participate in the battles directly, but she helped however she could, and their little five-person group was saving lives. In all her eighteen years, she would never have imagined she would come to do something so important.

"I can see trees!" Kazzak announced, interrupting Tara's thoughts.

"Thank Elilah," Sheik beamed, catching up to him.

Auni and Tara exchanged a relieved glance. Maybe they would stop and camp for a day or two and they could all rest up.

Fang did not seem content. He let out a slight whine and Sheik immediately turned to him. "What is it, boy?" Then, with a little fear in her voice, she announced to the rest of the group, "I think there's soldiers nearby."

Asroth glanced across the plains in all directions. "I can't see anyone."

"I don't either, but Fang senses something. Maybe he can smell them," Sheik replied with a shrug.

Asroth rolled his eyes. "That's ridiculous. How do you know he doesn't sense something else? Maybe he just smells his next meal."

"It's soldiers," Sheik insisted. Tara was not sure how Sheik knew either, but this was not the first time Sheik had interpreted one of Fang's barks or growls. Maybe it was some special talent elves had.

"Look, the forest is just up ahead," Kazzak interrupted before Sheik and Asroth could bicker any more. Tara was grateful. The last thing they needed was another argument between the stubborn Sheik and the know-it-all Asroth. "Let's quicken our pace just in case there are soldiers nearby. And if not, we'll get a little shelter from this sun."

At this, Asroth consented. It was the hot time of year and Asroth seemed to handle the heat the worst. It hardly bothered Tara. Omris was much hotter than Vesdar, and, despite it being late summer, it felt to her like a mild spring. Auni seemed to enjoy it, as he could go about shirtless like he used to on the plantation. Tara tied his unused shirts over her head to help cover her face. As much as she did not mind the heat, her skin was too pale to leave exposed.

In the shade of the forest, she was able to untie it and let her short hair fall into place. Sheik leaned against a tree and gave a great big sigh of relief. "Wow it feels nice to be in a forest again," she admitted.

Auni retrieved his shirt from Tara and pulled it over himself. "Are you cold?" Sheik asked with a laugh.

"A little. Plus there's bugs," he explained with a swat.

Asroth groaned. "I don't know how you can be cold in this temperature, but you're right about the bugs."

"Well of course you are going to overheat wearing those ridiculous robes," Tara laughed while she sat and rubbed her feet. Asroth always had gallant outfits. He had long flowing robes and kept a headdress on at all times, explaining that it was worn by distinct members of the Etmos clergy. It was not enough for him to be a powerful wizard, he had to make sure he looked the part. He sulked away at Tara's comment.

Kazzak, who had taken up the rear for a moment, entered the calm of the forest. "Sorry to bust up the fun, but Sheik was right. There's soldiers on the horizon."

Sheik lifted her eyebrows and mumbled, "What do you know," quietly enough under her breath that Asroth couldn't hear. Tara wished she could smirk with her, but the thought of soldiers sent a chill up her spine. She stopped massaging her feet and pulled on her boots, knowing she had to be ready to move.

"So what's the plan?" Kazzak asked.

Sheik thought in silence and Tara, Kazzak, and Auni stared in anticipation. Asroth was still pacing off by himself and Fang was nowhere to be seen. With each passing second, Tara got more and more nervous. "How far away were they?" she asked Kazzak anxiously.

"Plenty far off." He gave her a smile and a wave of his hand, like it wasn't something to worry about.

Tara looked up at the sky. "Well how long until they get here? The sun will start to set in only an hour or so." Fighting was scary enough in the daytime, she feared what it would be like at night.

"They might not be after us," Asroth interjected, suddenly reentering the conversation. "Look, here." He pointed to one of his maps. He and Kazzak were the only ones who could read the maps with any sense of accuracy as to where they were. "There's a town just south of us. The soldiers might be going there."

"Let's pray they're after us. If they make it to that town..." Sheik didn't finish her sentence, and it made Tara shiver. The New Prosper Army had visited many of the towns they had passed through between Calert and the forest. Most had surrendered, but one had not. Sheik did not let Tara and Auni enter the town and she would not talk about it after. Tara had no desire to know the details.

Recentering them around the current issue, Kazzak offered, "Well we can draw them towards us."

"Now come on," Asroth began to interject, but Sheik had already accepted the idea.

"Yes, it should be no trouble. Kazzak, where's your hunting bow?" He readied it and tested the string. It was not nearly as well-crafted as Sheik's bow, but it worked all the same. "Auni, maybe you can throw spears if we can carve enough? Asroth can warp holes in their armor. We'll start with bow and arrows, then switch to spears and pull back into the forest. Tara's right, it'll start to get dark in just a few hours. At that point, we'll reassess if we want to keep fighting or retreat. Either way they'll be after us instead of the town."

Tara held her breath. She had thought of the darkness as a drawback, not an asset, and now she was a little annoyed that she had mentioned it at all. But she supposed Sheik knew best. The rest of the group nodded at her plan and Auni got to work finding sturdy branches that could be shaved into spears. Tara followed after him, helping however she could.

"Feeling okay?" he asked as she struggled to snap a thick branch.

"Yeah," she lied. "You?"

He gave a nod. "We'll be fine. Sheik knows what she's doing." Tara smiled at the way he idolized her. "Just make sure you stay towards the back."

Tara always stayed towards the back and even still Auni would watch to make sure she was okay. It was silly. After all, she was the older one. But it was his way of showing that he loved her, and that meant more to Tara than anything in the world.

"You be careful, too, you know." As much as she believed in their cause and knew this fighting was the right thing to do, it still scared her. She did not know what she would do if anything happened to Auni.

They sharpened spears in silence until Sheik and Asroth joined them to go over details of the plan. Sheik and Kazzak would have their bows, Auni would have spears with Asroth's magic to make them deadly accurate, and Fang would guard Tara. Sheik had marked certain trees for rendezvous points and Kazzak had cleared paths so they could wind through the woods quickly and easily.

Tara waited at her designated spot when the sun began to go down and the army approached. Kazzak had given her a knife to wield if things truly became dire, but she honestly wasn't sure she could use it properly. Fang sat by her dutifully and she ran through the plan in her head, worried she might nervously lose her way or do something wrong.

After half an hour, Sheik and Kazzak jogged up to her. Tara grabbed her pack, ready to retreat further into the woods at their next designated spot. Kazzak shook his head and waved for her to set down the pack. "No need," he explained between breaths. "Half of the army retreated back north. There's so few of them left, we'll be able to fight them here."

That was good news at least.

"Any wounds?" she asked, though she knew they would not have been injured from merely firing arrows down on the army.

"Doing fine," Sheik reassured her. "Just be on the ready to pull back if any soldiers make it through Auni and Asroth."

Within seconds, Asroth came through the line of trees. "They're coming. Still twenty or thirty of them."

"Where's Auni?" Tara shouted, fear churning in her stomach.

The sorcerer looked around himself and shrugged. "He was behind me a second ago."

Tara lurched forward but Sheik grabbed her by the arm. "We'll go, Tara. You need to stay here." The order made Tara feel like a helpless child, but Sheik's face was stern and so she obeyed nonetheless. She could not fathom how Sheik stayed so calm in situations like these.

Kazzak led the way with his sword drawn. Sheik nocked an arrow to her bow and followed behind. Finally, Asroth, who had not fully caught his breath, turned back around. Tara knew she was supposed to stay put, but figured there was no harm in trailing behind them as long as she kept her distance. And Fang still guarded her, so she considered herself plenty safe.

She heard the sounds of combat before she could see them. Sheik was the first one she saw, set apart from the others, firing arrow after arrow into the chaos. Then she saw Auni and she was finally able to release a breath of relief. He was still standing, swinging a spear around wildly. If he was hurt, it could not have been serious. She stared for a moment, watching his movements, impressed with the intensity of his swings. Auni was always her priority and so she tended to watch him most in fights.

But she glanced towards Kazzak, who seemed to be holding his own, cutting down soldier after soldier as they came at him. Sheik was right about the tactical benefit of the forest. The soldiers were only able to approach a few at a time and could not all attack at once.

Asroth, too, was doing fine. Tara rarely watched him in fights. Auni had told her about the way he had used dark magic on a soldier back in Calert. It sounded truly awful, and she feared seeing Asroth use it in battle.

Now that she was close enough to survey the battle, Fang stopped guarding her and joined the fray. She hated watching him, too. He would leap onto soldiers, knocking them over, and then tear into their throats. It was a gruesome sight to see. Sheik's arrows were far less bloody and grotesque.

"Sheik!"

Tara had only just glanced over at her to find that she was in danger. A lone soldier had managed to avoid the combat and make his way towards her, and Sheik was far too focused on her target to notice. "Sheik!" Tara screamed again, but the elf either could not hear or refused to be distracted. The soldier brought his blade down across her back, knocking her to the ground.

Fang tackled the soldier and dragged him away by his neck. Tara seized the opportunity to move closer, trying to keep her body small and her eyes open for approaching soldiers.

"Sheik!" Combat clattered around her, but she dropped to one knee and gave Sheik's body a shake to see if she was still alive.

Sheik flinched and cried out in pain. At least she was alive and conscious. Tara could not tell how deep or long the cut was, only that there was blood and that it had to have been serious enough to knock Sheik down. Squeezing her eyes shut to prepare for healing, she placed a palm over the elf's wounded back. The pain crashed into her and her back spasmed, dropping her to the ground.

Could she move? She tried without success. But Sheik was on her feet in seconds, locking her arms underneath Tara's and dragging her away.

By the time she felt well enough to sit up, Sheik had managed to pull her to safety. She put a hand on Tara's cheek and said a soft,

"Thank you," before returning to fight. Tara took in a few deep breaths before standing, baffled at how Sheik was able to recover so quickly.

By the time she reentered the scene, the battle was over.

Auni was to her side in an instant. "Are you okay? I saw what happened."

She nodded and surveyed the damage. Most of the soldiers were dead, and those who were still alive had too severe of wounds to put up any more of a fight or pursue them once they left. Sheik collected what arrows were undamaged. Kazzak cleaned his blade.

Tara looked back at Auni. "Are you hurt?"

He made a face at her. "You just healed Sheik. You need time."

That meant he was hurt. She scanned him up and down and found the backs of his knuckles were cut and bruised. It was a minor injury, but she grabbed his hands anyway and absorbed the pain.

"Tara!" He scowled but it melted into a sigh. "Thank you. You don't need to—"

"Yes, I do. I want to help," she insisted forcefully.

He folded his arms for a moment, like he was cross with her. She ignored it. Now that the chaos of the battle was over, she found her normal, talkative self returning. "Come on, let's get away from here. We must get the packs. If we move quickly, we might be able to set up camp before it gets too dark to see."

Sheik, having gathered what arrows she could, caught up to them. "Tara, you saved my life back there. I can't thank you enough."

"It's nothing," Tara said coolly, though she had indeed been terrified out of her mind in the moment. "But you must be more careful, you know." Sheik and Auni laughed but she was completely serious. If Sheik did not watch herself better when she was aiming, she'd get hurt again. Or worse.

Tara glanced towards Kazzak and Asroth who were lagging behind. "Are those two coming? Do they need healing?"

"Fit as a fiddle," Kazzak retorted.

"And the Mighty Asroth?" Tara teased.

He raised an eyebrow, and she could not tell if he was flattered or annoyed. "I think I have more blisters from all this hiking than I do cuts from battle."

At this, she laughed. Kazzak agreed and began describing one of his blisters in gross detail. "Ugh, if you speak for a second more, I am not healing it!"

They laughed and continued to tease one another as they trekked further into the forest. After some time, Kazzak insisted they had put enough distance behind them, and no one disagreed. They set up camp in a hurry, everyone eager to get some sleep. Tara lay on her bedroll with a sigh of relief. Relief that the battle was over, relief that everyone was unharmed, relief that she was among friends. Then she drifted quickly to sleep.

———⋖◆⋗———

It was the middle of the night when Sheik realized that half of the army hadn't fled out of cowardice. They had fled to get reinforcements.

Fang had spotted them first and woke her. When she saw the soldiers' torchlights, she understood. She quietly woke everyone, put out their campfire, packed up their supplies, and led the hike through the forest. Everyone was too exhausted to put up a fight then and there, and Sheik didn't know how many troops they'd be fighting against. So they continued eastward through the night, hoping to outpace the soldiers.

It was late morning when Kazzak scouted ahead and discovered that they were marching straight towards another troop.

Sheik wasn't sure how it happened. The groups had to have been too far apart to communicate with each other. But she didn't have time to figure out the why or the how. They were surrounded and needed a way to escape.

"We need to find an opening," she suggested. As long as the troops were unable to completely surround them, they would be able to flee.

"And how do you suggest we do that?" Asroth asked, a hint of frustration in his voice. Sheik hated his negativity in times like these. It made her feel hopeless. It made her feel one step closer to death.

Kazzak came sprinting through the bushes. He had a bloody gash on his side, which Asroth quickly tended to. "The troops to the east are spreading out," he panted, trying to gain his breath back. "They're searching for us."

Sheik brushed her green hair out of her face and rubbed her temples, trying to think. She was sticky with sweat and utterly exhausted. They were in no shape to fight.

An idea struck her. "Come on, I have a plan. We need to find a hill." The men, though curious and confused as to what her plan was, followed her. They had learned to trust her tactics. Sheik had become their unofficial leader in times of battle. The group always listened to her orders; they knew it was in their best interest. She had proven herself to be an invaluable asset to their team.

"Over here!" Kazzak called, having spotted a good hill.

"Perfect," Sheik nodded, surveying it. "Go get Tara, Auni, and Fang. We'll defend from here." Kazzak sprinted away to gather the others.

"Defend?" Asroth asked, raising an eyebrow. "Sit in one location and fight off a few hundred men?" Their previous tactics had always involved movement. Running as they fought. They had never truly faced one of the armies up front.

She shrugged away his words. "It's simple, really." Bending over, she scooped up a handful of pebbles, playing with them in her open palm. "How far do you think Auni and Kazzak can throw one of these?"

He gave her a funny face, as if to notify her that she was currently insane. "I don't know, but I don't see—"

"What do we have that they don't?" Sheik interrupted.

Asroth rolled his eyes, smiling slightly. "A lunatic for a tactician?"

She chuckled at his stale humor. "Magic. You and I are both strong enough magic users we can warp these pebbles into boulders as soon as they've been thrown."

Asroth thought for a moment. "Like a catapult with better aim," he smiled. "Sounds good."

⸺◆⸺

Carlos whistled. He had spotted yet another boulder, flying through the air. "Lyle!" he called. "Keira!" He raised his hand, pointing at the giant rock. He had spotted one earlier, but the others had not seen it. "I told you! Someone is here, in these woods. They're fighting the army."

Lyle stared at the sky, watching for another stone. "We can't trust them, Carlos," he whispered. "Just because they're fighting the army doesn't mean they're our friends. We can't trust anyone right now. Let's just keep moving." He took the hand of the woman who stood next to him. "Come on."

Carlos continued to look upwards, even as his two companions walked away. "If there are people strong enough to oppose the New Prosper, they'll be able to protect us. I'd rather take the chance." Yet another boulder flew across the sky, this time in a different direction. Either they had multiple catapults or some sort of spinning device to pivot the catapult. Whichever it was, they clearly had a well-structured defense set up. A defense that could keep all three of them safe.

"We're leaving, Carlos. Stay in one spot too long and you'll get caught for sure. You can't hide from those soldiers. They'll burn down this whole forest."

"So, what? We just keep running?" Carlos asked angrily, following after the couple. "I'm going to find the people with that catapult."

Lyle stopped and turned. "Don't do it, Carlos. I'm telling you, it isn't safe. Nowhere is safe." He looked Carlos in the eye pleadingly.

Keira, holding Lyle's hand, pulled him along. "Come on, Sweetie. Let Carlos do what he wants."

Carlos' face began to turn red in anger. He was sick of Keira. He had been good friends with Lyle since birth, but ever since they had met Keira, Lyle had changed. He listened to everything she said, did everything she wanted. Now, she was pulling Lyle away from him once again.

Lyle stared at the woman for a moment longer. "Please, listen to me," he said, looking once again at Carlos.

"Listen to you?" he scoffed. "Listen? That's what got me into this whole mess! 'We'll be taken care of, we'll be wealthy.' Bullshit!" His heart raced, his anger growing out of hand. "You said we'd never have to work again. We'd just pretend we're nobles. Now we're being hunted. The army wants us dead." He half chuckled, overwhelmed with the concept. "They're going to kill us, Lyle."

Keira began pulling Lyle away once again. "Come on, Sweetie," she whispered softly. The man followed behind her like an obedient dog.

Carlos shook his head slowly. His best friend was gone. There was no more reasoning with him. "Well, I'm going to find those people," he pointed in the direction of the catapult. "I'm not going to die."

<hr />

Auni hurled another pebble and watched as Sheik transformed it into a giant stone. It came crashing down behind a group of fleeing soldiers. Her plan had worked beautifully. The soldiers had scattered into the woods, afraid of the sudden defense that Sheik had rigged up. He and Kazzak simply tossed rocks as far as they could and Sheik and Asroth worked their magic, making them gigantic and lethal.

It was strange how much Auni's life had changed in the past six months. He had just been a slave. Now he was fighting off armies, led by Sheik, who he thought was probably the smartest person in the world. Who else would have come up with such a plan?

He had learned to care about and trust this tiny group. All of them except Asroth, perhaps. But Sheik and Kazzak were the nicest people. He never would have guessed that he would be able to rely on anyone, but here he was, trusting them with his life.

He threw another rock and watched it grow. It crashed down past a pack of soldiers with intense speed. There were fewer and fewer charging towards the hill. Some of them had died. Most of them had fled. Sheik always tried to create tactics that would cause the fewest deaths. Auni found it admirable the way that Sheik tried so hard to stick to her morals, even in the midst of war.

They continued their rock throwing for another fifteen minutes to ensure that all the soldiers had truly given up. Auni contemplated how easily they had defeated an entire army because of Sheik's ingenious tactics. The group sat down together, resting. His arm was hardly sore, but Auni supposed Asroth and Sheik's heads might hurt. He did not fully understand magic, but he had noticed how draining it could be on them. Just as he pondered the thought, he spotted Sheik rubbing her temples, eyes closed.

He leaned in next to Tara. "You okay?" he asked her quietly.

She nodded instead of speaking and it wasn't very convincing. She was scared. She was always scared when the soldiers were close. He could tell she was embarrassed and tried to hide it from the others, but he found that terribly sad. It shouldn't be embarrassing to be scared and disgusted and traumatized at such violence. In fact, it should be the only sane emotion after watching people be killed. Especially for people as young as he and Tara. Someday, he told himself, they would live a life free of violence.

But for now, they had to endure it for the sake of many innocent lives.

He was about to give Tara's hand a squeeze, to reassure her that he was there for her, when a noise interrupted his thoughts.

A soldier remained. Auni stood and focused his hearing. A single person. Sprinting from the east, not caring about the noise they made.

Auni's hand went to his sword, but Sheik had already nocked an arrow to her bow. Fang let out a whine. Not a growl. "It isn't a soldier," Sheik whispered. Auni spotted him through the trees. He was too far away to see clearly—how could she know for sure?

When the man came close enough to see they were aiming weapons at him, his arms went up. Sure enough, he was no soldier. "Please," he said from the bottom of the hill. He took a cautious step towards them. "I mean no harm; I'm looking for the soldiers who were fighting the New Prosper Army. I thought they were this way."

His face was full of freckles, and he had shaggy hair roughly the same color as Kazzak's. Though the two looked the same age, he was much smaller than Kazzak. "We are those soldiers," Sheik spoke flatly and lowered her bow.

The man shook his head. "No, no," he whispered. "There are only five of you. There's no catapult here. I know they had a catapult."

"Why are you looking for people opposing the New Prosper Army?" she asked.

He sighed. "I need safety. Any enemy of the New Prosper is a friend of mine," he said reluctantly, as if he did not want to admit the full truth.

Sheik set down her bow and waved for him to continue the rest of the way up the hill. "Then consider yourself among friends. Whether you believe us or not, we are the ones who fought those men." She sat back down, no longer tense. "Kazzak, won't you get some firewood? The man looks tired, and I think we all could use some rest, too."

Auni, however, stayed standing, not fully trusting the man.

Sheik listened to the crackle of the fire. She enjoyed the relaxing moments of their travel, absorbing her surroundings. This forest, though different in so many ways, reminded her of home. It was not nearly as crowded with shrubbery, but rather spacious. The deciduous trees around her were beginning to change color.

When she was banished, it had been the frosty beginning of spring. Now, summer was bleeding into fall. The air was muggy. The weather was much warmer out on the plains than she was used to back in her homeland. She was looking forward to winter, but Kazzak warned her that the winters could be incredibly harsh. She feared that cold might be worse than heat. Her old forest was always temperate, calm. Not overbearing or extreme like where she was now.

She glanced around the trees as the fire's light cast designs on them. Finally, she turned to the newcomer. "So, tell us your name," she smiled, trying to be as friendly as possible. Auni had kept his hand on his sword since the man's unexpected arrival. But she did not want the man to feel unwelcome. He had not said a word, but simply glanced at them suspiciously as they got the fire started.

"My name is Carlos." He hesitated, like he wanted to say more but decided against it.

Kazzak smiled. "Nice to meet you, Carlos. I'm Kazzak." He introduced the others, then asked, "And how did you come to be running through these woods?"

Carlos glanced around uneasily. Asroth was slumped over, reading one of the books he carried with him, as if he was paying no attention. Tara was leaning against the distrustful Auni, nearly falling asleep. Kazzak and Sheik were the only ones who seemed interested in what Carlos had to say.

"I," he began slowly, as if deciding what to tell them. He sighed. "I was with two others. With the nobility fleeing because of the New Prosper rebellion, we thought we could get away with a little," he paused, "swindling." He watched their faces carefully before saying more. "Anyone against the army would help one who claimed to be a noble. We went town by town, pretending we were nobility in disguise, telling people in confidence so they would provide us with free food and room. It was perfect," he trailed off. "Until, of course, they found us."

Sheik listened closer. "They?"

He chuckled, pulling some grass out of the ground and playing with it in his fingers. Sheik stared at the bad habit, thinking about how disrespectful Atarius would have found it to Elilah. "The New Prosper Army, of course. They got wind of three nobles running around. I guess some of the people we stayed with ratted us out. We've been on the run for two weeks, even though we aren't even real nobles."

Kazzak nodded. "Ah, yes. The complexities of lying." He patted Carlos on the back, though the man awkwardly shrugged it away. "Welcome to the life of a rogue," he laughed, digging through his backpack for his pan flute. He played quietly so his terrible tuning would not disrupt the conversation.

Carlos gave him a slight grin, obviously happy to know they would not hurt him for his crime. In an ironic way, Carlos telling the truth about his past lies made Sheik trust him more. "So tell us about your friends, the other two," Kazzak added after a particularly out of tune note on his instrument. Tara had fallen asleep, despite the noise, her head resting on the ground next to Auni. It was beginning to grow late. Fang, too, was curled up next to Sheik, happy to get some sleep.

The man thought for a moment, as if he was once again considering how much to say. "One of them was my best friend," he explained. "The other was his lover." He paused for a moment, seeing if any of them were actually paying attention. "Well, my best friend, Lyle, he only thinks he's in love. The woman's a bitch, really," he stated flatly. Sheik's jaw fell open at his casual use of the word. Swears were so rare in elven—she wasn't even sure there was an equivalent phrase. "Always ordering him around and making us do something just a little more dangerous and risky than before." He shook his head. "I miss him, but at the same time I'm glad to be rid of them."

Sheik nodded and tried her best to ignore his harsh words. "Yeah, love can do that to people. Opens some people's eyes and blinds others."

Laughter interrupted her thoughts. "What, are those your words of wisdom for the day?" Kazzak asked, lowering his pan flute as he made fun of her. "Who have you ever been in love with? That man that banished you?"

At first the laughter was a shock to her. She really had loved Atarius. No, still did. No, had. She ignored the complicated thoughts building up in her mind and instead grinned at the man mocking her. "Hey, he saved my life. Isn't a girl supposed to fall in love with the man who saves her life?" she joked back.

"I saved your life too, you know." Kazzak tossed her a playful wink. "Don't fall in love with me too," he teased before continuing to play his pan flute.

Sheik laughed and took away Kazzak's instrument, insisting it was much too late to be making a racket. Kazzak rolled his eyes and looked back at Carlos. He seemed much more relaxed, knowing he was in the company of jokesters. "So what about you guys?" Carlos finally spoke up. "Why are you guys here, fighting an army all by yourself?"

"Someone needs to get the tyrant off the throne. He's wreaking havoc for no reason. We've come across multiple towns now where he has scared them into submission." Sheik paused, lowering her voice. "One town where he made good on his threat."

Thoughts of the horrible memory crept into her mind. Men, women, and children, slaughtered. Blood had stained the streets. There had not been a living soul.

Sheik tried to shut the thoughts away, but she could not. There were countless flies swarming about the carcasses. They had needed to watch every step so as not to tread on a dead, decaying body. Sheik imagined it looked similar to the village Atarius had found her in long ago.

Noticing that her thoughts were, once again, drifting to Atarius, she quickly changed subjects. It seemed sometimes she could never stop thinking about him. "So before this nobility trick, what did you do, Carlos?"

"I tanned leather until Lyle met Keira. She was a con artist and got us mixed up in it. Maybe I can find the two though. Shake some sense into him," he muttered. Sheik could tell he was getting frustrated just thinking about his best friend and the woman who had changed him so much. He continued pulling grass.

Sheik nodded. "Perhaps." She yawned and laid down against Fang, using him as a pillow. "Well, we've had quite the eventful day. I think we could all use some sleep." She stared at the stars for a moment before closing her eyes. Millions of thoughts were going through her head. Thoughts about Carlos and his friends. About how she knew Auni would be up until the stranger fell asleep. About the battle they had won. About the future battles they would face and how precisely they were to conquer Isandas.

But foremost in her mind was Atarius.

Sheik awoke to the smell of roasted fish and smoke blowing from the campfire. While most of the time they ate what Sheik conjured, the others liked to supplement their meals with some real food, especially meat. When they got a moment to breathe, Kazzak and Fang hunted or Tara and Auni gathered fruits along their journey.

Kazzak leaned down next to her. "Hey there's a stream not too far away, we've been taking turns bathing. You're up after Asroth."

She nodded, blinking her eyes. "I could use a bath," she replied, yawning. It seemed less humid than the day before and she planned on washing and drying her clothes, too. It had been a long time since they had gotten to really clean up.

Kazzak sat on a log and placed a small mirror on his lap so he could trim his overgrown goatee. He had clearly already taken his bath, his long hair dripping down his back. Sheik glanced at his shirtless body for a moment. It was powerful and muscular, his abs well defined and his back sturdy. He had a patch of hair on his chest and a line of it below his belly button. Elves did not have so much body hair and Sheik found it silly looking.

She looked away before he could notice her staring and gazed instead into the fire. Tara and Auni were still asleep, curled up next to each other. Fang sat several paces away, chewing on some sort of rabbit he had caught. "Where's Carlos?" she asked suddenly, realizing he was nowhere to be seen.

Kazzak finished shaving the corner of his chin with his knife, then glanced over to Sheik with a shrug. "His stuff was all packed and he was long gone when Asroth and I woke up. Wasn't at the stream either. Asroth thought maybe he'd run off with some of our supplies, but nothing is missing."

She frowned. "Strange."

Asroth entered the camp and, catching the end of their conversation, asked, "What, that Carlos boy? I still think he stole something."

"My turn." Sheik stood upon Asroth's return, grabbing her pack of clothing. "You should probably wake those two up," she motioned towards the half siblings, still fast asleep. "We need to discuss a battle plan for Isandas." With that, she took her leave, heading towards the stream.

⸻◆⸻

Asroth pulled off his headdress and fanned himself with it. Multiple hairs fell off as he did so. He had noticed his hairline had been receding. He was not sure if the myth was true or not, that those who had taken the Oath were marked by their hair loss. But to ensure the others didn't take notice, he kept his headdress on at all times. The others didn't know about him being excommunicated, and so he pretended to still be a member of the clergy, wearing his priest garbs day and night.

But in weather like this, it was exhausting. The humidity made him sick. Heat like this was rare in Darinshire, lasting only one week per summer at most. But south of Calert it seemed the whole summer was a heatwave. The only relief was a moment like this, the cool breeze from the stream dancing through his thinning hair.

He leaned over and dipped his headdress into the water before placing it back on his head and leaning against a tree. He sighed. This was not the life he had thought he would live after leaving his father's home. Running from an army, overheated, hiding his hair in the guise of a clergyman.

A voice distracted his thoughts.

Tara and Sheik, talking. They were further upstream, and Asroth got up and walked a few paces closer. The stream bended in such a way that he could see them without difficulty while staying mostly covered by the thickness of the forest.

Sheik was pulling her clothes on as Tara approached with a handful of laundry from their packs. Asroth glanced up and down Sheik's body as she finished dressing. He didn't know if all elves were unattractive or if it was just Sheik. She was tall and lean, her muscles well defined from overuse. It was completely unladylike.

Tara was the opposite. Her face was rather plain, but her body was nothing but curves. How he longed for her body. He watched her stoop over the river, scrubbing the clothes with soap. He was enraptured, mesmerized.

But Tara didn't like him. She turned away when he touched her and hardly spoke to him unless it was something directed to the whole group. He didn't understand. He had been nothing but kind to her, had rescued her when she was in distress back at Calert. The only logical conclusion, he supposed, was that she didn't realize just how great he was. Once she saw how powerful he was, she would come running to him. He only had to wait until she had seen him, the real him.

Until then, he would daydream and fantasize. And so he watched her finish laundry. Sheik helped her hang the clothes to dry and then left her alone. Tara glanced once to the left and then to the right before unbuttoning her blouse.

Asroth took in a sharp breath. He had to leave, and he had to do so quietly now that Tara was already half nude. But he paused to take a glance at her naked breasts. And though he knew it was wrong and she should be left her privacy, he couldn't help but stare. So long as he stayed hidden, who did it really hurt?

Tara slipped slowly into the water, one tiny step at a time because of how cold the river was. Asroth was more than grateful, as it gave him that extra moment to scour her body with his eyes. As long as she never found out, he thought to himself, no harm was done.

And so he situated himself into a hidden position where he could watch from behind the trees and bushes, dreaming of the day that she would see him for the attractive and powerful man that he was. The day she would give herself to him. How he longed for that day. He just had to be patient, to wait. Then she would be all his.

CHAPTER 11

Spike faltered for a moment. Paused. His appearance had to be intimidating if he was to get what he wanted. King Garret was a large man. Spike had to appear larger. Without warning, Spike burst through the doors and they swung on their hinges as he entered the room.

"Listen here," King Garret began before Spike even had a chance to speak. "My family has ruled the Tasvran Mountains for centuries. I'll not be conquered like the other nations—"

Spike cut him off. There would be no intimidating this man into doing what he wanted. No, he would try a different approach. "Nonsense!" he shouted, his voice booming. "I'd not hear of conquering you, King Garret." He lowered his voice. "You and I are men; we respect the same thing." Garret's eyes narrowed, trying to read him.

"Power!" Spike shouted as suddenly as he had come in the door. "I respect you for your power, managing to hold the Tasvran, and I pray to Justar you respect the power I have taken, too."

Garret nodded slowly. "Justar, eh?" he asked with a slight chuckle. "Why's that?"

Spike shook his head slowly. "Oh King Garret, you're far too wise to believe Ziad is the greatest god, aren't you? No, there is no good left in this world. Even you and I, we cannot enforce good. But we can enforce justice."

The man smiled at Spike's response. "I have believed the same for quite some time. It seems you and I are alike in many ways, um," he paused, "how may I address you?"

Spike merely waved his hand, as if dismissing the thought. "I'm only a man. You may call me Spike."

Garret nodded. "Spike it is then. So, if not to threaten me, why did you call me to Isandas?"

"No, please, you are my guest. We will dine before we speak of such matters." He knew such an approach would flatter him. If Spike was able to make the evening go perfectly, Garret would be honored to help him. He simply needed to please the man.

With a snap of his fingers, servants rushed to Spike's side. "I would like a red wine. Bring King Garret any kind of beverage he desires," he spoke elegantly, with a wave of his hand.

Garret raised his hand. "To you, Spike, I am only Garret, please." His attention turned to the servant. "I'll have a stout ale."

"Please, bring us some breads to start," Spike commanded with another snap of his fingers. The servant raced off. Spike glanced at Garret. The man was simpler than he had imagined.

Spike was well mannered. He held his head high. He was well groomed. He was clean, attractive, and intelligent. On the other hand, Garret was sloppy. Dirty. Stupid. In fact, the only thing that made him look at all like a king was the crown placed over his headscarf and his decorous clothing. And that was partially due to the Tasvran culture. Bright colors were commonly layered over white. Living in the snowy mountains, it made sense. One could shed their robes and hide easily in only white garments, or one could signal for help in a snowstorm with their bright outer layers of clothing.

Garret was a large man. Most people with Tasvran blood were hefty. Spike himself was a decent sized man, but he was puny compared to Garret's mass. Spike sat up straight while Garret hunched over, his face grotesque and unshaven.

The bread came, accompanied with all sorts of oils and spices. Garret immediately dug into the food, seemingly swallowing loaves whole. Spike tried to copy his disgusting, crude behavior. He did not want Garret to feel strange and unwelcome. No, he wanted the man to be completely content.

"Bring out the rest of the meal at once," Spike boomed, gulping his wine instead of sipping it as he usually did. He generally ate his meals in separate portions, the breads separate from the salads, separate from the meats, and so forth. He had a feeling, though, that Garret was used to meals all in one sitting.

Garret ripped chunks of meat with his bare hands, shoving the oversized portions into his mouth. It made Spike want to gag, but he did the same, stooping to the primitive level of the king. He would not compromise Garret's assistance by eating his meal daintily.

He mimicked the man, filling himself with breads, meats, and cheeses all at once. He pretended to drink more than he was, seeing how much Garret was drinking. Pies stuffed full of fruit were brought to the table. Even these, Garret dived into with his hands.

By the end of the meal, grease and juices dripped from his hands, which he wiped carelessly on the tablecloth. "Entertainment?" he asked Spike. "Surely your castle has after dinner entertainment? Dancers and argileh?"

Spike nodded, though he doubted anyone in Isandas had a Tasvranian argileh pipe. "After business," he said strictly, sick of playing games with the man.

Garret gave an annoyed frown. "Fine." He pulled a knife out from a hidden strap along his trousers and stuck it into the table in front of him. His frown grew into a smile as his fingers rubbed the hilt lightly.

It was clearly meant as a threat, but Spike continued anyway. Leaning forward, he whispered through a grin, "How would you like to own more than the Tasvran?" The man did not flinch but continued to stare at the knife. "You and I join forces and conquer together. You can have Masil and I will take Vesdar and Omris. Your family will prosper for generations with twice the land it has now. You want a good future for your son, do you not?" he asked coolly.

Garret spat on the floor. "Damn my son, I want a good future for me!" He smirked. "Why is it the great rebellion leader Spike now needs my help? You've conquered Etmos and half of Masil and Vesdar without difficulty. What hinders you now?"

Spike's smile faded as he debated whether or not to tell the man about the real problem. "As you said, you're too powerful to conquer. I knew I could never take the Tasvran, so I thought I would welcome you in alliance. You and I, we're the most powerful men in the world right now."

The king smiled a monstrous smile. "You are a smart man, Spike. I am happy to accept this alliance of yours."

"I'm happy to hear that. My men have been so focused on keeping the north-west secured, they've hardly had time for the south. There's been some small group apparently—hardly a trouble. If you would like to eliminate them, the rest of Masil should be easy enough to lock down and the territory is yours."

The group was much more than a small trouble. They were a mysterious bunch; no one was sure how many men were involved. He had heard numbers from three to a hundred. He first heard of them after one of his troops had been destroyed trying to take the city of Calert. Originally, he had assumed the mystery group played an insignificant role compared to Calert's soldiers. He figured they would be easy to track down and kill.

But now that he had thrown troop after troop against them, he realized they were a much bigger threat than he had once thought. He needed trained soldiers to fight them, and the best army was Garret's. By pretending the group was harmless, he could convince Garret to fight them simply so he would be able to show off his army's great strength. Garret's soldiers would easily tear the small group to pieces.

Garret nodded, understanding Spike's request. "Seems straightforward enough. What do you know about this group?"

Spike thought about the question for a moment. He shook his head slowly. "Unfortunately, I know very little. They are a small group. I've heard rumors that they are led by an elf," he scoffed.

The king raised an eyebrow. "An elf?" He chuckled for a moment. "Well how about we send this elf a little surprise? Let's say, wyverns?" Spike smiled, relieved to know his problem would soon be taken care of.

⚬

"That's the fifth one I've spotted," Jamen pointed, wincing as he looked into the sun.

Jason sharpened his spear on a whetstone. "Come on, let's go hunt the bastards down! We can take them!"

The man's twin shook his head. "No, you know our best shot is staying in this forest and waiting for whatever threat to come to us. That's how we've been winning the river battles. They keep coming and we'll keep destroying them."

"We'll never destroy them all, though, if we don't take the offense, Jamen." Like his twin brother, Jason's eyebrows furrowed when he was upset. The two were so similar in voice and mannerisms that the only way one could tell them apart was by their hair. Both of them had blonde hair, but Jamen's was cut short, while Jason's hung down to his shoulders and into his eyes.

"You listen to me, Jason," Jamen spoke suddenly, rising to his feet. "We and the rest of the troops stay in this forest. We know the woods better than any of those half-assed soldiers, and that's how we win battles."

Jason rolled his eyes. "You'll stay in this forest forever and be forgotten in twenty years. I'm not gonna let that happen to me. Someday I'm going to go out and really save people." He smiled. "I'll be a knight of honor."

Jamen laughed out loud. "You don't have honor! Before the New Prosper came along we were robbing whatever depressing bastards and widows happened to be passing by. We're only fighting these people to loot their dead bodies and you know it. Don't feed me any of that honor bullshit."

"Well, we are helping people. Just because we benefit from fighting the New Prosper doesn't mean it isn't an honorable thing to do," Jason retorted.

"Whatever. You can pretend you're in it for the honor all you want. I'm just protecting my turf, my men, and trying to survive."

Jason rolled his eyes and glanced towards the sky. "How about the wyverns? We're just going to wait for them to make the first move?"

Jamen shook his head before shrugging, implying he really wasn't sure what to do. "I'll tell the troops to train more with their bows and less with their skirns. Other than that, all we can do is wait." Then he left Jason alone to finish sharpening his spear.

Their camp contained roughly two hundred people. Just under half of them were the men who fought against the army under Jamen and Jason's orders. It was a ragtag group who had previously been simple woods bandits trying to survive. They would steal from whomever passed through the roads or sailed on the Canaen River.

But, ever since Spike took control, the woods bandits directed their attention to the New Prosper Army. They made just as much money from the soldiers as they did from innocents, and it solved their moral qualms about thievery.

A new platoon generally came through the forest every several weeks, by boat, which made them an easy target. Between their weak defense and the forest men's well-planned assaults, the New Prosper had no chance of making it through. But now, as Jason stared up at the sky, he feared everything was about to change.

◆

As they wandered the forest, continuing to head east, Sheik quickly learned that there were still soldiers in the area. She knew they hadn't killed them all with their giant boulders, just scattered them. That was all the damage she had hoped to do. But now she began to regret the choice, realizing that the soldiers were scouring the forest and could regroup at any time.

The safest option was to simply try and avoid them. It would have been easier if Sheik were by herself. She was used to the forest. Climbing trees and hiding was as natural as walking. But Tara, who

222

still tended to wear skirts instead of pants, wouldn't be able to climb easily. And Asroth would consider it a blow to his dignity.

Fang scouted for them most of the time. Through their mysterious means of communication, he relayed back to Sheik if soldiers were nearby. Then they would hunker down and find a place to keep hidden until the troops had passed. It saved them energy and it spared the soldiers their lives.

But sometimes the soldiers would become aware of their presence, and they were forced to fight. It had happened twice now. The first time was a quick skirmish, only eight soldiers. The second time it was twenty-two soldiers.

"The groups are going to keep growing larger and larger," Asroth explained.

"What do you mean?" Sheik asked, not sure there was any rhyme or reason to the number of soldiers they came across.

"I mean the longer they scout, the more times we engage with them, the more likely they are to figure out we're headed east. Once they know our direction for certain, they'll be able to block us before we can even reach the Canaen River." The Canaen River was their goal because it wound north, directly to Isandas. If they could reach it, they could stay along a water supply for the rest of their journey.

"So what do you suggest?" It seemed she was always asking Asroth that. The man liked to talk about problems much more than he did solutions.

He crossed his arms. "We should have killed more soldiers back when we had the chance. None of this pacifist crap."

"Okay, but what do we do now," Kazzak interjected on Sheik's behalf.

"Well, we could double back," Asroth suggested. "Make an obvious trail in a different direction so the soldiers think we're headed south or something." Then, quietly, he added, "Maybe not all of us. Maybe not the slower travelers?" He motioned towards Tara, who was chatting away with Auni, too oblivious to notice he was talking about her.

Sheik shook her head. "No that's ridiculous. What's Tara going to do out in the forest by herself?"

"Not by herself," Asroth snapped, like she had completely misinterpreted his comment. "I know I'm not the fastest either." It was true, although mostly because he insisted on hauling around several large books in his backpack.

"Well Auni isn't going to leave her behind, so he'd have to stay with her," Kazzak added. "But, yeah, I guess you three could hunker down for a day or two? Sheik and I can go make an obvious trail south and then sneak back this way?"

Sheik did have to admit it was a smart plan, though something about splitting up was unsettling. They had only been able to handle so many troops because they fought as a team. If they separated, who knew how well they would fare. Or was it only because it was Asroth's idea that she didn't approve of it? Perhaps if she had come up with it herself, she would have a little more trust in the plan.

But before she could decide on a course of action, Fang came running up to her. "There's soldiers," Sheik interpreted.

Asroth rolled his eyes. "How do you do that anyway?"

Sheik wasn't entirely sure how she understood Fang, and, even if she did, now certainly wasn't the time to explain. "Come on, we need to hide."

He made a remark under his breath that Sheik couldn't quite hear, but she tried her best to ignore it. Kazzak ran ahead to stop Tara and Auni while Sheik began scanning for a place to hide. Fang whined, trying to get her attention. She stared at him for a moment and sensed that he had a plan. Perhaps he had found a hiding spot?

She followed after him and Asroth reluctantly trudged behind her. Fang stopped abruptly and growled. "What's he saying now?" Asroth asked with a frustrated flail of his arm.

But Sheik knew instantly what it was.

Soldiers were just up ahead. She waved for Asroth to keep his voice down and began to turn back the way they had come. In three whispered words, she explained, "There's soldiers there."

"Where?"

"Right there," she said with as much emphasis as she could while whispering. "I mean two paces further, now come on."

Kazzak nearly crashed into her. "There's soldiers to the east," he explained before seeing the look of fear on her face. His voice lowered. "What is it?"

Sheik bit down on her lip. It was too late. The soldiers that she had just turned her back on had clearly heard them; they began hacking through branches with machetes and shouting that they'd seen something. Kazzak, realizing his mistake, mouthed that he was sorry.

Sheik's mind raced. Tara and Auni stared at her wide eyed. Asroth glared at Kazzak. "Come on, they'll be here any minute. We've got to run," Sheik ordered. They were in danger and that meant she was now in charge. In her element. She pushed past branches and led the way. "Kazzak, you said there were more to the east?"

He jogged up beside her. "Yeah. Want to go south?"

"No, let's push through. Keep an eye on Tara and Asroth." They were indeed the slowest of the group. "Fang and I will fight any soldiers who get in the way and try to make an opening." She could hear the metal armor of the soldiers as they gave chase. That armor would weigh them down, and even Tara would eventually out pace them. Sheik just had to make sure that nothing stood in their path.

Kazzak fell back to follow her orders.

Sheik kept her bow ready, aimed low. Despite Asroth's annoyance at her pacifism, she refused to compromise her values. They could win this war without stooping to Spike's level.

When a soldier entered her field of view, she aimed for his thigh. He let out a cry of anguish and began to scream, "They're over here!" Sheik hadn't anticipated this and wondered if she should keep moving quickly or stop to silence him with a gag. Fang made the decision for her, pouncing on the man and ripping open his throat.

Sheik winced and kept up her jog. If he had just stayed quiet, the soldier might have lived. She didn't want to have to kill these men. She just wanted to escape. She wondered if Asroth was right about her tactics putting them in danger. But she shrugged the thought away. They trusted her with their lives and Sheik had done a good job leading them.

By the time they reached the wall of soldiers Kazzak had mentioned, Sheik was beginning to tire. She couldn't imagine how Asroth and Tara were holding up. But they couldn't stop and rest—soldiers were hot on their trail. This was the moment they needed to be strong. If they could make it through the wall, they would survive.

Her jogging paused as she entered the scene, dropping to one knee and firing arrow after arrow.

The soldiers were caught off guard and it took them a moment to find her. One by one, she took them down. The area needed to be secure by the time Kazzak and the others caught up to her. She needed to clear the path for them.

Arrow after arrow thunked into the soldiers. Her magic warped away their armor for just a split second, allowing the arrow to pierce through. A knee. A thigh. An abdomen. She lost count at how many fell, and in the thick of the forest it was hard to tell how many were standing.

One rushed at her, but Fang tackled him to the ground and tore him apart. Sheik couldn't allow herself to be distracted by the violence. There were only a few more. The others would catch up momentarily. They needed to keep moving. She needed to take out the last few soldiers rushing towards her.

But as she reached back into her quiver, she found it empty.

"Fang!" she shouted, unsure if the wolf would reach her in time. She dropped her bow and drew one of Farin's throwing knives from her belt. It was no bow and arrow, but it would have to do. Her hand was sweaty and she was nervous to fight in close combat, especially with such a small weapon.

But as she readied her right hand to take a swing at the first soldier, he froze, clutching his neck and spitting out blood. "Go!" a voice yelled. "Run!" Sheik, though utterly confused, did not argue. She picked up her bow and pushed the dying soldier out of her way.

Three more soldiers came at her. Fang took down two and the other one fell to the ground in similar fashion, clutching a sudden wound.

Asroth burst through the forest, trying not to trip on his ridiculous robes while holding his headdress in place. Sheik was still stunned at how the last soldier had fallen, but she waved for him to continue running. After all, they had broken through the wall. As long as they kept moving, they would be free of soldiers.

Tara came next, Kazzak and Auni just behind her, ready to lift her up if she tripped. Why she insisted on wearing skirts, Sheik couldn't fathom. Sheik turned to Kazzak. "Keep going, I'll catch up."

He gave her a confused look. "They're not far behind us," he explained between breaths.

Sheik knew she shouldn't linger, but she scanned the woods for her mysterious savior anyway. "Hello? Are you there?"

Fang whined as a figure emerged from the cover of a thicket. "Carlos!"

The man smirked. "You seem pretty happy to see me."

"What are you—?" Sheik began, but realized there wasn't time. "There's more following us, we have to go."

"Go." Carlos held up a confusing hunk of metal. "I'll watch your back. There's a stream not far. Wait for me there."

Sheik didn't know what he was holding, and she wanted to tell him it wasn't a good idea. But Kazzak pulled at her arm, insisting the soldiers were just on their heels. So she nodded and began running once again.

They ran for only another ten minutes or so. Once they came upon the stream Carlos had spoken about, Sheik waved for everyone to stop. By this point, Tara was wheezing. Asroth hardly looked any better, but still managed to ask, "Why are we stopping?" between breaths. Tara seized the opportunity to drop to her knees and shovel water into her mouth with her bare hands.

"Carlos was back there," Sheik explained. "He saved me. He asked us to wait at the stream for him."

"Carlos?" Asroth asked in disbelief. "What are you talking about?"

Kazzak nodded, backing up her story. "Yeah, he said he'd keep the soldiers off our trail. But Sheik," he turned to her, "I don't know how long we can wait. If he can't pick off all the soldiers, they'll be upon us soon. We just ran all this way in hopes of losing them. We can't stop now."

"For a bit," Sheik said quietly. "We'll just wait for a bit."

"How long?" Asroth asked, his breathing beginning to return to normal. Tara still lapped up water. Auni hardly seemed winded at all.

"For a bit," Sheik insisted firmly. He rolled his eyes but said nothing. Good, she thought to herself. She was still the leader. They would follow her and she would keep them safe.

And sure enough, in another ten minutes, Carlos stumbled upon them.

"Carlos! You okay?"

"How far away are the soldiers?" Kazzak asked.

He took a moment to catch his breath and then explained, "I gave them the slip." They collectively gave a sigh of relief. "But there's more in the area. We should keep moving."

Sheik nodded her approval and they walked along the sandy bank of the stream.

"So what made you come back? We thought you went to look for your friends."

"I found them." He sighed and his fingers wrapped around a necklace she now noticed. "Unfortunately I was too late."

"They were—?" Tara asked, eyes full of concern.

Carlos nodded. "Dead."

Kazzak swore and put a hand on his shoulder. "I'm so sorry, Carlos."

He nodded again. "Yeah. I'm just glad I wasn't too late to catch up to you guys. I can join your little rebellion, right?"

"Of course!" Kazzak exclaimed before anyone could reject the offer. "Clearly you're a sharp shooter."

Sheik glanced between them. "Yeah, wait, how did you kill them?"

Carlos held up the same piece of metal and handed it over to her. "Crossbow," he explained. Sheik hadn't heard the word before. She inspected it carefully, trying to make sense of how it worked.

"Interesting," she said at last. He shrugged, like it was nothing, and took it back. "With weapons like these, you'll be a huge help. You can help us plan the assault against Isandas."

Carlos raised his eyebrows. "Going after Isandas itself, huh?"

Kazzak nodded. "It's the only way to truly put a stop to this madness."

"I suppose so," he muttered. "But that will have to be some plan if we six are going to destroy the whole lot of them. Any of you ever seen Isandas?" he asked.

The group glanced between each other, hoping someone would speak up. "I guess not," Sheik admitted, turning back to Carlos.

He smiled. "You're in luck, then. I used to deliver tanning goods there. I never went inside the palace, but I could draw up a map of the city and major walls."

Before Carlos could say more, a shadow loomed over them.

The group glanced upwards, scanning for the object in the sky that could have cast such a shadow. Another patch of darkness passed overhead. Sheik squinted, trying to see what it was.

"Oh no," Carlos whispered. "We need to hide." Sheik didn't know what it was, but she readily agreed. They dove through bushes, pushing further and further into the thickest part of the woods. Finally, hidden in brambles, Carlos motioned for everyone to stay quiet. He leaned in next to Sheik. "Have those things been following you?"

She shook her head. "Not that I've noticed. What are they?"

"Wyverns."

"I thought so," Asroth piped in. "I've read about them. Never seen one before."

Sheik gave a puzzled look to both men. "Well what are they?"

Carlos licked his lips and lowered his voice. "They're like dragons—" he began before Sheik quickly interrupted him.

"Dragons? Dragons aren't real," she stammered, now second guessing herself.

He chuckled. "They aren't, or are long extinct if they ever were. But wyverns, they're supposedly the descendants of dragons. They're smaller, but still large enough to kill you. About the size of two, maybe three horses." He glanced around, as if making sure everyone was listening. "They don't breathe fire or anything. And they don't have front legs, but they still have claws on the end of their wings that they can walk with. They're menacing creatures, with tough scales and the sharpest teeth."

Carlos reached just under his shirt and pulled out his necklace. The simple string was wound tightly around a sharp, finger-length fang. "It's a wyvern tooth."

Sheik stared in silence. Even bears didn't have such large canines. "Where did you get it?"

"It was Lyle's," he whispered, and she could tell he was holding back tears. He blinked a few times before continuing. "We used to live near the Tasvran Mountains, where wyverns are common. Wild ones rarely attack humans, they just go after goats and sheep. But King Garret's army, they capture and train wyverns. Ride them into battle. Those ones are trained to kill humans." He tucked his necklace back into his shirt and glanced upwards, though from where they were hiding the sky was hardly visible. "I've never heard of a wild wyvern being this far from the mountains. They're King Garret's soldiers alright. They're looking for something."

Sheik felt the echo of her heartbeat. King Garret, she understood from Kazzak and Asroth's lectures, was the king of the Tasvran Mountains, one of the only territories Spike had left untouched. And now, King Garret's men were suspiciously far away from the mountains, riding a horrific creature that Sheik had never even heard of.

"They're looking for you, aren't they?" Carlos whispered, practically reading Sheik's thoughts. "We're going to need to keep in the thickest part of the forest."

The entire group nodded in silence. Sheik had no intention of having a run in with one of these wyverns.

Chapter 12

Kazzak thrust the apple towards Sheik's face. "Come on, one bite?" he joked. She laughed and pushed his hand away. He took a juicy, crunchy bite. "It's delicious," he mocked, the chewed-up food still in his mouth.

"You're so gross." Her nose crinkled, watching him chew with his mouth wide open.

He smiled, holding the apple out towards her once again. "Come on, what changed? When we first met you ate tons of food in Calert."

She shrugged because she herself didn't fully know. "It just feels wrong. Besides," she added with a smirk and an apple formed inside her open palm. "Mine tastes better."

With every bite she made an exaggerated, "Mmm!"

The truth was, though, her magically created food just wasn't as good. She did not understand why. It still had taste, whether sour or sweet. In fact, she could even control its flavors and textures. But for some reason, the knowledge that the apple was not real impacted its taste. But she wouldn't admit so out loud, at least not while Kazzak was teasing her.

The apple disappeared as she finished her chewing. "Still food, still tastes good, and I didn't have to pick it from a tree."

Kazzak finished his apple and tossed the core to the ground. "But what's wrong with picking an apple from a tree?"

"Because it's taking something living." That was the reason Atarius and the elders had always given.

"Yeah, but it's going to fall off anyway!" Kazzak exclaimed, laughing.

"And when it does, then it's okay to eat," Sheik explained for what felt like the hundredth time.

He made a face. "What, after it's gone bad? Why? That doesn't even make any sense."

"Look, I don't make the rules."

"And who did? Atarius? You're not even—"

Finally, a point she could argue. She cut him off. "No, Atarius enforces the rules. He didn't make them. It was passed down by his ancestors, who were told by Elilah herself." Supposedly. Sheik doubted the rules really did come from Elilah, but admitting so to Kazzak only strengthened his argument.

"Well, I don't see why this goddess of yours wouldn't want you picking fruit," he said simply.

"Are you two still flirting?" Tara asked, pushing past the bushes and working her way in between them.

"We're not flirting!" Sheik blurted out. Kazzak merely laughed. She felt her face grow hot and, realizing how awkward and childish she had sounded, she mumbled, "Well we weren't."

"Guys!" Asroth shouted out from the underbrush behind them. "Wyverns!"

The conversation instantly ended and became a horrifying silence. Though they were traveling off the main road and the wyverns hadn't yet found them, the beasts continued to search. Most of the time the group was able to travel with ease. But once in a while the wyverns circled directly overhead. Before the horrid creatures could spot them, the group would submerge themselves in bushes, sitting sometimes for hours on end.

As they all pushed themselves against the ground, Sheik listened closely. The wyverns had a distinct screeching call. But they quieted down when they closed in on their prey. Right now, they made no noise.

Then there was a faint sound. A gust of wind. Again, she heard it, this time louder. The beating of the wyvern's heavy wings. They were closer than they had ever been before. Sheik felt chills run up and down her arms.

Sheik was not sure if the others could hear the wings of the wyverns. She knew she had better hearing than them. But as she glanced around, she saw the worried faces of her companions, practically holding their breath trying not to make any noise. From where she was, she could not even see the sky. Surely they would move on. But what if they didn't?

"Fang," Sheik whispered to get his attention. "Find out how many there are." The wyverns were searching for men; they would not pursue a wolf.

He rose to his feet and began to wiggle out of the thicket they had wedged themselves into. The group still did not fully accept that she could communicate with the wolf. They tended to believe her when Fang executed her commands, like he was currently doing, and then calling it coincidence when the situation was over. Fang trotted back and lay close to Sheik. She only had to stare at him for a moment to understand what he was trying to tell her.

There were ten beasts circling in the sky.

Sheik could not imagine trying to fight ten of the terrible creatures Carlos had told them about. Even seeing one up close, she feared, might scare her into shock. Certainly they could not defeat ten.

The group sat in the silence. Sheik didn't know how much time had passed. Ten minutes? Thirty? All she could do was pray for the beating of the wings to stop. "How long are we to stay down here?" Tara finally asked.

For a long moment no one spoke up. "As long as we have to," Carlos finally replied, his voice deadly serious.

"No," Asroth whispered. "They've been up there for too long. If they're circling us, then they know where we are. Maybe not our exact location, but still our general area. And the longer we hide the more time they have to surround us."

"If we run for it then they will know our exact location," Carlos retorted, fear rising in his voice. "We'll be wyvern food before you know it."

"There may be a way to buy us some time," Sheik interjected. She paused, thinking out her plan. "This is the last thing I want to do," she sighed, "but if we start a fire, they won't be able to see through the smoke and we'll have a chance to run. Hopefully we can get far enough away that they lose track of us."

The group thought about it for a moment. There were a lot of risks. But Asroth was right; if they continued to hide, sooner or later the wyverns would find them.

⸺◆⸺

Jason watched his brother intently as he addressed the small army. Two thirds of the group held bows while the rest wore bladed bracers and wielded javelins. "Jason will lead the archers!" Jamen yelled over the crowd. "You will shoot down whatever wyverns you can. When they spot you and are drawn towards you, you will pull back." He glanced over everyone, as if making sure they were listening. "That is when the skirns rush in, led by me."

Turning to the second group, he continued his speech. "You will get one shot with your javelin. If you do not throw it accurately and strong enough to pierce the wyvern's skin, you will have a difficult fight. If you succeed, though, then it will be wounded. The archers are to grab spears and join the skirns."

He looked out towards the rising smoke. "They have come too close to be ignored. That fire is in our woods, and those wyverns flying in our skies. They are the enemy! This is for our home and our lives! Grab your weapons and let us fight!" The crowd roared, eager to begin the hunt. Jason grabbed his bow and gave his brother a quick slap on his back before leading the rest of the archers.

After several hundred paces, the soldiers were silent. They did not stomp and beat their weapons together like most armies, but simply crept through the woods as quietly as possible. Their faces and clothing were painted deep green and brown colors, making them difficult to see.

Jason tasted the smoke in the air as he continued to walk. It had not yet obscured his vision, but he could still sense its presence. The wyverns had clustered just above where the fire had started. Originally there had only been eight or nine wyverns, but, as the smoke rose, others had joined them. Jason counted seventeen.

He froze, realizing he was just on the edge of the smoke. If he walked much further, he would become immersed in it and be unable to aim accurately. He pulled out an arrow and nocked it to his bow. The camouflaged men following him did the same, raising their weapons to the sky.

Jason's arrow whirred through the air. He doubted that he had hit any wyverns. He had never been well trained with a bow, but he let off another arrow. The army, too, released their arrows, aiming at the distant creatures. Jason watched as he spotted one fall to the ground, making a horrible screech. More arrows soared. Another wyvern fell.

The beasts' attention finally turned away from the flames and towards the hidden snipers. Jason and the archers were able to release three more times before the wyverns had completely located them. "Now!" Jason and Jamen shouted in the same instant. The archers turned and fled while the skirns rushed forward, waiting for the wyverns to dive.

As the creatures soared downwards, javelins flew to greet them. One wyvern fell dead. Some were simply wounded. Many javelins missed. Most merely snapped as they came in contact with the wyverns' tough hide. It was gruesome and chaotic, soldiers clashing weapons, wyverns ripping men in half. The smoke continued to grow, making it hazier every moment. The battle raged on.

⁂

Sheik led the group at a fast jog. Too much movement would give them away. Too little movement would get them caught up in the fire. As she ran, the sounds of combat increased. She was afraid what that could mean. Perhaps she was running into a trap of New Prosper soldiers. But she had no choice. She had to move forward, towards the noise.

Then, out of nowhere, a wyvern crashed down in front of her.

Its rider had died, several arrows sticking out of the man. But his corpse was still harnessed to the wyvern, flopping from one side to the other as the wyvern moved.

A javelin was lodged in the creature's side, yet it hardly appeared in pain. Its scales were thick, like small shields woven together. It let out a terrible screeching roar, lifting up its claws and gnashing its long teeth.

Sheik's heart skipped a beat. Her brain told her run, but her legs wouldn't react. The massive creature loomed over her.

It came down swiftly, and Sheik barely had enough time to dive out of the way.

The wyvern's face smashed against the ground. Sheik swallowed hard and pulled out an arrow, but she fumbled ever so slightly. She'd never fumbled with an arrow before.

There was no time to even pull herself onto her feet. The wyvern's long neck ripped around, its teeth snapping at the elf. She thrust her arrow into its jaw as hard as she could and then yanked back her hand before the teeth could get her.

The arrow tore through the creature's mouth and it screeched louder. But the wyvern wasn't deterred. Despite the broken arrow embedded in its jaw, the wyvern pulled back its neck, readying another attack.

As sudden as the wyvern had come, a man jumped onto the creature's back.

The wyvern let out another screeching roar. The man grabbed hold of the javelin jutting from the beast's side. It thrashed and the man swung about. He fell to the ground. Miraculously, he was still holding the javelin that had ripped from the creature's side.

The wyvern was quick as lightning, despite its injuries. But the man was quicker. As the beast went to pin him down, the man thrust the javelin into the wyvern's neck. It gurgled out a final cry and collapsed.

Sheik felt her heart beat several times before she was able to react.

Tara and Auni, who had been behind Sheik, finally caught up to the scene. Auni helped Sheik to her feet. "You alright?"

She nodded and pointed at the man, who had slumped against a tree once the wyvern had died. "Are you okay?" she called out to him. When he didn't move, she wondered if she had missed something in the combat, if he was injured or even dead. His face was covered in what looked like moss and mud, so she couldn't tell if blood was mixed in too. "Are you okay?" she asked again. Tara approached him, ready to check his vitals. He lifted his head and they sighed collectively. "You're unharmed?" Sheik asked a third time.

With a groan, he began to feel himself over, checking for injuries. "Seems I'm alive," he said with half a chuckle and rubbed his shoulder. He glanced between the three of them. "Who are you?" Before she had time to answer, he yelled, "Wait! No way. Ziad. You're the elf!"

She looked at him for another moment. "Are you sure you're okay?"

"You're the elf!" he laughed, sitting up. Auni extended his hand and the man pulled himself to his feet. "I had no idea you were a girl!"

Sheik gave him another puzzled look. "What are you talking about? Please, come on, we need to get out of here." Asroth, Carlos, Kazzak, and Fang had all caught up and encircled the man. "Are you okay to walk?"

He nodded and began to lead the way. "Follow me, I'll get you behind the skirns. The wyverns won't get past the skirns." Trotting through the smoke, he motioned for them to stay close. The group exchanged a quick glance. They had no idea what he was talking about but followed quickly after.

After a moment, the sounds of battle had faded and the man sat down in a patch of moss. "So what is your name, elf? You've been my idol, yet I don't even know your name," he chuckled. "I never would have guessed you were a girl."

"My name is Sheik." Confusion lingered in her voice. "How do you know of me?"

"Everyone knows of you. The elf that's been leading a rebellion against the New Prosper. There's been countless rumors. I am more than happy to meet you, Sheik," he smiled. "My name is Jason. I've also been fighting the New Prosper with my own army."

She was taken back. "There's rumors of us?" Kazzak, like her, stifled a laugh.

"Of course. You're famous. The mysterious elf fighting the New Prosper Army. You've certainly been an idol to me and to many of my men."

"Jason!" a voice shouted. A man, nearly identical to Jason, burst through the woods. "What are you doing not fighting?"

He smiled as he casually stood up. "For your information, I killed three wyverns. Now please, I would like to introduce you to someone." He waved his hand, displaying Sheik and her comrades. "Sheik, the elf that has been rebelling against the New Prosper Army."

The man stared her down for a long moment. "You're the reason those wyverns have been circling these woods. You caused the fire. Do you know how many dead men are lying in this forest?" he screamed suddenly. "We risked our asses thinking those soldiers were attacking us, and all we were doing was protecting you?"

Once again Sheik was taken back. Jason, too, seemed shocked and tried to defend her. "Please, Jamen, they're fighting the New Prosper. They're our allies."

"I'm not fighting the New Prosper. I'm not fighting those wyverns. I'm fighting anyone that threatens my life." He locked eyes with Sheik. "And right now, your presence is threatening all of us." He looked over each of them and then stormed off the way he had come.

"What in the name of Ziad is wrong with you?" Jason screamed out after his brother. He turned back to Sheik and her friends. "I'm so sorry about him. Please, just ignore him, he'll lighten up. Stay with us awhile, our village is right nearby."

Sheik glanced at Kazzak and the others. Despite the uncomfortable reaction from the man's twin, they agreed out of complete exhaustion. "One night certainly wouldn't hurt." Her legs were tired from hiding and running. She still felt adrenaline pulsing through her veins from fighting the wyvern. She was covered in dirt and sweat and was eager to have the pleasantries of staying in a town again.

Jason began to lead the way. "Our village is hidden. We build our houses in the bases of trees and in tunnels in caves," he explained. "We've been fighting the New Prosper." He pushed past bushes and tree branches, guiding them through the woods. "Here we are," he announced suddenly.

Sheik instantly recognized the homes. It reminded her of Atarius' village, the way they were carefully carved to be invisible. Unlike her old home, though, everything was built close to the ground instead of high up in the trees. The carved-out trees were partially dug up, their roots covering large tunnel rooms. Apparently it worked, since none of the others seemed to spot the houses like Sheik did.

Several other forest soldiers were walking back to the area, tossing their odd shield-like weapons into a large pile. "What are those?" Asroth asked before Sheik had a chance to. All of them were curious besides Tara and Auni, who instead watched the soldiers filing into the many hidden homes.

"Oh, we call them skirns," Jason explained. "My father invented them actually." He picked one up to show them. It consisted of two bracers which protected the arms. On the left arm, the bracer had two wooden boards extending from it. "See, these two boards on the left arm can slide straight into two holes on the right arm." He showed how easily they slipped in. "Then the bracers can form a shield.

"But it's easier to fight without them connected, so they pull apart easy too." The left arm also had spikes rising out of the front of the bracer while the right arm had a long, sword-like blade jutting from the bottom. "The left side is weighed down by the boards," Jason explained, "but it can still be used for bashing into an opponent. The right side only has a single leather strap which you hold on to. It's not tied to my forearm so I can flick it out with my wrist. It's just as effective as a sword and much easier to defend yourself with."

Asroth, Carlos, and Kazzak, still intrigued, continued to ask questions. Sheik, losing interest, glanced about the village. The homes seemed to be built around a central clearing, where four strong men were currently dragging one of the wyvern carcasses.

Tara leaned in next to Sheik unexpectedly. "He has been looking at you, you know."

"What?" Sheik asked, confused.

"Jason. He is cute, don't you think? He has been looking at you this whole time."

She laughed, ignoring Tara. "Sure." She turned back to Jason. "How many people live here?"

He had been in the middle of a sentence but stopped to answer her. "Oh, well there's about two hundred of us. They're divided into five camps like this one, with their own clearing for cooking and stuff. They're all within a three-league radius of both each other and the river."

"The river?"

"Yeah," Jason said slowly, looking at them like they were hopelessly lost. "The Canaen."

The group exchanged gleeful looks. "We had no idea we were so close to the Canaen!" Kazzak explained. They only needed to follow the river north to get to Isandas.

Jamen warily approached them. "Jason, we are cooking up the wyverns if you could help." Jason nodded, said goodbye, and trotted off to help the others. Jamen stayed a moment longer. "Um, I'm sorry for being so upset earlier," he mumbled awkwardly. "The river is just east of here. If you all want to wash up, you're more than welcome to join us for dinner."

Sheik smiled a warm smile. "Thank you. Who wants to go to the river first?" she asked the rest of her comrades.

"I'll come with you, Sheik," Tara spoke up. "I'll help you get ready for Jason," she whispered into her ear. Sheik rolled her eyes but gave her an approving nod.

⁓◦⁓

"Stop pulling so hard!" Sheik complained.

"Oh, just sit still," Tara laughed.

The river was smaller than the Great River, but still quite deep and difficult to bathe in because of the heavy pull of the current. But now they both sat safely on a rock, Tara tugging at Sheik's green hair.

"I wish I had long hair like yours," Tara chatted idly. She had been talking for the past half hour.

Sheik shrugged. "Yours is just as pretty." It actually hadn't been very pretty during their travels. Tara's hair was too short to put back properly, and her bangs clung to her face messily when she was forced to march for hours on end. But Sheik remembered how perfectly combed and properly styled it had been in Calert, as it was now. Her bangs were parted just right and the light brown hair curled slightly in front of her ears. "Besides, mine takes forever to brush out."

"Oh but certainly it is worth it," Tara insisted. "You can do fancy braids and all sorts of things with it!" Sheik rarely did a thing with her hair besides tie it back. She winced as Tara pulled together another lock of hair. "So what are you going to say to Jason?"

Sheik laughed. "I'm not going to say anything I wouldn't say to you, or to Auni, or Carlos, or anyone."

"What is the matter with you? Do you not find him attractive?"

She thought about it for a moment. The man was about her age, maybe a few years older. He seemed strong and sturdy, and had shaggy hair and the beginnings of a beard. He had all of the classic human traits—the different skin hue, the creased eyelids, the strangely brown hair. Sheik wasn't sure which features were and weren't considered attractive among humans. With a shrug, she finally answered, "I guess so."

"He's amazing," Tara gushed. "He's so big and strong. And his facial hair," she smiled, getting lost in her thoughts, "it's so manly without being an actual beard. And his hair—"

"Maybe you and I have different tastes," Sheik chuckled. Even if he was good looking, Sheik didn't think she'd be able to find anyone attractive without knowing them for longer than twenty minutes.

Tara sighed. "If you say so. Well, I am almost finished with your hair." She continued to pull it back and braid it tightly against Sheik's scalp. "It feels nice to finally have gotten a good bath. I'm so tired of constantly walking and hiding and fighting."

Sheik stopped her and turned around. "Tara, you don't have to come with us. You and Auni are free to go at any time. I mean, you two are so young, this isn't something you should have to do." Sheik wasn't much older, but since this adventure had begun she felt she had aged a lifetime.

"No way," Tara grinned, pushing her back so she could finish her hair. "Of course we are going to see it through to the end. We're not going anywhere."

Relief washed over her. Sheik didn't want them to feel forced into this war, but she was also glad to have them. It was hard to remember when they had all first met in Calert, but Sheik had been so afraid of losing them. She had so desperately wanted a family, a home. Now that she had found it, she hated the idea of them leaving.

But they weren't a family. Not really. They were a group of soldiers. Hesitantly, Sheik asked, "What about when this is all over?"

"We were just talking about it the other day. Auni knows a lot about farming from when he was on my parents' plantation. Maybe we could start up a farm of our own." Sheik wondered who 'we' included. Asroth? Doubtful. What about Carlos? Did it at least include Sheik and Kazzak? "It is only a thought," Tara continued. "I really don't know for sure." She finished the last strand of Sheik's hair. "All done!"

Sheik stood up and looked at her reflection in the still water. She looked surprisingly different. Her hair was now pulled out of her face, two separate braids against her scalp culminating in a bun. "Wow, it's beautiful. Thank you."

She helped Tara off the rock and the girl gave her a hug. "We should do this more often."

Sheik smiled back at her. "Yeah, we should."

Tara left cheerfully, unaware of the fear and anxiety sinking into Sheik's bones. As much as they had all grown to love each other, Sheik realized now that she still was not home.

Someday this war would be over. And when it was, Sheik wasn't sure what would happen. Even if they all liked each other, they were all very different people. Carlos could return home once the New Prosper had been defeated. Asroth undoubtedly had his own goals and aspirations. Would Kazzak also go his own, separate way? Would Sheik?

She thought of Tara's plan to live on a farm. It seemed quaint, yet it did not feel quite right. And the more Sheik thought about it, the more she realized the only place that felt like home was Atarius’ village. And that was a dream that was long gone.

Even if Atarius were to end her banishment and accept her back, she wouldn’t want to go back. She couldn’t return to someone whose love was conditional. Unless he owned up to it all, admitted how wrong he had been, and truly gave the apology of a lifetime, there was no way she would return. And the idea of Atarius pleading for her forgiveness? It simply wouldn’t happen. He was too stubborn. Too proud.

The past was the past. She needed to focus on the present and the future, just as she had after losing her memories over a year ago. But would she ever be able to find a new home? To have a family, to feel secure, to live a simple life? She wasn’t sure.

All she could do was continue to keep the group together. To lead them onwards. And as she thought about what lay ahead, about wyverns and storming Isandas, suddenly finding a place to call home felt very, very far off. Would any of them even survive this war?

CHAPTER 13

"Here you are," Jason smiled, placing a wooden dish before Sheik. "Wyvern meat and some of our local vegetables."

Kazzak, who was sitting to her right, leaned in and whispered, "You're going to have to eat meat if you want to impress your boyfriend over there." Then, louder, he announced, "Looks delicious!"

"He's not my boyfriend," Sheik whispered back as she watched Kazzak dig into the meat. She tried not to gag. "I don't actually eat meat," she stated quietly. "Or vegetables. Well, I mean, I'm just not hungry."

The rest of the group, being used to her odd diet, simply ignored her. But Jamen stared. "So how long will you be staying with us?"

Jason elbowed his brother. "He doesn't mean it like that," he smiled at Sheik. "You can stay as long as you'd like."

"Well thank you, but we should be leaving right away." She glanced at the others to see if there were any objections, but her companions said nothing and continued to eat.

"It's winter in only a couple of weeks," Jason stated quickly. "You don't want to travel in the middle of winter. You should stay until the end of the season."

Jamen nearly spat out his drink. Coughing for what seemed like several minutes, he shook his head no. "You probably want to be on your way before then," he said sharply, emphasizing that they were still not welcome.

Sheik understood his fear that the group would bring more troubles to them. She spoke up before Jason could say anything. "No, you're right. We can't stay all winter. We need to get to Isandas as quickly as possible and just put an end to all this nonsense. Spike, the New Prosper Army. Too many people are suffering."

"Wait, you're attacking Isandas?" Jamen interrupted. She nodded. He studied each of them for a moment.

"Is there something wrong with that?" Asroth asked finally.

"You're going to die."

Carlos shook his head as he chewed on a piece of meat. "We aren't just marching up to the gates. We'll come up with a plan," he explained.

"No, it's not that," Jamen mumbled. "You won't make it to the gates of Isandas alive. Those wyverns will keep coming, and you won't have the forest to hide in for much longer. I know you are famed for fighting the New Prosper, but those soldiers are weak. We've bested them countless times as well. King Garret's wyverns are different. They're trained. You get cornered by his men trying to march up to Isandas and you'll die."

Asroth chuckled. "You underestimate us. We have something on our side that they don't. Magic."

Jamen shook his head, frustrated. "I don't care what magic you have, you don't stand a chance. There's a reason Spike struck an alliance with King Garret. He knows you can't get to him while those wyverns are following you; they'll trap you. Only way you can defeat them is fighting them on your terms, which—"

"Buys Spike more time to defend against us," Sheik finished for him. Jamen was right. Spike was not as stupid as she once thought. And now she was being forced to play the man's games.

"What other choice do we have?" Asroth asked.

They glanced between each other, no one having any strong suggestion. Sheik had one, but she hated to say it out loud. She bit down on her lip. Had war really warped her mind so much that her first solution was assassination? Finally she spoke up. "If we got close to King Garret himself," she whispered, not wanting to finish the sentence.

Asroth gratefully did it for her. "Of course! Assassinate him. Transitioning to a new king might create chaos. They might want to renegotiate terms with Spike. Even if it only buys us a few weeks without wyverns, it will be enough to get into Isandas."

Sheik looked down at the table, ashamed that she was the one to come up with the idea. She could feel Kazzak's eyes on her, but she refused to meet his gaze. He interrupted Asroth's excitement. "But King Garret's castle is way up in the Tasvran Mountains. There's no way we can make it up the mountains without dying of cold or being eaten by wyverns. Then when we get there, how are we supposed to get inside? It's going to be easier to get to Isandas and kill Spike than it would be to assassinate King Garret."

"That's true," Asroth admitted. "If Jamen's right that the wyverns will kill us, then how do we make it to the Tasvran without being hunted by them?"

"You would have the advantage though," Jamen argued. "They'd be searching for you along the Canaen."

The group dissolved into a bickering mess. Sheik slipped away as soon as she possibly could, eager to get a moment alone with her thoughts. The idea of assassination weighed heavily on her mind. Especially because she had suggested it. As quickly as she entered the chilly outdoors, Jason followed after her. "I'm coming with you," he said quietly.

She shivered, rubbing her arms to keep her warm. "Your brother is here. The rest of us, we don't have family anymore. I can't ask you to abandon your family."

"You aren't asking me, I'm volunteering," he stated simply. "I'm a trained fighter. I can help you, whether you're marching straight to Isandas or going after King Garret's army."

"We'll head to the Tasvran," Sheik replied after a moment of thought. It bothered her, but she tried her best to justify it. An assassination would ultimately cause the least amount of killing. "If we can stop King Garret's wyverns, maybe we have a chance at really ending this war."

Jason smiled. "Sounds like a dangerous mission. You'll really need my help."

Sheik forced herself to smile. He simply wanted to make a difference. To help stop the suffering. That was all she had wanted. Surely Jason had that right, too. "Your brother isn't going to like this."

"I'm old enough to make my own decisions," he replied forcefully. "My brother and I are twins. He has no authority over me."

"Then welcome aboard."

"You'll be joining us, will you?" It was Kazzak.

Sheik nodded. "Looks that way," she answered for Jason. He smiled at her once again and, not particularly having anything else to say, she added, "Well I'm tired. I think I'm going to go to bed." Jason had previously shown them to several empty rooms where they could stay for the evening. Sheik wished him and Kazzak both a pleasant goodnight before heading in that direction.

Kazzak lingered to tease, "But you haven't eaten a thing!"

She rolled her eyes, turning back towards him. "I find it difficult to eat in the company of such slobs," she retorted with a sly smile.

"Touché." Taking a step closer, his hand reached out and his fingers glided over one of the braids Tara had done in her hair. Her heart began beating faster under his touch. "Quite the job Tara did," he inspected. "Looks nice."

Sheik laughed. "I should hope so, considering how long she pulled at it."

His fingers trickled lightly down her hair, to her neck, her shoulder, her arm, until finally he was holding her hand. Sheik's mind flashed to the time in Calert when she had panicked after her first kill, when he had held her. He had held her hand then, too, she thought to herself. "Goodnight, Sheik." Before she could gather her thoughts together and say goodnight back, he had already let go of her and walked away.

———⚬———

Tara was relieved when Sheik announced that they would stay an extra night. It would give them an additional day to recover from their hard travels and it would give Jason time to say his goodbyes. Jamen was adamantly opposed to him leaving the village to travel with a group who he predicted would not survive. But Tara thought it was silly that he had such little faith in them. Perhaps if he had seen them in action he might be convinced.

Jason gave arguments as to why he needed to leave. How their little group desperately needed him and how he would be truly making a difference in the world. But Tara knew plenty well why Jason was coming with them. She saw the way he stared at Sheik, practically drooling over her.

Tara was not particularly jealous. She just did not understand why Sheik didn't reciprocate. How could she not see how gorgeous this man was? How absurdly devoted he was to her? He was the kind of man she had wished to find back in Omris. But somehow she had only managed to attract crude, immature boys or men after her father's wealth.

Perhaps now that she was detached from her father's name, she could find a man without worrying about his intentions. Perhaps now that she was older, she would find a mature man. Maybe a handsome man like Jason. After all, she was attractive herself, and she had lost weight during their grueling travels. Unfortunately, her breasts had shrunk as well. But still, she was good looking, and she hoped she might find someone built big and muscular. And that they would be as obsessed with her as Jason was Sheik.

She smiled, wondering who her future love might be someday, when Auni disrupted her thoughts. "Weird sleeping under a tree, huh?" he asked, climbing into the burrow alongside her.

"Better than marching at least." She scooted over to make room for him. The burrow was meant for one and was obnoxiously tight with two people. But Jamen was so on edge that Tara did not dare ask him for another sleeping space.

Auni gave her a lopsided grin, though his face was hard to see in the shadows. "Sheik says her whole village sleeps in trees. Isn't that crazy?"

"I don't believe it. What tree is big enough across to sleep in?"

He shrugged. "I don't know, but that's what she says." Auni idolized Sheik and believed everything that she said. Even that she could speak to her wolf, Fang. It was silly but it was also sweet, and so Tara never argued with him.

"No sign of wyverns?" Tara asked, changing the subject to something far more serious. Jamen's men were posted to stay up and watch, but Auni did not trust them to do a good enough job. So he had stayed up and craned his neck to search the skies.

"Not that I saw. I sure hope we don't come across anymore."

Tara could not agree enough with that sentiment. "What do you think of the plan? To go to the Tasvran and kill King Garret?"

He said nothing for a long minute. Then finally, "I guess if that's what they all think is the best idea, then it's probably the best idea." He did not elaborate and Tara could tell he didn't like something about it.

But she pressed it no further. "You're going to need your shirts back," she said, wondering if they were in his pack or hers. "And we should see if we might get some coats from some of the people here." When they had left Calert, their supplies had been few, and they had not even thought to prepare for winter. But leaves were now turning orange. It would be cold soon, and even colder in the mountains.

Normally Omris winters were only cold enough to leave a bit of frost. But Tara remembered one time when a whole blanket of snow poured down on them. She had only been eight or nine at the time. It had been so magical, the experience dampened only by her father worrying it might ruin the crop that year.

It was only in reminiscing about the crop that she realized Auni had been there for that same snowfall. It was easy to forget that he had been there, even when she was young. Before she had ever known he had existed. Her whole life, while she had lived on the manse on the hill, he had lived down in the slave camp below. She shuddered.

In a quiet voice, she asked him, "Do you remember the year it snowed?"

He nodded. "Yeah. I do."

She remembered jumping in it, playing in it. Lying down in the snow and spreading her arms to make an imprint of herself with wings. She hesitated, but forced herself to ask, "Did you get to have fun in it?"

A smile lit up on his face. "Yeah. All us boys had a snowball fight."

Tara tried to imagine a little six-year-old Auni throwing snowballs. "I wish I could have joined you."

"Me too."

They sat in silence for what felt like forever. Tears welled up in Tara's eyes. "I'm sorry, Auni." He glanced her way. "I'm sorry we did not get to be siblings. I'm sorry for the way my family treated you. I'm sorry you did not get everything I got." He listened to her as she poured out her apology. But she was not just apologizing on behalf of her family. She was apologizing for herself, too. "I'm sorry I did not do anything about it sooner."

"Hey, hey, it's okay." He patted her shoulder like he was trying to put out a fire.

"No, no it's not," she interrupted, breaking into a full sob. "I knew for months. I knew for like eight months and I didn't do a thing. I don't know why. I was scared." Scared of confronting her father. Scared of leaving behind a life of luxury. "I was selfish. And I just watched you, watched you work every day, and I didn't do a thing about it. I'm sorry, Auni. I'm so sorry."

Her body shook as she sobbed. Auni said nothing, just reached out a hand to comfort her. She wanted to push him away because she did not deserve his comfort—she did not deserve anything from him. But she didn't push him away. She needed him too much.

"I forgive you," he stated quickly. Too quickly. How could he forgive her just like that?

She cried into his chest and he wrapped an arm around her the best he could in the tiny space.

"Will it snow in the mountains?" he asked. The question caught her off guard and it took Tara a moment to recollect herself. She stopped her crying as soon as she could and nodded that there would indeed be snow. "Maybe we can have a snowball fight. Like siblings."

Tara wanted to burst into a sob all over again but allowed herself to smile instead. "I would like that." And eventually she drifted into a deep sleep with dreams of snow.

When she awoke the next morning, Auni was gone. She cleared her eyes of crusts and went straight to the river to clean up, knowing she was likely puffy from crying.

There were several other of the town woods people at the river, washing or doing laundry, but thankfully no one she knew. It might not be so bad if Sheik saw that she had been crying, but she would be terribly embarrassed if one of the boys knew.

Tara splashed a little cold water on her face, letting it soak into her puffy eyes. She wondered if Sheik, with her differently shaped eyelids, ever suffered from puffy eyes when she cried. She had a hard time imagining Sheik crying. The woman always appeared so strong.

When she felt her eyes had returned to normal, Tara flagged down one of the women doing laundry. "Pardon me, you don't have any kohl, do you? For your eyes?"

The woman exchanged glances with a girl who looked to be a year or two younger than Tara. "Iseult, you have kohl, right?"

The girl nodded, handed over what she was washing to the older lady, and motioned for Tara to follow her. "Iseult?" Tara confirmed. "I am Tara. Thanks for letting me borrow it."

Iseult nodded. "If it gets me out of laundry." Then, after a pause, she asked, "So which of the men is yours?"

"What do you mean?"

"The men you're traveling with. There's four, right? Which one are you wearing kohl for?"

Tara laughed. "I am not wearing it for them, only for me."

They reached a tunnel and the girl motioned for Tara to stay put. In a moment she returned with the kohl, a stick, and a small mirror. "Be careful with it," Iseult said cautiously. "We don't get many chances for trading."

Tara took the mirror gently and applied the kohl in as thin a line as she could manage around her eyes. Wiping the edges clean, she decided that was about as good as she could get it with the crude thickness of the stick. It was not like what she was used to at home, where she had several kohl applicators, powders, and rouges. This village was clearly poor and did not have the luxury of such things.

She licked her finger and wiped a little kohl into it. Rubbing it the best she could on her eyelashes, she managed to bring them from a light blonde to a dark brown. She took one last look in the mirror before handing it back. "Much better!"

Iseult smiled at her. "And you aren't trying to impress any of those men?"

"Ziad no," Tara reiterated. "One of them is my brother, for starters. The young one."

"The one with the very curly hair?" Tara nodded and Iseult's face went pink. "I'm sorry, I didn't realize. I'd have guessed you two were together. He's the cutest of them anyway."

Tara's nose crinkled at the thought. "Gross, no. No if I had to choose, I would probably pick," she paused to think a moment, "well Kazzak I guess. The one with the goatee. He is funny at least."

Iseult laughed. "Him? The one who's always wearing the headdress is much better looking."

"Asroth?" He did have a handsome face with soft skin and beautiful blue eyes. But Tara would never be able to get past his personality. "No, trust me, when you spend more than five minutes with him, he is no longer attractive," she insisted.

The girl laughed again and Tara smiled. It had been so long since she'd had good company to talk to about makeup and boys. "And the last one? Skinny with the freckles?"

"Carlos," Tara nodded. "Hmm. Maybe." Carlos was not particularly handsome, but he was not unattractive either. She had not put much thought into him because she had not gotten to know him. None of them had really. He used to be a tanner or a tanner's assistant or something. Besides that and his pretending to be Isandas nobility, she knew nothing else about him. He was always so closed off and quiet.

"Well he's cute," Iseult spoke up again. "Maybe the kohl will help catch his eye."

"Maybe." She was lost in thought but gave Iseult another smile. "Thanks again. I had better go find them all." They said their goodbyes and Tara wandered for a bit, lost in the camouflaged village. Occasionally she spotted a tunnel dug into the base of a tree, but she could never tell one apart from another.

Amidst her wandering, she heard yelling. She glanced at the sky, afraid it might mean wyverns, but saw nothing. As she continued towards the sound, she realized it was not screams of peril, but angry shouts.

A hand grabbed her by the shoulder.

Tara's heart jumped, but she found it was Carlos. He held a finger to his lips. "It's Jason and Jamen."

"Fighting still?" They'd been fighting since the night before, when Jason had told his brother he'd be leaving with their group.

Carlos nodded and motioned for her to move closer. "I'm trying to get the details."

She grinned and followed after him, watching carefully how he moved to avoid snapping any twigs. Between his quiet nature and small frame, eavesdropping suited him quite well.

Once close enough, she could hear the specifics of the argument. "It's a suicide mission," Jamen shouted. "You can't go. I forbid it."

"You can't tell me where I can and cannot go," Jason retorted. "And it is not a suicide mission. Sheik knows what she's doing."

"Oh please. Winning a few fights against the New Prosper Army is one thing. But you think she can manage an assassination of King Garret and then... then what? A full-scale invasion of Isandas?"

Tara felt her stomach flop and turned back the way she had come. Carlos shot her a glance, listened a moment more, and then chased after her. "What is it?"

She walked until they were out of hearing range. Finally away from the twins' heated debate, she whispered, "You don't think he's right do you? Jamen, I mean."

Carlos shook his head. "Of course not. You think I'd be traveling with you all if I thought it would get me killed?" he laughed.

She gave him a slight smile. "Yeah okay. But what about Isandas?" Their normal tactics involved movement, distance, and whittling down the army. None of that would work for invading a palace.

"I still have some connections there. I can sneak us into the city. Then we lay low for a bit, see if maybe Kazzak or Asroth can get a job in the palace. It might take some time, but we'll find a crack." He gave her a gentle nudge with his elbow. "Don't worry, Tara. We'll be fine."

"What makes you so sure?" she asked, a little curious and a little skeptical of his optimism.

"Sheik," he replied simply. "She's in charge, right?"

Tara shrugged. It was not formal, but she had indeed become their leader, at least in times of combat.

"She's in charge," he reiterated. "And she cares about you. All of you guys. She won't put you in danger, not real danger. That's the difference between her and Keira."

"Keira?"

"My friend Lyle's girl. She was the one who got us caught up in all this impersonating nobility business. She would drop you in a heartbeat to save her own skin."

They stared at the ground for a second, Carlos suddenly silent and Tara not knowing what to say. "I'm sorry," she finally managed. He nodded but still said nothing. "You must miss him."

"Yeah. I do." Tara could not imagine coming across a friend's dead body. Knowing they were truly and totally gone. She wondered if that might be part of the reason Carlos was always so quiet. Maybe he was still processing everything that had happened.

She was about to ask about his friend when more shouting interrupted them. Jason. He thundered through the forest like he was trying to be as loud as possible. Upon spotting them, he marched straight up to Tara and Carlos. "Go pack your things, we're leaving right now," he ordered.

Carlos raised his eyebrows but said nothing. Before Tara could reply, Jason had already stormed away, leaving as loudly as he had come. "Hopefully he doesn't stay that mad," Carlos mumbled as he began to lead the way through the well-hidden village. "The last thing we need is another Asroth, right?"

Tara laughed in agreement. Maybe she did not want a gorgeous man after all—it seemed all the handsome ones were moody and short tempered.

As they wandered through the village, Tara finally began to recognize things and orient herself. "Well this one is mine," Carlos motioned to one of the dug out homes. "Better get packed before we get in trouble." He gave her a boyish grin. "Nice talking to you."

"Yeah, you too," Tara smiled before hurrying to pack her own bags. She hated being the slowest one of the bunch and forced herself to rush so she might not be the last one ready.

***

Faris paced through the garden. The guards were watching him from only twenty steps away. He could never be alone. Though he knew they were there for his safety, he also knew he could no longer trust anyone. Not anymore.

"Prince Faris," one of them spoke up. "The king has instructed that you spend an hour practicing on your wyvern."

The crown atop his headscarf shifted as he spun around to face the soldier. "My father is gone," he said sharply. He instantly felt guilty. It wasn't the soldier's fault. It was his father's fault. "I'm sorry. Please, I am in charge when my father is absent. I will do as I please." He paused. "I wish to be alone now. Actually alone." It was strange that, despite having no friends, he always felt surrounded.

"Sir, what about assassinations?" the guard whispered. "We're here to protect you."

Faris chuckled despite how much he wanted to cry. "I'll take the risk." The guard gave a solemn nod and exited the gardens, leading the other soldiers with him. The prince glanced around before collapsing against the main fountain, bursting into tears. "What am I going to do?" he sobbed.

His coming-of-age ceremony was in spring, but he still felt like a child. Compared to most Tasvranians, he was scrawny. He had not even learned to ride his wyvern yet, something all men in the palace were trained to do. He was shorter and less muscular than most men, he had no facial hair, and his eyes were a mysterious blue color, an extremely rare feature for Tasvran men. All of his traits were strictly feminine, weak, pathetic, and made his father completely disrespect him.

Yet still, Faris could not believe that his father wanted him dead.

The man was arrogant and violent, but Faris had always believed there was still some good in him. Until he had recently overheard his father give orders to poison Faris' food while he was gone. Upon tasting only a small portion of his breakfast, Faris had thrown up nine times in his bedroom.

Now that he had stopped his vomiting, he wandered the gardens in hope of some sort of solution. He had thought of running away. That was his response to most of his problems. But he had nowhere to go. He had never experienced the outside world, and he had heard rumors from servants that many people hated King Garret. Surely they would despise the cruel man's son as well.

Besides, how was he to escape with the guards always watching him? He hated the way they lurked around him. He was not sure how many were faithful soldiers, willing to die for him, and how many were eager to do his father's bidding and murder him. It was such a complicated mess that Faris wanted to ignore it altogether. But he had to come up with a plan before his father returned and killed him with his own two hands.

Faris had heard rumors that one of his father's concubines was pregnant. Perhaps, Faris thought, his father saw this as the opportunity to raise a new, stronger child who could claim the throne. He wondered if the rumor was true. There was no way to find out. He rarely spoke to his father, and their conversations usually consisted of no more than grunts.

He did not understand how he could possibly be Garret's son. The man was a monster, full of rage and ugliness. Faris was tender and sweet hearted. It had taken him six months to learn how to mount a wyvern because he was afraid of hurting the creature.

But his father did have one trait that Faris admired. Something he greatly lacked: courage.

Faris was much too timid to ever stand up to his father or any of his training guards. Instead, he preferred avoiding those who caused him troubles and strolling through the gardens which had been abandoned since his father had first taken control of the kingdom.

The gardens were once well cultivated and delicately refined. Over the many years, they had grown wild, weeds conquering the entire pathway and choking the life out of the more fragile plants. Still, the garden was refreshing and beautiful compared to most of the sights Faris had to watch day by day.

He spotted several clumped-up weeds and pulled them aside to see what they could be obstructing. Uncovering the object they had wrapped themselves around, he discovered a small fountain. There were countless fountains throughout the gardens, hiding in different areas under plants, some even buried in soil and rock. He sighed, sitting and leaning against it.

Unexpectedly, it moved.

Faris turned back around and examined the fountain from top to bottom. All of the fountains in the garden had some sort of hose which allowed water to flow through them constantly from a spring located right outside the garden, though many had been severed or broken many years ago.

This fountain had no hose.

Faris thought about it for a moment. What good was a fountain with no water running through it?

There was a small inscription in it. Faris tried to make it out, but it was written in Old Tasvranian. If anyone still spoke it, they would have had to have been very old, older than anyone Faris knew. Yet somehow, as Faris stared, he recognized the words. Where had he seen those words before?

Grave markers!

Though he did not know the language, he remembered that he had seen the exact same characters on grave markers. "Here lies," he read aloud. That was what they always said. Here lies, followed by a name. It didn't matter what language they were in, whether it was an ancient forgotten one or the common tongue.

"Here lies," he whispered. Could it be a secret grave? He glanced about to make sure no guards were watching and then he pushed the fountain aside with all his strength. Below the fountain was a hole, though Faris knew neither how deep it was nor where it led.

Before he had time to study it further, a shadow flew over his head. Faris gazed up at the sky. He could hardly see it, the white object juxtaposed against the mist and clouds. He squinted. It was unlike anything he had ever seen before, and it was flying directly towards him.

⚬

Sheik stared up at the mountains towering before her. She pulled her arms close to her body, trying to fight off the cold. Unfortunately, she knew it was about to become much colder.

The trip from the forest to the mountains had been done in much haste. Occasionally they would spot wyverns in the sky and be forced to hide. So far, none of the beasts had discovered them. They assumed King Garret's wyverns were searching along the Canaen River, expecting them to be marching towards Isandas rather than the Tasvran mountains. In any case, they had been extremely fortunate not to encounter the creatures again.

The journey was an awkward one. Jason had left his village after hours of fighting with his brother. It had made the entire group uncomfortable and there had been limited conversation among them over the past several weeks of traveling.

Instead of walking alongside the others, Sheik walked ahead of the group, just her and Fang. Despite how lonely she had felt after being banished by Atarius, she missed traveling with only Fang. Kazzak was nice to talk to in private, but they rarely got a moment alone together. And Jason never seemed to stop smiling at her.

Her conversations with Fang were a relief. Sheik still was not sure how they communicated; it didn't matter if she spoke to him in elven or human, he always understood the emotions and concepts behind her words. Yet he was unable to comprehend anyone else. And likewise, so long as Sheik was actively focusing, she was able to understand what he was trying to communicate when no one else could. It was something strange and special. Some form of undiscovered magic that made their relationship unique.

"Are you ready to climb?" Asroth asked, interrupting Sheik's thoughts.

They had already begun ascending. But it was nothing compared to the mountains that rose steeply just east of them. They had been traveling alongside those mountains for days now.

When Sheik said nothing, Asroth explained, "King Garret's castle should be just northeast of that ridge." He pointed to a particularly steep crest.

Carlos jogged up beside them. "We aren't climbing yet, are we?" Sheik nodded and Asroth pointed out the peak once again. "But there's a passageway from the north." Carlos showed them on the map as he explained, "If we hike around the edge of the mountains, we can take the main road. Clearly they aren't expecting us to be entering Tasvran territory or we'd have run into wyverns by now. If you disguise that you're an elf, we can sneak in with merchants and travelers."

Asroth shook his head. "What, you want us to double back west, go all this way north, then all this way east? That'll take weeks!"

"Maybe so, but there will be no struggle up the mountain if we stick to main roads."

Everyone had caught up now and huddled around the debate. Sheik glanced between the two men. "How long will it take to make it to the castle from where we are now?"

"Maybe a few days?" Carlos said, uncertain.

Asroth rolled his eyes. "Two days, tops."

"The quicker we can assassinate King Garret, the quicker we can stop Spike and the New Prosper," Sheik decided. "Let's cut across from where we are."

"Maybe Carlos is right, though," Jason interjected. "It may take longer, but it's winter now. There might be blizzards, snowstorms."

"Yeah, if the other way is safer, maybe it's worth the time," Kazzak added as well. "I mean a few days of mountain hiking versus a main road?"

"This will cut down our time tremendously," Asroth argued, backing up Sheik. It wasn't often that their opinions aligned. "And ultimately, the quicker we get there, the quicker we solve the wyvern problem. This is safer in the long run."

The group began to argue between the two options. The northern passageway was safer, but taking longer meant more time for the New Prosper to build, conquer, and kill. And Asroth insisted that taking a main road meant they could be discovered easier. Carlos swore that plenty of people took the path and they could blend in. Asroth doubted that they would blend in successfully since word had spread about them.

Sheik pulled her coat tighter against her face as she listened to their arguments. Jason had managed to sneak them all fur coats when he left his village. At first Sheik had objected to wearing fur. The thought of it was sick. But now that they were hiking higher and higher and snow began to dust the ground, she relented.

"And what if they notice Sheik's an elf? What then? They'll know who we are and kill all of us," Asroth exclaimed.

"She doesn't even have to be visible. We can buy a cart and she and the wolf can hide in it when we enter the city," Carlos pushed back.

"Oh, like they aren't going to search a cart for contraband," Asroth rolled his eyes.

Finally Sheik threw her arms up in the air. "That's it! I'm heading up right now. It's going to be quicker, and we'll be better hidden from any wyverns if we take the harder route."

"So, what, we aren't going to discuss it anymore?" Carlos asked, his tone accusatory.

Sheik shrugged and added, "Look, it won't take all of us to assassinate King Garret. If you don't want to hike the mountains, you can stay behind and we'll meet up after."

"Okay, but—"

"My mind's made up," Sheik said firmly. She was the leader during battles. If they trusted her in times of danger, then they should trust her now, too. "Anyone who is coming, let's go. Anyone who doesn't want to go, you're welcome to stay."

Asroth immediately followed, alongside Fang. Kazzak sighed and rolled his eyes. Mumbling curses under his breath, he began to walk behind her. Auni and Tara, who did not have much of an opinion on the matter, fell in line.

Carlos and Jason hesitated, muttering between themselves. But eventually they, too, caught up to the rest of the group.

Sheik couldn't help but smile. She was their leader. They trusted her. They followed her. They would not leave her.

———⦾———

Faris dropped to the ground, trying to avoid the object flying at him. Upon hearing the loud thud of it landing, he jumped back up to his feet. "What in the world?"

It was a pegasus.

He had heard of the creature before. A horse with wings. Nearly everyone had heard of such beasts in myths and tales. In such stories, pegasi were friendly creatures, but for some reason Faris was afraid to approach it. He had lived around wyverns, terrible looking creatures, yet here he was afraid of a winged horse.

He moved towards it slowly. "Hey there little guy," he whispered. The pegasus whimpered. "Are you okay? You don't need to be afraid." Faris laughed out loud. The creature was shaking, absolutely terrified of him! No one had ever been scared of him before. "It looks like you hurt your leg," he cooed, moving closer and closer to the frightened creature. "Let me help you."

He bent down and examined him. To his surprise, the pegasus didn't put up any kind of a struggle. It submitted peaceably and allowed Faris to bend its leg. It was not actually the leg that was damaged, but rather the hoof. He had watched farriers work on such hooves before. "Stay here, okay? Stay," Faris repeated calmly. Running out of the garden he yelled at a nearby guard, "Everyone is to stay out of the garden, understood? On penalty of death."

The soldier, confused, gave a quick nod, accepting the order. Faris continued to sprint towards the blacksmith. But he slowed his pace and whispered, "The library." He changed directions and burst open the doors of the dusty library. It, like the garden, had not been accessed in years.

He glanced around trying to understand how it was organized. Scanning down the aisles, he found what he was looking for. "Pegasi," he smiled, grabbing a small book and running back towards the blacksmith.

By the time he had found the tools he needed, it was almost dark. "Hey," he whispered into the dimly lit garden. The pegasus was still there, laying down in a patch of soft wildflowers. "You aren't used to this rocky area, huh?" Faris asked, noting how many rocks were stuck in the hoof. The pegasus was more compliant than any horse Faris had ever seen, extending its leg comfortably across his lap. Faris pried the rocks out carefully, making sure none of it hurt the creature.

When he was finished, he grabbed the book he had gotten from the library and leaned against a wall. "Let's see what I should know about you," he mumbled, scanning through it. "Pegasi are supposedly native to a region called Aldena, located in the Wilds," Faris read aloud. The area east of the Tasvran Mountains was known as the Wilds. Very few men had explored it and returned. No one knew quite what existed in the foreign land.

"So what made you fly all the way across the Tasvran?" he asked, as if the pegasus would give him an answer. He continued to glance over the book. "Looks like you eat the same stuff horses do. That shouldn't be a problem. Oh, it says here pegasi desire companionship and should be named. What would you like your name to be?"

The pegasus let out a small nicker. Faris chuckled. "How about Percy?" The pegasus nudged him. "Percy it is."

Then Faris remembered what he had discovered just before spotting the pegasus: the fountain that he had moved to reveal a deep pit. He ran back to it and gazed into the darkness. Percy followed behind him, curious. "I wonder what's down there," he mumbled out loud. A moment later he added, "There's only one way to find out."

He was not sure what made him do it. He was not normally adventurous. He dreamed of adventures, fantasized about them. But he rarely acted on such impulses as he did now, lowering himself into the dark hole.

As he extended his arms, fear overcame him. He realized he could not touch the ground, and obviously could not see it in the darkness of the hole. He struggled to pull himself back up, but his arms were growing weak and his hands kept slipping.

Closing his eyes, he let go.

The falling sensation lasted a brief moment before he landed on his feet, completely unharmed. With a decent jump he could still reach the rim of where the pit began. He nearly laughed at how scared he had been when the fall had been so harmless. Percy peered down at him, wondering what he was doing. Looking around, a tunnel appeared out of the darkness as Faris' eyes adjusted to the poor light. Curious, he began to follow it.

It seemed to go on forever. Faris wondered if he should turn back but decided against it. He thought of his father, wanting him dead.

This tunnel might be an escape route. This tunnel might one day save his life. He had to know what was at the end.

So he continued to walk further and further into the darkness. Soon, he was unable to walk at all. He had to crawl, the ceiling growing closer to the floor. He felt like he might not be able to breathe; that the tunnel would collapse on him and he would suffocate.

Still, he pressed on, crawling on hands and knees. A quarter of an hour passed by before the tunnel grew brighter. He was approaching some source of light. Faster and faster he scrambled through, excited to see what it was.

Then, as suddenly as he had found the mysterious tunnel, he emerged into the bright moonlight. The ledge he stood on was narrow and frightening, overlooking the mountains and the dangerous drops they contained. His heart beat rapidly. To his right was a small bush, its leaves dead. To his left, a perilous drop off.

CHAPTER 14

The snow was blinding. Sheik remembered winter in her forest homeland, where there were light dustings of snow. It was never like this. This snow was painful. Sheik tried to cover and protect her face from the sharp icy stings. Everything was a white blur.

The first day had not been so bad. It had simply been cold and difficult to trudge through the thick snow. By the second day, though, the group was exhausted. Sheik was afraid perhaps she had made the wrong decision. Now she felt lost and hopeless. She could only see a few paces ahead of herself. For all she knew she was no longer even heading east.

But she kept her worried thoughts to herself and continued the trek. From the way the others had made it sound, King Garret's palace would be easy to spot, towering high into the sky.

She was proud that the others had followed her despite most of them disagreeing with her. In that instant she knew she finally had a place, or rather a group of people, to call home. They all trusted her and would follow her to the death. Not that she would ever put them at risk. It was simply a relief to know that they would follow her. That they wouldn't leave her. No matter how much they disagreed or fought, they would still stand by her side.

Sheik paused. A low rumbling interrupted her thoughts. She listened closely, but it was hard to hear with her ears bundled up to avoid frostbite. Suddenly there was a loud, terrifying crack. She turned to glance at the others, though they were difficult to see in the thick snowfall. "Did you hear that?" she yelled.

She heard several voices shout back but she could not make out what they were saying. Facing forward again, the ground started to shake. A strange hissing began to build. It grew louder. Stronger. The ground continued to rumble.

Then she saw it.

Far in the distance, snow tumbling down the mountainside.

It came upon her quicker than she thought possible. The snow plowed into her, sweeping her away. She held her breath, but snow still managed to force its way into her mouth, making her cough and choke. The whiteness of the snow blurred her vision.

Fang, who had been next to her only moments ago, let out a whimpering cry. He had been swept too far away for Sheik to try and grab or help him. She tried to help herself, swimming with the flow of snow and ice, but it seemed futile. She tried to create a barrier with her magic, but it wasn't strong enough and flickered out of existence as the snow piled up against it. The snow was a powerful creature, grabbing and holding her still as she suffocated.

Her lungs burned. Her body was trapped and compressed. She felt as if she might be ripped to shreds by the violent flurry. Pain accompanied by fear echoed through her body. She did not know which way was north or south, east or west, up or down. It viciously shook her and pounded her against rocks and trees. She tried to grip them, but the snow was too powerful and simply tore her away.

After what felt like an eternity of struggling to hold her breath and not get ripped apart by the snow or jagged rocks, the sickening turning stopped. Her left hand was stuck, but she quickly used her right hand to free her mouth of snow before she choked on it.

Everything was black. She was trapped. How could something as light as snow be so constricting? She created a flicker of flame to at least see her surroundings. But then she realized what a small space she was crammed into. She couldn't keep a fire going—she would run out of air in only moments.

Elilah, she would run out of air.

Her breathing became frantic. She disappeared the flame but couldn't help but gasp in deep breaths, hyperventilating. She had to calm down. She had to calm down and focus.

Her breathing steadied.

First, she had to figure out which way she was facing. She recreated the fire for only a moment, just enough to melt the snow above her. It dripped down. Good. That was good. That meant she was right side up.

The air was getting thinner. And she still didn't know how far away from the surface she was. *Don't panic,* she told herself. She focused her magic around her stuck left hand, turning the ice and snow into water. Finally, it was free. Now she could dig upwards.

Her left arm was throbbing, as was her head, but she had to stay focused. She was getting dizzy. She couldn't breathe. But she had to keep digging. She concentrated on the snow above her with her magic, turning it into water, letting it rain down on her. *Stay awake.* Using her magic in such a weakened state might cause exhaustion. But if she passed out, she would die. Unless she reached the surface, she would die.

A crack of light broke through as snow began to disappear. Sound resonated throughout her small cove. Air streamed in. She took in a lungful and sighed. Painfully, she pulled herself out of her prison and into the frigid air.

She was wet from melting the snow. Then she looked at her left hand and realized it wasn't just water. She was covered in blood. Her left arm had been torn open. But there wasn't time to deal with it. She had to find the others. She had to get out of this weather and get dry before she froze to death.

All she could do for right now was put pressure on her arm to stop the bleeding. Though her arm was the worst of her injuries, her entire body was littered with cuts. She pulled the now-ragged fur coat against her to try and keep herself warm and protected from the wind. "Is anyone here?" she yelled, hoping they could hear her. They had seemed so close before, but the flood of snow must have separated them.

Then she heard a bark. Fang! "I'm here boy! Bark!" He let out another muffled bark. "Good boy!" she called back, crawling on her hands and knees searching through the snow, hoping to find where he was buried.

He barked again. The snow was piling up higher and higher, but Sheik pushed past it, frantically searching. Another bark, this time much closer. She placed her ear against the ground. One more bark echoed throughout the layer of snow. She tried using magic first to melt it away, but her head began to spin and once again she feared passing out. And so, she began to dig with her raw, wounded hands.

Thankfully Fang was not buried terribly deep. It took Sheik only a few minutes to get him out. "We need to get away from here," she explained, helping him stand upright. "Another snow slide might come any minute." The two began hiking back down the mountainside from where they had come.

<hr>

Asroth pushed his way past the snow. Most of his body had not gotten buried, and he had easily pulled himself out of his stuck position. He did not bother searching for the others.

Sheik's idea had nearly killed him. He would not risk his life again searching for the others. His life was more valuable. More important. It would be like a king risking his life to save six pathetic peasants. It would be a waste of time.

He did not much care for the group, anyway. Tara he desired, but Sheik and the men he did not like. They were an obnoxious bunch who did not treat him with the respect he deserved.

Jason had proved that they were getting the fame he wanted. Their name had spread across nations. But of course it was Sheik's elven heritage that got the attention.

It was unfair. He hated the woman sometimes. She was adored by the others. Respected beyond belief when she deserved none of it. He deserved their respect. He was wise, talented, powerful, handsome. It simply was not fair.

He grimaced angrily, trudging through the thick snow. He was so special and unique, and yet nothing had ever come easy to him. His mother had died when he was so young, his father had cast him away. He had fought off countless soldiers, run from wyverns, and now had managed to survive an avalanche. It was no life for someone as impressive as himself.

However it did go to show that he was truly indestructible. When men tried to kill him, he was always left unharmed. Now, even nature had sent disasters at him and he hardly had a scratch. He could not be defeated. He could not be conquered. Not by man or nature.

Asroth spotted something in the blinding flurry of snow. He inched closer to it, trying to see through the thick wind and sleet. It was a hand, emerged from the snowfall of the avalanche. He watched it wriggle for a moment. His pathetic comrades were so much weaker than him. It brought him a sense of satisfaction knowing that they were struggling for air.

Then a thought came to him. What if it was Tara? If he saved her life, she would be eternally grateful to him. She would throw herself at him, eager to sleep with her savior. He smiled, praying it was her under the snow, and began to help dig her out.

After a moment, the person's head emerged, gasping in deep breaths of precious air. It was Carlos. "Asroth, boy am I glad to see you!"

Asroth frowned. He had wanted to save Tara. He did not want to save Carlos. He didn't like Carlos. He didn't even trust Carlos. The man was a con artist and could betray them at a moment's notice. Frankly, Asroth thought he should be put to death for his crimes of impersonating nobility. Asroth would be happy to be the one to do it. But the rest of the group would never permit such a thing.

And then it dawned on him; the rest of the group was not here.

His frown turned into a smile. He placed a hand on Carlos' cheek. The dark power formed in his eyes and dripped down his throat. It slid into his chest and absorbed into his heart. The pain was worth the satisfaction. He no longer felt the snow beating against him. It was like he was in his own separate world, just him and the power.

As it extended from his heart into his palm, he heard Carlos scream.

It was faint, as if Carlos was leagues away instead of right there with him. Asroth smiled as he felt the pleasure of the man's suffering. He was too stuck in the snow to twist away from Asroth's hand.

When he awoke from the strange state, Carlos was long dead. Half of his face was decayed and deteriorating. Asroth had never gotten to use his magic on someone for so long. It was a pleasurable experience, getting to feel their pain until their last breath.

He stared into Carlos' dead eyes for a second longer. The exhilaration was beginning to wear off and a pit filled his stomach. What had he done? How horrified the others would be if they knew.

They wouldn't know. He wouldn't let them find out. He would sink Carlos back into the snow. And, if Asroth ever even reached the others, he would tell them the truth: he had found Carlos' dead body buried in the avalanche.

<hr>

Auni pulled himself out of the heavy snow. He had managed to cling to a large rock and most of the thicker snow had been pushed to one side or the other. It was still a scramble to get completely free, but he certainly considered himself lucky. "Tara!" he shouted instantly.

She was not far from him, lying half buried in the snow. "Tara!" *I forgive you!* He started to dig her out of the snow. *I forgive you!* He was screaming it inside his own head. She was unconscious. *Please don't be dead, I forgive you!*

He had said the words back in Jason and Jamen's village. They had come to him so freely at the time. After all, it hadn't really been Tara's fault that she was born a Mainlander and Auni was born an Islander. She was never to blame for his circumstances.

He lifted her head out of the snow and felt for her breathing. She was still alive.

I forgive you.

He had said those words so quickly, so easily, because it was the thing to do. You were supposed to forgive people, right? And he loved Tara. She was his sister. Yet when he had said it, he had felt an emptiness in his stomach.

He lifted Tara's limp body. She was still breathing. He held her body close, trying to keep her warm.

I forgive you.

He didn't know what the emptiness had been. It wasn't anger. Bitterness? Maybe jealousy? She had lived such an easy life. He had been born into a sadistic system where someone else owned his body. It wasn't that he blamed her, but it was impossible not to have some animosity for the differences in their circumstances.

He adjusted Tara in his arms and began walking down the mountain, hoping he was going the right direction.

I forgive you.

For these past weeks he had sat with this unnerving feeling in his stomach. This knowledge that he had said the words yet part of him hadn't completely meant them.

But in the moment that the snow had cascaded down on them, the emptiness had dissolved.

"I forgive you."

Tara was his sister. She was his world. And despite her privilege and sometimes ignorance, despite her role and complacency, and despite everything he had endured, he forgave her.

"Auni?"

His eyes stung with tears. "Hey," he yelled over the roaring wind. "You alright?"

She blinked several times. "I think so. Are we the only two that—?" She stopped herself, as if saying it would make it true.

He hadn't had time to process that. He shook his head. "I'm not sure." But Tara was alive, and for now, that was enough. She tried to climb out of his arms, but he stopped her. "I'll carry you, don't worry. I don't want you to get cold." He held her against his body, trying to keep them both warm. The last thing they needed was frostbite.

It was amazing how easy it was to carry Tara. He had always been strong, but since he had left the plantation he had grown much taller, larger, and bulkier. He no longer went without meals like he used to. If they could not catch or find anything to eat, Sheik's magic provided them with whatever food they needed to sustain themselves.

Now he was nearly the same height as Kazzak, who had once seemed big to him. It was like all of his growing had been repressed until the night he and Tara escaped. Carrying her was practically nothing to him. He pulled her closer as she started to shiver.

But then he spotted it. "There's something up ahead." Auni placed her back down in case they needed to run.

A figure stood only thirty paces in front of them.

Sheik and Fang struggled through the snow together. They had heard more avalanches since wandering back west, but thankfully had not been caught up in any. Having not come across any of the others, Sheik felt a pang of guilt welling up inside of her.

If they were harmed, if they had died, it was her fault. She had forced them to take the hard way up the mountain side. The remorse beat through her veins. She could feel it throughout her entire body, weighing her down. Only an hour ago, she had cared about being the leader. About the others following her, no matter what. It seemed a stupid thought now. How immature had she been? She had wanted this group of people to call home, to call family, and yet she hadn't respected a thing they had said. What good was a family if she had gotten them all killed?

The thought of them dead hit her in the gut. They weren't dead, were they? No. She would find them all. They would be okay.

But when they escaped from the mountains, she was unsure what she would do. She certainly wouldn't be the leader. Part of her felt she was far too weak to continue on this journey at all. The reality had hit her during the avalanche. She was not invulnerable. She had nearly died.

It seemed as if the world had gone dim and lifeless. Everything she was fighting for had been shattered. She thought she had the power to save thousands. Did she even have the power to save her comrades? Part of her wanted to lie down in the snow and fall asleep, never to wake.

Something told her not to. Something picked up her feet and moved her forward, step by step.

She did not know why.

The more she thought about it, the more she realized that she had nothing to live for. After all, that was why she had started this crazy journey. All she had wanted was to find a place to belong. But the truth was, she did not belong.

Atarius had banished her.

He had cast her out, not wanting her. She had a hard time believing he really sent her to rescue the Sword of Elilah. He had given her no map, no direction. She hardly knew the lands she was traversing. She was too weak, too powerless to accomplish such a task. Atarius had probably made it all up just for an excuse to send her away.

And no one had ever asked her to fight the New Prosper. She was trying so hard to fight for these humans who she hardly understood. What was the point? Perhaps she would simply live as a hermit, just she and Fang, in one of the many forests. Perhaps that was where she belonged. Not with those who would cast her out. Not digging into human affairs. Simply on her own.

Perhaps that was the life she was meant to lead.

Focusing on her thoughts and merely staring at her feet, she had hardly noticed how far she and Fang had come. The weather was improving, the sleet easing up. It was still difficult to see. She glanced straight ahead, brushing her cloak out of her face. To her surprise, a figure was not far off. "Hello?" she called out.

It was Auni, holding Tara close to himself. "Dear Elilah!" she yelled, hope flooding into her cold body. "You aren't dead!" She sprinted towards them through the snow, Fang just behind her. "Is she alright?"

"I'm fine," Tara said. "Are you okay?" Sheik nodded. "Thank Ziad. We thought we might be the only survivors."

Sheik, in her excitement, hugged the two, relieved that at least they had lived. "I don't think we're too far from the edge of the mountains. The snow will lighten and it will be easier to see. Perhaps the others are okay, as well." It felt as if her entire body had been warmed with sunshine, though she knew very well she was not far from hypothermia.

The four continued down the side of the mountain, the journey slowly becoming easier and easier. Still, they were exhausted and freezing. Sheik was frigid from being buried alive, and Auni was growing noticeably tired.

"Do you want to take a short rest?" Sheik asked, now that they were out of the heavier weather. Auni nodded, and so she broke some bark from a tree and got a small fire going. They gathered around closely, trying to warm themselves. They ate a quick meal, consisting of Sheik's magic. It exhausted her to start the fire and then feed them all, but Sheik didn't complain about the growing headache. She deserved it. This was all her fault. "It shouldn't be much further until we're out of the snow," she muttered, trying to keep their morale high. "Then we can have a good rest. Find a cave or something."

The two nodded, both shivering. They all bundled together, trying to fight off the frigid weather. Even with a fire, the longer they stayed in the snow the likelier they were to freeze to death.

"Hey!" a voice called suddenly, startling them. It was Asroth. The large man seemed to travel easily through the snow, quickly reaching them. "Glad you all survived. Shouldn't we be hiking down, though?"

Sheik nodded. "We were just resting. You come across anyone else?"

"Carlos." He looked away, like he was afraid to make eye contact. "He was already dead by the time I reached him. Like I said, I'm glad you all survived."

"What?" The news hit her like an arrow in the chest. Dead? She held back tears. Carlos had not been with them long, but he had still saved Sheik and continuously helped everyone. He had been trying to turn his life around. He was a good man. He was dead. He was dead and it was Sheik's fault.

"We should keep hiking." Asroth's voice was monotone.

They rose together without a word and continued down the mountainside. They traveled in complete silence. Sheik let the numbness wash over her, because it was better than guilt. But she couldn't ignore reality. Carlos was dead. He had wanted to go around the mountains. She had said no. She had said no, and it had cost him his life. He had trusted her. And now he was dead. It was hard to believe. After all these bloody, violent battles they had fought without casualty, Carlos had died in the snow.

It was not long until they had broken away from the steep mountainside. The snow crunched beneath them without difficulty. Their vision was clear with no sleet to obstruct it. Knowing wyverns might be in the area, they quickly found a cave. They needed to rest up before making any decisions about where to go or what to do.

Sheik was not sure if she wanted to go anywhere or do anything. She was far too miserable to continue her fight against the New Prosper. All energy and hope that she had gained when she spotted Auni and Tara had been sapped out of her once again with the news of Carlos' death.

⁂

Jason shuffled around awkwardly, trying to loosen the snow packed around him. He waited for a moment, trying to figure out if he was upside down. Sure enough he was, the blood rushing into his head. He slowly turned himself right side up.

He had been traveling with his left arm skirn on. His right one was attached to his backpack, which he was unable to reach, but it was the left one he needed. Thrusting his body upwards, he beat against the solidifying snow with the bracer's spikes. With several more slams, the ice began to break apart and he dug his way out.

Lifting himself out of the pit, he looked around in hopes of spotting someone. "Hello?" There was no answer. "Dammit," he muttered, starting his trek down. Who knew where the others were. Perhaps dead, perhaps lost, perhaps still buried.

He headed westward, knowing he needed to escape the perilous mountains. After that he did not know what to do. If the others had died, there was no point in continuing the attack against King Garret. Perhaps he would simply accept the humiliation and return to his brother.

The skirn made it easy for him to travel. When he started to slip or fall, he simply needed to throw out his left arm and the spikes secured him. He could actually slide down some areas easier than hiking them.

In the distance, he spotted something, half buried. He quickened his pace, trying to get a better look. Finally, sliding down a slope with his skirn to help brace him, he recognized what it was.

Kazzak's lifeless body, lying in the snow.

CHAPTER 15

Faris overlooked the calm whiteness. There had been a blizzard two days ago. This was good. His father's return would be delayed, which would buy him time.

Someone was still poisoning his meals. He had needed to sneak food from the kitchen to keep up his strength. Despite his efforts, he was continuing to lose weight and constantly felt the pang of hunger.

Percy's leg was no longer troubling him, but the creature still had not left the garden. Faris was trying to come up with a way to get him out without the guards shooting him down. He had his own way of escaping. The secret tunnel underneath the fountain could be used in a pinch, even if the drop at the end did terrify him. But he could not leave Percy behind.

"Here," he mumbled, handing the pegasus a carrot. Percy took it gently. He was always gentle, unlike the wyverns Faris was forced to ride. He could not stand the clumsy beasts. They made such horrible screeching noises and beat their wings clumsily. They took unexpected turns and were difficult to control.

Fog was beginning to roll in. Perhaps the guards would not spot Percy. The wyverns could see fairly well through the fog, but the soldiers could not. It was the only chance Faris could think of. "Can you fly home?" he asked the animal, as if it understood him. "You know, fly?"

The pegasus stared at him blankly.

"Oh please," he cried, begging Percy to comprehend what he was saying. "Please, you need to fly away. If someone sees you, who knows what they'll do to you. Can't you go home?"

Faris sat down with a sigh. If only Percy could understand him. Maybe if he simply left, the pegasus would leave not long after. But he couldn't risk that. He didn't want the poor animal hurt.

A noise interrupted his thoughts. It was a low horn, echoing over the mountains. A sound Faris was all too familiar with. A deep, echoing call that was recognized by everyone in the palace.

It was the king's horn.

Faris felt his stomach tighten with sickness and fear. The world around him was spinning. How could his father be back so soon? He thought the blizzard would delay him at least another two or three days.

His father would soon find out that Faris had not died from the poisoning. The man would strangle him to death with his own two hands; the familial bond they shared meant nothing to Garret. The boy buried his face in his hands, trying not to cry.

Percy nudged the crown atop Faris' headscarf and gave out a small whine. "Oh, not now Percy. You don't understand," he whispered in an inaudible voice as he straightened his crown. Percy whinnied, pushing him harder. "What?" Faris asked, looking up at the pegasus.

The creature's head was lowered in a submissive fashion. Faris had read in the book what this stance meant. The pegasus was ready for a rider. He stood up, looking at Percy carefully. "I can ride you?" he asked as if expecting a response. "Won't I hurt you?"

The pegasus continued to keep his head low. The boy carefully pulled himself onto the creature's back, afraid of crushing him. Percy was stronger than he had expected. He pushed off the ground and beat his powerful wings. The pegasus began the ascension slowly, staying below the garden walls, as if allowing Faris a chance to get used to the concept of flying.

Faris knew flying all too well from riding wyverns. But Percy's movements seemed to flow, moving swiftly yet safely. When the pegasus finally started off, taking to the sky, Faris sighed in relief. They would escape together.

The sound of wyverns screeching echoed below them. The beasts could see through the fog. To the wyverns, Percy was an unfamiliar creature, meant to be attacked. They pulled at their chains angrily, snapping and screeching. But to the oblivious soldiers, the wyverns were simply growling at the air.

Faris held his breath, paranoid they might hear him exhale. Percy, though, soared high above them through the wintry air. Before he knew it, the pegasus began his graceful descent down the mountain side, far away from the palace.

"Where are we going?" Faris asked, realizing he had not been guiding the creature at all. He did not really know where to go. The castle had always been his home. He had never been anywhere else, and so, with a shrug of uncertainty, he allowed Percy to continue flying as he pleased.

━━◆━━

Sheik let out a large sigh, watching water drip from a stalactite. She, Fang, Tara, Auni, and Asroth had camped out in one of the many caves at the base of the Tasvran Mountains. Several days had gone by since escaping from the treacherous avalanche that had killed three of the group's members.

She stared at the dripping water. It splashed into a small dip on the floor of the cave, and then from there spilled over after precisely one hundred and twenty-four drops.

While she was bored beyond belief, she hardly had the motivation to leave the cave. The others went out repeatedly to hunt or simply get a breath of fresh air. While Asroth and Auni left her alone, Tara and Fang urged her to do something.

"Hey Sheik," Tara whispered into the darkness, pushing her way towards the back of the cave. "How are you feeling?" Sheik continued to count the drips of water, ignoring the young woman. "Please? Just answer me?"

Sheik let out yet another sigh. "Tara, you know plenty well."

The girl bit down on her lip, not wanting to upset her. "It's just that, Asroth was kind of wondering when we were going to move out. You know, continue fighting Spike. Or King Garret. Or whatever you had in mind."

"We aren't," she replied flatly.

Tara looked at her for a moment. "Sheik, please—"

"No," Sheik snapped, interrupting her. "*We* are not going any-where. *You* can leave whenever you want, but I'm staying here." She continued to stare at the dripping water as Tara left with a sigh.

Sheik simply did not have the energy to continue the trek. To fight in combat seemed unrealistic, as she could hardly lift herself from the rock she leaned against. It was uncomfortable, but she did not feel like she deserved to be comfortable. She deserved being cramped up alone in a dark, damp cavern.

She was responsible for their deaths.

Carlos, who had simply wanted to start a new life. Jason, who had so eagerly volunteered to help in their noble cause. And Kazzak, who had made her feel so safe, so welcome. The man who had joked with her, teased her, saved her, and treated her so kindly. And now they were all dead.

It made her want to cry, but she had been crying for days. She had no tears left, her eyes in a constant red and blurry state, swollen and tense.

Her body felt like it was shutting down. She had gotten sick and was hardly eating any food. Anytime she magically prepared food she would get a severe headache. Such simple magic had been easy when she was healthy, but now even the smallest bit of magic was physically and mentally draining. And sitting in her cramped position made her muscles sore and her joints ache. It was as if everything inside her was screaming misery. Nothing could bring her joy or relief. Her body, her mind, and her soul were all slowly dying.

She listened closely as Tara began whispering to Asroth. "She says she isn't leaving," the girl's timid voice spoke weakly.

"What?" Asroth roared. "She isn't—no! I'm sick of being cooped up in this little cave because she feels guilty over a few men. Three men are dead—three! And how many are dying as we waste time rotting in this forsaken mildew-stained cave?" The anger in his voice caused Sheik to glance over, wondering what the man might do.

Tara feebly replied, "I know. I am tired of it, too, but I think—"

"I don't care what you think!" he screamed, pushing her down. Tara fell, scraping her arms on the rock, and cried out. Auni leapt to his feet and punched Asroth in the face. The sorcerer's nose spewed blood. His hand first went to his face, instinctively protecting his bloody nose; then he swung back at Auni.

Sheik scrambled out of her stuck position as quickly as possible. "Stop!" she shouted as loudly as she could, her hoarse voice burning her throat.

Asroth spat the blood that had leaked into his mouth at Auni, who merely wiped it away with a glare. The boy retreated to Tara's side, helping her up and making sure she was okay while Asroth turned his attention to Sheik. "Oh good, you're willing to talk," he yelled at her. "Are we going to die in this damn cave, or are we going to fight?"

Sheik yelled back. "Hey, you're allowed to leave whenever you want. I'm not stopping you. No one is stopping you."

"Fine!" he retorted. "I'm more than happy to leave. You, you led us like a flock of sheep! Made us follow all your orders without wanting our opinion on any of it!" His face grew red as he screamed at her. "And now look, your stupid decisions got half of us killed! If you'd listened to the rest of us—but no! You make these decisions and force us into it. You can't ever just think things through, can you?" He stood there for an awkward moment, breathing heavily, blood still dripping from his nose. "Well, I'm done with you!" he finally concluded, turning and leaving them behind.

The three stood in silence. They had always dealt with arguments, but nothing like this. Sheik held her composure for a moment before sitting down and bursting into tears.

As much as she hated to admit it, everything Asroth had said was right.

Auni examined Tara's scraped up arm for a second longer, then bent down next to Sheik and whispered quietly, "What he said isn't true."

Sheik did not bother lifting her head up, too ashamed and depressed. She wanted to acknowledge his words, but she could not even bring herself to grunt without her nose running.

"Yeah," Tara piped up. "You know Asroth. He's just mad." She let out a small grin. "He's always mad."

Sheik managed a small tearful chuckle before growing serious again. "He's right though. I... I'm," she stuttered for a moment. "It's my fault they're dead. I failed." She said it again, this time with more force. "I failed all of you. You'd be better off without me, so just leave."

Tara laughed. "We are family, Sheik. We are not going to leave you."

She glanced up at their faces. They were both so young but had grown so much since Sheik had met them. "Really?"

"Of course! Why else do you think we are here with you? We aren't sheep, as much as Asroth likes to think that we might be that stupid. We are not following you thoughtlessly. They..." she trailed off for a moment, tears coming to her eyes. "They did not die following you against their will. They wanted to follow you to the death." She paused. "And so they did."

Tara began to cry and Sheik couldn't hold it in either. She was too overcome with emotion. Thoughts of her friends dying. Had they really thought of her as family? Had she finally found the family she had always wanted, only now to lose them?

She tried to dry her tears and calm her puffy eyes. "I just," she stuttered. "I just want to stop. I want to forget all this fighting nonsense."

Auni leaned in close to her. "Do you remember when you asked about the R on my shoulder?" Sheik gave him a puzzled look. It was so long ago. But she did indeed remember the morning they had sat together on the rooftop in Calert. She nodded. "It means runaway," he explained. "That's what it stands for. I was a slave, and I tried to run away. They caught me and branded me. That was the lowest moment of my life."

Sheik said nothing. Now she understood why he had responded so curtly when she had asked about the R. What a terrible question she had asked him. She sucked in her breath as he said more.

"I didn't want to live with an R branded into me. Slaves with R's get more work. They get beaten for practically nothing. If it had been up to me, I would have lay there until I died. I wanted to die." He glanced over to Tara. "But then Tara helped me get back up. She made me try again. And we're here to help you try again, too. Don't give up yet, Sheik."

The elf, contemplating his words, remained silent, and so Auni continued. "I know what you feel like. It's different, but you've got an R right now too. I know you feel like you can't go on. Like life itself has beaten you." Everything he said echoed inside her. The avalanche had shown her how powerless she was. This was a war she couldn't win.

"But you're only beaten when you quit. The men that died believed in you. Don't let them down. Tara and I, we still believe in you. Don't let us down. And even if you don't feel like it right now, you believe in yourself, too. Don't let yourself down."

He was right. She couldn't give up.

Spike was still out there, his army destroying town after town. Their job wasn't done yet. She felt weak, empty, and hopeless. But she had the power to stand back up. The power to rise despite her failures. To conquer despite her fears. She overruled her own life; it did not rule her.

<hr>

Asroth stormed out of the cave into the cold, open air. He still could not believe that the boy had struck him in the face. He had wanted to use his dark magic. To kill him. To feel the life sucked out of him. Yet something had stopped him.

Even still, he desired to turn back around and burn a hole through the boy's heart. He did not bother though. He never wanted to see that group again. It had all been a great big waste of a time. For the past six months he had endangered his life for them, and what had he gotten out of it?

Nothing.

He had wanted fame, but for some reason the stupid elf had stolen all of it. No one had appointed her their leader, and yet she was. And because of her unique race, everyone remembered her, despite that Asroth was much more talented and experienced. He deserved the fame and glory for their successes.

He had also wanted money to begin a study. To further his knowledge. But he had hardly gotten a single coin since joining up with the group. He would have been better off simply fighting in the arenas back in Calert.

Asroth thought for a moment. If he had stayed in Calert, he would not have had the pleasure of Tara. But then he rolled his eyes and faced the truth: he had gotten nowhere with her. It would have been better if he had simply spent his time in whore houses.

It was time to move on now. As much as he wanted to seek revenge against them, the proverb of Ziad echoed in his mind: the best revenge was living well. And it would be. Sheik would suffer the consequences of trying to get along without him. Perhaps someday they would come crawling back to him, begging for mercy.

He smiled a bit.

It would only be a matter of time before they realized how essential he was to their little group. He was one of two healers, one of two magic users, and the sole sorcerer able to command the power of death. He was an unstoppable force and, if they ever got out of that damn cave and entered combat again, they would realize how imperative he had been. They would be slaughtered.

In that moment he went so far as to consider joining this man, Spike, who wanted them dead so much. With how talented Asroth was, the man would probably pay him plenty. And then Asroth would have the pleasure of fighting Sheik in battle.

He imagined the moment. Watching her eyes widen as she saw the foe she was facing. Being the cause of her death. It sent a pleasurable chill down Asroth's spine.

No.

He reminded himself of the proverb. He must simply move on. The others would struggle without him and that would be punishment enough.

As he muttered under his breath, trying to decide where to go and what to do, something caught his eye. A strange white shape floating in the sky. It was difficult to see with the thick fog swirling about, but he could tell it was moving too fast to be a cloud. It was too large to be a bird. He craned his neck and squinted, trying to examine it.

Then all of a sudden it was heading straight towards him.

Asroth dove to the ground, attempting to get out of its way. It barely missed him, flying just over his head. The creature was a white horse with large wings—a pegasus! He had heard of such beasts before, though only in books and stories.

Atop the creature was a young Tasvranian boy, perhaps fifteen, whose body launched forward as the pegasus landed. His chest plate clattered against the ground and a chunk of his armor seemed to pierce into his side. Gilded armor, Asroth noted, seeing how fancily the gold was etched into the shoulder plates. Under his armor, his clothes were thick and flowing, covered in patterns that Asroth could only assume were typical of the Tasvran. The wounded boy clutched his head in pain with one hand and his ribs with the other.

Asroth stared at him blankly and rose to his feet, confused where a pegasus would have come from and why someone so young and wealthy might be riding it. The boy was only conscious for a moment before his arms fell limp. Asroth pulled the chest plate off him. It had bent and pierced into him because of the hard impact with the ground, and now blood began to gather up in a puddle around his side. It was too much for Asroth to heal alone.

The pegasus bent over and whined, nudging the dying boy's cheek with its nose. "Tara!" Asroth shouted, running back towards the cave. He needed a second healer, and with the strange occurrence, he had completely forgotten about their fight. Completely forgotten about the anger that had been pulsing through his veins only minutes ago. "Tara!"

CHAPTER 16

Sheik had pulled herself up from the ground and completely dried her eyes. Though they were still puffy from crying, she smiled. She had been thanking both Auni and Tara before the shout interrupted her. "Tara!"

What in the world was Asroth doing back? He looked frantic as he ran towards the mouth of the cave. She wanted to say a snide comment, something rude to encourage him to turn around and leave them be. She honestly thought they might be better off without the man. But before words could form in her mouth, he continued his shouting.

"Tara, quick, I need a healer." The girl folded her arms and glanced him up and down, as if implying that he did not look wounded and that she was not planning on healing him even if he was hurt. "No, not me!" he explained. "A boy, he just fell from the sky on a pegasus!" Sheik was not even sure what a pegasus was, and seeing Tara and Auni's expression, she guessed that they did not know either. "Aren't you going to help?" Asroth demanded again. "He looks like he's rich and, well, aren't you curious?"

Ah, Sheik noted. He was curious. She thought there had to be some sort of ulterior motive for him to want to heal someone. He usually was not fond of helping others unless it got him something in return. "Come on," she answered with the slightest roll of her eyes. Tara, too, acted put off, and Auni held a serious composure as the small group followed Asroth.

Sure enough, there was a young boy bleeding terribly. And next to him an odd, winged creature, much like a horse. Sheik had never seen anything like it. "Whoa!" Tara exclaimed, walking up to it like she might pet it.

Asroth jerked her away, pulling her towards the boy on the ground. "Come on, help me heal him," he muttered angrily, upset with her lack of focus.

"Right," she replied. She opened her mouth to say more but closed it again when she realized she was speaking to Asroth. Still mad, she helped heal the boy in silence.

Sheik and Auni watched them. They both let out a small wince as they healed the boy. His wounds were severe, and the pair quickly grew exhausted. Auni leaned down and took Tara's hand, making sure she was alright.

Fang, who had followed the group, carefully trotted around the pegasus in a circle, viewing it both as predator and prey. He let out a low growl and the pegasus returned it with an arrogant snort. "Not now Fang," Sheik mumbled, but turned her attention away from the animals as the mysterious boy coughed.

"What's going on?" he asked, glancing at the four surrounding him. "Who are you, what's happened?" His accent was thick, but Sheik could easily discern the fear from the expression on his face.

Asroth spoke first. "You fell off your pegasus when it landed. We've just healed you." There was a quick moment of silence before he began questioning. "So who are you, what's with the fancy outfit, and how in Ziad's name did you get a pegasus?" he asked all at once.

The boy looked up at them either too terrified to answer or perhaps merely unsure. Sheik bent down next to him. "Don't worry," she replied with a smile. "I'm Sheik. This is Asroth, and Tara and Auni." She glanced to Asroth. "Let's get him back to the cave. We can figure out who he is then," she offered gently.

Asroth nodded and pulled the boy to his feet. He let out a gasp, clutching his side. Sheik winced, watching him limp. Auni silently went to his side and helped him alongside Asroth. It sure had been a strange day, Sheik thought absentmindedly, as Fang and the pegasus trotted behind them, warily eyeing each other.

***

Sheik gazed into the burning fire. It was warm, something she had not felt in quite some time. She snacked on her own food while the others ate something they had hunted earlier. The boy ate eagerly, as if he had eaten as little as Sheik had over the past week. Aside from his clear hunger, he was perfectly healthy now that Asroth had done a second round of healing.

She studied him silently. He was clearly human, with the typical rounded ears and creased eyelids. His skin was golden brown, almost the color of Auni's. His hair had a slight curl to it and Sheik had trouble telling in the dim lighting if it was black or dark brown. He avoided eye contact, and Sheik wondered why he seemed so terrified of them.

"So will you tell us your name now?" Asroth asked.

The boy glanced at them again before nodding. "I'm Faris."

"It's nice to meet y—" Sheik began before she was rudely interrupted by a shout.

"The prince?" Asroth exclaimed. "Faris the prince, as in, King Garret's son! That's why your armor has gold and why you're riding a pegasus!" he shouted wildly.

Tara and Auni's jaws dropped in surprise. Faris averted his eyes once again. Sheik caught him glancing towards the cave entrance and she worried he might make a dash for it.

Asroth let out a cruel chuckle. "Well, this makes everything easier. We'll just hold him hostage to get his father to surrender. And King Garret's little army of wyverns will soon dissolve," he said with a smile.

Sheik was about to speak up that she would not allow taking the innocent boy hostage, but Faris interrupted first. "Your plan won't work!" he yelled. "My father wants me dead. He'll be happy for you to do it for him!"

Asroth merely replied, "Sure, kid," with a roll of his eyes. Sheik couldn't tell if Faris was lying to save his own skin. There was no way to know for sure. But why would a prince be out on his own?

"I'm serious! Please! He tried to have me poisoned! That's why I was running away! He doesn't want me," he finally whimpered, tears welling up in his eyes.

Asroth glanced at Faris. The boy's cheeks were stained with tears, though he emitted no sound of crying. He merely sat still, his eyes averted as they misted over. "Fine," Asroth replied. "We won't hold you hostage. Just," he hesitated, as if unsure what to do with the boy, "just stop crying."

Sheik was shocked at Asroth's sudden change of heart. She didn't think she'd ever seen him so sympathetic.

She lifted an arm to Faris' shoulder and gave it a squeeze. "Don't worry, none of us are going to hurt you. Why don't you get some rest? You seem exhausted."

Faris gave a quiet nod and left the fire to go lay by his pegasus, who was just at the mouth of the cave. Sheik stood and went towards the back of the cave where she had been staying in her lonely depression. She felt much better now. Kazzak lay heavily on her mind, along with Carlos and Jason. But she did not feel hopeless.

It was still her fault. She had made a poor decision, and she had made it without everyone's consent. It wouldn't happen again.

Tara and Auni's devotion to her, the fact that they had stuck with her despite her errored judgement, despite her depression, had shown her just how much they cared for her. She didn't belong because she was the leader, the tactician. She belonged because they loved her and were going to stand by her side.

And together, they were going to stop King Garret's wyverns. Together, they would stop Spike's tyrannous reign.

Asroth, sulking as usual, stayed sitting by the fire while Tara and Auni came towards Sheik at the back of the cave. "Hey guys," Sheik said with a light smile, trying to prove she was okay. She did not need the two worrying for her anymore.

"Hi," Tara replied simply, glancing at her as if to check if she was crying. She wasn't.

"So you think he's cute?" Sheik asked, trying to lighten the mood. Tara thought every guy they came across was cute, so Sheik considered it a valid question. She was surprised when Tara only shrugged.

"I suppose so," the girl replied. "Why?" Suddenly her face lit up. "Do you like him?" she asked excitedly.

Sheik couldn't help but laugh. "I think he's a bit young for me," she grinned instead of quite plainly saying no. The boy looked about fifteen, though she could not say for sure, and Sheik was now twenty and a half.

Tara laughed too, though it seemed like she was merely happy to see Sheik smiling and joking again. "Yeah, I think he is a bit young for me, too. I am eighteen you know," she added matter-of-factly.

"Well, he's the perfect age for me," Auni chimed in with a smirk.

Tara and Sheik laughed some more. "Is that so?"

Auni shrugged. "Sure. I think he's cute. Besides, he's a prince. That's gotta count for something." Sheik couldn't quite tell if he was serious or joking to make her feel better. It didn't really matter much to her; she was just glad to be talking and laughing again. Of course, joking around reminded her of Kazzak.

She tried not to think about him. She forced herself not to think about him. She consciously told herself to not think about him, but her thoughts were interrupted by Tara's voice. "What?" Sheik asked, realizing she had completely missed what the girl had said.

Tara laughed. "Forget it," she said, waving it away. Sheik figured it was just another comment about the prince, anyway. "I'm going to sleep. You should, too."

Sheik nodded, knowing a long night's rest would do her good. Despite how bored she had been in her depression, she had hardly allowed herself to sleep. But if they were going to wage this war against King Garret, she would need to be in good health. "Goodnight," she said quietly as Tara and Auni moved to their own section of the cave.

⚬

Sheik leaned over and gave the boy a light shake on the shoulder, waking him up. "Faris," she spoke gently. "Er, Prince Faris," she added, thinking it might be rude to address him without his formal title.

The boy blinked several times, allowing his eyes to adjust to the morning light. "Yes?" he asked, his voice a bit hoarse. He looked like he might be scared, or perhaps just not used to being woken up. "Sheik, wasn't it?" he said as he sat up a bit.

"Yeah," she replied, crouching down next to him. "I thought maybe we could go for a walk?" It sounded odd as the words left her mouth, and Sheik was reminded of her conversation with Tara the night before. She was glad the girl was not awake to hear her, or else Sheik might have gotten teased for the strange request.

He gave her a curious, almost suspicious look before nodding. "Alright," he said in a cautious tone as he picked himself up off the ground. She led the way and he followed carefully behind her, glancing back nervously as if someone might be sneaking up on him.

Once they were far enough away from the others, Sheik began speaking. She was glad she was the first one to wake. The first to talk to Faris. Asroth would have simply scared him. "Do you know where you're going, Prince?" Sheik asked, not knowing how else to start the conversation.

"Huh?" he replied, unsure what she meant.

"You said you were running away. I believe you, but do you know where you're running to?" she clarified.

Faris' face turned blank. "Oh. No, I guess not," he replied. Asroth would have instantly taken that as a sign that he was lying about running away. But she just felt sorry for the boy. He reminded her of herself, when she had first left Atarius' village. "I just wanted to get away from my father," Faris added when Sheik did not reply. "I didn't have any plans after that."

"I see." Sheik thought for a moment longer. "I would love for you to come with us so we can help you find somewhere, but I'm afraid we cannot," she explained as gently as possible. "Do you know who Spike is?"

The prince nodded. "My father has been having meetings with him. He's the leader of the New Prosper."

Sheik frowned a bit, unsure if Faris thought of the man as a villain or a hero. "Well, the New Prosper has been going town by town, recruiting and killing. We're trying to stop them. To stop Spike. Your father," she trailed off for a moment, not wanting to frighten him. "Your father has been aiding Spike," she finished finally.

Faris was silent for a moment, as if in contemplation. "I know," he spoke up quietly. It was clear he also knew what this implied—that Sheik and her friends were trying to kill his father. They walked several more paces in silence until they reached a stream. Faris bent over it to get a drink and wash his face, and after watching him a moment longer, Sheik did the same.

She had not ventured this far from the cave before. She had not even known there was a stream. There were trees around, but they were sparse compared to a real forest. Still she took in the beauty of it before continuing the morbid conversation. "So that's why you can't exactly come with us."

He nodded, listening carefully. "How is it you're going to stop my father?" he asked, his voice still quiet.

Sheik let out a small sigh. "I'm sorry, Prince Faris. I'm sure you already know the answer to that." It hurt her knowing that the man they were going to kill had such a sweet son. Perhaps they could simply reason with him, she thought. After all, she hated killing. But then she remembered King Garret was nothing like his son. He wanted Faris dead.

The prince interrupted her thoughts. "I know you're going to kill him. I meant how are you going to climb up the mountain, get into his palace, and assassinate him without being killed yourself?"

She paused, staring into the water of the stream as she found a rock to sit down on. Despite that they were off the mountain, the air was still extremely cold. After all, it was winter, and everything was covered in light snow. Kazzak had told her the winters out on the plains could become quite treacherous. She could not imagine anything worse than the snowy mountains, but she knew to prepare herself for something similar as winter wore on.

She looked back up at Faris with the slightest smile on her face. "I guess neither of us really thought out our plans very well, did we?"

He let out a small, almost depressing chuckle. "Guess not." The two of them listened to the sound of the stream. Sheik let out a small shiver. "Want to get back to the cave?" Faris asked, noticing her chills.

She nodded. With a small fire going, the cave warmed up quite well. She stood up and waited for Faris to follow. He did not, and instead continued to stare at the water. "Faris? I mean, Prince Faris?" she asked.

He chuckled again. "You don't need to call me prince," he said softly. "Just Faris will do." He turned to face her and paused, hesitant to say something. "May I ask what you are?" he finally asked.

Sheik smiled a bit. She supposed with how far away they were from elven lands, Faris might not have known. It was obvious there was something different about her; her hair was green, her skin a different hue, and her eyelids without a crease. "I'm an elf," she explained. "I'm pretty far from home."

"Oh?" he asked. "Why is that?"

She thought for a moment, not really wanting to get into Atarius banishing her. She was growing sick of telling that story. "I suppose you could say I ran away, too," she said finally.

Faris seemed to think about this for a moment. "Do you ever wish you had not?"

Sheik exhaled sharply. "I guess so. But only because I wish the circumstances could have been different." She wished Atarius had proposed. She wished he had told her how much he loved her. She wished he hadn't provoked her into a standoff where they both stubbornly refused to back down.

"Me too," Faris said wistfully. "I wish my father wasn't the man he was. I wish I didn't have to do this."

"Do what?" Sheik studied him.

He sighed and stood back up. "I wish I didn't have to help you."

Sheik shook her head. "You don't have to help us. You can stay here. Or you can run. We aren't going to hold you captive."

But Faris shook his head. "You're going to do this regardless. I might as well help. I don't want any of this to be the way it is. Like you said, I wish the circumstances could have been different. But if my father is going to be the man he is, you need to stop him. And if you need to kill him, then I should be there to assume the throne. I'm not going to run away."

"If we fail," Sheik whispered, "he's going to kill you."

"I will not run."

⸎

Faris finished his quick sketch onto the frosted dirt and tossed the stick aside. "There," he said, announcing it was done. It was crude but would serve its purpose.

On their walk back to the cave, Faris had explained how he had never confronted his father before. He had led a life of running. But he was not going to run anymore. His father had always hated him because he was weak, timid, and afraid. But now, Faris would prove his father wrong. He would be strong, bold, and courageous.

Sheik, though admiring his new-found strength, did not want the boy to be the one to kill his father. Faris did not argue with her, only insisting that he should come to take charge immediately after the deed was done. With luck, he could prove his power to his soldiers, and they would follow him as obediently as they followed his father.

"Come look," the boy said, motioning for the others to gather around him. They glanced at his sketch. "There's a secret trail here

322

for if soldiers get knocked off their wyverns on the southwestern side and can't fly back. The normal south entrance is here, but over here is another entrance in that leads straight to the palace gardens. No one knows about it besides me. It's a tunnel, though, so I don't think Asroth could fit." He looked up at each of the others, studying their build. "The rest of you should be fine."

Auni gave a simple nod. "We'll go if you need us, Sheik."

"No," Asroth interrupted. "Tara should stay behind. She might get in the way, if she got hurt or something."

Tara shook her head. "What if they got hurt? They'd need someone to heal them."

"Maybe Asroth's right," Sheik spoke up, mostly to avoid another argument. They had all forgiven each other, though not formally, and were working together again. The last thing they needed was another fight. "It might be better if she stayed behind."

"Then I'm staying too," Auni added sternly.

Faris gave Sheik a small smile. He knew nothing of their previous fight, and so found their disputing funny. But Sheik noted the tension between everyone. "So just you and me?" the boy asked her.

"Looks like it," she replied, trying to smile back, hoping everyone would get along while she was gone. A part of her feared coming back to a fight between the three. "Leave tonight?"

"Actually, we should leave right now," he explained. "It will be night by the time we get close enough for them to spot us. Especially since it's winter."

Sheik nodded and turned back to the other three. "Well hopefully we'll see you tomorrow afternoon or so," she said as enthusiastically as possible, so they would not think about the possibility of their death. Tara gave Sheik a hug, which the woman chuckled at but returned. "Don't worry."

Scratching Fang behind the ear, she whispered to him, "I'll be back tomorrow." He let out a small whine, upset she was leaving when she had only recently started to feel better. "Goodbye," she said again to all of them, following behind Faris.

<hr />

Sheik pulled herself on top of another ledge, letting out a long exhale. "How much further?" she asked Faris, who scrambled just a bit ahead of her.

She was not used to the rockiness of the mountain, nor the bitter cold and the slippery ice. Even with gloves, the snow made her hands freeze as she pulled herself higher up the mountain, and the ice made her feet slip out from under her occasionally. It would be so much easier to scale using her magic, but she was afraid of how it might affect her. She hadn't fully recovered and the last thing she needed was a splitting headache as they ascended deadly cliffs and snuck into enemy territory.

Faris glanced back at her as he pointed a ways up. "See that bush there?" he asked, pointing to a leafless, dead plant. Sheik gave a nod.

"That's right where the entrance is. It's just buried in snow," he explained, as they were unable to see it from where they stood.

The elf looked down, seeing how far they had come. At first the path had been easy, ascending at a slow rate, as if they were merely walking uphill. But the closer they came to the kingdom, the more they needed to stay away from the path. To stay clear of any soldiers or wyverns.

And now, as she looked downwards, she saw how steep it was. They had begun climbing at a nearly vertical angle since leaving the path, hiding behind rocks and patches of snow. She inhaled sharply upon seeing the descent. "Don't look down," she muttered quietly.

Faris merely chuckled. "We're almost there," he reassured her, pulling himself up a bit higher and extending an arm to her. He helped lift her up alongside him. "But it looks like we'll need to jump," he mumbled as he examined the gap between where they were and where the bush was.

Sheik rubbed her forehead. "I'll create a ledge with my magic," she offered. Jumping across an icy ledge was far too dangerous to attempt. It would be worth the headache.

"You have magic?" he exclaimed.

She nodded. "Yeah, just give me a second."

"What are you going to do?" he asked cautiously. She noticed his stance had changed. He had taken a step back, like he was scared.

"I told you, just create a ledge. What's wrong?"

He took in a deep breath. "I've never met a magic user besides healers. They're dangerous. If there are even rumors that someone can use magic, my father has them put to death."

Every time she learned something new about King Garret, she hated him more and more. "Magic is dangerous," she admitted. "But it's also incredibly helpful." She focused carefully on the small space between their current ledge and the ledge they needed to reach. Rock protruded from the mountainside and formulated in the air, providing a small but sufficient path for them to cross. She motioned for Faris to go first.

The boy studied her for longer than she would have preferred before taking a nervous step onto the magical ledge. With his back hugging the side of the mountain, he sidestepped across quickly. Her head throbbed. She crossed as fast as possible so she could drop her magic.

Together they dug at the snow to reveal the tunnel. "Come on," Faris said, entering it headfirst. He was completely submerged into the darkness, and Sheik hardly could keep up with him as he crawled further and further in.

"How long is it?" she whispered. The sun had just set as they entered the tunnel, and she hoped the sky would be pitch black by the time they reached the opening.

Faris gave as good of a shrug as he could in the tight, cramped space. "I'm not sure, to be honest." It seemed to stretch on and on. Knowing he had been through it before, she at least was not worried that they might suddenly reach a dead end. The tight walls were restricting, and panic welled up inside her. But there was no chance of getting lost. Just one simple tunnel leading inside the palace. The gardens to be exact, Sheik remembered.

The boy had told her they were quite beautiful, despite that they were overgrown with weeds and the fountains were cracked and old. She had never seen a garden, cultivated by people instead of nature. She thought it an interesting concept and was curious to see it.

"Here," Faris announced, standing up to his full height. Sheik could see dim light, either from stars or the moon, flooding into the tunnel. It was no longer as tight or cramped, and she could smell burnt ash.

"What's that smell?"

"I'm not sure. Help me up?" Sheik scrambled over to him, giving him a push off so he could reach the solid ground above them and climb out. "Dear Ziad," he whispered.

"What is it?" Sheik asked, still trying to pull herself out of the tunnel and into the garden. Faris stuck out his hand, which she accepted, and helped her up. Brushing herself off before looking around, it took her a moment to notice what Faris had so instantaneously discovered.

The entire garden had been reduced to ash. Any plants that might have once existed here had withered up and gone, intentionally burned. Several smaller fountains remained intact, but the main fountain had been smashed apart. Faris' eyebrows furrowed. He made no sound, simply staring at his defiled garden.

After a moment, Sheik laid a light hand on his shoulder, but he shrugged it off and silently turned towards one of the archways that led into the palace halls. She followed after him, quickly and quietly. With a glance towards the dark hallway, Faris led her through the shadows. He seemed to have better night vision than she did, and so she trusted his every step. Likewise, he relied on her good hearing to stop him when she could hear the footsteps of a guard approaching.

Between long pauses in the shadows and silent creeping through the many complicated halls, Faris eventually stopped at a door. Sheik went for the handle but found it would not turn. It was locked. And unlike most locks she had seen that were separate from the handle and could easily be warped away with magic, this one was built into the door handle.

Great. How were they supposed to sneak in? If she used magic to disappear the handle entirely, she wasn't sure she could open the door. And if she disappeared the hinges at the same time, the door would clatter to the ground and Garret would hear them.

She remembered how Kazzak had told her about the pins inside locks, so long ago in Calert. Perhaps she could pick the lock? But she didn't have anything like Kazzak's tools on her. No slim strips of metal with curves and grooves.

Perhaps, though, her magic could substitute a lock pick. She had never worked magic on something she could not see, but she thought she would give it a try. It was simply a matter of being able to imagine inside the lock as if it were in front of her like any other object.

She concentrated for a moment, imagining the inside of the lock. She thought back to that day in Calert, how Kazzak had helped guide her hand to move one of the pins. A minute went by before she knew she was altering the right thing.

Then the pins in the lock clicked as she changed their positions with her magic. She quickly grabbed and twisted the handle before she lost her concentration. Faris, still astonished by her magic, stared with wide eyes at the lock Sheik had managed to get open. He followed carefully behind her as she entered the room.

It was the largest room Sheik had ever seen before. Everything was elaborate, laced with golden designs. Along the walls hung many weapons, mostly lances, but some swords and axes, too. It was astounding.

And in the center of it, emitting a loud snore, was King Garret. He laid on top an oversized bed, covered with several blankets made of animal furs. She edged closer to the monstrous man.

"Sheik!" Faris whispered sharply. But his warning came too late. As Sheik took a step closer to the bed, she tripped over a small wire running along the floor. Tied to several weapons on the wall, the string pulled tight and caused them to come noisily crashing down.

King Garret awoke groggily, rising from his bed slowly until he locked eyes with the intruder. Sheik hardly knew what else to do, so she fumbled with an arrow, nocking it clumsily to her bow, and letting it fly towards the beast of a man.

It pierced Garret's left shoulder, but he ripped it out with ease, as if he hardly felt a sting. Climbing out of the bed, he revealed his great size. He was twice as wide as Sheik and towered over her despite a hunch.

Sheik aimed another arrow, straight for his heart. His heart. He would die in an instant.

She hesitated and loosed the arrow just to the right. With enough arrows into his arms, he would be unable to fight. It merely grazed the large man's thick skin and she reminded herself that she was not here to disarm him. She was here to kill him.

The king's fist flew at her. It was quicker than she had expected, but she managed to dodge it. When she tried for the third arrow, his other hand came crashing into her.

For a split second she felt fear.

Then pain.

Garret's fist, large enough to hit both her eye and her nose in one punch, seemed to shatter the left half of her face.

Her nose made a sickening crunch and blood spewed out. She could feel it draining down her face, but she could not see it. Her eye felt like it had burst, the left half of her vision cloudy with blood.

She slumped to the ground, the pain overwhelming, and clutched her eye and nose protectively. Her nose was bent out of position and hurt far too much to touch. And as blood continued to gather up in her swelled eye, she knew she was soon about to lose all vision. The last thing she would ever see was Garret's massive body stepping closer to her.

CHAPTER 17

Faris watched in horror as his father shattered Sheik's nose and eye. She crumpled to the ground in a bloody heap. He was not sure if she was dead or unconscious or simply in too much pain to move as his father towered over her.

The man reached out to grab Sheik by the hair, to pull her to her feet. But Faris was quicker. Pulling a lance from the wall, he slapped the tip of it against Garret's hand. "Father," he said simply, watching the man's eyes.

Garret let out a low rumble of a laugh. "You're back. Where have you been?"

Faris glared. "I know you tried to have me poisoned."

"You didn't want to be poisoned, but you're okay being killed by my bare hands?" he asked with a sadistic smirk.

"I do not plan on dying. And I do not plan on running." His legs were shaking, but he forced his voice not to waver. "You always wanted me to be strong, to be courageous. Well, grab a weapon," he said, motioning to the many weapons still on the wall.

The massive man did as he was told, grabbing a halberd from the floor, where it had fallen when Sheik had sprung the trap. He swung it quickly and unexpectedly, but Faris jumped back in time. He had never been offensive when he was forced to spar, but dodging was something he could do.

Garret swung again, the halberd smashing into several weapons on the wall. With all the noise, several guards had come to Garret's room. But, after discovering the assassin was the prince, they stepped away from the battle. None of the knights knew each other's allegiances. Revealing their loyalties by helping Garret or Faris could get them killed.

"This is precisely why I wanted you dead," Garret boomed. "All you can do is dodge, little mouse. Fight me!" He lifted his arms, taunting Faris, testing him, proving he was too scared to strike.

But Faris was not afraid. He lunged forward, piercing Garret's leg. The man cried out in pain. He grabbed the spear and ripped it out, throwing Faris to the ground along with the weapon.

"So the mouse can bite, eh?" Fear pulsed through Faris, but he quickly hopped back onto his feet. "But you are no leader."

"And you are?" Faris screamed back. He tried not to cry, but tears always sprang to his eyes when he yelled. "Your own soldiers despise you!" He grabbed another lance to defend himself with as Garret rushed at him once again. "Look at them," he pointed vaguely at the crowd that had gathered. "Why aren't they helping you?"

This seemed to strike a nerve. Garret roared and swung about wildly. Faris continued to dodge and deliver quick strikes for several minutes. It was like taking down a wyvern with dinner utensils. No matter how many times Faris stabbed Garret, and no matter how much the man bled, he continued to fight back, hardly showing signs of pain.

"You are not fit for the crown! I will not allow it!" Garret shouted as he stumbled back, slightly out of breath.

Finally, Faris saw his opening. The king had left his chest exposed. With a thrust as quick and powerful as lightning, Faris drove his spear into the man's heart.

Garret's head snapped upwards, looking Faris in the eye. For a moment, Faris was afraid that perhaps even a blow to the heart could not kill the tyrant. But he was wrong. The king slumped to the ground, though his head continued to look up into Faris' wide eyes.

He looked like he might say something, but his face was still. The man's unclosing eyes made it difficult to tell if he was dead or not, and it took Faris a moment to relax the hand that still tightly held one end of the spear.

He looked to Sheik's motionless body. "Healer!" he cried out to the nearest guard. They probably assumed it was for him. To his own surprise, he did not seem to have even a scratch on him. The knight took off and Faris went to Sheik's side, placing a hand on her head. "Sheik?" he whispered quietly, listening to her breathing carefully. At least she was alive.

Faris stood back up and went to a chest of drawers where the king's horn was kept when not around Garret's neck. Faris placed the string over his neck and breathed a loud call through the horn.

Soldiers came rushing towards the sound and, despite the many guards already surrounding Faris, he continued to blow the horn, calling everyone to him as he marched out of the room. The halls were big enough for everyone to hear him.

Raising up the king's horn, Faris watched as soldiers bowed down to him on one knee. He felt fear in his stomach at the speech he was about to give to these hundreds of men. But he thought of the courage he had in facing his father and tapped into that strength once again.

"I have slain my father!" he began, his words loud, echoing through the halls. "I am your new king. I have displayed the strength and bravery it takes to rule you as my father did. However, I also plan to do what my father did not."

He took in a deep breath, as people listened carefully, curious as to what he was going to say. Faris himself hardly knew what to say. "I will show kindness and mercy," he decided after the long pause, trying to think of the things he had always wanted from his father. "And freedom," he added, thinking about all the people his father had ordered to be killed for speaking against him.

"This has always been a nation of fear. But no longer. This will be a country of peace. That does not mean I am afraid to go to war," he explained. "But I will not lead soldiers into war for the sake of land, for the sake of treasure, for the sake of bloodshed and death. I will only lead soldiers into war for the sake of peace."

⎯⎯ ◆ ⎯⎯

Asroth warmed his hands by the small fire. He hated that Auni had stayed behind with Tara. The boy was no better than the wolf or the pegasus. They were all animals. Especially when compared to Asroth himself.

Tara was napping towards the back of the cave while Auni just stared into the fire. The tension was awkward, Asroth and Auni often glancing at each other then quickly averting their eyes. They both knew they disliked each other, if not hated each other. And yet they worked together for Ziad knew why. Perhaps to destroy the New Prosper. Perhaps because of Sheik. Asroth hardly knew why he was back with this group when he had been so close to leaving before.

Auni stood up. "I'm going to get some more firewood," he mumbled as he left the cave, eyeing Asroth carefully.

Asroth merely nodded his head in reply. Waiting for the boy to leave, he moved towards the back of the cave. He stood over Tara's quietly breathing body for a moment.

Tara was a heavy sleeper. Auni snored, but Tara always managed to sleep through it. Asroth knelt next to her, his fingers running through her hair. How he longed for her. If she could only see him for the great and powerful man he was, she, too, would long for him. He ran a finger across her cheek, down her neck. She turned but did not wake. His heart pounded, ravenous for her flesh.

If he kissed her, she would stir. She would pull his lips closer and kiss him back. She would throw herself on him, rip the clothes from her body, beg for him to take her right then and there.

He steadied his breathing and sank back to reality.

She would do no such thing. If he were to kiss her, she would push him off her, maybe strike him like her worthless, nuisance of a brother had. His fingers lingered on her cheek.

Did he care?

So what if she pushed him away? Asroth was much stronger than her. She had no magical protection. She had no physical strength. He could hold her down. He didn't need her permission.

What was he thinking? His hand pulled away from her, recoiling in disgust. How could he think to do such a thing?

But then he remembered the moment in the mountain. When he had killed Carlos. Even if he had felt empty after, how exhilarating had it felt in that moment? To drain the man's life away, to steal his very essence. How much more exhilarating would it be to have his way with Tara?

"Asroth!"

He jumped, startled at the sound of Auni's voice. The boy dropped an armful of sticks near the fire that had almost gone out. "Auni!" Asroth called back, trying not to let his voice show fear. He had to think of a lie. And quickly.

"What are you doing so close to my sister?" Auni asked as he made his way to the back of the cave. Asroth rose to his feet while Tara stayed sleeping, peacefully ignorant of all that had transpired.

"She had a fever. I was healing her," he lied. Auni was too stupid to know that sickness could not be healed with magic.

And sure enough, the boy believed it. He gave a watchful nod and knelt down next to his sister, shaking her a bit. "Tara?"

Before the girl could wake up, Asroth left the cave. "I'm going for a walk," he called back. Auni did not bother replying and Asroth let out a breath of relief once he was out of ear's reach.

⁓ ◆ ⁓

"Sheik?"

It was Faris' voice. She was afraid to open her eyes but did so anyway. Surprisingly, she could see. Faris was leaning over her, gently shaking her shoulder. "Sheik?" he asked again.

"What happened?" she replied, jumping to her feet. She remembered Garret towering over her, about to crush her.

"One of my father's healers fixed your eye and nose," he explained. "Can you see okay? You were bleeding pretty bad."

Sheik nodded, looking up at him. He was wearing some sort of headscarf that covered his hair and holding it in place was a beautiful golden crown. "What about King Garret?"

Faris rubbed his neck. "He's dead. After you fell, I killed him." Sheik's heart sank. She was supposed to kill Garret. But she had failed. Her hand had faltered when aiming. Her arrows had not been steady or quick enough. And so Faris had ended up having to kill his own father. "Are you okay?"

She rubbed the bottom of her eye where it felt like it had shattered. "I think so." It was sore, something the healer obviously could

337

do nothing about, but everything seemed in place and there was no more blood. "I guess I must thank you, then. I thought I was dead for a moment there," she said with a weak chuckle.

"Same," he added with a lopsided smile. "Are you ready to get back to your friends?" He opened a door that led to the main hallways.

Sheik still had so many questions. She didn't think she had lost consciousness right away—she remembered bits and pieces of things. Fighting, the sound of a horn. But the pain had been so overwhelming she had been unable to focus on anything else. "What about the soldiers? They aren't a threat? Did they accept your authority?"

His smile widened a bit. "Of course. I am their king, after all." It was then that Sheik noticed two silent guards in the corners of the large room. Their hands rested on swords, ready to draw and defend their new king. They were big, bearded men, dressed in armor and wearing the same headscarf as Faris, though it was held down by a black cord rather than a crown. "And I've already begun giving orders."

"Oh?" Sheik laughed, her attention drawn back to Faris.

"Absolutely. I demanded the garden be restored to its former glory."

Sheik smiled. That was a pretty good order, she thought to herself as the new king led her out of the room.

They wandered the halls, and the two guards followed behind without a word. It made Sheik uneasy having soldiers following their every step. These soldiers who had been their enemy only hours ago. But Faris continued to wave for other men to follow as he passed them.

He eventually led Sheik to a stable. Sheik hadn't seen any horses since they'd left the open plains. Calert had been full of the large but docile beasts. Though Sheik hadn't ridden one, she had pet them at every opportunity. But now Faris presented her with one, holding out the reins to her.

She gave him an uneasy look. "We can't walk?"

"It would take us all day again. This will make the journey quicker." Then, under his breath, he added, "Trust me, it's better than riding a wyvern."

At that, she consented. She couldn't imagine riding one of the snapping monsters that had hunted them back in the southern forests. With a little coaching, she climbed onto the horse and Faris led her and the group of nearly two dozen soldiers he had accumulated out of the palace. The horse was not particularly comfortable to sit on, but she supposed it was better than walking down the mountainside.

It started as a narrow path, meant for soldiers who had been knocked from their wyverns. When the trail was wide enough, Faris beckoned Sheik's horse closer so they could talk. "I want you to know how much I appreciate what you have done for me."

"I'm not sure I did a thing," Sheik confessed. The assassination had gone so poorly.

He shook his head, and the crown atop his headscarf shook with it. "That isn't true. Two days ago, I would never have had the courage to—" He didn't finish the sentence, and instead said, "I didn't think anyone could ever oppose him. He was invincible in my eyes. But you helped me to see," he paused, "other options."

Sheik hated that she had put murder in this boy's mind as a solution to his problems. But she wondered if there had been any other way. Leaving King Garret on the throne of the Tasvran was as dangerous as leaving Spike in power in Isandas.

"I want you to know I consider you my ally," King Faris continued. "The truth is, I have yet to discover how loyal my subjects are. I don't know if there will be attempts on my life. If you and your companions were to stay for a month, or at least a few weeks, you might be able to help me weed out any threats. In exchange, I'll happily provide you some soldiers to fight against the New Prosper."

The trail narrowed again, forcing Sheik's horse to move behind his. Faris gave her a glance, as if to ask her to think it over. Sheik knew better than to try to continue the conversation, as they would have to speak up to hear one another and risk being overheard. So she considered it in silence until the trail widened again.

"I'm not sure we can spare a month," she explained. "Every day, Spike grows stronger—"

He raised his hand to silence her. "I understand you have an important mission." He hesitated, like he wanted to say more. After a pause, he added, "I'll still lend you the troops, regardless of your decision. But I hope you consider it. It's the middle of winter. We've already had one blizzard." Pain flooded through Sheik. He did not know of the loss they had experienced due to that blizzard and the avalanche it had caused. "I don't want you to get caught up in another. I've heard the plains are as harsh as the mountains in some ways. It might be in your best interest to stay, at least until the worst of it is over."

Sheik wanted to say something, but she felt the breath had been taken from her. She stared at the path in front of them and listened to the clip clop of the horses' hooves until her breathing had returned. "Ask my companions, not me," she finally managed.

Faris gave her a sideways glance. "Aren't you the one in charge?"

She shook her head. If she had ever been their leader, she hadn't been a good one. "They're in charge just as much as me." If it wasn't true, she wanted it to be. She would not lead them into disaster, not again.

Faris nodded and gave an impressed look, but all Sheik felt was guilt. The rest of their descent was traversed in silence. The path appeared more and more familiar as they reached the beginning of the trail that Faris had led Sheik through only the day before. By midday, they spotted the caves where her companions camped.

"Sheik!" Tara called out.

Sheik struggled to climb down from the horse and then collapsed into Tara's hug. "Auni, Asroth," she added, greeting the two others. "And Fang," she laughed, the wolf jumping up to lick her face.

Auni gave her a wave, but she noted his eyes on the soldiers, taking in their thick armor and many weapons.

"I see you're alive," Asroth stated simply.

"Barely," Sheik sighed, though her face still held a smile. "King Garret is dead and the Tasvran is officially no longer a threat."

Faris hopped off his horse to get Percy. "I've asked Sheik if you all would like to stay with me in the palace for the next few weeks. Until midwinter has passed. What do you say?"

The three glanced between each other and Sheik avoided eye contact, wanting the decision to be made without her input. Tara and Auni nodded and Asroth gave half a nod, half a shrug. "A short break in a palace might be nice."

Tara gave Sheik a long look. "Sheik?"

"If that's what you guys want," she nodded, "then it might be best. Better safe than sorry," she whispered lightly, trying to forget about those they had lost.

<hr>

Auni awoke to the sudden cold of a snowball falling onto his face.

Tara giggled above him.

"Wake up! The courtyard is full of snow!"

She sprinted away and Auni brushed the snow off his nose and cheeks and tried to orient himself. They had ridden horseback through the evening along the same path Sheik and Faris had come from. When they finally reached the palace, it was night. Faris led each of them to their own room, though Auni had insisted on staying with Tara. After a long day of travel and upon discovering the luxury of the palace beds, he had collapsed into an easy sleep.

Only to be woken by a snowball to the face.

He rubbed his tired eyes and chased after Tara. There was a trail of wetness where she had tracked in snow that made it easy to follow.

Upon turning a corner, she smacked him with another snowball, this one thankfully in the chest.

So this was the courtyard. There was no ceiling, and snow was falling in thick flakes. Before she could strike again, Auni bent down and scooped up a handful of snow and threw it back. Tara ducked and ran behind the center fountain.

Snow was not new to them. The mountains had been full of it. But snow had represented a harsh journey of frostbite, hypothermia, and overall danger. The avalanche of snow had taken three of their friends' lives.

But here, safe within the walls of King Faris' palace, Auni saw snow in the same light as he had back when he was six years old. He smirked as he hit Tara with a snowball. Here they were, just two siblings having a snowball fight.

And by the end of it, the two of them were freezing and couldn't contain their laughter.

When Auni finally found himself shivering, Tara suggested they change into fresh clothes and go exploring. They didn't exactly have any fresh clothes. Tara had tried to wash their clothes once during their time in the cave after the avalanche, but they had frozen stiff and so she hadn't washed them since. So they changed into their dirty but dry clothes and began to wander the magnificent palace.

It was a place completely unlike anything Auni had ever seen before. It wasn't just that it was a royal building of incredible luxury and size, although that was foreign to Auni as well. But the structure of the rooms themselves was something new. Everything was massively tall. The ceilings towered above them, further than anyone could reach. The hallways began with arches and the rooftops peaked with domes and spires.

And Auni could tell when he left common areas and approached the king's hallways. The walls became intricate. The stones were not flat and smooth, but ornately carved in beautiful designs of spirals and flowers and circles and more.

Tara traced her hand along the patterns as they walked, as awestruck by their beauty as he was. He could only imagine that this area was highly restricted, but none of the guards stopped them or even questioned their presence. King Faris must have given them full access to the entire palace.

Eventually they found their way to a kitchen. Workers and chefs bustled in and out. Like the guards, they, too, wore headscarves with a thick black cord. It reminded Auni of the headdress Asroth wore, though these men looked nothing like Asroth. If anything they looked like Auni. Bronze skin, black hair.

"Pardon me," Tara spoke up and Auni stopped his staring. "I don't mean to interrupt. We are guests of King Faris. Is this where we would go to get food?"

One of the chefs nodded and replied in a thick accent, "Yes, of course. You are his guests. Anything you want." It was quite clear that King Faris had asked them to be treated like royalty. The thought of it was bizarre. If anyone from his old life were to hear that Auni had stayed in a palace and been treated like a king, well they wouldn't ever believe it. He certainly wouldn't have. "Do you want a specific food?"

Auni shrugged. Tara was the pickier eater, but even she shook her head no. "I don't know. What do you have?"

The man smirked and shouted out a few orders to the kitchen workers around him, rattling off a list of unfamiliar words. Then he hurried Auni and Tara out of the kitchen through another tall archway and into an extravagant room filled with nothing but a low, long table and dozens of pillows.

Tara gave Auni an unsure glance as the chef left. "Where do we sit?"

"On the floor, I think." He went ahead and did so. "This is probably the king's table. Maybe we're supposed to be lower than him, you know?"

She joined him on the floor, squishing together some pillows to try and create a backrest. "I guess so. Where do you think he is, anyway?"

"No clue. I'm sure he's busy. Probably too busy to see us. Should we get Sheik and Asroth? And Fang?" Though it probably wouldn't be acceptable to bring a wolf into the king's personal dining room.

Tara shook her head. "No, Sheik had already left her room by the time I was up. And I don't want to eat with Asroth." She didn't have to explain why. They talked to him as little as possible since the fight in the cave.

"Hey, were you sick two nights ago? The night that Sheik and Faris left to—" he cut himself off, realizing how inappropriate it was to discuss the assassination.

"What? No. Why?" Tara raised an eyebrow, confused.

"Remember how you went to nap in the back of the cave? I left to get firewood," he explained. "And when I came back, Asroth was real close to you. He said he was healing your fever."

Tara stared at the empty table for a moment, like she was lost in thought. "No, I felt fine. I was tired. I was tired from healing Faris—King Faris," she corrected, "the day before. But I did not have a fever."

"Hmm." Auni didn't like it. A gross feeling swirled in his gut. Why would Asroth pretend to be healing her? Had he been hoping to hurt Tara and Auni had interrupted him just in time? "I don't like him. I don't know what he's up to but he's getting stranger and stranger."

"And meaner," Tara concurred. "But it is what it is. We don't have to put up with him for much longer. We just have to stop Spike, then we can go our separate ways."

Auni gave her a curious look. "All of us?"

"I'm not sure," she admitted with a sigh. They had talked about several options. Going on their own, starting a farm just the two of them. Or staying with Sheik and Kazzak, their core group from Calert. But now Kazzak was gone. "Certainly we can part with Asroth."

He laughed and might have said more, but the chef returned carrying a giant tray that billowed steam and smelled of meat. Auni's mouth watered at the smell, though he hadn't a clue what half the foods were when the chef placed the platter on the table. "Enjoy!"

They took it in for a moment, inhaling the delicious scent. And then they dug in.

There was a pile of warm flatbreads with half a dozen dipping sauces ranging from spicy to sweet. Hot, thick stew that tasted of lamb. Cheesy flatbread with eggs layered on top. A rice blended with vegetables and nuts. Mint and honey tea. And sweet, flakey pastries filled with smashed fruits.

After consuming only half of the magnificent spread, Auni felt his stomach swelling from overeating. If this wasn't the king's table, they were certainly dining like kings.

"Auni? Tara?" Sheik stared at them from the extravagant archway.

Fang pushed past her at the smell of the food. There were still some strips of lamb in the stew and so Auni placed it on the ground for the wolf to lap up. "Hey Sheik!" Tara smiled. "I know you do not care for food, but you drink tea at least, right?" She poured a little more into her cup and held it out for the woman to try.

"Dear Elilah, how much have you eaten?" Sheik exclaimed.

"A lot," Tara laughed.

"The man said it was okay, that we're King Faris' guests." Auni popped another pastry into his mouth, though he could probably have gone a week without food after such a meal.

Sheik dropped to her knee to get in close to them. "You don't understand." Her voice was a harsh whisper. "King Garret tried to have Faris poisoned."

Tara gave her a shrug. "Yeah so? King Garret's dead."

"Yes, but there still very well might be people who don't want Faris on the throne. People who would poison him."

Auni's heart pounded with realization. If they wanted King Faris dead, surely they would want his companions dead too. If someone were to poison the food, they'd poison all the food. Suddenly he felt sick, and he wondered if it was poison or just the thought of it.

Tara's forehead crinkled as she gained understanding. "So what are we supposed to do, not eat?"

Sheik sighed. "Exactly. I was in King Faris' room just now making him breakfast with my magic. I was going to do the same for you two."

They said nothing for a moment, Auni wondering if they had just doomed themselves. But the silence was broken by the chef who had served them reentering the room. He carried a large object that looked something like a candlestick attached to a glass vase. Coals glowed red at the top and a tube hung from the center. It smelled awful and Auni peered at the chef, wondering if this man was their murderer.

The man extended the tube to Auni, then to Tara. They stared back blankly. "You have never had argileh before? You must try it!"

"Do you think it is poison?" Tara tried to whisper to Sheik, though her comment was quite audible.

Auni held his breath, wondering how the man would respond to the accusation. To his surprise, the chef merely laughed. "It's no poison, see?" He demonstrated, putting the tube to his lips, sucking in a breath, and blowing out a cloud of smoke.

"Oh, it's a pipe!" Tara exclaimed with sudden realization. The chef nodded and extended it to her. Before she could take in a breath, Sheik placed her hand over the tube.

"I'm sorry," she explained, "but we don't know this is safe. Are you the one who served these two their food?"

The man gave a nod of understanding. "You're worried the king's chefs might poison one of your comrades." Sheik said nothing. "I assure you, my staff and I are loyal to the new king and anyone who serves him." He hesitated, but then added, "I have heard rumors involving poison. There was a chef, Chef Bezru. He went missing yesterday. If the rumors are true, I have a feeling that is why Bezru fled. I would be happy to speak with King Faris directly if he has concerns."

Auni noticed a bit of tension release in Sheik's stance. She gave the chef a forced smile and added, "That might be helpful. Let's go see if we can find him."

The man nodded and Sheik led him out through the tall archway, casting one last look at Auni and Tara as if warning them to be careful.

And they were careful. For the rest of the afternoon, they retired to their room, fearing the strike of poison. But nothing came and by evening their stomachs were grumbling once again.

Sheik eventually came and brought them food, ensuring that it had been prepared under her supervision by only chefs that she and King Faris had personally questioned. Tara ate quickly while Auni was cautious, tasting every bite suspiciously now that he knew to be on his guard.

"The food is safe, I promise," Sheik said with a smile, as if reading Auni's mind. "And Faris—King Faris—has sent soldiers to track down Bezru. Once they find him, he'll be questioned and we'll know if there are any others who were loyal to King Garret."

Auni ate a bit more. "Then what?"

"What do you mean?"

"When you're done helping King Faris catch all the bad guys. You know, make sure he's gotten rid of anyone who wants him dead," Auni clarified. "What's the plan after that? Are we going to keep marching towards Isandas without Kazzak and the others?"

The mention of Kazzak made Sheik's face drop. Auni wished he could take it back and say something different. She glanced between him and Tara. "What do you two want?"

"You know what we want," Tara said softly. They wanted to stop Spike. They wanted to see this thing through. "But we don't want you to do something just because we want to." Auni nodded, agreeing with her sentiment. Sheik was the one who had wanted to stop fighting back in the cave. She was the one who had wanted to give up. She had to be the one to decide to keep going. "We are going to stick with you no matter what you decide."

Sheik crossed her arms. "Well, I don't want to make the decision all by myself."

Tara crossed her arms, too, then gave Sheik a warm smile. "Fine. We shall decide together."

"Deal." Sheik took a seat on their bed. "I think we all agree Spike needs to be stopped. Right?" Auni and Tara nodded in unison. "Faris—King Faris," she corrected herself again, "he's offered us soldiers. Do you want to continue just us and try to sneak into Isandas, or do you want to take him up on his offer?"

"He did? Wow, that is nice!" Tara immediately gushed. Auni said nothing but thought the proposition over. While he liked the dynamic of their small group, he knew they would be safer with an army. Ever since the others had died in the avalanche, he had realized how dangerous this mission might become. Sheik's magic couldn't keep them safe from everything.

"I think we should accept his help."

Tara agreed and Sheik nodded. "Okay. And when do we want to move out?"

At this, Auni had no idea. But Tara seemed to have a response. She fetched a thick parchment from a desk in the room and held it up. Though Auni couldn't read any of the words on it, based on its four circles with corresponding symbols—a snowflake, a flower, a sun, and a tree with no leaves—he could only assume it was a calendar. Pointing along the snowflake circle, Tara explained, "Well we are here right now. If we can wait two more weeks, we would be past the solstice. Then presumably it will not be as cold."

Two weeks sounded like plenty of time to recuperate, help King Faris, and plan some battle tactics, and so they all agreed.

But by the end of the second week, Auni regretted not moving out sooner.

In so many ways, it was a wonderful two weeks. Once the chefs had been thoroughly vetted, they continued to eat great heaps of delicious foods. They even tried the argileh pipe, though Asroth insisted it was a disgusting habit. With the exception of mealtimes, Asroth made himself scarce, much to Auni's relief. All in all, he had a marvelous time.

But it set him on edge to be on vacation from war. He had grown accustomed to beds and living indoors, and he knew how excruciating it would be to begin marching and camping in the wilderness once again. He wondered if his reflexes had grown dull and his muscles had become weak from the lack of fighting. And so while it was perhaps the best two weeks of his life, Auni dreaded what dangers lie ahead and feared how unprepared they might be when they faced them.

Spike watched the messenger carefully. "So the rumors are true," he muttered. He had heard word of King Garret's death, but it had now been confirmed. Spike thought for a moment, pondering what to do. "I suppose they'll be coming. Especially if it was that elf's army who killed him."

He had been relying on King Garret to eliminate them. Now all he could hope for was the new king staying neutral in the affair. "We'll go offensive," he announced to the messenger. "Go ready a troop. Not one of those we've rounded up, some of the loyalists. And magic users, healers."

The messenger raised an eyebrow. "How many?"

"As many as it takes!" Spike demanded. "All of them if you must. We have them outnumbered but they're able to beat us with tactics and magic. Now we'll show them our own tactics and magic."

"Of course. Is that all?" the man asked after a moment's pause.

Spike was about to send him away when he smiled. "Yes actually, there is one more thing," he added quietly. "I've heard the elf leading them is a woman." He waved away the messenger's look of shock. "Yes, I know it's absurd. But I'd like you to find out if these rumors are as true as King Garret's death. If so, I've got a plan for her."

Chapter 18

Auni approached the group at a light jog. "They're still a ways away," he explained as Sheik looked to him for information. "They might be here before nightfall, but even then the sun would set soon after."

Sheik nodded. Their plan would work perfectly. "Alright, don't forget that they might have magic users among them," she added, speaking over the crowd. "If you see someone using magic, try to kill them immediately." Her qualms about killing still nagged at her, but not as strongly since the night of King Garret's assassination. If she hadn't hesitated to kill him, Faris wouldn't have had to take the life of his own father. It had been her fault, her mistake. It wasn't a mistake she would make again.

"Armor is useless against them," she continued, trying to drive the point into the soldiers' heads. "A magic user can warp it away and kill you in an instant," she said with a snap of her fingers.

"The torches are here," she added. "Everyone take as many as they can gather and light them before the troops arrive. We may need to work quickly."

Since moving with the men Faris had provided, it was easy for Spike to locate them and send an army their way. But with the extra hands Sheik had been given, more tactics were available for their use. Their current plan was setting up countless torches so the approaching army would not know how many men they were up against and where they might be. The enemy would attack a cluster of torches to find no one there, giving Sheik's troop an opportunity for a sneak attack.

It was a well-constructed defense, and no one had raised any objections to it. Sheik made a specific point of asking. She was not ready to make another mistake that would cause more deaths. She was careful to ask advice of the troop leaders, but not a single man could find a major flaw in the plan.

Still, she wished they had more magic users. But King Faris had explained that his father had put any regular and dark magic users to death. Only healers were permitted to live because they presented no threat to him. A simple man with a simple but brutal plan, Sheik thought. Spike was not so simple—he would use every magic user he could get.

Sheik watched over a hill as the sun grew closer to the ground. It was late winter now. They had left King Faris' castle just after the solstice and then traveled another month and a half. Though it was still cold, and frost coated the ground, it was not the horrendous temperatures they had faced before. The temperatures where toes and fingers could freeze, and people could drift easily into death.

As much as she tried to just focus on the battle ahead and pray for success, it was often difficult. Her thoughts were always wandering. It seemed something was always on her mind. The avalanche, the assassination. Killing, surviving. Several soldiers were near her, lighting torches and tying them onto the trees to give the appearance they were being held. She glanced to check how realistic they looked.

Somewhat bored and curious, she turned to a knight as she strapped one of Farin's throwing knives to her thigh. The rest were located on her belt, but she thought it might be a good idea to have one on her body in case the belt somehow tore off. "What do you normally do before battle?" she asked as she finished securing it.

"Not talk," he replied, smirking a bit.

"Oh."

He laughed. "It's alright. I guess I double check everything, my weapons, my armor. Think about the people I love." He paused for a moment, thinking. "When the battle is really close I think about the people I hate. The people I want to kill, something to get my blood boiling."

Sheik nodded. That seemed reasonable. She took his advice, thinking about those she cared about. Those she deeply missed. Atarius and Farin. Kazzak. Carlos, Jason. Even the family she was unable to remember.

Then she heard the sound. It was a collective stomping, a march. Soldiers united together, a shield of strength. She only needed to hear the sound of their feet to guess they were better trained than any group they had fought before. When she saw them, she knew for certain.

They walked like one terrible beast. Their armor and weapons were varied, but it was to serve a purpose, not because of a lack of resources. Shields rose together in a solid movement as they chanted a command, ready to deflect arrows. They broke into organized groups, not frantically but like a rushing river dividing into two.

Sheik's eyes grew narrow as she nocked an arrow to her bow. Her thoughts of loved ones shattered apart and were replaced with thoughts of killing. "Time to think about hate," she heard the soldier behind her whisper. The last rays of the sun's orange light disappeared and the darkness emerged.

—◆—

Eighteen, nineteen, twenty, she counted in her head. Slipping away from the main bunch of torches, Sheik watched the enemy work. The way they maneuvered, all their backs facing each other so they could not be taken by surprise. But with the shock of finding eight torches being held by trees and not people, they darted around, seeking out the trap they had clearly walked into.

Her arrow slammed into one of their backs. Another. It was not until the third man fell down that they realized where the arrows were coming from and charged.

A dozen Tasvranian soldiers stepped out of the darkness, their weapons striking the enemy from behind. Sheik rushed towards the combat, ripping an arrow out of one man's side and sticking it into another's. She no longer aimed for knees and ankles. She aimed for throats and hearts.

"Sheik!"

She turned to see Tara, stumbling away from a pursuing soldier. In an instant, her arrow was ready, aimed, and loosed, catching the man in the neck. Tara let out a breath of relief and rushed to Sheik's side. "Is anyone injured over here?" she asked. She was one of few healers they had, running from each cluster of torches to see if people needed her services.

"I think we're fine."

"Your plan is working perfectly," Tara smiled. "There have hardly been any wounds since we do not have to deal with their soldiers all at once."

The words brought relief to Sheik's ears. She was glad to hear there had not been any problems and that the enemy was falling into their trap as planned.

But then a scream broke the silence.

One of the Tasvranian soldiers had fallen without warning. A knife jutted out of his chest. A knife that was too short to have pierced his armor. "Magic!" Sheik shouted.

But it was too late. The enemy was upon them. One soldier's armor locked up as he swung. The ground bent so another soldier tripped. The helmet of one soldier started to melt onto his face and his screams echoed in the otherwise silent forest.

Sheik aimed and fired an arrow, but the magic user merely willed up a wall to block it. Two soldiers swung at him, but their swords disappeared, and he bent their armor against them. The metal crumpled against their ribs and Sheik could see them gasping for air.

She loosened the dirt and sunk the magic user into the ground. When he realized what was happening and focused against it, he lost his concentration on several of the soldiers he had been restraining. One swung quickly and, with a spray of blood, the chaos ended.

The sorcerer was dead.

They caught their breath for a beat. "Help them out of their armor!" Sheik instructed, realizing the two with crumpled breastplates were still gasping. Tara felt for pulses amongst several of the fallen soldiers, but Sheik knew it was futile. She winced at the sight of the man whose helmet had been melted against his face.

"Shit," one of the soldiers mumbled.

She nodded. How many were there? How many had they killed and how many were left? "Be on your guard," she said, though they knew plenty well. Magic was what had allowed Sheik's group to decimate armies. Spike's magic users were just as deadly.

Tara gave Sheik a look, as if wondering whether she should stay or continue her rounds. Sheik gave her a nod. "Go ahead. I'll be right behind you." While Tara left cautiously, Sheik helped the soldiers readjust the torches and reset their hiding spots. Then she took off after Tara.

Sheik's bow hung idly by her side, though she held an arrow between two knuckles, ready to raise it at any moment. It was strange hearing the sound of distant conflicts. They echoed throughout the wintry woods, and it was difficult to discern their individual locations because of the randomly scattered torches. The forest could be filled with dozens of men or hundreds. It was impossible to tell.

Footsteps approached. "Tara?" Sheik asked, peering towards the sound. Her sight was far worse than her hearing.

"That's the elf."

It was hardly a whisper, but her keen ears were able to detect it. A man's voice, no Tasvranian accent, ten paces away from her. Sheik's bow raised, the arrow finding its position, and she let it fly towards the man and whoever he might be speaking with.

A cry of pain indicated that she had hit one of her targets. "Go!" someone whispered harshly. Sheik heard their steps before she saw them emerge, sprinting like lightning.

They were not normal soldiers. They were cloaked, wearing no armor. They did not even hold weapons. She loosed as many arrows as she could before they reached her, but there were at least fifteen men, even if four or so had now fallen to the ground. Dropping her bow, she pulled a knife from her belt and stuck it into one man's shoulder.

But she was surrounded. Two men grabbed her arms. Still Sheik fought. She kicked one man in the gut and continuously thrashed, hoping to get loose from the men's clutches.

It was no use.

Their grasp grew tighter around her biceps. She cried out for help, but immediately felt a fist slam into her stomach, knocking the wind out of her. He struck again even though Sheik had grown silent. And again.

"Stop it." One of the men grabbed her assailant's arm after he punched her a fourth time. "He wants her in good condition," he snapped.

"Who?" Sheik gasped, having trouble speaking after the blows to her gut.

The man smirked. "Why Spike, of course. You're a lucky lady," he mocked, shoving a gag into her mouth.

Sheik used her magic to warp the gag and make it small enough she would be able to spit it out. But she felt it grow large again, her magic fighting an unknown force. Then she realized it.

They were magic users.

No matter what magic she used, one of them could use their own magic to counteract it. It was hopeless. She was a prisoner, gagged and now tied and being carried by several of the men. No fighting could help her. No magic could help her. She would soon be delivered to Spike.

Tara bit down on her lip, tears welling up in her eyes. She wanted to run at those men. She wanted to kill them. She wanted to save Sheik, but she knew she could not. And so the only thing she could do was hide, feeling cowardly, frightened, and terribly powerless.

Tears began to cascade down her cheeks as the men left, taking Sheik with them. She waited an extra minute just to be sure they would not spot her, and then rose from her hiding place. Bending over, she grabbed Sheik's bow and belt of knives that had been thrown to the ground.

Then she ran.

She was not sure what to do or where to go precisely, but she ran towards the nearest cluster of torches, where she had been heading before she heard the men attacking Sheik. Running there felt like forever. Choking on tears, it was hard for her to keep up the sprint, and the light of the torches almost seemed to grow further and further away. By the time she finally stood in the center of the torches, she was panting and out of breath.

A soldier stepped out of the black, raising a sword to strike her down. She ducked and screamed out. The soldier stopped. "Tara?"

She wiped several tears from her eyes and looked up at him.

"I didn't realize it was you, sorry," he continued, realizing that she was too frightened to speak. He was one of King Faris' soldiers, an ally. "We don't have any wounded," the man explained.

"No," she stuttered. Between catching her breath, trying not to cry, and recovering from her shock, she could hardly get out a word. "Sheik, she was taken," she finally managed to spit out.

The soldier raised an eyebrow. "What do you mean?"

"Kidnapped, captured! Some men with hoods. They took her, said they were taking her to Spike," she explained the best she could. The thought of it made her stomach drop. She felt like she was trapped in some horrific nightmare. She prayed she might wake up and realize it was all only a dream.

But it was no dream. She had seen Sheik grabbed, beaten, tied, and carried off. "We have to do something," she added, hoping the soldier would give her a reaction of some sort. Part of her wanted him to get a troop together and go after her. But that was unreasonable. The men who had taken Sheik were long gone, and their tracks would be impossible to follow in the darkness.

Another soldier ran up to the two. "They're retreating!" he called out enthusiastically.

"What?"

"They're retreating. We scared them off I guess; didn't you see the signal in the sky?"

Tara, who had been so focused on running, had not seen much of anything. "Signal?" she asked, completely confused.

The soldier nodded and pointed up. "They sent off some sort of fire signal and then they all began retreating."

She understood, now. Dear Ziad, she understood. The entire battle had been a setup. A plot to capture Sheik. And now that they had what they wanted, there was no more reason for them to fight.

⊷

Sheik landed with a thud against the solid rock floor. For most of the journey they had kept a bag over her head. Anytime she tried to remove it with her magic, the other sorcerers merely used their own powers to secure it. Despite not being able to see, she was able to keep track of how many days had passed: three.

They had been a painful three days. The men had first carried her back to the main army. She was then loaded onto a wagon, enduring a fast journey. Her legs felt weak from lack of walking, as she was only permitted to stand and leave the wagon a few times a day. Surviving off of only a few gulps of water and food, her stomach growled and her throat burned.

It hardly mattered anymore, though. She knew she was either being transported to be tortured or merely executed by Spike himself. She hoped it was the latter, so she would at least be given the mercy of a quick death.

But now, as her body slammed against the stone floor, somehow she knew she would not have the pleasure of an execution. The bag was removed from her head and she blinked at the surprising amount of light in the room.

A man stood over her. He wore an elegant white shirt and tight pair of pants with a fully buttoned golden vest. His skin was an attractive tan, contrasted by the light color of his clothing and his long black hair. It was hard for Sheik to see his face, but as he bent down next to her, she saw he was quite handsome, from his green eyes to his solid jaw.

"I am Spike," he spoke calmly. Even his voice sounded angelic, Sheik thought. "Who, might I ask, are you?"

She bit down on her lip, not wanting to respond. But he would learn the answer sooner or later. "Sheik," she answered reluctantly.

"Sheik. You've caused quite a bit of trouble for me," he said with a smile. "I find it rather strange, since you're an elf. Aren't you a little far from home?"

Her face turned away.

Spike let out a chuckle after realizing she wasn't going to reply. "You're lucky to be an elf, though. You'd be dead if you were human." He paused, but finally lightly turned her chin towards him. "I'm a forgiving man, Sheik. And despite all the problems you've caused, I have decided to spare you your life." He ran his hand through her hair but quickly removed it and clicked his tongue several times. "You're rather dirty, I'll have someone prepare a bath for you."

"Why?" Sheik retorted angrily. "I know you plan to torture me. Why do you want me clean for that?"

"Torture? I'm not going to torture you," he said with a hint of surprise in his voice. "No. You are to be my wife."

Sheik couldn't quite fathom it. Why would he want her as a wife? Perhaps it was just to humiliate her. He only wanted to rape her and to watch her suffer a different kind of torture. She kept her mouth closed, refusing to let him see the fear on her face.

He smiled a bit. "I know, after being enemies for so long you must be confused." He paused and then asked, "Did you know that elves outlive humans by nearly thirty years?" Sheik found the question strange. She wasn't sure if it was true or not—she didn't know how long humans usually lived. "It's true," he continued. "Elves have many other desirable traits, too. Excellent hearing. A stronger affinity for magic.

"Once all the territories are under control, I will need an heir to keep them united. One with elven blood would certainly be desirable, don't you think? A son that would live longer, that would easily command magic, that would have heightened senses." He looked her in the eye, his voice growing suddenly stern. "Considering your current position, I think it would be wise for you to accept my offer."

She looked back into his green eyes, contemplating what to do. She didn't want to be tortured, but her pride and defiance told her to fight back. Feeling around her leg as Spike stared into her eyes, she found what she wanted.

The knife she had strapped to her thigh before battle, four days ago.

In one quick motion, she pulled it from its sheath and thrust it towards Spike's heart. She had been waiting to reveal it for the perfect moment. The opportunity to see Spike face to face. To stab him. To kill him, even though she knew it meant her own death.

But she had not expected him to be so quick. He reached out as fast as she, grabbing her by the wrist and preventing her from letting the knife meet his flesh.

The knife suddenly grew intensely hot, searing her skin. It wasn't until then that she even realized there were other people in the room with them. All she had seen before was Spike.

There were four people. Obviously all sorcerers. It was their magic heating the knife, making it impossible to hold. Sheik was forced to drop it and watch Spike frown as it clattered against the stone floor. "I'm so disappointed in your choice," he whispered. Then, to the sorcerers, he announced, "Administer the toxin."

"What?" Sheik cried out in a panic. One of the men pulled out a long needle connected to a vial. She tried to scramble away, but Spike reached out and smashed her head against the ground, holding it down firmly. She summoned her magic, creating barriers between her and the needle, throwing rocks at Spike and his sorcerers. But her magic dissipated in mere seconds as the sorcerers had her outnumbered. They could warp away her magic just as easily as she could create it.

The needle slammed into her neck, piercing a vein. The liquid injected into her, pumping painfully through her blood stream. Spike covered her mouth with his free hand and explained over her muffled screams, "Calm yourself. This doesn't have to hurt. This is merely a precaution so you won't hurt me or yourself." He rambled on about the poison that was now coursing through her veins, but Sheik had stopped listening.

This was her chance. Even as the poison was so quickly shutting down her body, she knew that this was her chance. Everyone was focused on her neck, watching the poison enter her, making sure the procedure was properly completed.

Gathering the last of her strength as she felt her limbs growing numb and lifeless, she grabbed the knife that had fallen to the floor.

In one quick motion, she thrust it into Spike.

With her head held down against the floor, she could not quite see where she had struck him. But by the sound of Spike's screams, she knew it had to have been important. He released her and fell backwards.

The needle ripped from her neck as the sorcerer finished injecting the liquid and ran to Spike's side. Sheik barely managed to lift her head to see where the knife had hit him. A small smile spread across her face as she watched him pull the knife from his crotch, blood rapidly staining his pants.

She could hear him curse and scream for healers as her head slouched down. Her body grew limp and heavy until she could no longer move at all. Still, her smile remained. As Spike continued his yelling, the sorcerers reminded him that he had sent all his healers with the army. It would take them at least another week to return.

Finally a medic was brought in to tend to Spike. Even if not a magical healer, he could stop the bleeding and bandage the wound. Sheik couldn't move her head enough to glance towards him and see how much damage she had done, but hopefully it was enough to keep Spike from forcing himself on her.

She continued to listen to his cursing, but his words began growing fainter in her mind, like they were something distant. Everything became blurry, her eyes heavy despite how hard she tried to keep them open. "Give her the cure before she dies," she heard Spike's voice yell between his swears.

Someone turned her head for her and forced her jaw open. A liquid tasting like a sweet honey poured into her mouth. It was not a lot, perhaps three spoonfuls. She felt it drip down her throat, having difficulty swallowing it normally.

It only took a moment before it began to work, her hearing and sight becoming suddenly clearer. As it focused, she realized Spike was standing over her.

"I offered you a chance," he said harshly. He did not bother bending down to talk to her this time. Her body still tingled with numbness, but she managed to crane her neck to look at him.

He didn't look angelic anymore. In fact, he looked more like a demon.

Though he still wore his shirt and vest, they were splattered with his own blood. From the waist down he was naked. Between the black stitches of recent surgeries and the horrific scars and keloids covering his body, Spike looked like he had somehow crawled out of the abyss itself. Crimson blood trailed down his now bandaged wound, highlighting his frightening image.

"I offered you a chance and you rejected it," he repeated, as if he could sense that she wasn't listening to his words. "Your life is now mine, Sheik. You're mine," he growled before delivering a swift kick to her skull, sending her back into the blindness and deafness she had only just recovered from.

CHAPTER 19

Sheik had anticipated the curses and being spat upon by Spike's men. What she hadn't expected was the look of disdain and absolute confusion.

Her presence had obviously been announced throughout the castle; everyone knew who she was. It wasn't difficult to spot her: an elf constantly surrounded by one or more sorcerers. The sorcerers were there to prevent her from escaping or harming anyone, but they were also there to keep her safe. They administered her small doses of the cure to keep the poison from killing her. And they were there to ensure that none of Spike's men lay a hand on her.

Sheik quickly discovered that some of the sorcerers did their job better than others. The first soldier to watch her did not let her out of his sight, rarely spoke to her, and never let others speak to her. But the next sorcerer, a much younger soldier with a scar across his forehead, hardly cared who spoke to Sheik. He also didn't care if they struck her or spat on her.

The scar sorcerer was one of those who looked at her with disdain and confusion. After several hours with him, feeling particularly defiant, Sheik finally blurted out, "What? Why are you looking at me that way?"

The man's nose crinkled. He said nothing for a while, as he was supposed to. Then finally he relented. "How could you stab him?"

"What?" The question genuinely caught Sheik off-guard.

"I just don't understand why you'd want to. How can you be so hateful?"

Sheik's stomach churned at the accusation of her being the hateful one. "Spike's hurt a lot of people. Killed a lot of people. How can you serve him?" she retorted.

The scar sorcerer rolled his eyes. "Is that what you've been told?"

"It's what I've seen!" she shouted back. Images of the decimated town ran through her mind. The threats on Calert from the New Prosper Army. Spike was slaughtering innocents. He was a monster.

"You're on the wrong side of this fight," the man said simply. He shook his head and gave out a small chuckle. "It's sad, really. You're an elf, you're from the west. You don't even know what you're fighting for." Sheik said nothing. "Spike's a hero. He's liberated this land. Our land."

It was then that Sheik noticed the resemblance. The scar sorcerer was different looking, but he had the same tanned skin, green eyes, and dark hair as Spike. "Our land?" she asked cautiously.

"The royalty in Isandas was evil. Spike attacked them and their army, yes," he admitted, "but not without just cause. They stripped our people of everything, taxed us until we had nothing. The people of the northern plains were dying because of the monarchy. Spike put a stop to all of it. Now we're equals. And soon all the people of all the lands will be equals."

Sheik didn't know anything about the nobles in Isandas. She had no knowledge of Etmos history and who had suffered before Spike came to power. All she knew was that Spike killed people. But now, doubt faltered in her mind. "Even if what you're saying is true," she said hesitantly, "Spike is going about it all wrong. The ends do not justify the means. He's a murderer."

At this, he scoffed. "Do you know what happened to my cousin when he refused to pay the increase in taxes?" Sheik stayed silent. "The sheriff sent troops to make an example of him. They cut open his belly and pulled out his intestines. In front of his own children." Sheik swallowed dryly, wanting desperately to believe it wasn't true. "Spike gave that troop a swift death. It was far more than those swine deserved. So, yes, he's a murderer. As am I," he said with half a shrug. "There are far worse things one can be."

"Yeah?" Sheik retorted. "How about him holding me here? He's soon to be a rapist, you know," she added, knowing that once Spike recovered from his injury he would force himself on her.

The scar sorcerer slapped her, hard. "Don't you dare speak of him that way. We'll see if he even makes it through the night because of you."

But Spike did last through the night. His wound had not grown infected. It would take weeks to heal naturally, but his healers would return much sooner and then he would have his way with her.

She didn't see Spike at all for the first couple of days. Sheik was paraded through the castle for meals and then returned to a small cell where a sorcerer always watched her. She did as she was told and ate the food, even though it wasn't prepared with her magic. She had to keep up her strength.

Sheik began to regret more and more her decision to stab Spike. From the few days she had been there, she had heard nothing but good things about him. It wasn't that she wanted to accept a fate of being married to him, but she wondered now if she might have been able to reason with him. He was supposedly this kind and rational man, this liberator. Surely, she could have come to some sort of agreement with him?

Sometimes she thought she was crazy. Here she was, this pacifist, this woman who aimed so carefully for ankles and knees, yet she had tried to stab Spike in the heart. Who was she? Who was he? What if he really was a liberator who had saved the masses from an evil monarchy? Yes, perhaps he was in the wrong for killing to get what he wanted. But then, wasn't she in the wrong too?

She reminded herself that she was his prisoner. She used the thought like a whet stone, sharpening her resolve against him. Spike was evil. Good people did not keep prisoners. But she only heard more and more rumors of his wonderful deeds.

Until the whisper of a serving woman brought her back to her senses.

The woman delivered Sheik a plate of food in the dining hall. Sheik sat on the floor next to whichever sorcerer was in charge of her at the time. The dining hall was always bustling with noise and the sorcerer always occupied with his own meal, so Sheik was practically invisible.

And that was when the serving woman mouthed two words to Sheik: "Thank you."

The woman looked terribly frightened and when Sheik replied, "What?" she hurriedly left with no reply.

For the rest of the day, Sheik pondered what the woman might have meant. Maybe Spike had raped this poor woman? And now he could not do it again because of the injury Sheik had caused. It was the only explanation that made sense, and it brought Sheik the reassurance that she needed.

Spike was evil.

Spike was a murderer. Spike was a rapist. Even if he had conquered Isandas for virtuous reasons, even if he had helped people, he had hurt many others. He was continuing to hurt others. He had to be stopped.

And so, the next day, Sheik began to look for patterns. When the sorcerers switched shifts. Where hallways were unguarded. Items that could be used as weapons. Perhaps with enough time she could escape.

But deep down she knew escape was futile.

Even if she managed to get away from the sorcerers and soldiers, even if she could sneak out of the palace, she was still poisoned. It started as a dull headache. Then the numbness set in. After that, blindness and deafness. The only senses she would be left with were her taste and smell. And then... death.

The only cure was the honey-sweet medication. Apparently the small doses they gave her each day were only temporary cures. She was still dying. It would take a much larger dosage to cure her permanently, and even then she wasn't sure if there would still be side effects. Not that it mattered, though. She assumed Spike would never give her the full cure.

Unless she became pregnant.

As much as she dreaded the moment his healers returned, she knew sleeping with Spike might be her only chance. If she became pregnant, Spike would not want any poison in her system for the sake of the child. And once she was administered all the medicine, perhaps she could find a way to escape.

<hr>

It wasn't long until Sheik met the serving woman again. The woman came to her cell with a bucket and sponge. She explained to the sorcerer on guard that she was supposed to clean Sheik up because Spike wanted to meet with her. The way she said "meet with her" gave Sheik a small burst of hope that perhaps Spike would be willing to reconsider, to negotiate.

But this was the woman who had whispered "thank you." Spike was evil. There would be no negotiation.

The sorcerer let the woman into the cell. She set down her bucket and stared at him for a long moment. "Well?"

"Well, what?" he responded gruffly.

"Well, I'm bathing the woman. You need to step out."

His brow narrowed. "It's my job to watch her."

"If you chain her up against that wall and stand just outside the door then there's no need for concern." After a short pause she added, "I'm only trying to follow Spike's orders."

The man sighed and did as he was told, chaining Sheik's right arm to the wall and stepping outside. Sheik wondered if her magic was strong enough to warp the metal of the chains holding her. But with the poison in her blood and the sorcerer just beyond the door, now was not the time to escape.

"Did Spike's healers arrive?" Sheik asked hesitantly as the woman began to remove her tattered clothing.

The woman shook her head lightly. "No, not yet." Relieved that tonight was not the night, she asked the woman her name. "Marjorie," the woman said with a small smile. "And you?"

"Sheik. Marjorie, why did you thank me the other day?"

"Shh, shh," Marjorie hushed her. She continued in a low whisper, "You helped a friend of mine escape." Sheik gave her a look of confusion, and so she added, "What you did to Spike. He was in the infirmary for two nights. We'd been planning but we could never predict when he'd come by. Then suddenly we had our window and," she gave Sheik a smile that looked like it might dissolve into tears, "and she made it."

Sheik didn't know who this person was, but it gave her hope that there really was the potential for escape. "How?" she asked with excitement.

"Rumor has it," Marjorie whispered, "that she lured a guard into her room. Somehow," she said pointedly, "the girl had obtained a knife. They found the guard dead in her cell, his throat slit. She took his keys, and no one has seen her since." Sheik wondered if Marjorie would be willing to do the same for her. But Marjorie dashed her hopes by explaining, "She wasn't poisoned like you."

"Ah." Sheik's hopes dissolved away. There wasn't any hope. Not until she was given the full cure. Not until Spike had impregnated her. She banished the thought and forced a smile for Marjorie. "I'm glad your friend is safe. Who was she?"

Marjorie gave a long sigh as she continued to bathe Sheik. "Oh child, you don't want to know."

"I do," Sheik replied, now even more curious.

There was a long pause, like Marjorie truly didn't want to say it out loud. "Sophia. Spike's sister."

Sheik's jaw dropped. "His sister? Why would he take his sister prisoner?"

"To torture her. He does all sorts of awful things to her. Beats her. Shaves her head." In a low voice, she added, "He rapes her. She's been his prisoner for years now."

Sheik nearly vomited. How could anyone do such a thing? "How can all these people follow Spike, claim he's a good person, when he's…" she couldn't even finish the sentence.

Marjorie gave a slow shake of her head. "From what I've pieced together, when Spike first began the New Prosper Army, Sophia tried to stand against him. Spike was very distraught to have to take her prisoner. Like it was a terrible sacrifice, but necessary for the movement. I don't think anyone knows what he's been doing to her ever since. I'm one of the few who sees her. Everyone else seems to think he's being merciful by keeping her alive." She sighed. "It would have been more merciful to kill her a long time ago."

Sheik felt like all life had gone out of her. This sick man who had raped his own sister was soon going to rape her. How would she survive this? "I can't believe it," Sheik admitted. She didn't want to believe it. People were following this man. People would die for him, believed him to be their liberator, their savior. How could such a dichotomy exist?

"I told you you wouldn't want to know," Marjorie said quietly.

"Yes, but if we know the truth we can use it against him, can't we? Surely if word gets out no one will follow such a man." Maybe Sheik wouldn't need to escape after all. Maybe all she'd have to do is turn Spike's own men against him.

Marjorie gave her a sad smile. "It's a nice thought. But who would believe a serving maid over a man like Spike?" She let out a long sigh. "There isn't much you can do against men with so much power. All we can do is just try to stay alive." A bang on the door interrupted their conversation. The sorcerer shouted for them to hurry up, that Spike was waiting. Marjorie helped Sheik get redressed and then gave her hand a soft squeeze. "Stay alive, child."

⸺◦⸺

Atarius looked out into the water of the river. They sat at the quiet, still part, where the stream moved slowly and calmly. It was peaceful, no one there but the two of them. She always relished every moment she got alone with him.

Normally they talked. But now they were quiet. They simply sat side by side, watching the river, listening to its sound. The sun shined through, highlighting Atarius' face perfectly. His soft skin, his silver eyes, his dark hair. As she looked at him, she knew everything was perfect. The late autumn weather was perfect, their beautiful surroundings were perfect. He was perfect, and the moment he looked down at her felt eternal.

He reached out and grabbed her hand, his fingers gently gliding over hers. She leaned back, taking his hand with her, implying that he should lie down on the sandy bank next to her. He did so, propping himself up with one arm while the other continued to hold her hand. The sun made her want to close her eyes but she couldn't stop staring at him.

Atarius let go of her hand. She was afraid the moment was over, but to her surprise he reached out and brushed her bangs out of her face. "Sheik," he whispered quietly. Something in his voice sounded

380

like he wanted to say more. He didn't though. Instead, he leaned forward, his palm resting on her cheek and his lips resting on her own.

The kiss lasted longer than she had expected. Her heart pumped fast and irregular as he breathed through her parted lips. As she returned the kiss, she savored the taste and gentle feel of his mouth on hers. After a long moment his lips broke away, though they continued to hover passionately close as their eyes stared into each other.

"I love you," she whispered faintly, as Spike's fist struck her again. That was what she had wanted to say. And what she had wanted him to say. Instead, Atarius had simply lain down next to her while she rested her head against his shoulder. It was so long ago, but she still remembered it so clearly.

She gasped for air and continued to focus on the memory of Atarius. The time he had kissed her. How perfect it had been. She clung to that memory like it was the only thing keeping her alive. And perhaps it was.

The thoughts of Atarius helped dull the pain. Sometimes even after the beatings she would still retain the slightest smile on her face, just remembering those short moments she had been with him.

Spike hit her again. Ever since he had been cleared from the infirmary, Spike brought Sheik into a new chamber for beatings. His injuries were still significant enough he couldn't force himself on her, but he had recovered enough of his strength to beat her senseless.

The first night was the worst. It was the night she had spoken to Marjorie. And Sheik suspected it was the night that Spike had first learned that his sister was missing.

He had screamed and cursed and beat her with such fury she wasn't sure she would live through it. Sheik could tell it wasn't a tactful form of torture. He was incredibly angry, and it seemed Sheik was his new victim for releasing that anger. He stopped only when he had physically exhausted himself and then he left Sheik alone in the chamber for hours.

After his initial rage, the beatings grew less severe. But Sheik's living situation had changed. She was now held in a new chamber. She wondered if it might have been Sophia's chamber. She no longer was given trips to the dining hall. Her food was delivered with the changing of her sorcerer guard. Aside from them, Spike was her only visitor.

Despite the lack of visitors, he was careful not to hit her face. Her torso was bruised from her collarbones down to her gut. Her arms had markings from where he had grabbed her and flung her about. Her ribs and back ached from being kicked on the floor. But her face was spotless, and she fully knew why: when she returned to the public eyes, none of the common soldiers would know how she had been mistreated.

Every time he beat her, she was administered medicine. Not enough to give her the strength to fight back, just the right amount that the numbness would fade. So she could feel every painful strike of his hand.

She no longer had any doubt about him being good or evil. His diplomatic side faded away the instant the sorcerers left them alone. All that was left was Spike's rage. He was no longer charismatic. There was no more façade. This was him. The man that none of his soldiers could see. The man that Sophia had seen every day.

It seemed Sheik was Spike's new Sophia.

But there was relief in knowing that Spike was beating her out of anger. Sheik could think of far worse ways to be tortured. It didn't seem Spike cared about her suffering; she was just an outlet for his rage. And his rage died when he was physically exhausted. Since he was still quite injured, it didn't take long before he would tire or rip out a stitch or hurt himself in some other way.

Sheik went into her trance. She focused on thoughts of Atarius. On peaceful thoughts. Of that perfect day, so long ago.

Time began to melt away. Since she never saw daylight and no longer had regular mealtimes, she was not sure how much time had passed. Perhaps hours, perhaps days. Her life was simply a timeless box, a rotation of beatings and food.

A voice snapped her back into reality. "Spike!"

The violence stopped and Spike composed himself. "Yes?" he replied, leaving the room.

It was a messenger, completely out of breath. "Your healers!" Sheik sucked in. "Only two survived the retreat," he explained as quickly as he could. "They are waiting for you in your chambers."

"Only two?" he asked in surprise. Sheik wasn't sure how many he had originally had, but obviously her army had killed a fair amount of them. It gave her at least a small piece of satisfaction within the terrible news that the messenger brought: Spike would be healed, and Sheik was soon to bear his child.

⸺◦⸺

The water rushed over her head as she sunk downwards. She had never had so many eyes on her naked body. This time, she did not have the luxury of Marjorie giving her a bath. At least the sorcerers were being gentle, though. It was surprising, considering how rough they normally were with her. Spike had probably given orders for her to be treated kindly.

Kindness hardly mattered. She knew what was about to happen. What she was being prepared for. A hand ran through her hair, scrubbing it with soap. She was pulled back out of the water quickly. With the poison, she had difficulty holding her breath for any period of time. They had to keep her from drowning.

Again, she sank into the water. It was warm and would have been refreshing if not for the circumstances. Another hand wiped some dirt and blood from her. Her eyes stayed shut to avoid making her blurred and painful vision even worse.

The hands continued to move about her body for what felt like forever. She tried to stay calm, to accept their gentle touch, but she could not help but squirm. And she knew this would be the highlight of her evening.

Spike would not be nearly as gentle with her.

At least, she couldn't imagine that he would be. After all the trouble she had caused and all the pain he had suffered because of her, she could only assume that he would bring her as much grief as he could. The more she thought about it, the more she squirmed under the touch of the hands cleaning her.

Finally it was finished. They brought her out of the water, throwing a robe around her bare flesh. She clutched it as hard as she could and made sure it covered her well. Clinging to it brought her some sort of relief.

Then she was doused in perfume and her hair was combed out. Once again they were gentle. They kept their hands close to her scalp as they worked out tangles, taking caution not to pull too hard as they tied and braided her hair. All this concern for her wellbeing when she was only being prepared for abuse.

The men led her out of the foreign room into a more recognizable hallway. She shivered a bit, her hair still damp, her robe hardly providing her with any warmth. The sorcerers did not seem to notice, or they simply didn't care. Following the familiar hallways, she was led to a room that, while she had never been inside, she instantly recognized.

It was Spike's bedroom chambers.

Spike was waiting for her just outside the grand double doors. "Is she clean?" he asked the sorcerers, as if she was some disgusting rat that he was afraid of catching disease from.

"Absolutely," one of the men spoke up, pushing her towards him. Sheik had difficulty standing on her own because of the poison, but

Spike caught her with ease. He grabbed her chin and turned her face up towards him, inspecting it.

"Very well, you may leave us now," Spike instructed, watching the sorcerers turn and go. He let out a small chuckle as he looked back down at Sheik. "It will be just you and I for the rest of the evening."

Sheik swallowed a lump in her throat but said nothing. She was far too weak from the poison to resist when he opened the doors and pulled her inside.

It was a magnificently large room. Flashbacks of King Faris' palace came to mind, but even that was not as beautiful. The walls were covered with glorious murals, depicting various triumphant battle scenes. The floor was made of a beautiful wood but included a carpet that led directly to the bed. Spike pushed her down the carpeting like she was walking to her death. Finally she fell against the soft bedding.

Despite how well-crafted it was, how pleasant it smelled, and even how comfortable it was, Sheik's body remained tense and full of fear. She knew what was coming, and no matter what her surroundings were like, she would not be able to relax. A small tear escaped her eyes.

Spike began undoing the buttons on his finely tailored shirt. Sheik bit down on her lip. As much as she wanted to close her eyes, something made her keep them open. She had only seen him in long-sleeved shirts, and thought perhaps his upper body would be covered in as many scars as his lower half had been.

Sure enough, it was. He was littered with war wounds. He was like some sort of walking undead creature, unable to die no matter how often he was injured. The scars, keloids, and bumps rose out of his skin in a messy pattern. It was almost fascinating how inhuman he appeared.

Her breathing grew heavy as she panicked, thinking about what he was about to do to her. More tears ran down her face, though she tried not to make any noise for fear it would upset him. As his shirt fell to the floor and he began working on his pants, Sheik looked away.

That was when she first noticed the ceiling. It was fully glass, revealing the night sky above them. The moon was nowhere to be seen. Whether it was a new moon or simply out of sight, she wasn't sure. But the stars gleamed bright above them.

Fully undressed, Spike climbed onto the bed next to her. As he pulled away her robe, she didn't bother fighting him. It was a fight she knew she would lose. He explored her naked body first with his eyes, then his hands.

She tried to focus on one of the stars, praying it would give her comfort. She prayed to Elilah that that star would somehow get her through this night. That by merely focusing on it perhaps the pain would melt away and she would by some miracle survive the torture she was about to go through.

But then the star disappeared.

"Look at me," Spike spoke firmly, turning her face towards him.

She pulled her head away from his grasp, looking back up at the night sky, curious how the star had vanished. How was that possible? The stars were disappearing. Then reappearing. What was happening?

"Look at me!" he demanded again. "I want you to watch what I do to you." He gripped her jaw, forcing her to face him, but still her eyes remained on the stars. She couldn't look away from the blinking sky.

He slapped her again and again, harder, trying to get her to focus on him. "The stars," she managed to whisper between his strikes.

Spike stopped what he was doing and turned to look up into the night. He did not see it at first, but then suddenly he gasped. Pulling himself away from Sheik, he quickly redressed.

She was confused for a moment why it had stopped him. Why was he not forcing himself on her? But then she realized what he saw: the stars were not disappearing and reappearing. They were being blocked out by objects flying in the sky.

Wyverns.

Isandas was under attack.

CHAPTER 20

Kazzak glanced towards the sky. The wyverns themselves couldn't be seen, but one could spot them by the stars that disappeared when they passed under them. It was an incredible sight to watch. Hundreds of stars flickering in and out of sight because of the gigantic swarm of wyverns.

He waited patiently for the moment of attack, strapping on the skirn that Jason had taught him to use. Spike and his army certainly knew an attack was coming. Their soldiers were positioned just outside Isandas. He likely thought it was better to take the defensive, as the palace had a moat and tall walls that would be difficult for foot soldiers to breach. But Spike hadn't known that they had wyverns.

The plan was for the wyverns to take out as many of the outside guards as they could until the castle realized the attack had begun. Then the foot soldiers, wielding their skirns, would form a defensive wall and march on the bridge to the palace. With the skirns serving as a perfect defense and the wyverns a perfect offense, it would only be a matter of time before Isandas fell.

And then they would find Sheik. If she was still alive. No. Kazzak forced the thought out of his mind. She had to be alive. He still had trouble believing she had been captured at all.

It had been a strange turn of events.

Kazzak vividly remembered waking up in the snow after the avalanche. He had been knocked unconscious, and when he awoke Jason was standing by his side. Though they had searched for several hours, they had been unsuccessful in finding any of the others.

After escaping the mountains, Jason hardly had a plan of what to do. It had seemed hopeless. But Kazzak assured him that Sheik and the others were alive. Somewhere out there, he knew they had survived. Or at least he had hoped with every fiber of his being.

And so Kazzak had managed to convince Jason to travel back the way they had come and recruit the man's brother. Jamen was not nearly as easy to persuade. But then they received the news of King Garret's fall, and Kazzak knew deep down that Sheik was alive and responsible for the assassination.

Not long afterwards, with a little of Kazzak's diplomacy, Jason and Jamen were leading their forest bandit troops upriver to connect with Sheik's army. But they were too late. They had missed the battle in which Sheik was kidnapped by only a few days.

Kazzak refused to give up. A messenger was sent back to the Tasvran and almost immediately King Faris sent an army of wyverns to assist them. Between the wyverns, King Faris' foot soldiers, and Jamen and Jason's troop, they were sure to win. To rescue Sheik.

He was terrified for her safety. Being the slave of Spike himself. Kazzak couldn't imagine what she'd gone through.

And he missed her, too. He hadn't realized how close they had grown until the day they had become separated. These past many weeks had been so lonely. He wanted nothing more than to see her smile or feel her warm embrace.

But now he had to focus on the battle before him. At the first sound of Isandas being aware of the attack, he had to be ready to fight. And he had to be ready to implement his own plan.

He hadn't told the others, but he had no intention of staying in their defensive wall. As soon as it was safe enough, Kazzak planned to drop the skirn and get inside the palace as fast as possible. The others had to stand their ground, fight until the last New Prosper soldier was dead. But Kazzak had to find Sheik.

As he watched the impossibly-hard-to-see wyverns, he waited anxiously for the Isandas guards to realize they were under attack. He silently wondered how Spike had taken over the castle. Did he have enough men disguised within the castle to destroy it from the inside out? Or had he found a way to get past the moat? He wondered why anyone would have followed Spike in the first place. For the longest time he was just a nobody, his rebellion hardly posing a threat. Then, seemingly overnight, he had conquered Isandas and then Etmos itself and was now taking over all the other countries one by one.

Of course, the same went for Sheik. Back in Calert she was nobody. And now, if not her name, her legend had spread across the lands. The one fighting off the New Prosper. One of the few people brave enough to stand up to Spike. Kazzak winced as he thought about what the cruel man could be doing to her.

Focus, he reminded himself. He looked at the blinking stars in the sky, disappearing and reappearing because of the wyverns. Then he saw another light appear from the castle. A torch. Another lit up.

They were aware of the attack. Jamen's voice boomed over the soldiers. "Into position, go, go!" he chanted, and immediately the foot soldiers moved. They walked in a silent march, appearing out of the darkness and heading towards the main road. Side by side, they formed a perfect shield.

The fight was about to begin.

⁕

Sheik sat up in the bed weakly. She dressed herself, tightening the robe around her body. Spike was gone, and he had not bothered to send any sorcerers into the room to watch her. For the first time in the past two weeks, she was free.

But when she stood up, her face flushed and her legs wobbled. She hadn't had medicine in hours. The poison was too strong throughout her body.

Falling onto the floor, she crawled feebly, shaking as she pulled herself around by her arms. Her arms were often stronger than her legs, or at least worked for longer than her legs could without medicine. She had hoped to find some sort of weapon, but the room was huge and filled with countless dressers, drawers, and closets. She had no idea where to even start searching.

Her head ached something awful, and numbness soaked into her body. It started with her toes. They slowly began to lose feeling. Then her feet and fingers. She knew what was coming next. After the numbness came the blurred vision. Sure enough, as she scrambled to grab onto something, she could no longer keep her eyes in focus. Everything felt strange and disorienting. The objects around her swirled confusingly into one large image, like a painting splashed with water.

Then blackness began to surround her. The numbness continued to crawl up her arms and legs. The strange sensation felt like a beast sucking the life from her body. She had felt this way several times before. But she had always been administered medicine before the numbness could find its way to her center.

When was the last time she had been given medicine? She could hardly remember. The foggy blackness clouded her vision, shutting off the world around her completely. She was numb, immobile, and blind. She had never been this bad before. She had never gone this long without the medicine.

She was going to die.

<hr>

Kazzak winced as the blood splashed up against his face. He ripped the left half of the skirn out swiftly, the spikes tugging free of the corpse. It was difficult fighting like this. It was not how he was used to fighting. Perhaps simply because he was used to using different weapons. But that wasn't the only thing that made this battle different.

The whole world smelled like blood and death. For some reason, prior to this battle, Kazzak had the strange notion that he wouldn't die. He simply hadn't ever put any thought into death and the high chance he had of dying. Even after the avalanche he had hardly considered the concept.

It wasn't until he had gotten word of Sheik's capture that he really thought about dying. Losing. They were the good guys, and good guys always won in the end. But when Sheik had been taken, his faith wavered, and he could now sense death in the air.

He ripped through another soldier with the right blade of his skirn. He wanted to sprint ahead and kill all of them at once. But, of course, he couldn't. The point of the skirn was to fight defensively. To jump out, make a kill, and immediately click back into the wall of shields all around him.

But rage pounded in his heart. Not adrenaline. He had felt adrenaline many times in arenas and battles Sheik had led. But he had never felt such a deep anger for his enemies. Hatred.

They had Sheik. Behind those walls, she was suffering. And there was nothing he could do about it. He had to stay and fight with the rest of the foot soldiers, at least for now. The more he thought about her being tortured, the more he wanted to break through and kill everyone in the castle.

But he tried to stay rational, to not let his emotions overtake him. To stay patient. To stay calm. He would get his chance eventually.

Another swarm of soldiers headed his way. Block. Push. Dodge. Strike. It had become almost mechanical. A routine that he had performed now perhaps fifty times. They were unused to fighting against the skirn and didn't fully understand how it attacked. They didn't know where to guard, where to attack, or when to be prepared. Block. Push. Dodge. Strike. It was so simple and yet so deadly.

But even with their strong defense, Kazzak had still taken some blows. One enemy had managed to cut open his right shoulder. Though not a bad wound, it continued to bleed and throb. And his arms were sore, a large bruise beginning to form from ramming into his opponents with the skirn. With every hit he felt his arm might snap. Yet he refused to let the pain slow him down. Block. Push. Dodge. Strike.

More blood splattered against him. He was starting to hate war. As much as he believed in the cause they were fighting for, the constant bloodshed was sickening.

He smashed into yet another soldier, knocking them to the ground. Now able to see ahead, Kazzak glanced at the enemy still coming at them. A wyvern plowed into a row of men, sending them flying off the bridge and into the moat below. This was his chance. The space left open gave him his opportunity to get inside the castle.

Hardly able to run with the skirn strapped to his arm, he yanked the weapon off and instead drew a short sword. It would protect him without hindering his movement. Speed was key.

Several of the men next to him gave him strange looks as they watched him change out his weapon. When he took off at a full sprint, they let out shouts of confusion. He didn't look back though. He didn't care about sticking to the plan.

A sword came down on him as he ran forward. He pushed into the man, knocking him down, and continued his sprint. More soldiers leapt at him, but he dodged them without much difficulty and made his way through the pockets of men.

As he entered the large castle gates, breathing a sigh of relief that the mad scramble to safety was over, he discovered just how many soldiers there were. Crowded into the main hall were hundreds of men preparing for the battle waiting outside the castle. "Dear Ziad," Kazzak mumbled under his breath as all eyes turned to him, shocked that he had entered the palace on his own.

The sound of weapons being drawn echoed throughout the busy hall. Kazzak inched back against a wall, realizing he was surrounded and cornered. The world felt suddenly hot. Sweat trickled down his forehead.

Then he noticed why it had grown so warm.

Directly to the right of his head was a lantern. Grabbing it with his free hand, he threw it down in a swift motion. The flames spread as fast as he'd hoped, creating a barrier of fire between him and his enemies.

Once again, Kazzak was sprinting. The soldiers might still pursue him, but the fire would slow them down and at least give him a better chance to escape. He was beginning to regret breaking away from his formation. It certainly wasn't working as he'd imagined. But it was too late now; all he could do was hope that somehow he could make it to Sheik alive.

<hr>

Spike watched the battle below him. He was in one of the tallest towers, able to view both the defensive wall of foot soldiers and the many wyverns circling the castle. One creature plowed against the tower, shaking it horribly and causing Spike to fall to the floor.

"Sir!" a soldier cried, bending down to help him.

"No sirs, how many times must I remind everyone?" He picked himself up and dusted off his fine clothing. He was not dressed in armor, but rather his usual gold and white outfit. Unlike the others fighting below him, fighting like beasts in the wild, he was graceful and elegant.

Taking another glance at the battle below, the long pause of silence was ended. "We need to leave."

"What?"

"This tower, this castle, this place. We need to leave," Spike instructed seriously. "Gather all of my wizards, all my healers. As many loyalists as you can. We must depart at once."

He began to stroll away casually, but the many soldiers around him called out in protest. "We'll be left vulnerable to the wyverns! We'll be ripped to pieces!"

Spike held up his hand, demanding silence. "We'll escape the same way all the lords and ladies of Isandas did when I conquered this castle. Through the north tunnel." He waved for his soldiers to follow. "Come, we must gather what troops are left. Kill any servants you come across. If we kill anyone who may know about the north tunnel and conceal the entrance, we might escape without being followed."

⸻◆⸻

The door creaked open casually. Sheik tried to lift her head towards the sound. Not that she would be able to see who it was anyway; her vision was completely gone. Could Spike be back so soon? She had imagined he would be gone all night commanding his army. Apparently not.

A hand brushed against her head. It wasn't Spike. She had gotten to know Spike's touch. His hands were soft and smooth, as if they were constantly oiled and manicured. This man's hand was rough and calloused. "All alone?" the man spoke.

The voice sounded vaguely familiar. Of course! It was one of the sorcerers. One of Spike's wizards in charge of her medicine. Medicine. She was going to receive medicine. Her vision would come back. Her strength. Maybe she would be able to escape after all.

"It's a good thing I came to check on you," the man spoke again. His hand moved through her hair. It was gentle at first, but then, with a sudden yank, he pulled her face up so he could look at her.

398

Sheik's eyes snapped open at the pain, but still could see nothing. Vague splashes of distant light, perhaps, but she had no idea what the man looked like.

He paused. "Blind, hmm?" Obviously her eyes had clouded over or gave some sign of her vision going. "You're pretty close to death," he said flatly. "Don't worry, though, you'll be better in—"

The man coughed before he could finish his sentence. Liquid dripped into her mouth. She closed her lips to savor the sweet honey taste of the medicine.

She cringed. It tasted like a salty copper. It was not medicine—it was blood.

The man fell on top of her, more of his blood dripping onto her. Glass shattered against the floor. "What's going on?" Sheik managed to whisper, unable to see or even feel around to get a clue of what was happening.

Then the man's weight was lifted off her. "Sheik?" Another familiar voice, but she could not quite identify it. "Sheik!" The man kneeled to the floor instantly, wrapping his large arms around her. His scent hit her. That was one sense unaffected by the poison—her ability to smell. And now she inhaled his familiar aroma, shocked beyond belief.

"Kazzak?"

"Of course! Can't you see me?"

How in Elilah was Kazzak alive? How was he here, sitting with her? Was this a trick? Questions bubbled through her mind, her confusion overwhelming her. No, she had to stay calm. She was about to die, and if she was going to live she had to stay calm. Her voice was weak, but she forced the words out of her mouth. "I'm poisoned. Need medicine. In vial."

"Vial? Oh, that? It shattered," Kazzak mumbled.

"What?" Sheik asked, frantic. Shattered? The medicine was gone? She was going to die. She had just learned Kazzak was alive and now she was going to die? He had come for her, come to keep her alive, and in his haste had killed the man who was actually saving her. He had sentenced her to death. A small tear escaped her eye, but her face was too numb to feel it roll down her cheek.

"Calm down, don't worry," Kazzak whispered soothingly. "It's okay."

Tears streamed down her face. "It isn't!" she cried out, her voice hoarse from all she had endured these past weeks. "I'm dying. I thought you were dead." Her thoughts began to muddle together. How was this happening? Since she'd arrived at Isandas she had expected death. Sometimes even wanted death. But now that it was actually happening, she couldn't fathom it.

"I love you."

She hardly even realized she had said it. It had simply blurted out, as if she had no control over her own words. Perhaps she had always wanted to say it but hadn't found the strength until now. Now that she was going to die.

Kazzak was silent for a second. Unable to see, she didn't know what his reaction was. Was he in shock? Had he even heard her? Did he not care? Then finally he spoke up. "Just calm down. Drink this the best you can."

Before she could reply, his fingers were in her mouth. She didn't understand at first, but then she tasted the honey-sweet liquid. The medicine. He had scooped up what he could from the broken vial.

With his other hand, Kazzak brushed her bangs out of her face. It reminded her of Atarius. He used to do that. Atarius. She would never see him again—the amount Kazzak had given her was not nearly as much as a normal dosage. She was still going to die.

"Sheik." Kazzak's voice snapped her back into reality. "Do you know where the medicine is kept? I can get you more."

"No," she managed to whisper, swallowing the last of the medicine he was able to give her.

"Okay, well let's think about this rationally," he said, taking a deep breath. She imagined he was just as panicked as her, simply trying his best not to show it. But then something interrupted both of their thoughts.

The clattering of armor, echoing down the hallway.

Soldiers.

"Oh Ziad," Kazzak trembled, his voice shaky. The medicine was enough to still off the numbness, but her vision was still black. And now soldiers were upon them. Kazzak left her side and pulled his sword from the corpse next to them.

But then, as the doors burst open, instead of combat, Kazzak exclaimed, "Jason?"

"Kazzak!" the familiar voice called back. "What in Ziad's name were you thinking running off like that?" A pause. "Most of the troops surrendered. Spike and some others found a way out of the castle, we're all searching for them. What are you doing in here?" He obviously had not noticed who Sheik was and must have thought she was just another dead body.

"They've fled?" Kazzak asked, ignoring Jason's question. Relief was obvious in his voice. "Sheik needs a medicine. Tell them to abandon their mission and start searching for vials instead. It looks like this."

"Sheik?" Jason asked. Then he must have seen her because he yelled her name again. "You're alive!"

"Stop!" Sheik pleaded. "If it's between me and killing Spike—"

"I would choose you every time," Kazzak interrupted. There was defiance in his voice. "We're searching for the medicine and that's final. Jason, go inform the troops."

Jason took off at a sprint, not even bothering to reply, eager to obey his orders. But Sheik gave out a frustrated cry. "Kazzak!"

He bent down by her side and lifted her head. "I didn't come here to kill Spike, I came here to save you. I..." he trailed off for a quick moment. "I love you, too. And I'm not going to let you die." He leaned over, giving her a rushed kiss.

Chapter 21

Sheik didn't remember passing out. She had felt faint. Her skin had gone completely numb throughout her entire body—someone could have stabbed her and she might not have felt it. And she had been completely unable to see and hardly able to breathe. But she didn't remember the actual moment she became unconscious.

And now she was awake. Perhaps more important than being awake, she was healed. Before she had even opened her eyes, she knew she had received the cure. The sense of poison, the toxic feeling beating with her heart, was gone. For the first time in weeks, she took in a deep breath, relieved to be alive and well.

Tara was lying to one side of her and Fang the other. Both were asleep and Tara looked particularly exhausted so Sheik decided not to wake them. Sitting across from them all was Auni, who jumped to his feet upon seeing Sheik turn her head. "You're awake!" he smiled. Sheik almost laughed, as she had never seen him so excited before.

His exclamation woke Fang who, upon seeing Sheik conscious, licked her face repeatedly.

"Auni, Fang! I've missed you both!" she smiled, giving Fang a hug and then waving for Auni to come next to her. He did and they shared a quick embrace. "Where's everyone else? Is everyone alright?" She had so many questions to ask. After all, she had been gone for weeks. And with such a large battle all sorts of things could have occurred.

Auni sat down on the bed and thought for a moment. "Well let's see. Asroth hasn't left the library since discovering it. Oh, Kazzak and Jason are both alive! I'm not sure if you remembered that. And Jason's brother is here, too. His troops and King Faris' troops are mostly digging out the tunnel."

"The tunnel?" Sheik asked, confused. She was confused about a lot of things, but she decided to only ask about one.

Auni nodded and breathed a sigh of relief. "Glad I'm not the only one who hasn't heard of it. Apparently it's common knowledge around here. Some north tunnel that all the Isandas royalty escaped through. Well Spike must have known about it because he and almost all his men have disappeared."

"I see." She was still a bit overwhelmed, but things were beginning to make some sense. "Is Tara alright? She looks sick or something."

"Well," Auni began with half a sigh, "the medicine healed your sickness but you were still pretty beat up. The army only had a few healers, and they were all tending to the rest of the soldiers. So Tara had to heal you all on her own and I guess it exhausted her."

Sheik raised an eyebrow. "What about Asroth?"

"I'm not sure, really. It was strange, he tried healing you. Tried healing some soldiers, too. For some reason he just couldn't. No matter how hard he tried, it was like he lost his magic. He wouldn't talk to anyone about it, you know how he is. And then he found the palace library and now he's too busy with that to talk at all." He gave a shrug and half a smile. "Not that I mind."

She laughed and, stretching, climbed out of bed. Tara had clearly done a good job; Sheik hardly even felt sore. Fang bounded down and paced around her and she gave him a strong scratch behind the ears before turning back to Auni. "Do you know where Kazzak is?" One of the last things she remembered was him saying he loved her and then kissing her. She wasn't sure where to begin with that. She didn't know what it meant. Or even what she wanted it to mean. All she knew is she wanted desperately to see him.

⟡

Asroth glanced over the hundreds of thousands of books. He had once thought the library in his hometown, Darinshire, was huge. It was miniscule compared to this. There were three levels to the library, the topmost being restricted. But, of course, now that both the original guards and Spike's guards had been driven out, there was no one to enforce the law. And so it was the top floor that Asroth began browsing first.

It was nice to have the luxury of staying in a castle again. It was a life he could get used to. Since no one else had claimed it, he slept in the greatest of rooms: the king's room. The room where Spike himself had stayed. Sleeping in the center of the castle, beneath the glass ceiling, made Asroth feel like a god. Finally he was receiving what he was long overdue.

He had joined this whole mess for two things: money and fame. Money he had seen none of. He wanted to be able to buy a study so he could be alone all the time, learning more of his magic and growing more powerful. And fame? Sheik had taken all of that.

There had been a hopeful moment when she had disappeared. He thought then that he might be able to take over the army. Instead of 'the rebellion led by the elf' it could be 'the rebellion led by the wizard.' But no, as they invaded Isandas they discovered that Sheik was still alive. And, worse yet, instead of chasing after Spike, Kazzak managed to convince the entire army to stop and search for medicine to keep Sheik alive.

It simply didn't make sense. How could they stop their entire mission for one person? Especially someone as useless as Sheik. After all, she had allowed herself to be kidnapped. Asroth would never have been so stupid. He would have defended himself. It was pa-thetic, really.

He hated that he was still with this group. But it wouldn't be for much longer. Something would change. What, exactly, he couldn't place. It was like he was arguing with himself all the time. Did he want to abandon them quietly and let them struggle without him? Did he want to kill them with his dark magic? Or was he still determined to aid them against Spike? Did he want to take Tara by force or win her affections with his strength? His mind spun with the possibilities, the conflict. He didn't know what he would do, but he knew things couldn't go on as they were, not for much longer.

He simply had to wait for his perfect moment. To find what it was he wanted and to claim what he deserved. Glancing across another aisle of books, he finally found the section he was looking for: dark magic. But his smile faded into a frown.

The section was empty. Someone had taken them. Every last book on dark magic, gone.

⸻ ❖ ⸻

A smile came to her mouth after finally finding him. Fang trotted along by her side. She raised her hand to shield her eyes from the sun so she could be certain it was Kazzak. Sure enough, he sat below a tree playing his pan flute. "Kazzak!"

He looked up and returned the smile. "Sheik!"

She couldn't help but laugh at his silly grin. "Never thought I'd be so happy to hear you play your pan flute."

"They told me I had to be outside the castle walls if I wanted to play," he joked. "How you feeling?" He patted the ground next to himself, encouraging her to sit.

"Pretty good considering you saved my life. Again," she replied with a shrug.

He watched her as she took a seat next to him. Putting away his pan flute he replied coolly, "I'd say it was a joint effort. Again." He shot her another grin. "Fang was the one who actually sniffed out the medicine. I guess me and him make a pretty good team when it comes to rescuing you, huh?"

A wider smile spread across Sheik's face, both at Kazzak's teasing and Fang's efforts in saving her life. She chuckled and looked down at Fang, petting his head. "You saved me again, huh boy?" His mouth opened into a smile and she scratched behind his ear before turning back to Kazzak.

Something about his face was serious. His grey eyes stared directly into her. They were different than Atarius', but it felt similar, the way they pierced through her.

He leaned forward and her heart began to pound, her breathing suddenly frozen. "So," he began slowly. "About that kiss."

She was relieved that he was the one to mention it. She wanted so badly to ask him about it, to ask him what his feelings were, to know what it meant. But she couldn't bring herself to ask. It would be too embarrassing and, although she knew it was silly and childish, she wanted him to be the one to state his feelings first. She wanted him to tell her he cared about her, to ask her to be with him. Just like she had always wanted from Atarius.

"I'm sorry," Kazzak disrupted her thoughts. "When you said I love you, I thought you meant like, in a relationship sort of way. But if you didn't mean it in that way, then I'm sorry."

"Oh," Sheik replied flatly. "So you didn't mean to kiss me?"

"What? No." He stumbled over his words. "No, that's not what I'm saying." Regaining his composure, he explained, "I meant what I said. I love you, Sheik. And if you feel the same way, then I'm glad I kissed you. But even if you don't, well I'm just so relieved you're alive." He chuckled, but Sheik noticed tears welling up in his eyes. "I really thought I'd lost you."

At this, Sheik, too, nearly cried. She squeezed her eyes together and leaned her head against his shoulder. "I thought I'd lost you too." He wrapped an arm around her, pulling her close to him. "I'm so glad you're okay."

"Me too." They stayed wrapped in each other's arms for a moment. Sheik thought about how she had mourned his death after the avalanche. How certain she had been that she would never see Kazzak again. And then, after being captured by Spike, how certain she had been that she would never see anyone again. Yet now here they were.

Kazzak moved his hand from her shoulder to her head, his fingers stroking her hair. She turned towards him and stared into his grey eyes. With a smile, he said, "So now that we aren't seconds from death, how about we try this again. Sheik, I like you. Do you like me too?"

She nodded and her eyes crinkled as she smiled. "Yes. I like you too." She liked his honesty. His directness. She liked how much he cared for her. She liked the way he held her and brushed his fingers through her hair. She liked the way he stared at her like nothing else in the whole world mattered.

He leaned closer. "Can I kiss you?"

Her smile grew. "I'd like that."

And then he closed the gap between their lips.

Her eyes closed and her heart raced as he pressed against her. His lips were firm, more confident than the night before, and she relaxed into him. He drew a breath and kissed her more. She wrapped her arms around him and pulled him close, leaning into him, feeling his chest against hers. His hand slid around the back of her neck and his lips slowly peeled away from hers.

Then, in one rapid and sudden movement, he jumped back and pulled his hand off her.

"Tara!"

Sheik's eyes snapped open. Sure enough, the girl was only a few paces away, staring at them. Her jaw hung open in a shocked fashion, but something about her face retained an ecstatic childlike grin. The astonished expression faded away into a simple look of amusement.

"Whatcha doing?" she enunciated mockingly, not bothering to hide her smiling face.

"Oh Ziad," Kazzak mumbled, burying his face in his hands. Sheik could feel heat rushing to her cheeks.

Tara paced around them, still beaming as she glanced down at the two. "I was just thanking him for saving me," Sheik quickly blurted out.

The girl shot her a look of skepticism. "Oh really?" Her expression quickly returned to a childish grin. She reached out and grabbed Sheik by the arm, pulling her to her feet. "Well come on then, you have a whole army full of men to kiss—oh, I mean, 'thank,'" she corrected herself, her smile never fading.

As Tara dragged her away, Sheik glanced back just in time to see Kazzak lift his head up and raise his hand in a pathetic wave goodbye. Fang hopped to his feet and quickly trotted after Sheik. "Dear Elilah," she muttered to herself, embarrassed beyond belief.

"Why didn't you wake me when you woke up?" Tara pouted when they finally got a good distance away from Kazzak.

The elf rubbed her eyes, a bit disoriented. "What? Oh, Auni said you were exhausted from healing me. I thought you'd want your rest."

"Well," Tara began, suddenly a bit quieter, "I had not exactly finished healing you. That is, I am not sure if I did. I didn't inspect," she paused, "everywhere. But if Spike hurt you in, um, certain areas, well I certainly do not mind healing you."

Sheik understood instantly. "Oh! No, no. I'm fine. He didn't get a chance to... I mean," she stuttered awkwardly, "I'm not fine." How could she be fine? She had been subject to humiliation, her privacy violated. He hadn't had time to rape her, but that didn't make her okay. "Physically I'm fine." Emotionally? She didn't know when she would recover. There was no magic for that.

Tara let out a sigh of relief. "Good. That is good." The silence lingered awkwardly for a moment, and she quickly changed the subject. "So since when do you like Kazzak?" Her grin returned.

Sheik's hand went to her forehead as she let out an embarrassed sigh. "I don't know. When he saved me last night—"

"Two nights ago," Tara interrupted, correcting her. "You were asleep for a while. The attack was two nights ago."

Sheik shrugged it away. "Whatever. I thought I was going to die. And all these thoughts were racing through my mind. Everything I wish I could have said to everyone. And then without even realizing it I just blurted out 'I love you.'"

"Wow. Pretty bold." The girl seemed almost impressed.

"Not when you think you're going to die," Sheik laughed. "It doesn't matter much then. But anyhow, after I said—"

"Lady Sheik!"

A troop of ten soldiers approached the two women. She recognized Jamen and Jason but the rest of them were unfamiliar Tasvranian soldiers. "Who are they?" Sheik asked quickly, before the men were in hearing range.

"Oh those are all the commanders or generals or whatever," Tara replied nonchalantly.

They approached rapidly. The Tasvranian men took a knee upon reaching them, but Jamen and Jason remained standing. "It's nice to see you again, Miss Sheik," Jason said with a charming smile.

She returned the smile politely. "Of course, you too. I'm relieved you are alive and well." Though she still wasn't particularly fond of his constant smiling and waiting on her.

"Lady Sheik, we were given orders by the King to follow your command," one of the Tasvranian men she did not recognize spoke, rising to his feet.

Sheik didn't know what to say. She wanted to explain that they probably knew better than her. As cunning and resourceful as she had been in fighting Spike, she really didn't know a lot about warfare. "Well, I was told you all believe Spike to have gone through some north tunnel. Have you found him yet?"

"We found some servants who could show us to the tunnel. But unfortunately he and his men must have done something to trigger an earthquake. It's been completely blocked off. We have a crew digging at it, trying to clear the dirt. Once it's clear we can go after him."

Sheik didn't think it was possible to trigger an earthquake. Perhaps with magic? And Spike certainly had magic users. She sighed. "Well, the most important thing is to find Spike," she concluded simply. "I don't mind helping clear the tunnel as well; my magic might speed up the process."

Another soldier spoke up. "With all due respect, as important as it is to eliminate Spike, we cannot merely abandon Isandas." Sheik looked towards him, curious what he had to say. "We have the castle on lockdown right now. With the exception of familiar faces," he motioned towards Tara, "no one goes in or out. If we were to leave? An empty castle full of treasures is just asking for a riot, Lady Sheik. We need to keep soldiers posted here until we can get order established. Otherwise another rebellion like Spike's could begin all over again with Isandas in an even weaker state."

She hadn't thought of that. She had spent hours analyzing how to conquer Isandas, but now she realized that she had never put any thought into what to do afterwards. She knew nothing of kingdoms or how they functioned, or what it would mean if suddenly the throne was empty. So she deferred to the soldier's judgement. "Understood. Keep digging out the tunnel. When it's clear, I'll go with as few men as possible. The rest of your army," she said, motioning towards Jamen and Jason, "and King Faris' army will stay here."

Sheik still didn't know what would come next. She knew that she couldn't ask King Faris' troops to stay in Isandas indefinitely, at least not if he wasn't gaining any territory for his trouble. But she didn't know who else could be on the throne and restore order to the city that had been through so much.

"Carlos." A sudden wave of sadness hit her, realizing now that he was the only one who had not escaped the mountains. "Carlos had said something about the nobility fleeing when Spike took over. If several soldiers could take wyverns and spread word throughout the countries that Isandas is no longer under his reign, maybe there are still a few..." Her sentence trailed off as she realized she did not like the idea after all. What if Spike's soldiers had been telling the truth about the Isandas nobility being evil? If Spike truly was a liberator, she couldn't possibly put those same people back on the throne, could she?

But her thought was already out and the Tasvranian generals gave dedicated nods. "Will do, Lady Sheik," one spoke before she had a chance to redact her suggestions. Sheik didn't stop them. Perhaps Spike's soldiers had been wrong about him. Or perhaps only some of the royalty were corrupt. Or perhaps Sheik could question whatever royalty they found and make sure they would not oppress the northern plains people again. There were a million possibilities and Sheik didn't want to go back on her suggestion now. "We will declare martial law and begin a conscription to raise an army to defend any royalty we are able to find and reestablish order." Then the generals began marching away.

Jason lingered. "When they've cleared the passage, might I accompany you?"

Sheik was still lost in thought about Spike and politics and Isandas royalty. She wanted to simply ask him to leave her alone, but of course she couldn't bring herself to be so rude. "You and Jamen are the only ones here with experience running a town. These soldiers may be talented and strong, but you two are far more qualified to be keeping the city prosperous. I want you two to stay here and keep an eye on things," she explained.

He gave somewhat of a sorrowful nod, but Sheik tried to ignore it. "If you'll excuse us," she said, trying to retain a friendly smile, and turned back to Tara, "Where were we?"

***

Tara caught Sheik up on all that had happened. How Kazzak and Jason had survived the avalanche and joined up with them only three days after the battle where Sheik was captured. How they had sent back a message to King Faris and he had immediately supplied them with more troops. How Tara had dutifully carried Sheik's bow and belt of knives strapped to her until she was able to return it to Sheik herself.

The weapons were back in the room Sheik had been staying in while unconscious, and Tara led the way, eager to return them to her. But when they arrived, Sheik was surprised to find a stranger in the room, folding up the bedding.

"Who are you?" she asked defensively.

The man took a step back. "I'm just a servant. We were given orders to change the bedding for the soldiers."

"Oh." Sheik let her guard fall as she turned to Tara. "The servants are still here?" She wasn't sure what she had thought would happen to them, but she didn't imagine that they would continue working for King Faris' soldiers.

Tara nodded. "Remember? The castle is on lockdown. Most of Spike's soldiers surrendered instead of fleeing. Faris' soldiers are still trying to sort through the castle and make sure they have all of Spike's troops locked up."

"Locked up?" Sheik asked next.

"Yeah. They wanted to execute them but Kazzak and I told them you would never permit it. So they have them in the dungeons."

Sheik sighed. At least they hadn't been executed. "They shouldn't even be prisoners. Most of them were probably recruited by force and just want to go back to their homes." She glanced over at the servant who was tending to her bedding. "And so you servants aren't allowed to leave either?"

He looked nervous, like he was scared to say the wrong thing. With a shake of his head, he replied, "No, Miss."

"Well, we'll have to fix that," she replied, wondering what else they needed to fix. "You don't happen to know the serving woman Marjorie, do you?"

The man gave her a look of surprise. "Marjorie? Marjorie Hamond?" Sheik didn't know, but gave a nod. "Yes. Do you want me to take you to her?" he asked cautiously.

"Yes, please." The man led her through the halls that Sheik only vaguely recognized from her time as a prisoner. Tara asked who Marjorie was and Sheik summed up how she had met the woman. The dining hall looked as she had remembered it, full of soldiers, though now they were from a different army. Servants bustled in and out of the kitchen.

"Marjorie!" Sheik called out upon seeing the woman.

The woman took her in with surprise. "Lady Sheik. I had heard you survived. I'm relieved to see you with my own eyes."

"Do you have a moment?" Sheik asked, hoping to speak with her in private rather than in the busy kitchen.

Marjorie laughed. "Aren't you the general in charge? If you say I have a moment, then I have a moment."

Sheik frowned, uncomfortable with the idea of overseeing so many people. She had once enjoyed being in charge of their small party. But after her mistake in the mountains, she feared such responsibility. To think that she oversaw the whole army, the whole city of Isandas, was a terrifying thought. "I need to talk to you. Can you take us somewhere quieter?" Marjorie put down her tray of food and led Sheik and Tara through another maze of hallways and doors until they had found somewhere private.

"Marjorie, this is Tara. Tara, Marjorie," Sheik quickly introduced. They said their pleasantries and then Sheik moved on to more pressing matters. "Marjorie, I'm afraid I've a very big favor to ask of you." The woman looked at her with cautious uncertainty. "You're the only person I know in Isandas. The only person I can trust," Sheik explained. "If I have the soldiers round up every servant, will you be able to identify them?"

Marjorie let out a low whistle. "That's quite a task. I've been working here for six years, I certainly know most of the workers. But I can't say I know all of them. Why?"

"Well, perhaps between you and several other people you know for certain you can trust. The soldiers have the castle on lockdown because they don't want any of Spike's men escaping. If you can identify all of the servants, verify that none of them are soldiers for Spike, then we can let you all come and go as you please."

"Really?" Marjorie sighed in relief. "If it means going home, then yes of course. I'll find a few others who I know aren't loyal to Spike and see if they can help."

"Fantastic," Sheik sighed as well. "I'll introduce you to the generals and we'll get that orchestrated. Then we'll make sure you're all being paid for everything you're doing for Faris' soldiers while they stay and everything can go back to normal for everyone in the castle."

They walked through the halls for a few moments, Marjorie thanking Sheik profusely. "Please, you're doing me the favor," Sheik laughed. "I'm just grateful you spoke to me that day." She paused before voicing the next thought on her mind. "I know it's only been two days, but you haven't heard from Sophia at all, have you?"

Marjorie shook her head. "No, I'm afraid not. I know she made it out of the castle, but she's probably still running. Probably hasn't gotten word yet that it's now Spike who's on the run."

Tara shot them both a confused glance and Sheik merely waved it away. "Well, I'm sure she'll find out soon enough. Marjorie, there's something else I need to ask you." The woman looked at her expectantly, but Sheik hesitated, not sure how to broach the subject. "I heard a rumor that the Isandas nobility oppressed the northern plains people. Spike's people," she explained for Tara's sake. "And that Spike was the one to liberate them. But that can't be true, right?" Sheik asked hopefully. "It's just something he told his men, right?"

The serving woman gave a knowing nod. "Yes, I suppose in a sense it's true."

"Wait," Tara interrupted, catching on. "Are you suggesting Spike created the New Prosper Army to actually help people?"

"I try not to follow politics," Marjorie admitted, "but from my understanding, the northern plains people haven't been exactly treated well by the throne. They're a very simple people. They don't have cities or anything. They weren't contributing enough to the monarchy in the way of science or progress, so the king decided to increase their taxes. I'm just a maid," she said, as if trying not to get involved, "I can't really say what's fair or not fair, but of course the northern plains people disagreed with the king and Spike started a riot. That was the beginning of the New Prosper Army."

"Huh," Tara said simply.

Sheik sorted through her thoughts. Perhaps the king was being fair on the northern plains people and Spike and his men had just stirred up dissent over nothing, she considered. But she shook the thought from her head. She was only trying to justify her hatred of Spike. She had wanted the truth, even if that meant that Spike had once been a hero. "So, the northern plains people, they really are better off now?"

Marjorie shrugged. "I'm not sure. Like I said, I'm not much one for politics. Things have been too chaotic for me to bother with listening to news of the north."

"Fair enough," Sheik conceded. Marjorie had given her enough information anyway. Whoever took the throne next needed to be someone who would not repeat the old monarchy's mistakes.

When they finally found Faris' generals, Sheik quickly explained that Marjorie would be able to identify the servants and could aid them in the process of returning Isandas to a normal state. One general pushed back, but Sheik stood her ground. "These people have been through enough. You will rule them as a government, not a military. If they are serving you, they are to be paid and allowed to leave the castle. Also," she continued, "I want the prisoners released, too."

At this, every general interrupted her.

"I know, I know," she laughed, trying to calm them down. "Hear me out. Most of the men serving Spike, certainly most of those he abandoned, were forced into his army. They did not want to serve him and they pose no threat of rebellion."

"But if they are loyalists," a general interjected, "then there will be further rebellion."

Sheik nodded. "I've considered that. I want them released in small enough numbers and escorted from the city. Make it clear that they will be imprisoned if they stay in or return to Isandas. If they were indeed conscripted, they will want to return home anyway. Even if some of them are loyalists, they won't be able to raise an army if they're released in small enough groups. Say twenty men a week?"

The generals seemed reluctant. But they did not press the matter further and agreed to follow Sheik's decision. Sheik reminded them once again that Marjorie was in charge of all matters involving the servants, thanked the woman profusely, and left with Tara.

"You have become quite the leader, haven't you?" Tara said, either shocked or impressed.

Sheik gave a disappointed sigh. "Apparently." Leadership came naturally to her. But it also worried her. The last time she had made a dissenting decision it had ended in an avalanche.

The next few days passed by quickly. Sheik constantly received updates about the servants, the prisoner release, the lockdown, food and water supplies, and other trade. Sheik rarely knew what she was doing and simply wanted to continue in her quest to track down Spike.

But unfortunately, there wasn't much she could help with regarding the tunnel. She had tried to use her magic to clear it but exerted too much of her strength and passed out. She needed rest. So the men continued clearing the tunnel with shovels and Sheik had to accept that it was a slow process that she was unable to speed up.

Instead, she was kept busy with maintaining the state of Isandas and trying to keep the palace and city a perfect balance between safe and free. She didn't understand why everyone deferred to her judgement, but she accepted it because of how well Tara and Kazzak helped her. The two rarely left her side.

Yet as much as Kazzak was always near her, she rarely got a moment alone with him. They showed no outward signs of a romantic relationship. Only small gestures. When no one was looking he would give her hand a squeeze or toss her a wink from across the room. As sweet as it was, it wasn't enough. Sheik wanted a real relationship. She had hoped things would be different with Kazzak, different from how they were with Atarius.

Finally, after several long days of being surrounded by soldiers and servants, they managed to get a morning alone together.

It was early, the sun just peeking through her window, when the tap of a pebble caught her attention. Though she was used to waking at dawn, having such a comfortable bed encouraged her to sleep in a bit longer. But she made her way to the window to investigate the sound and found it was Kazzak tossing the small stones.

"What are you doing?"

He raised a finger to his lips. Then he pulled a rope from a small basket next to him and tossed it up to her, waving for her to come down.

She gave him an inquisitive look but obeyed, tying it off and scaling down the side of the castle. When she reached him, she noticed he looked different. His goatee and hair were freshly trimmed, and he wore a nice coat, a pattern interweaved along the seams, that Sheik knew he had never worn before. "What is going on?" she asked with a laugh.

"There are already generals waiting at your door," he explained. "This way we'll at least get a few hours before they figure out you're gone." With a grin, he took her by the hand and led her from the castle to the neighboring woods.

It wasn't anything near a forest. Compared to her home, it was merely a cluster of trees, but, when juxtaposed with the large city and palace of Isandas, it was paradise.

"So what else is in the basket?"

"Wouldn't you like to know," he said with a smirk. "We've got to a find a perfect spot first."

And so they wandered the woods together.

"When did you have time to plan this all out?"

Kazzak shrugged. "Past couple of days. The generals don't bother me nearly as much as they bother you."

"I don't know why they insist I'm in charge." She rubbed her arms, wishing she had grabbed a coat before joining him. "I'm not sure I've done anything to warrant it."

"From what Tara and Auni told me, you did a lot to earn King Faris' trust. Besides, you were always kind of the leader, even back in Calert, right?"

She frowned. Back then, she had desperately wanted to be the leader. But only because she was afraid of losing them. She had feared if she was anything less than a perfect, heroic leader, that they might all go their separate ways. "I don't want to lead armies or be some war hero." She thought back to Atarius' village. How she had wanted to bake acorn bread, to beat bark from trees. It struck her suddenly how much she missed that simple life.

"What do you want to do then? Do you want to stop?"

She turned to him. "Stop what?"

He gestured vaguely back towards the castle of Isandas. "Stop this. Tracking down Spike. Fighting a war." She blinked at him for a second, surprised. Was that even an option? "Look, we finally found each other, safe and sound, after we both thought the worst. We can just walk away."

"No." She stopped him before he could say anymore. To just stop all of this and live a happy, simple life? It was too beautiful a thought. And if she entertained it for more than a moment, she might truly consider it. "No, we have to see it through." She paused, unsure if she wanted to continue her train of thought.

Sheik hadn't admitted it to anyone, but she'd been having nightmares. Horrible dreams about Spike having his way with her. Dreams about if Kazzak had not come to her rescue and she'd been trapped there for the rest of her life. Terrors of pain and suffering and hopelessness.

"Are you okay?"

Kazzak's voice pulled her back from the edge of the abyss.

She took in a bit of a breath before replying. "I'm fine." He looked down at her with his deep grey eyes, obviously wanting to hear more. "I'll be better when we've found him," she added quietly. What she wanted to say was *when we've killed him*.

Kazzak wrapped an arm around her and gave her a kiss on the head. "We'll see this thing through. I promise."

Sheik sighed and melted into his embrace. How nice it was to have him back. He was this calming force, this strong serenity. She wiped the tears welling in her eyes and looked back at him. "But when this is all over? We'll still be together?"

He smiled down at her. "Of course. Like back in Calert." She wasn't sure if he meant it literally, that they would return to Calert. The city that had turned on her so quickly when she had defended it. She wondered if she could live there. Or if she really wanted to live in any human city. The forest was the only place she could truly imagine as home. And she wondered if she stayed with Kazzak, with Tara and Auni, if she would ever see Atarius' village again.

"This will do," Kazzak announced suddenly, as they entered a clearing. He set down his basket and pulled several blankets from it, much to Sheik's relief. Winter was transitioning into spring, and while there had been no snow since she had arrived at Isandas, the ground was still icy.

"Praise Elilah, I was freezing." Kazzak laid one blanket on the ground and Sheik bundled herself up in the other.

He put an arm around her and she gladly buried herself in him, both to be close to him and to keep warm. Sunlight shined down on them, but it was still too early in the day to feel its heat.

"So do I get to know what else is in the magic basket?"

"Alright, well I'm afraid it isn't terribly exciting. Because I know you don't really eat food, but you have mentioned wine before and since the grapes have nearly fallen by the time they're picked," he reasoned, "I thought it might be romantic if you'd be willing to try it." He revealed the rest of the basket contents: a wineskin, a loaf of bread, and several wrapped cheeses.

She smiled at him and the idea that he had packed all of this to be romantic. "Of course! I'd love to." Memories came back to her of her and Farin sneaking drinks. "It isn't such a big deal. The grapes I mean. You know, I had a friend who made wine with picked grapes instead of fallen ones."

"Oh?" he asked with a raised eyebrow as he tasted a sip of the wine. He passed it to her. "I thought all the elves followed your rules?"

She had a small sip and was caught off guard by the sour taste. She hadn't had the drink since leaving Atarius' village, and it took her a moment to adjust to the flavor. "No, my friend Farin never followed the rules except around Atarius. Most of the younger ones didn't." She thought for a moment and then let out a small laugh. "It's silly, isn't it?"

"What is?" Kazzak asked, breaking off a bit bread and balancing some cheese on top.

"Just the rules about eating. They seemed so important at the time." Because she was trying to please Atarius. He represented the rules, and if she wanted to be with him, she had to follow them, no matter how inane they might be. But that chapter of her life had closed. She might never see Atarius again. She didn't need to follow his rules any longer. "Can I have some?"

"Feel free," Kazzak nodded, passing her the loaf and cheeses.

She tasted the bread first. It was fluffy and light, like the bread Tara had made her try back in Calert. But this one was sour and salty to the taste. It was altogether different from the acorn bread from Atarius' village. The cheese added another element of sour, but was also smooth and soft, unlike anything she had ever tasted before. Kazzak laughed at her reactions to the flavors and Sheik laughed at how extraordinarily strong they were. She wondered if Atarius tasted such food if he could really continue to enforce the bizarre tradition he clung to.

As Sheik finished the small meal and continued to sip on the wine, Kazzak started a fire. "They'll find us soon, anyway," he conceded. "Might as well make it a little easier on them."

Knowing it was the truth, that the soldiers would soon see the smoke and discover where they had gone, Sheik decided to make the best of their last few moments together. She took Kazzak by the hand and gave it a squeeze. "Thank you. For planning all of this. I needed it."

She hadn't realized it until now, but she had needed it desperately. An escape from her responsibilities and the generals' constant questions. A quiet moment in a forest, the only place she could call home. A friend to distract her from her fears and nightmares. And reassurance that she could count on Kazzak, be with him, even after this was all over.

"Of course." He smiled at her, his grey eyes crinkling, and pulled her close to him. Her stomach fluttered. She had to remind herself to breathe, her heart pounding away inside her chest.

His face drew closer to her, their noses almost brushed up against one another's. Then he closed the gap between them, kissing her gently. Her arms wrapped around his back, one hand feeling the nape of his neck, her fingers wrapped in his soft hair. He brushed a strand of hair from her face and kissed her again. And again.

They clung to each other as they lay by the fire, Kazzak's body over hers. His kisses moved from her lips to her neck and her fingers remained tangled in his long hair. She held her breath with his every touch and savored the taste of him on her lips.

The sound of soldiers disrupted their passion.

"Lady Sheik!"

She let out a sigh at the distant voices. Kazzak chuckled and gave her one last kiss. He sat up first and then extended his hand to help lift her to her feet.

"Lady Sheik!"

The soldiers were close now and she called back, "I'm here," though her eyes never left Kazzak's. The thought of them leaving this war behind reentered her mind and she had to push it aside.

The soldier finally came into view. "I'm here," she said again, giving Kazzak's hand one last squeeze and then letting go. "What is it?"

"The tunnel is clear!"

Her eyes brightened. The interruption had at least been an important one. "Well, we should set off at once," Sheik replied immediately. She glanced at Kazzak, adding, "Do you want to find Auni and Tara?"

The soldier began the trek back through the woods. "They've been informed and are already packing. The wizard, too."

"Asroth?" Sheik asked.

The soldier nodded. "He requested to join you."

Sheik hadn't even seen Asroth in the past week. Based on how scarce he had made himself—and the fact that he hadn't visited Sheik a single time—she had assumed he would want to part ways. She glanced towards Kazzak, the surprise obvious on her face.

"I guess it will be like the old gang," Kazzak said simply. He gave her a grin. "Like back in Calert where this all started."

Chapter 22

"Look at me." Sheik winced under his touch. Her eyes were closed tight and so she couldn't see him, but she knew who he was all the same. "I want you to watch what I do to you."

Spike.

She could tell from his voice. That perfectly angelic voice that chilled her to the bone. She squirmed with his every touch, trying desperately to get away from him. Get away. Get away. He was a snake, twisting around her, feeling her flesh.

Get away from me!

She wanted to scream but couldn't make the words come to her mouth. His touch made her skin crawl. Pain. Sickness. Vomit.

Then sunlight.

It was the sunlight that made her open her eyes. She could feel it on her face and now she looked up. Up through the glass ceiling. This time there were no stars. It was sunny and there was someone there. Someone familiar.

He was hard to see, it was so bright. He was reaching down at her. Green hair. Soft skin, gentle eyes.

Atarius?

It was Atarius! He was here to save her. She called out to him. Atarius!

Sheik awoke with a jump.

Everything was dark except for Kazzak's face, illuminated by his lantern.

"Are you okay?" he asked.

She nodded, though she hadn't completely gathered her thoughts. I am in the tunnel, she reminded herself. Kazzak is here. Auni and Tara are here. Fang is here. Asroth is here. We are in the tunnel, but we are okay.

Kazzak outstretched his hand and she accepted it. He pulled her to her feet. "Let's get moving, okay?"

He left, taking the light of the lantern with him. Sheik blinked several times, trying to see in the dark as she collected her things, rolling up the bedroll and tying it to her backpack. It was the third time they had slept, though none of them could be certain if three full days had actually passed. Maybe more, maybe less.

"Bad dream?" Tara asked. She tried to keep her voice quiet, but everything was loud in the tunnel. Again, Sheik merely nodded. "Need any help?"

Sheik finished tying her last knot and then threw the pack over her shoulder. "Nope. Let's move out." She was still disoriented from her dream and didn't feel like chatting. Not to mention that there was very little privacy with the echoing walls and limited space.

The tunnel was smaller and darker than Sheik could have ever imagined.

Kazzak took the lead, still holding the lantern. Sheik followed in behind him and, despite the light, had trouble seeing her own feet. Tara followed next, then Auni, who also carried a lantern, followed by Asroth.

Taking up last was Fang, who was not fond of the tunnel. Not that any of them were, of course. Sheik hated being without daylight. The air was dusty and dry, the space was confining, and the darkness made her feel like they were walking nowhere at all. Perhaps into the depths of the abyss. She had been in caves before and had never found herself claustrophobic, but this was like being completely consumed in darkness. Kazzak and Auni's lanterns offered her little comfort.

She knew Kazzak had better vision than her. That did bring her a slight amount of reassurance. She trusted Kazzak and could tell by his hand, always resting on his sword, that he was ready to spring into action should they come across something in the dark.

Her hand, too, constantly went to her knives. The knives that Farin had given her. She was better with her bow, but in this light she figured it would be a lot easier to stab someone than aim an arrow at them.

The tunnel seemed endless. And it always seemed to move downwards. They had already climbed down a wooden staircase at the entrance of the tunnel, so it was strange they were still traveling downwards. Either they would have to walk upwards again or Isandas had rested on a hill that Sheik had hardly noticed.

Another possibility nipped at Sheik's mind—maybe the tunnel did not lead back to daylight.

Maybe they were just traveling to their death. A perilous trap that Spike had marched into that they were now following him into as well. Perhaps thousands had died in the tunnel, assuming it led somewhere when it simply didn't.

She wondered if it was possible for her to die like that. Others could die of starvation if the tunnel truly did lead nowhere and they ran out of rations. But she had her magic. She could create food and water.

Her mind wandered to the hopeless time she had spent in the cave, mourning the loss of Kazzak, Jason, and Carlos. With the stress she was under, she hadn't been able to use her magic for more than a few seconds without a splitting headache. She could only assume, if they never did reach daylight, eventually the stress and pain of traveling would prevent her from using her magic at all.

And so thoughts of death constantly crept in the back of her mind.

Hours passed by slowly. They rarely talked. Occasionally Sheik tried whispering with Kazzak, but he seemed agitated. She thought to ask him what was wrong, but then realized what a stupid question it would be. They had been wandering a tunnel for presumably days with little rest. All of them were agitated.

They took few breaks. Sheik hadn't had to march like this in months. Blisters formed but she hated to bother Tara for healing and Auni had mentioned something about Asroth having difficulty healing. Besides, they probably all had blisters. If the others managed not to complain, then Sheik wouldn't either.

All they did was march. When someone had to relieve themselves, they let the others pass ahead and then caught up. They didn't stop for meals. Sheik made food with her magic or the others dug dried meat and nuts out of their pack and ate as they walked. They stopped only to sleep or relight a lantern when it went out.

Tara invented a guessing game but Asroth seemed annoyed by it and Kazzak suggested they keep their voices down in case they came across Spike and his men. Sheik didn't think it was possible. Perhaps the most maddening thing about the tunnel was its absolute silence. There was no ambient noise aside from the sound of their own steps. If Spike and his men were up ahead, Sheik could only assume she would hear them in an instant.

But she complied and continued to only talk in whispers and only when necessary. By the sixth day, or at least what they all assumed was the sixth day, Tara finally blurted out, "I need to stop." Though she said it in a reasonable tone, it seemed like shouting compared to the whispered voices they had been using for the past week.

"Has it been that long since our last rest?" Kazzak asked.

"Not to sleep, just to sit for at least half an hour and please for the love of Ziad let us talk!" Tara exclaimed. Sheik couldn't help but laugh, knowing this was probably the longest Tara had gone without talking in her whole life. Auni laughed too and then it made Tara laugh and finally Kazzak cracked a smile and relented.

"Fine, we can talk," he said, and for an instant his annoyance melted away. "But use your inside voice."

At this, Tara began laughing all over again. She and Auni sat, trying to hold in their giggles. Kazzak watched them with a smirk, and seemed happy to sit as well, taking off his boots and rubbing his feet. Sheik was just relieved to see a spark of happiness flood through them, even in the darkness of the tunnel. She leaned against Fang, who was eager for the break though confused by the sudden change in tone.

But Asroth had no time for joy and took the lantern from Kazzak silently, stepping around the pair of laughing siblings. He glanced at them like they'd lost their minds and continued to lead the way, calling back, "You can catch up when you're done resting."

Sheik and Auni shared an eyeroll, but Kazzak seemed to take his words seriously. "We really should keep going," he added, retying his boots.

Again, Sheik wanted to ask what was bothering him, but she supposed he was just eager to get out of the tunnel. "Kazzak's right. The faster we go the faster we're out of here."

"Guys come here!" Asroth's voice pierced the silence.

"What is it?" Kazzak asked, jogging up to him. The others pulled themselves to their feet and followed after.

"It's a dead end."

Sheik felt her heart flop. "What?"

"The tunnel, it's a dead end," Asroth said again.

That was impossible. It couldn't just end. They hadn't run into Spike. And there weren't any turns or branches. It didn't make any sense.

"Wait, there's something there. Hold up the light," Kazzak instructed. Asroth lifted it up and Sheik peered, trying to see what Kazzak had seen. Built into the dirt ceiling was something made of wood. "It's a trap door," Kazzak said with a sigh of relief. "Keep the lantern there, I'll see if I can get it." He fidgeted with it for a moment while the others crowded around, holding their breath. Finally it popped loose, the wood swinging down and almost smacking him in the head.

Light burst from above them.

It wasn't very bright, obviously not the direct sun. But it was everything. It was a source of light, something they hadn't seen in days.

Kazzak reached for the top and pulled himself up. A hardly audible, "Oh Ziad," escaped his lips. He scrambled to lift his legs up and then turned around to offer Sheik a hand.

The smell hit her before she could even pull herself into the room. "Don't breathe in," Kazzak called down to the others as he continued to help them up one by one.

Dead bodies littered the floor. And though the decay was enough to make one vomit, the stench was not what left Sheik so shocked.

It was the way they were mutilated.

They had cuts and wounds on their bodies, like they might in a normal fight. But, unlike a regular skirmish, each and every one had their skulls smashed open as if with rocks. And, even more bizarre, none of the skulls leaked brain matter. As if it had been scooped out. Collected.

Sheik gagged and closed her eyes, trying not to faint at the sight. Kazzak continued to help the others out of the tunnel, but she found herself unable to move. All she could do was stare at them. Just stare at the bodies. So many bodies. Finally she counted them.

Fifteen. At least in this room. Perhaps there were more in the other rooms that she only now began to notice. She glanced around. The ceilings were extraordinarily high, somewhat like the palace of Isandas. Nothing else about it was grandiose. It looked dark and stained with dust and cobwebs. The windows were all boarded up with thick planks of wood, though the wood placed over the front door had obviously been broken through.

She pulled herself to her feet and began to wander into the other room, stepping carefully over the bodies to reach it. It looked completely empty and branched into several more equally empty rooms. There were a few empty barrels, several beds, and a pile of bodies in a corner. Their skulls, too, were smashed open in the same fashion as the others. But there was one difference: these were the bodies of women and children.

Tara's crying and gagging interrupted her search. "Oh Ziad," she sobbed, "Justar." It was not as if her eyes had never seen dead bodies before. But these were certainly different. Mangled and decaying, riddled with insects, their skulls beaten out and their brain matter for some unknown reason stolen away.

Asroth and Kazzak were the only two who didn't seem to be in shock. Kazzak was lifting Fang out of the tunnel in silence. It was Asroth who spoke up first. "Who do you think they were?"

They were all in silence for a moment before a thought sprang to Sheik's mind. "Nobles."

Their clothes were too torn apart and full of dust and grime to tell if her assumption was correct. Identifying the type of fabric they were wearing would be both difficult and disgusting. But it was the only thing that made sense. "They must be," she continued. "The nobles that fled from Isandas. At least some of them. Spike must have slaughtered them all."

No. That couldn't be right. Spike would have come here only a few days before them. The bodies looked as if they had been rotting for weeks.

"Not Spike. Centaurs," Asroth spoke up.

Kazzak gave a nod, as if agreeing with him, though he didn't say a word.

"Centaurs? Why?" Sheik asked.

Asroth shrugged. "Why not?"

She glanced at the two men's faces before letting out a sigh of exasperation. "What are you talking about?"

"Centaurs aren't the regal creatures you might have heard about in your forest," Kazzak explained. "They may look half human, but they're beasts."

Asroth took over. "Legends say a tribe of people cracked open human skulls and ate what was inside. The gods cursed them and gave them the body of a beast. I doubt it's true, but it was always the explanation for why centaurs are attracted to the taste of brains. Just look at the bodies," he added with a wave of his hand.

Kazzak nodded. "And the boards here. The nobles must have realized they were in centaur territory and boarded themselves inside. Eventually the centaurs found out about the people inside this building and broke in," he felt along a board, noting how it was bent, broken from the outside in. "The men fought to their death..."

"And the women and children hid in the back room," Sheik finished for him. It all made sense. As sick and horrifying as it was to think about, it added up. She had never put much thought into centaurs, but she wouldn't have ever guessed that they would be such dark, evil creatures.

"Well, we need out of here," Sheik whispered after a long silence. "It smells awful. Besides, we need to find Spike. He's probably quite a few days ahead of us now."

Auni finally spoke up. He had pried loose a board so that Tara could breathe outside air. Peeking through a space between the wooden boards, he mumbled, "It's a swamp out there."

Kazzak and Asroth turned to glance outside. So it was. "Elena Swamp," Asroth muttered.

"Elena Swamp?" Sheik asked.

"Yeah," Asroth spoke up again. "It's dangerous from what I've read. Between centaurs and the lack of sunlight and sinking mud holes," he listed on. He glanced at the nervous faces and then gave a slight shrug. "I'm sure it's not that bad, but we should all be cautious."

Tara remained petrified. Perhaps she was still stunned over the bodies, or perhaps Asroth had just frightened her back into another state of shock. Sheik couldn't quite tell. She gave her a slight pat on the shoulder, urging her to relax. "We've made it through worse," she said confidently. "We'll make it through this, too."

⁘

The swamp was not as horrible as Asroth had made it out to be. It was, essentially, a thick forest with the occasional mud hole. So far they had not spotted any centaurs, though Sheik had noticed hoof prints in the mud. She couldn't imagine this swamp was home to horses. But something that feasted on brains? Something evil like centaurs most certainly would lurk in a forest like this.

Spike's soldiers' footprints were also fresh in the easily imprinted mud. It looked as if they had passed by only hours before Sheik's group had arrived, though she knew the tracks had to have been at least a few days old.

It made them easy to follow. For once, something was easy. Until now it seemed Sheik was always doing the running. Now they had Spike running. He was in fear of them catching him, not the other way around. It was only a matter of time, really.

And on the second day of travel in the swamp, they discovered his group was growing smaller.

They found six bodies. They all had the same tanned skin and long black hair that Spike had, but the faces could not be identified. All six had their skulls smashed in and brains scooped out. "How do we know if any of them are Spike?" Asroth asked.

"Check their chests. Spike has a scar from here to here," Sheik explained, indicating where she remembered his scars had been. So they tore open the shirts of the dead men, but none of them matched. Spike was still out there.

"Still, good to know their numbers are being whittled down," Kazzak offered.

Sheik nodded. They just had to catch up to Spike. Then she could kill him. She could have her revenge. She could put a stop to the nightmares.

The darkness of the swamp made it difficult to travel, but Kazzak and Fang, with their excellent vision, took the lead. There was a lot more freedom now that they had escaped the tunnel. Tara and Auni walked a pace away, talking to themselves quietly. Asroth sulked in back, like usual, though he did share his knowledge of Elena Swamp, and how it had been named after a runaway princess who had been killed in the swamp by the centaurs. Generally, though, Sheik tended to converse with Fang or Kazzak, or sometimes both.

As strange as Kazzak found it that she could communicate with the wolf, he no longer questioned it. But although he had come to accept the strange ability of hers, he was hardly able to grasp their method of conversation. The understanding was not so much in the words that Sheik spoke but the emotions and thoughts hiding behind the words themselves. But Fang simply could not comprehend all the concepts that she could, and so she was happy to have Kazzak to speak with, too.

They didn't talk about anything deep or personal. He still seemed distant. Sheik couldn't quite place it. But she felt a general uneasiness after seeing the damage centaurs could cause, and she supposed he might feel similarly. And so their discussions focused around battle plans for when they found Spike, when they might take their next break for food or rest, or even something as simple as complaining about the latest mud puddle they accidentally stepped in.

"Hey," Kazzak interrupted Sheik. She had been in the middle of saying something unimportant, watching the tracks of Spike's men as she walked along. "Look!"

She glanced upwards to discover they had made it. They were out of the swamp.

A cool stream flowed downhill from the dark bog they had been stuck in for the past week. There were still trees covering the land, especially bordering the brook, the ground hidden in brush and tall grass. But the sun had just fully risen, its pink glow lighting up Kazzak's smiling face.

"We made it!" he sighed with a smile. "I thought it would never end." He gave out a small chuckle. Sheik took in a breath of fresh air. Behind her was a dark thicket of forest; in front of her were light woods, bursting with spring.

The group had spread out quite a ways, Tara and Auni far behind and Asroth no longer even in sight. Sheik let out a whistle to get their attention, but Kazzak made a quick motion that cut her short. "We're still in centaur territory, don't get too loud," he reminded her.

She rolled her eyes at his crinkled forehead. He hadn't been himself lately. Anxious and on edge. But finally, they were in the light. As Tara and Auni came close enough to hear, Sheik called out to them, "We're going to go fill the waterskins at the river. Will you go find Asroth?" The pair nodded and handed their waterskins off to her before heading back towards the swamp. Sheik only needed to glance at Fang for him to know that he was meant to stay with the siblings. Then she turned to Kazzak. "Come on, that'll at least buy us a few minutes alone."

His worried look melted away into a soft smile. That cute, boyish grin he used to always have on his face. She grabbed him by the hand, but he winced. "What's the matter?"

He turned his hand over to show her. "I accidentally grabbed a sticker bush back there," he explained. The cuts ran up his palm all the way to the middle of his forearm, several burrs still stuck in him.

Now it was her turn to frown and be worried. "Why didn't you say something? Tara could have healed you right then." Kazzak waved the thought away like it wasn't a big deal. "Come on, let's clean it up before it gets infected."

When they reached the stream, they were eager to splash themselves with water like little kids on a summer's day. Kazzak took off his shirt and dipped it into the water, handing it over to Sheik. "Alright, go ahead. Clean away." He winced, giving her his injured hand.

Sheik inspected it and pulled out what remained of the burrs. The larger cuts had dried blood that were now forming a yellowish film. She pressed the cloth against it, letting it cool the area first.

"Ow!" Kazzak exclaimed.

"Sorry, it's about to get worse." She bit down on her lip as she scraped it clean, dipping the shirt back into the river with every piece of dirt she removed. "You really don't mind me using your shirt?"

He shrugged. "A little blood never hurt anyone. I don't care. Or do you just want me to put it back on because you're intimidated by my rugged physique?" he asked, raising an eyebrow.

She rolled her eyes. But, in all honesty, seeing his half nude body did cause her heart to flutter a bit. Cleaning off the last of the wound, she tied it up with a bandage from her pack. "All done."

"You mean you aren't going to kiss it?"

She made a face, her eyebrows furrowing in confusion. "Huh?"

Kazzak laughed. "Do elves not do that? You know, you kiss an owwie to make it feel better!"

"An owwie? No thanks," she laughed too. "But," she added once she stopped her giggling at him, "I could kiss you to make it feel better." He raised his eyebrows and his mouth curled into a half smile. Her hand moved first, reaching around his neck, her fingers burrowing in his hair. Then her face followed, leaning forwards until her lips pressed lightly against his.

He kissed her back, his lower lip cupping around her own lower lip. His body began to lean into the kiss until she felt his bare skin pressed against her. Naturally her body fell slowly backwards. Before she knew it, she was lying on the ground next to the stream, her hands wrapping around his back as he continued to kiss her.

It reminded her of the time Atarius had kissed her. The setting of the cool water. The way his body lay lightly on top of her. The way he kissed her. Her lips parted and he breathed through them. She felt herself breathing harder.

He bit down ever so slightly on her lower lip before she felt the touch of his tongue. Once again, something reminded her of Atarius. Why was she thinking of Atarius? She was kissing Kazzak, not Atarius.

This wasn't right. She shouldn't be kissing Kazzak and thinking of Atarius. Why in the name of Elilah was she thinking of Atarius? He had asked her to leave. Banished her. And yet, the more Kazzak kissed her the more she realized she was in love. She was in love with Atarius.

His mouth moved away from hers. She took in a deep breath, preparing herself to tell him to stop.

But he stopped on his own. There was a long silence. Kazzak sat up and looked at the ground, avoiding eye contact. "I'm sorry."

"What?" she replied after a moment, sitting up.

"I'm sorry," he repeated. Finally he looked her in the eyes. "I can't do this."

"What?" she said again, still confused.

He let out a long sigh. The two of them fully sat up. "Look, I really like you. You're funny and smart and kind and beautiful. But it's pretty obvious you're in love with someone else."

Was it that obvious or was he just a mind reader? Again, "What?"

"Back in the tunnel. You were having a nightmare. And I was trying to wake you and you called out to Atarius. You still think about him." She did still think about Atarius. And Kazzak knew it. There was a long pause. "I love you, Sheik. But you... you still love him, don't you?"

Sheik thought about her kiss with Atarius. By the stream. Her perfect moment. It was all she could cling to when she was trapped in Spike's cell. Tortured. Lost. In that lonely, desperate place, she had clung to her memories of Atarius.

In a small voice, she finally whispered, "I do."

Kazzak nodded a few times. "I thought so."

Sheik held her breath. "I'm sorry. I didn't realize it until now. I didn't know I had said that, back in the tunnel." Now she understood why Kazzak had been so quiet. Why he had seemed distant. She sighed. "I'm really sorry, Kazzak."

He shook his head, like it wasn't a big deal, but she could tell it was. "You're a really great guy. You mean so much to me," she began. But she stopped herself. It didn't matter how much she cared for him if she was still in love with Atarius. He deserved better. So she just said again, "I'm sorry."

After a long moment, he gave her a small smile. "I know. I'm sorry too." He stood up and offered her his uninjured hand, pulling her to her feet. Then the seriousness melted away and he returned to his usual joking self and stated rather simply, "I'll be taking my shirt now."

Sheik couldn't help but laugh at his silly expression and she tossed the shirt at him. "Come on, we should check up on the others. What could be taking them so long?"

Their conversation was cut short as Tara let out a scream.

"Tara!" Sheik cried out, and she and Kazzak sprinted back into the darkness of the swamp, towards the sound.

Tara was backed against a tree, shrieking for help.

Auni was on the ground, his legs trampled and covered in blood. Still he continued to fight off their attackers: a pair of centaurs.

The centaurs were larger than Sheik had imagined. The beast half of their body was taller than any horse Sheik had seen, nearly reaching the top of her head. Adding the human torso, the creatures towered over all of them, even Asroth and Kazzak.

They were not as horse-like or human-like as she'd imagined centaurs were. Their lower half was covered with thick, shaggy fur rather than the short, silky fur of a horse. Their upper half, too, was covered in fur, starting at the center of their chest and blending down into their lower half. And the hair on their head continued to grow down their neck and spine until it met with the rest of their coarse, disheveled coat. Everything seemed to be covered in hair, even their arms, hanging down almost twice as long as a normal man's.

But the scariest thing about them, Sheik thought, was their faces. They were gnarled and snarling, large fangs protruding from their mouth. Their black, beady, animalistic eyes were hardly visible, sunken in underneath their hairy brows. In place of their nose was a small bump and two slits that blended in with their leathery, cracked skin.

Despite her fear, she readied her bow. Kazzak's reflexes had been faster than hers, his sword out and stabbing the darker of the two beasts. Sheik let her arrow fly towards the lighter one that was on top of Auni. Asroth stood to the side, but Fang had already jumped into the battle. He latched onto the dark centaur's leg.

It delivered a kick to Fang, sending him flying. Still the wolf managed to tear a chunk of flesh from its leg, causing the creature to falter and stumble. Kazzak slashed into it once again, but his sword hardly seemed to pierce the thick fur.

The other centaur continued to stamp at Auni, who desperately rolled between its trampling hooves. The arrow Sheik planted in its side didn't seem to slow it down.

She had to protect Auni. The ground melted around him and then rose up and covered him. The centaur reared back, startled by the movement. Then she hardened it. The ground was like steel, forming a protective shield around Auni. The centaur continued to kick at him, and she loosed another arrow. It didn't even bother the creature. She aimed at the monster's throat, but the centaur thrashed about, and her arrow missed entirely.

Fang managed to get back on his feet and helped Kazzak tear the dark centaur to the ground, gripping its already wounded leg. It didn't quit fighting. With every draw of Kazzak's blade and every splash of black sticky blood, the centaur kicked, thrashed, and grabbed at him.

Sheik, realizing how useless her bow was, dropped it in favor of one of Farin's knives. Her heart pounded as she leapt against the centaur still kicking at Auni despite her magical shield. With all her might, she thrust the knife into its back.

Its attention switched from Auni to Sheik, now bucking to try to get her off.

With her left hand, she clung to a clump of the centaur's fur, hoisting herself on top of the creature. With her right hand, she held desperately to her knife. It let out a snarl and bucked more.

Though the rest of her body was being flung about wildly, her arms remained steady. Every second she was able, she ripped the knife out and replanted it a palm's length higher. After about four stabs, the knife rested in the centaur's neck. Black blood gushed out. The liquid splashed onto her knife, loosening her grip. She tried to hold on but before she knew it, she was on the ground.

"Look out!" Tara called out frantically.

The dying centaur was still trying to trample her. Sheik rolled out of the way and scrambled to her feet. It chased after her. She ran, dodging between trees, trying not to trip on a root or get herself stuck in a mud hole. Her heart raced. Each breath exhausted her. But finally the struggle ended as the centaur collapsed, clutching its neck.

Though she wanted to catch her breath, Kazzak was still wrestling with the darker centaur, hacking into it as it flailed around. Fang had taken several more kicks from the beast but continued to tear its flesh apart.

Sheik feared getting in their way. Instead, she focused with her magic. She made mud stick to the centaur, then made it grow heavy. Weighing the beast down the best she could, she gave Kazzak and Fang the advantage. With a few more swings of Kazzak's sword, the centaur fell lifeless to the ground.

The group stood panting, the adrenaline still pumping in their veins.

"Is everyone alright?" Sheik asked, thinking first of Auni, who seemed to have been horrifically injured. Tara had already rushed to his side and Sheik turned to see how severe his wounds were.

But Kazzak turned to Asroth. "What in Ziad's name are you doing?" he screamed. Sheik had never heard the man lose his temper like this before. "You just stood there while the rest of us almost died, you bastard!"

Asroth yelled back something about being in shock and too overwhelmed to fight. Sheik ignored their screams and leaned down next to Auni and Tara. "Are you two okay? What happened?"

Tara wiped away her terrified tears. Auni shook his head and motioned to his shin. "They trampled my legs before you guys came," he explained. Tears streamed from his eyes. "I can't walk." His legs were a gnarled, bloody mess. "It hurts," he winced, biting on his lip to disperse the pain.

"Asroth!" Sheik yelled over the wizard's argument with Kazzak. "Come heal him!"

The two stopped screaming for a moment to look over at the boy, who was trying not to burst into a complete sob. "I can't heal," Asroth growled bitterly.

"What?"

"I can't heal! Tara will have to do it. I don't know why, I just haven't been able to lately!" his voice raised to yelling again. Kazzak looked like he was about to take a swing at the man.

Before he could, Asroth moved next to Auni and said with a mumble, "I can still help." He bent down and felt the boy's leg, despite it causing Auni to scream out. Tara moved a bit closer, nervous to do her part. Sheik watched anxiously, chewing on her lip. Asroth poured his waterskin out over the various cuts on Auni's legs. Blood and dirt washed away, revealing the extent of the damage. Auni screamed out once again. Tara healed him one cut at a time, crying out with each bloody gash she helped repair.

"The right one looks okay, but the left one is in bad shape," Asroth explained. "Most of the bleeding has stopped, but there are a few more places that need to be healed. I think Tara needs a little time to recover, though," he added, glancing at the girl.

Sheik listened intently. "Let's get out in the sunlight. Then she can rest a minute."

Kazzak nodded and helped Asroth lift Auni up and carry him into a patch of sunlight outside of the swamp. Auni's jaw remained clenched, trying not to make too much noise despite the obvious pain. Sheik glanced back at Tara who was coming along slowly, Fang limping behind her.

They were all so beaten and bruised. And now Kazzak and Asroth were out of breath. How would they make it any further?

"I'm out of water. Where's the rest of the waterskins?" Asroth
asked.

Sheik wondered if he really had the audacity to ask for their
waters after he had hardly helped in the fight. But she kept her
mouth closed. "I left them at the stream," she realized. "I'll fetch
them."

"Fill mine too?" he asked, and sadly the fact that he asked instead
of ordered was a pleasantry of its own, so she accepted the waterskin.

Kazzak glanced between them and then said, "I'll help," and
followed after Sheik. She thought it odd he would think she needed
his help to carry a few waterskins, but she said nothing until they
were out of earshot.

"It's my fault."

"It is not," Kazzak responded sternly, waving his hand at her like
she was crazy. But she was the one who had sent Auni and Tara
back into the swamp. So that she could have a moment alone with
Kazzak. And he had warned her even! He had said not to whistle,
he had said they were still in centaur territory. He had— "There's
something wrong with him."

"What?" Sheik was spiraling and hardly registered his words.
"Who?"

"Asroth. There's something wrong with him. Like he's hoping
we get hurt."

Sheik gave half a snort. "And then can't be bothered to heal us."

Kazzak nodded, but then said, "He wasn't able to heal at Isandas, either." After a pause, he added, "Do you remember back in Calert, that soldier? The time he used dark magic?" Sheik shuddered. She didn't like to think about it. "He couldn't heal that soldier, either."

Sheik nodded. "So?"

"It's weird, isn't it? What was his reason back then?"

"I don't remember," she admitted. He had given her an explanation—what was it? Kazzak tromped through the stream, gathering the waterskins they had entirely forgotten to fill during their first visit. He splashed the sweat off his face, took a long drink, and then filled it again. "Maybe Tara would know."

He shrugged and tossed the waterskins into his backpack. "I don't know. Let's just keep moving. We can sort it out once we're a little further away from nightmare-territory."

"Fair enough. But we should discuss it." She watched him as they began the trek back. His eyes had that tired look once again. "Maybe when we set up camp, I can take the middle watch? Wait until he's asleep and then we can—" Her thought was cut short. Kazzak put a hand on her shoulder, indicating for her to stop. Her mouth snapped shut as she saw it.

A centaur watching their group.

Then another came into view, peering at them from the swamp. Then another. "What do we do?" Kazzak whispered as they emerged. "Fight or run?"

"There's too many to fight," Sheik mumbled, trying to count them all. She currently spotted eight between the brush and trees. They had hardly managed two. "And Auni can't run."

"Well," he said, his voice full of annoyance, "what other choices do we have?"

She wasn't sure, really. But they had to at least get back to the others. Grabbing Kazzak by the hand, they crouched and stalked silently towards their friends, all the while keeping their eyes on the centaurs. The creatures continued to gather, eagerly awaiting the feast of blood.

They were barbaric monsters, Sheik thought to herself. They were a rabid carnivore, a wild beast. And then she thought of it. An option besides fight or flee. Who knew if it would work, but it was their only chance. "Asroth!" she called once close enough.

They were on edge, also watching the beasts gathering. Asroth and Tara stood while Auni sat helplessly on the ground. Fang growled a deep, stern growl. "Asroth!" Sheik said again, this time her voice fiercer so he might reply.

"What?" he demanded angrily.

"Can you still use magic? Standard magic?"

The centaurs began stomping their hooves as if it was some sort of ceremony that deserved the beat of drums. "I think so!" he yelled over the sound. "Why?"

Sheik was about to explain when they charged. From almost every direction the centaurs galloped towards them. Some held nothing while others swung tree branches around wildly. "Follow my lead!" was all Sheik managed to scream out before she knew she had to act.

CHAPTER 23

The man opened his door slowly. "Yes?"

"Bishop?" a young woman asked.

He nodded. "Come in, come in." He led her inside his home and pulled a teapot off the fire. "Tea?"

"Oh." She seemed taken back, almost surprised by his generosity. "Yes, sure, that would be delightful."

The bishop let out a chuckle. "If you're hungry I can prepare some food."

"Yes Mom, please!" a small boy, perhaps six or seven, cried out. He had been tucked carefully behind his mother's skirt, the man not even noticing the boy's presence until he spoke.

The woman looked at the child for a long moment. "Very well. Yes, we have been hungry. If it is too much effort, though—"

"Not at all!" the bishop replied eagerly as he went through his cupboards to find something for the two to eat. "So how may I be of service?"

As he motioned towards an empty chair, she sat herself at the table and pulled the boy up on her lap. "If we are any inconvenience you may ask us to leave at any time. I only pray you do not report us."

He raised an eyebrow as he listened carefully, curious what crime they could have committed. "Ziad forgives all sins," he replied cautiously, urging her to confess.

"It is not a sin," she sighed. "We are some of the only noble survivors." She paused, but the bishop gave her an understanding nod, urging her to go on. "I didn't know where else to go." Her eyes watered. "I prayed the church at least would take pity on us. Please, oh Ziad, please." Her words faded out into a tearful muddle of begging and pleading.

The bishop extended his arm and raised her chin with his fingers. "You are safe now, child."

⸻◆⸻

Fire shot into the sky. Sheik's arms waved about wildly. It was not necessary for her to move at all, but she wanted it to be obvious that *she* was the cause of the fire. That she had the power to create a flame and then extinguish it with her sheer will.

More fire bubbled up around her. She made it dance about, creating designs like a piece of art. It drew lines across the ground, and she had to create water to keep the flames from spreading as they danced along the grass. She had never been good with fire, and her mind was beginning to tire already. But she could not allow herself to weaken.

Asroth joined in, understanding what she was doing. He was much better with magical fire and he created great images before them. They would last for a moment before falling to the ground as ash. Fiery paintings of circles and triangles appeared and fell.

It worked. The centaurs stopped in their tracks, suddenly full of uncertainty and fear. They trotted around slowly, examining the group. Sheik's mind blurred with pain, but she would not let her magic stop. For the sake of all their lives, she and Asroth had to appear like gods, beings capable of controlling the elements.

"Let's take the offensive," Asroth blurted out suddenly. He shot fire forward at one of the centaurs. Though the flames disappeared before it had time to burn, the creature let out a horrid shriek and quickly scampered away, fearing for its life.

Sheik had to hold in a laugh. These terrifying beasts were afraid of them. She, too, sent forth a burst of fire, though it was not nearly as strong as Asroth's had been. The centaurs all jumped back, gnashing their teeth together and letting out growls. After several more circles around the group, they finally began to trot away.

Her head was aching, but still she managed to smile as the last centaur disappeared back into the swamp. It had worked. "Sheik, that was amazing!" Kazzak yelled out, running to her side. He gave her a slap on the back. Already feeling dizzy and lightheaded, it was enough to knock her unconscious.

The ground was moving. Why was the ground moving? Sheik lifted a tired hand to her head, rubbing it lightly. Everything seemed a bit hazy. Auni was lying next to her. "You okay?" he asked quietly.

She blinked about five times. "What's going on?"

"You passed out," he explained. "They built something to pull us with since I can't walk and you've been asleep."

It was just a few thick sticks tied together with some loose rope, which Asroth and Kazzak pulled with one arm each. "Oh good," Asroth announced. "You're awake. You can walk now." He stopped pulling so she could climb off.

"Asroth," Kazzak chastised.

"No, it's alright," Sheik interjected, pulling herself to her feet. "What happened?"

Asroth was the one to explain. "You exhausted yourself using magic. Tara wanted to heal you, but you just can't heal exhaustion. You've been out for half an hour now."

She remembered the day Alta had died giving birth to Fang. Some things simply could not be healed with magic. "And Auni? She can't heal him?" she asked.

He shook his head. "No. She healed the rest of his cuts up fine, but one of the bones in his left shin is obviously shattered. She tried her best, but if it isn't attached it simply can't be healed; it needs surgery. Once we find a city where we can buy some tools, I don't mind doing it myself."

"She healed my hand though!" Kazzak smiled, raising his palm to show where a hardly visible scar had replaced the wound she had cleaned earlier.

"Thank Ziad I was able to help at least one person," Tara chuckled dryly. Her face was pallid, and Sheik wondered how long she had tried in vain to heal Auni's broken leg.

The sun was low in the sky, but Kazzak and Asroth kept pulling the contraption Auni lay on. Sheik wasn't sure if they simply weren't tired or if they were worried about running into more centaurs. Either way, she didn't complain, but walked dutifully alongside the group despite still being a little lightheaded.

They reached the top of a hill as the sun began to set, and from it they could spot a small town across the plains. "I'll go see what kind of medicines and surgical tools they have," Kazzak offered, dropping his rope that pulled Auni. "You guys can set up camp." And with that, he took off, running at a quick jog towards the distant buildings.

Sheik got right to work. Tara seemed exhausted and Asroth was as unhelpful as always. Still, she managed to set up some sheets of cloth along the side of a tree in case it rained during the night and then got a small fire going.

"You doing okay?" she asked Auni, helping him underneath one of the sheets.

He nodded. "Sorry I've been such a hassle."

"What?" she exclaimed. "Don't be ridiculous. It's my fault. I shouldn't have sent you back into the swamp. I shouldn't have let you out of our sight." Then, after a slight pause, she added, "I'm really sorry."

With a weak smile he replied, "It's alright. It's not your fault." It certainly felt like it though. It felt like every time she made a decision it was the wrong one. "You didn't know."

Sheik sighed. Tara had already fallen asleep. It was only natural after being so exhausted. "Can you get some sleep or are you in too much pain?"

He shrugged. "You don't need to fuss over me, you know."

"Well what am I supposed to do?" she chuckled. "You're sure there's nothing I can get you?"

"I'm back!" Kazzak announced, out of breath. He doubled over, his hands resting on his knees as he tried to steady his breathing. "Here," he handed Auni a small pouch. The boy opened it and pulled out some leaves, rubbing them between his fingers, confused. "They weaken the pain. It was all their doctor could offer me. He doesn't do any kind of surgeries."

Sheik's face dropped, disappointed they wouldn't be able to get Auni the help he needed. "But!" Kazzak added, "I have good news too! First off, we're out of centaur territory. They said it's rare enough centaurs would come out of the swamp like they did; they definitely won't travel as far as we have.

"And second," he continued, "we aren't far from one of the largest cities in the area. He said Darinshire is only a few days' travel west. They'll have a surgeon there where we can get Auni's leg fixed up."

"Darinshire?" Asroth interrupted. Sheik had hardly noticed he was around, let alone listening.

"Yeah why?"

"Nothing," the man replied firmly, turning around and storming off.

Kazzak raised an eyebrow. "I don't know what that was about," Sheik mumbled. He shrugged and bent down next to Auni, giving him instructions on how to chew the leaves. Sheik remained quiet, glancing off in Asroth's direction and wondering what could have possibly upset him so much.

Several days passed before they reached the outskirts of Darinshire. As it was nighttime, they were forced to wait until the next morning to find a doctor to operate on Auni's leg. They were all asleep except Fang, who had left to hunt, and Tara, who was currently standing guard.

This was his chance.

Asroth rose casually, glancing at the others before approaching her. "Beautiful night, isn't it?"

Tara jumped at the sound of his voice. "Ziad, Asroth!" He raised his hands to calm her, to show he hadn't meant to startle her. Then he waved for her to step a few paces away, so they might not wake the others. "What is it?" she asked, and just by her tone he could sense she was annoyed with him. What had he done to put her in such a bad mood? He had hardly spoken to her in the past couple months.

But he paused and took a breath. "Isn't it a nice night?" he asked again. He would win her over.

She shrugged and rubbed her arms. "It's freezing," she muttered bitterly.

He smiled, knowing exactly what she meant, exactly how she wanted him to interpret it. He put his arm around her, ready to pull her in close to him. To feel her skin against him, to share their warmth.

But Tara pulled away. "Not that cold."

He glared at first, annoyed with her mixed signals. But this was the game women played, subtle signs that they wanted you while having to act coy to maintain their innocence. "Oh Tara," he chuckled. "You don't have to be that way with me."

She stared back at him, nothing to say. Just silence. There was longing in her eyes, he could sense it. Her full lips, pouty, just begging for him to kiss her.

And so he did. He lurched forward, his arms around her, his mouth on hers. She let out a yelp and pushed against him, pushed his face away from hers. "Asroth, what in the abyss!" she screamed.

He shushed her—she would wake the others screaming so loud. "Tara, what are you doing?" he whispered sharply. She continued to protest and so he covered her mouth with his hand. She bit down.

Asroth held his breath as he shook the hand, trying not to cry out at the pain. He hardly even noticed that he had slapped Tara. It had just been a reflex. She had bit him and he had slapped her. But now he had to get her quiet. "Tara shut up, you're fine," he cooed, trying to cover her mouth again, though this time he was much more careful to keep her jaw shut with his hand safely on the outside.

Tara squirmed under his grasp and pushed her hands against his face. Asroth jolted his head back to keep her from jabbing him in the eye.

And in that motion, his headdress fell.

He moved quickly to catch it—not quickly enough though. She had seen him. She no longer twisted and turned, she no longer even screamed. She stared at him, jaw agape, stunned by the bareness of his head.

There was a twinge of shame. His hairline was receding, a bald patch resting in the center of his head. She had seen him, seen this mark of evil upon him.

But soon it was replaced with rage.

He slammed his fist into her gut and she doubled over in pain. Then he took the headdress and shoved it into her mouth, gagging her before she could call for help again. That instant she had been stunned into paralysis was all he needed. He grabbed her arms tight against her sides and dragged her away.

What would he do with her? She had ruined everything. Here he had hoped to woo her, to finally get his night with her. And instead she had ripped the cloth from his head and realized exactly what he was. She wouldn't sleep with him now. And she would tell the others. And the others—what would they do?

He threw her to the ground. She immediately went to pull the gag out of her mouth, but he put a quick stop to that. He drew a dagger from his belt and slammed it through her palm.

Even through the gag he could hear her scream. He closed his eyes at the sight, the sight of her crying, the knife pinning her hand to the hard ground. "What have you done?" he whispered over and over. Finally he opened his eyes. "Do you see what you've done, you bitch?"

He had to kill her now.

There was no other option.

She had put him in this horrible position. She had to make a scene. She had to be difficult. And now he knew there was no other way. He had to kill her.

A small grin creeped across his face. As much as he had wanted Tara alive, as much as he had wanted to bed her, at least he would bathe in the sensation of his dark magic once again. He hadn't felt it, really and truly felt it, since Carlos. The pleasures of the flesh were only skin deep. But the pleasures of his magic? They coursed through his veins, through his soul, through his everything.

He placed a hand across her cheek, which was marred now either by tears or sweat. "Goodbye, Tara."

But the power did not come to him in time.

Something slammed into his back. It took him a moment to realize what was going on. Pain washed over him. Something sharp, something throbbing in his back. He ripped it out. A sword. Auni's sword.

Auni had fallen to the ground, hardly able to walk. The force of striking Asroth with the sword had caused him to stumble. Asroth couldn't take advantage of the boy's crippled state, as much as he wanted to. He was bleeding. A lot. His body became numb and weak.

"Tara!" Auni cried. The boy was too worried about his sister's safety to pursue Asroth. And so Asroth hobbled away, clutching the horrible wound. He knew he was dying. He knew what he had to do.

There was only one man who could heal a wound like this.

They weren't far from Darinshire. Even with his limping he knew he could make it in time. It would take him a while before he lost enough blood to die, and the lights of the city were just down the hill. As long as he didn't lose consciousness, he would live.

Thoughts rushed through his mind. Fear of dying. Anger at Auni. His chance at Tara slipping away. His magic. Dark magic was always at the forefront of his mind.

He would still get a chance at his magic. Once he was healed, he would return. He would kill them all.

But for now, he had to focus on being healed. The thought of healing reminded him of his own magic. His magic was strong, both standard and dark, and growing greater every day. But his healing powers had slipped away from him as his empathy had dissipated. He didn't care enough about Faris' soldiers in Isandas or Auni and the others in the group. He wondered who he might still have empathy for. If he came across a wounded infant? Could he even heal an innocent child? All of humanity had begun to sicken him.

But his thoughts were distracted by pain. Each step was agony, his life slipping away. He knew the town, though. He had lived in Darinshire all his life. He knew the quickest routes, the back alleys. And before long he reached the far too familiar cottage and burst in, knowing it would be unlocked.

The old man was dressed for bed but came out in a hurry at the sound. "Asroth? Dear Ziad, what has happened to you?" His voice was laden with shock and horror.

"Father." Unlike the bishop's expression, Asroth's voice was devoid of emotion. He was here for only one thing. "Heal me."

The man hesitated but eventually stepped forward. "Son," he whispered, feeling Asroth's hair, where it had become so thin.

"Heal me," Asroth said again, this time with more force and anger.

Tears welled up in his father's eyes. "Who has done this to you? How did it happen?"

"Heal me!"

Now he was fully crying. "Son, you know I cannot." He knew plenty well that Asroth's wound had been deserved. Still the bishop embraced him in a hug, as if wanting to comfort him in his death.

But Asroth would not accept the embrace. If he would not heal him, then he was useless.

With a forceful push, he shoved the old man to the ground and pounced on him. The darkness came to him effortlessly. In only an instant it sank from his eyes down into his heart. Then it soared through his veins and melted away at the bishop's throat.

Asroth's pain was replaced with pleasure as the darkness enshrouded him. It consumed him, comforted him. Even as he was still bleeding to death it brought him both relief and excitement. There was only him and his father's rapidly decaying throat.

But when he awoke from the trance, the thrill was gone. Though his father's throat was black and rotten, his face looked the same. The dead eyes stared up at him. And in that instant, all Asroth felt was an unfathomable emptiness.

"Father," he whispered. He stared at him for what felt like an eternity until he realized his eyes were welling with tears. Somehow his empathy had resurfaced. But it was too late to heal him now. The Bishop of Darinshire was dead.

So many were dead. And part of him still wanted to kill. The darkness was tearing his soul, begging him to kill, as if that were the only thing that would make him whole. But as he stared into his father's dead eyes, he didn't want this anymore.

The darkness was returning, he could feel it swirling through his brain, gripping at his thoughts once again. But he didn't want it. He wanted to be free.

"Ziad, please," he cried out into the darkness. "Let me be free."

Then, before the darkness had a chance to talk him out of it, Asroth removed a knife from his belt and thrust it into his own heart.

CHAPTER 24

Sheik put another log on the fire. It was still cold despite being mid-spring. The plains were often covered in frost in the morning. She glanced over at Tara and thought to ask her how she was doing. But of course she already knew the answer. Tara wasn't okay. How could she be? Sheik still wasn't okay from when Spike had nearly raped her, so how could Tara possibly be when it had only been hours since Asroth had assaulted her. Tears welled up in her eyes, wondering if either of them would ever be okay. Clearing her throat, she finally broke the silence with a quiet, "How's the hand?"

Tara raised her bandaged palm to look at it. "Seems okay. The blood is no longer leaking through." She had grown calm since Auni had given her his pain killing leaves. He sat by her side, his hurt leg stretched across the cold ground.

"And you?" Sheik turned to Auni. He merely shrugged, not in the mood for talking. It was understandable. What was there to say? Sheik sighed. Back at Isandas, it had felt like it was only a matter of time before they caught Spike. Now everything was falling apart.

Auni couldn't walk, Tara's hand was unusable. Asroth, after assaulting Tara had run towards Darinshire.

Kazzak, too, was in Darinshire. Sheik had thought it would be better for her and Fang to stay with Tara and Auni and keep them safe, so Kazzak entered the large city alone. He was to find a healer for Tara and a surgeon for Auni. And of course he wanted to find Asroth, though Sheik begged him not to go looking.

As resourceful as Kazzak was, Asroth could kill someone in an instant with his magic. Kazzak promised he would steer clear if he saw him, but Sheik wasn't certain he'd be able to. After all, if she came across Asroth, she wasn't so sure she could restrain herself. She would not aim to impair—she would aim to kill. None of them had really liked Asroth. But now they hated him. To think that they had traveled alongside such a sick, twisted, evil for so long. She would kill him in a heartbeat.

But for now she could do nothing. Just wait patiently for Kazzak to return, trying to keep the other two's morale up even though she could not sustain her own.

They sat in silence for a bit longer before Sheik noticed Asroth's backpack. Auni's attack had wounded him so grievously he hadn't had time to grab his things when he fled. Sheik dumped out its contents.

Clothing, coins, and books fell to the ground. Nothing particularly useful. No flint and steel, no extra waterskin. The clothes might fit Kazzak, although the thought of him wearing Asroth's clothes made her stomach churn. The rest of them wore neutral colors, practical clothes that fit to the body, lined with pockets. Asroth's garments were the long flowing robes of the clergy. Kazzak wouldn't be caught dead in them. She set them aside along with the coins before grabbing one of the books and glancing at the cover.

Dark magic.

She rolled her eyes and grabbed another. The Practical Application of Dark Magic. Theories on the Oath of Power. Exercising Moon Magic in Combat. All of his books: dark magic.

Sheik thumbed through the pages of one. Notes in Flesh Magic. This one was not printed through a press like the others. It was handwritten, mostly in ink and occasionally in graphite. Was it his journal?

Opening to a random page, she read an entry. *Hairline is receding and shedding continues. I must find a solution quickly, for my people are a superstitious people. My sister's hair would be a perfect match. Perhaps I have a use for her after all.*

Sheik hadn't even known that Asroth had a sister. She rolled her eyes at how callously he viewed her. Asroth had always been narcissistic, but it ran so much deeper than Sheik had ever realized.

She flipped to a new page and found a diagram of a human body with large black dots drawn sporadically atop it. The neck, the upper thigh, the shoulder, certain parts of the torso. She stared at the image, confused until she read the title of the diagram: *Locations where moon magic damage is fatal. Note: avoid these sections when employing flesh magic for torture.*

Sheik took in a sharp breath and snapped the book shut.

For a moment, she thought she might vomit. She didn't want to read any more. Gathering the books, she dumped them onto the fire. "What's that?" Auni asked, glancing up at her from where he was seated.

"We're out of firewood," Sheik lied. The boy didn't need to know.

Why had she thought going through Asroth's things would be a good idea? She accepted the silence without complaint and tried not to think about him.

Several hours passed by. Sheik considered going after Kazzak. Something could have happened to him. Asroth could have found him. And killed him. But she urged herself not to worry. She had to stay calm, at least for Tara and Auni's sake.

Finally, by mid-afternoon, Fang hopped to his feet and began barking. People were approaching. She sprinted towards them to find a small crowd, Kazzak leading the way. "Thank Elilah, I was beginning to get worried!"

"Sorry it took so long," he replied, catching up to her. "I got quite a bit of information in town." He looked tired and disheveled, like he had a headache. "We need to talk. But first thing's first." Motioning towards Auni and Tara, he explained some things to several of the people.

Sheik looked them up and down. The healer was obvious, wearing clergy garments like the ones Asroth wore. The surgeon, too, she could make out as he was carrying a box of tools. But one woman stood quietly towards the back, carrying a sleeping child. Sheik raised an eyebrow, wondering who she could possibly be.

"Okay!" Kazzak interrupted her thoughts. The surgeon made his way to Auni, immediately asking the boy questions. The clergyman merely went to Tara's side and, with a quick wince of pain, had her hand healed up. He then turned and listened in on the surgeon's conversation, as if he would be a part of the operation.

Sheik watched them studiously until Kazzak's fingers snapped in front of her face, trying to get her attention. "Hello? Sheik?"

"Sorry," she turned back towards him. "Just making sure they're okay. What is it?"

"I went to the church right away for a healer," he began explaining, "only to find out their bishop had been murdered last night." Then, in a single word, he summed it up. "Asroth."

"I witnessed it," the woman finally spoke up. "I was staying with the bishop when the man broke in. He was covered in blood and demanded to be healed. But the bishop wouldn't do it." She hesitated and added a quiet, "I don't know why. And then the man used magic on him—dark magic—until the bishop was dead. Cyprian and I, that's my boy, we were hiding." Her voice was lost, frazzled, like she was remembering the pieces of a bad dream. "The man, the murderer, he killed himself afterwards."

Sheik finally let out a sigh of shock, confusion, and relief. Kazzak spoke up again, "I identified the body. It was Asroth alright." He hesitated. "There's more. He had this on him." Reaching into his pocket, Kazzak produced a string necklace with nothing but a long, white tooth. A wyvern's tooth.

Carlos' necklace.

A sinking feeling in the pit of her stomach left her speechless. Why did Asroth have Carlos' necklace? When Carlos had died in the mountain, it was Asroth who had found his body. He wouldn't have taken the necklace to mourn him—Asroth couldn't have cared less about Carlos.

He had taken it as a trophy.

Sheik reached out and touched the surface of the fang, as if she was touching Carlos himself. "He killed him. Asroth killed Carlos."

Kazzak let out his breath and quietly said, "I think so."

Asroth had traveled with them for months. And he had murdered their companion. And he would have killed Tara. How could she have spent so much time with this psychopath and not known? She had seen all these little signs: his irritability, his dark magic, his arrogance, the loss of his healing magic. She had never liked him, but she hadn't imagined this. Pure, unrestrained evil. How had she not put the pieces together?

Suddenly she was reminded of Spike. All of his followers. They all traveled with him, obeying his every order. Did they know? Or were they as blind and ignorant as Sheik, walking alongside a monster without ever seeing him for what he really was?

"Sheik." Kazzak's calm voice brought her back to reality. "Stay with me, Sheik. There's more we have to deal with right now." He glanced towards the woman with the heavy child in her arms. "Go ahead. Explain why you were with the bishop."

The woman looked at him, holding her breath. She looked down. "My name is Lady Isul. I was a duchess in Isandas and fled through the escape tunnel to Elena Swamp. My husband Duke Cyler was one of the only ones brave enough to go through the forest. He died protecting me and my son from centaurs. We," she hesitated, finally making eye contact with Sheik, "I think we're the only survivors among the nobility."

Sheik's eyes widened. The only ones with any rightful claim to Isandas. "You certainly did find a lot of information," she said to Kazzak, overwhelmed.

He smirked. "I know. I also asked around about Spike. A small army was spotted about a week ago moving north-west. Only thing I could think of nearby is the north bridge."

"North bridge?"

"Yeah," he replied with a nod, "into the forest. Elven land."

Her face dropped. She understood now. She had wreaked havoc on Spike's life; now he was going to wreak havoc on hers. Biting down on her lip, she tried to ignore the thought of him searching for elven villages, burning them to the ground merely because he knew it would hurt her as an elf. "Okay, first we need to deal with you," she turned back to Isul.

"What do you mean?" Her voice was weak, and her arms tightened around her boy.

"Isandas is still in a state of chaos and confusion. They need some stability and leadership. They need someone on the throne," Sheik explained. Lady Isul nodded in understanding. "But," Sheik continued before the woman got her hopes up, "I need to know something first. The royal family, did they oppress the northern plains peoples?"

Kazzak, who knew nothing of what Sheik had learned about Spike's history, gave her a curious look. But Sheik could tell by Lady Isul's body language that the duchess knew exactly what she was getting at. The noblewoman tensed up. "The northern plains people needed guidance," she spoke carefully.

Sheik rolled her eyes and turned to Kazzak. "I'm not sure about this."

"Wait!" Lady Isul interrupted, loud enough to wake her son. She placed him on the ground as he asked what was going on. "Listen, I was only a duchess. I wasn't a law maker."

"I didn't ask if you were directly involved," Sheik said pointedly. "I need to know the truth. Did Isandas royalty tax the northern plains people at a higher rate than any other group of people?"

Lady Isul gave her a small nod, followed with an attempt at justification. "Yes, but they needed a heavy government presence. It was necessary for us to help them, to educate them."

Sheik raised her hand to silence her. "That government 'presence,' as you call it, is what caused Spike to revolt against you in the first place. If you want Isandas to flourish, to be unified, you need to recognize your government's past mistakes and do better than they did," Sheik said forcefully. "If you keep treating certain groups unfairly, it's only a matter of time until there's another revolution. And people like us," she added, motioning to herself and Kazzak, "might not be there to save your city for you."

The woman stared back at Sheik with an incredulous look upon her face. Her young boy pulled at her skirt. "Mom, I don't like this," he began to whisper.

Lady Isul quickly cooed her boy to be quiet. "Fine," she said sharply. She took in a deep breath and let out a sigh. "I understand. I owe you a great debt."

Sheik shook her head. "I just want to know that if we allow you to retake the throne that this will not happen again. That you will let the northern plains people be. That they won't be further punished for one man's crimes. That you'll treat everyone in Etmos fairly."

"I understand," Lady Isul replied.

Sheik's stomach turned. Somehow she knew it wasn't enough. Lady Isul didn't feel right for the throne. But Sheik didn't have time to sort through the nuances of leadership and find a worthy heir. She didn't know anything about politics or ruling a country. All she wanted was to continue on her quest to kill Spike. She just wanted Spike dead.

Then Auni let out a scream. Politics and thrones left her mind as she rushed to his side. Beads of sweat gathered along his forehead and dripped down his black, curly hair. He clung to his sister's hand and squeezed it with such force that Sheik was surprised Tara could take it. But Tara hardly seemed to notice, focused only on her brother. "Auni," she muttered, watching the boy wince.

The surgeon cut into his leg, slicing the skin evenly apart with a clean, sharp knife. Sheik winced herself. Auni took in deep breaths and tears welled up in his eyes. "Give him more pain relievers," Tara demanded.

"He can't have more, it could make him very sick," the surgeon explained. "It will be over soon." Once the leg had been cut open, he pulled out several large splinters of bone, tossing them in a bloody pile on the grass. He quickly fastened a thin metal rod against the bone, propping it perfectly into position to strengthen the section that had splintered.

"Heal," the man instructed to the clergyman who sat at his side. He did as he was told, the skin pulling together around the bone and metal rod with his magic. "It's completely fractured, all the way through the bone. That's why it can't be healed. But," he continued as he stood up, "the bones that broke off are out now and with a metal bar reinforcing the leg it should reconnect itself in time."

"When will I be able to walk again?" Auni asked quietly after he had regained control of his breathing.

"Right now," the surgeon replied. "We just need to find a pair of crutches your size."

※

The madness had begun to calm down. Lady Isul agreed to stay with the clergy of Darinshire until she and her son Cyprian could be escorted to Isandas. Tara was slowly becoming her old non-stop talkative self. And Auni was adjusting to walking with crutches.

For the first time, Sheik felt like she could breathe without being constantly plagued with worrisome thoughts. It was refreshing.

But even now, as they slowly marched towards the north bridge, she considered what Spike was up to. She hated to think that her actions were punishing thousands of innocents. What could she have done differently though? If she had never made any attempt to stop Spike, he would have ended up hurting many, many more.

If Atarius had never asked her to leave, she would have never been in Calert to do anything. Perhaps no one would have ever been courageous enough to stand up to Spike. Atarius had sent her away to retrieve a sword, but it wasn't necessary. It didn't take a magical sword to save countless lives. It was because of her actions, not because of prophecy.

All they had to do now was find Spike. Not only so she could stop him from hurting people, but so she could stop the trauma that replayed over and over in her head.

"How much longer?" Tara whined, dragging her feet to walk at Auni's pace.

Kazzak waved from a hilltop not far away. He tended to scout ahead, preferring to move at a quicker pace than what they had been reduced to because of Auni's injury. Even though the bridge was only a few days from Darinshire, they had been traveling for a week without spotting the Great River. Letting out a long whistle, Kazzak finally called out, "We're here!"

The rest of them caught up slowly, Fang doing circles around Sheik and the other two, tired of walking so leisurely. Sheik had seen the Great River before when she crossed it approximately a year ago, but the bridge was something magnificent. It was ancient but still stood strong. It was elegant and tremendous. It had stood for hundreds of years and she assumed it would stand for hundreds more.

And then, with a deep breath, Sheik felt her body relax: she was in her old forest.

They were much further north than Atarius' village, but it was the closest thing she had to being back home. This was home. After crossing the bridge, Sheik constantly pointed out various animals and plants. With how slow they traveled because of Auni's injury, it was easy for her to spot everything.

Even Fang seemed at peace. He knew he was home, too. Hunting became easier for him, and he dragged extra kills back for Kazzak to prepare for everyone.

Everything seemed as it should be. She was with friends traveling through her homeland. As much as Sheik knew she still had to find Spike, he was no longer a constant thought pounding at her mind.

"You're making too much noise!" she whispered sharply at Kazzak. The two of them were closing in on a chipmunk, acorns in their extended hands. Sheik used to be able to get them to come up close to her, but Kazzak was making it difficult.

He made a face at her but said nothing. As much as he tried, he simply couldn't make his steps any quieter. The chipmunk darted back a few paces. "Just wait here," Sheik laughed at him. She moved closer and closer, but the critter was still wary. Following it easily, she soon realized Kazzak was out of sight. She sighed, knowing he wouldn't believe she had fed it out of her hand if he didn't see it with his own eyes.

But before she could turn around and call out, a hand wrapped around her mouth. "Shh," a voice whispered. "Don't scream."

<hr>

Spike glanced at the great walls. Pulling his hood a little further over his head, he stepped towards the main road. He had never thought an elven city would look like this. Trying his best to blend in, he kept his eyes focused on the ground, lightly pushing past people until he reached the castle.

A soldier stopped him. "What's your business in the palace?"

He was slightly shocked. The man hadn't spoken elven. Spike looked up, risking his identity being discovered, to look the elven man over from head to toe. The man wasn't an elf at all—he was human, as normal as could be. "You're not an elf?" Spike whispered quietly.

The man scoffed and spat on the ground. "Karthais, no!"

Again, Spike was shocked. "Karthais? You worship the god of war? Not Ziad or Justar?"

The burly soldier laughed. "Failures pray to gods of goodness and justice, but victors pray to the god of strength."

Spike glanced around himself. There wasn't a single elf in sight. In fact, as he lowered his hood for a better look, he realized most of the men were quite large and powerful. "What is this place?"

"The palace and city of General Grathios."

"I would speak to him."

The soldier laughed again. "Speak to the general himself? You're joking."

He frowned. "I am Spike, leader of the New Prosper Army. I'm sure you've heard my name. I have a proposition for your general."

The man crossed his arms. "New Prosper Army? Haven't heard of it."

"I've singlehandedly conquered all of Etmos and half of Vesdar and Masil. Everyone has heard of me."

The soldier gave him a long, skeptical look. "Not here we haven't. We aren't exactly connected to the affairs of the eastern nations."

Of course not. How could they be? After all, Spike had never heard of humans settling in elven territory. He had no idea who this General Grathios was, and so it was only natural that he hadn't heard of Spike either. "I assure you, I'm quite famed on the other side of the river," Spike insisted. "Why don't you fetch your general and I will wait here for his presence."

The soldier's eyes narrowed, but he did as told. Spike waited patiently, glancing around the castle entrance and the parts of town that were within sight. How a fully functioning human civilization beyond the bridge had come to exist he had no idea. But here it was, bustling with commotion, as normal as any other city he had ever seen. He wondered why a general would want to carve out a piece of land, a bustling city, and then isolate himself.

"Spike." He turned to find himself glancing up at a formidable man. A tall man, with strong features, his black hair slicked back behind his scowling face. "My last scouting team brought back rumors of you. Conquering territory by territory. Is this how you do it? Come to the front gate and knock?"

He smirked and gave a light chuckle. "I'm not here to conquer. I have a feeling only a fool would try to conquer you."

The comment seemed to win him over. His frown faded into the slightest curve of a smile. "I am General Grathios. If you aren't here for war, then tell me, why are you here?"

Spike was used to talking smoothly and spinning tales. He could have someone believe him in an instant, convince them of some lie and have them ready to do his bidding. But for once he found the truth might suffice best. "I came here originally for revenge. I planned to burn your city to the ground, to make every last citizen suffer." He watched the man's eyes grow dark and narrow. "But this is not the city I imagined it to be."

Suddenly the general seemed to understand. "You discovered it to be a city of humans."

He smiled. "I am in need of assistance. I have a bit of an elf problem. I have many powers and many riches. If this elf can be exterminated, I guarantee I will make it worth your while."

The general stepped forward and slapped him on the back, guiding him into the palace. "You've come to the right place, friend."

Sheik bit down on the hand as hard as she could.

"Ow! What are you doing?" As he let go and Sheik pushed him away, she was shocked to discover her attacker's appearance; he was a scrawny elven boy of perhaps only fifteen.

"What am I doing? What are you doing?" she exclaimed.

"I'm saving you, now keep your voice down!" he whispered back sharply.

She couldn't help but laugh. "Saving me from what?"

"The humans," he motioned towards where she had come from, where Kazzak was still waiting for her. "Aren't you their prisoner?"

Again, she laughed. "Of course not, we're friends."

"Oh." Suddenly his demeanor changed. He appeared instantly more relaxed and gave her a broad smile. "My mistake. I'm Jesse Torith!" he introduced himself, sticking out his hand. She had never seen an elf shake hands before and found it rather peculiar.

Nevertheless, she accepted it. "I'm Sheik," she said cautiously. She studied him a moment. Although it was clear he was an elf by the point to his ears and the color of his hair, something about him was off. His skin wasn't the same hue as hers, almost like Kazzak's. And his eyelids had that extra crease that she had only seen in humans.

"Pleasure to meet you, Sheik," he said excitedly. "What are you doing out here? I mean, with humans. It seems kind of strange."

He was a curious one. Despite her reservations, he seemed harmless, and so Sheik answered him honestly, "Well, we're actually looking for an army."

"The humans that passed through here? You're with them?"

"No," she shook her head, "we're against them. You've seen them?"

In a quick movement he spun around, picking a branch off the ground and holding it out like a rapier, pointed towards Sheik's chest. His eyebrows furrowed into a look of disappointment. "In that case, you're my enemy."

Sheik didn't bother refraining from laughing a third time. "What are you talking about?"

"The army you speak of is marching towards a human city I happen to want destroyed."

"Human city? Hold on, slow down." She took a step forward but he pushed the stick against her, as if threatening her not to move any closer. Using her magic, she shrunk it down so it no longer poked her. His jaw dropped at the sight of her magic. She pulled the stick from him and threw it on the ground. "Look, this is all rather confusing for both of us. Why don't you come sit with me and my friends and we'll talk this whole thing out? No need to draw any weapons," she added with a giggle.

Reluctantly he nodded.

Tara watched Jesse curiously as he ate the meal Kazzak had given him. He had long, teal, almost aqua hair, tied back into a ponytail with his bangs flopping unevenly across his forehead. Tara did not know such a hair color existed. His thin lips almost always seemed to form some sort of grin or smile. Though he was scrawny, she still thought him cute and wondered how old he might be.

He said very little, just introductions and the occasional thank you between bites once he started eating. By how fast he ate, Tara wondered if he had been starving. She was happy to have him join their group. Things had been different ever since Asroth's attack.

At first it had just been this unspoken, dark cloud of trauma that hovered over them. Fear, at how close Asroth had come to killing her. Anger. And the others felt guilt, she could tell. Sheik and Kazzak had never taken Asroth as seriously as they should have.

And Tara felt guilt of her own, for Auni's broken leg. She had been helpless to defend him in the centaur attack and then unable to heal him after. And now they traveled so slowly as they chased after Spike that Tara thought the idea of ever catching up to him was hopeless.

Sheik and Kazzak were no longer together. Tara did not know when it had happened. But she could tell by their distance, the way they chose their words. On the plains everything had been tense and uncomfortable.

When they entered the forest, it started to mend. Sheik seemed happy. Tranquil. She and Kazzak were like they had been before the avalanche. Like kids flirting. Tara thought to tease them but decided not to disturb the peace. Auni smiled again, too. And even though Tara still feared Spike was too far away to catch, everyone's attitude was infectious. She could not help but smile and laugh and talk. It was like her old self was coming back.

And Jesse only added to it all. He had a positive, cheery energy about him. And most importantly, he brought news of Spike's location.

"So Jesse," she finally spoke up. "You live around here?"

He shrugged. "I guess so."

She was not quite sure what that meant. Sheik followed up with, "Well do you want to tell us about this human city?"

"What's there to tell?" he asked between bites of food. Then turning to Kazzak, he added, "Thanks again, it tastes real good."

"No problem, glad you like it," Kazzak smiled, watching the boy eat. "I wasn't aware there were any cities occupied by humans on this side of the river."

"Used to be elven. Most people don't know about it," Jesse explained, though his explanations tended to just bring about more questions.

"Used to be?"

He nodded and took a break from eating, watching their expressions. "Did you want me to tell you the whole story?"

"Yes!" everyone exclaimed all at once.

Jesse let out a chuckle. "Well let's see, about twenty years ago I think it was, an army came led by General Grathios. They took over the city. Looking for something I think. All the elves had to run and to this day Grathios doesn't allow an elf past the walls. Doesn't allow them anywhere, really. You bring in an elf head and you get gold coins."

Tara's heart sank at the thought, and she wondered, "Then why are you so close to the city?" She hated the thought of him, this boy no older than Auni, being hunted.

"'Cause I don't think it's right and instead of running like all the other elves did, I want to kill Grathios."

Kazzak looked at him skeptically. "So you're out here all by yourself, huh?" Jesse nodded. "Then how is it you know about this if it happened twenty years ago? You couldn't have been around back then. And you couldn't have gone into the city if you're an elf."

He smiled a mischievous grin. "But I'm not an elf." They leaned in, even more curious. "I'm half an elf, half a human." Sheik gave a nod of sudden understanding, like she had guessed as much. Tara would not have known a thing if he hadn't said it outright. Besides the hair color, she figured Jesse looked as much like Sheik as any elf might. They could be siblings for all she knew.

"When Grathios' army first took over," he continued, "all the married men sent word for their wives. My mom came and lived there for a while until her husband died. She stayed widowed for a bit but then met an elf when she was outside the city. My father. She never told me much about him or how they met. I don't even know his name," he said with a lopsided frown.

"She had to leave when she became pregnant. When I was born part elf, I would have been killed and she would have been tortured until she told Grathios where the elves were. So she just ran away into the forest and raised me until she died last year.”

The story was terribly sad. “How come she didn’t go to live with the elves?” Tara asked.

He shrugged. “I used to ask but she never gave me much of an answer. Just that things were complicated. But anyhow, it’s Grathios’ fault she had to leave and I’m not going anywhere until he’s dead.”

“So that’s why we’re enemies,” Sheik said with a feeble smile. “The army passing through was marching towards the city, so you hope they’ll kill Grathios.” He nodded, watching her carefully. “Well,” she explained, “the leader of the army is a man named Spike, a very cruel and wicked man. Sounds a lot like this Grathios fellow. Who’s to say they won’t join sides?”

“Well, if that’s the case,” Jesse replied with a smirk, “I guess that would make us allies instead of enemies, now wouldn’t it?”

CHAPTER 25

Jesse used a small stick to trace lines across the dirt. The drawing was crude but accomplished what it needed to. "So over here are some caves," he explained, motioning with the stick. "They get flooded, so we'll have to swim at one point, but they lead right under the castle. If we can find a weak spot, we can break through the top and be inside the palace before anyone knows what's happening," he explained.

Kazzak shrugged. "It's worth a try, anyway."

Sheik, too, nodded. "Well Jesse can show me the way and then I'll sneak in by myself."

"Excuse me?" Kazzak retorted with raised eyebrows. "I'm coming."

"Me too," Jesse piped in. "I hunt every day, I'm a good shot," he added, holding up his bow.

"And me," Tara added.

"Whoa whoa whoa," Sheik shook her head. "Absolutely not. You and Auni are staying here," she declared. "Fang, too." The wolf's head popped up, hearing his name, but he immediately rested it back down, not particularly concerned.

"Agreed. But I'm coming," Kazzak stated matter-of-factly. "Even if you can assassinate Spike and Grathios all by yourself, it's not enough damage. New leaders will emerge. We have to wipe out the majority of their soldiers if we want to end this."

Jesse nodded. "You, me, and him."

With a sigh, Sheik finally gave in. Tara continued to complain and whine about not being able to help, but Sheik refused to allow her to come along on such a dangerous mission.

By the time the sun was beginning to set, Tara had quit her pouting and wished them luck as they stalked off into the darkness. Fang had wanted to come, too, but was compliant when Sheik asked him to watch over Tara and Auni in her absence.

Jesse led the way to the caves. They were closer than Sheik had imagined. The opening was tall and wide, Sheik hardly having to bend at all to walk inside them. But as they came closer to the back of the cavern, it grew tighter, and she crouched her way through. Jesse didn't have much difficulty, but Kazzak ended up crawling on his hands and knees, his shoulders almost being too broad to get him through some areas.

The echoes got louder as they continued, and everything slowly grew damp. Then suddenly Sheik's hand fell into a puddle. She ripped it back, startled by the cold temperature of the water. Jesse merely laughed at her. "It's gonna get worse," he smirked, pressing forward until they were soaked up to their knees.

Now that their surroundings were pitch black, Jesse lit a torch to reveal their next obstacle.

The water grew deeper as the cavern walls grew narrower. As Jesse moved forward, he shuffled around so he was swimming instead of crawling. His head stayed on the surface of the water but couldn't lift any higher without touching the ceiling of the cave. He passed the torch off to Sheik.

"We have to swim?"

"Scared?" he asked with a sly grin.

Sheik took in a deep breath and followed, plunging into the water while keeping the torch aloft. At first, it was only the shock of the cold that startled her. She adjusted to the temperature quickly and her head surfaced. But there was barely enough space between the water and the ceiling for her to breathe, and the tunnel grew tighter and tighter. The torch sizzled until it finally went out.

Stay calm, she reminded herself. Should she need to, she could always use magic to help herself out.

But it wasn't necessary. The tunnel opened wider and wider. She found the source of the water, rushing in from a crack in the wall, and, as she started to climb upwards, the water receded and left her on dry land. They were in a much more spacious area now, with plenty of room to stand. She pulled herself out of the way as Kazzak followed not far behind. "Thought I was gonna get stuck in there!" he exclaimed, calming his breathing.

Jesse laughed at the two. "Oh, it wasn't so bad."

"Except it was freezing!" Kazzak retorted. "Besides, you aren't wearing a cloak," he pointed out, motioning to Jesse's light shirt and pants. Sheik wasn't wearing anything too heavy, but Kazzak had a hooded mantle on. He pulled it off, wringing it out and whipping the tip against Jesse jokingly.

Sheik grabbed it and pulled it away from him. "Alright children," she teased, tossing the wet cloak over her shoulder. "Where to?" Her eyes were beginning to adjust to the darkness and she could see multiple paths winding in different directions.

"You can make fire with your magic, right?" Jesse asked, already on his feet.

"Yeah why?"

"We'll freeze to death if we don't dry off at least a little." Jesse pointed to a corner where loose sticks were already piled up. Sheik realized now that he had been preparing long before he had met them. She made a small fire and, after wringing out their clothes, they huddled around it. They weren't dry by any means, but at least no longer soaked. Sheik finally felt warm enough to look around.

Jesse pointed to the cavern wall. "That's how we'll track where we've been." Sheik didn't know what he was motioning to until she was right in front of it; there was a torch held up by an iron ring laid into the wall.

"Weird." She hadn't expected the cave to have been previously discovered. Using her magic, the torch lit with a small flame. Glancing around, she now noticed elven runes carved into the walls. It had been many years, but these caves had once been used quite regularly.

"Well," Kazzak moved up next to them and pulled the torch out. "I'll take this and go one way, you guys can go another way and light torches as you go so I'll be able to find you."

Sheik nodded and motioned for Jesse to lead the way. He meandered through the cavernous hallways and Sheik lit up torches as they came across them. It all seemed mostly the same, the walls etched with small prayers for safety or courage or pure hearts and other generic virtues. Jesse wandered a bit quicker than her, while she walked at a slow enough pace to glance over the prayers.

"Whoa!" he suddenly called out. "Come here, come here!"

She came at a sprint, worried something might be wrong. When she reached him and saw that he was fine, she scolded him. "You shouldn't shout so loud if you aren't in danger."

"But look!"

She stepped a little closer. It was hard to see what he was pointing at, as the last torch she had lit was quite a ways away. "What is it?" Then she saw it.

Elilah.

Instantly she knew that was who it was.

It was a large statue—Sheik had to crane her neck to see the top of it. It was made of a smooth, black graphite, though crackles shot through it, the statue having been damaged many years ago. She reached out and touched Elilah's stone skin, which, while cold, felt strangely full of life.

It was incredible.

Her flawless features, graceful posture, outstretched hand, flowing hair, and free spirit.

"Look there's gold down here," Jesse commented, though Sheik didn't bother looking. "Ooh and a book. Oh, it's in elven I don't know what it says," he mumbled after picking it up.

He handed it to her and Sheik glanced at it quickly. "That's not elven," she said nonchalantly, looking away.

Wait.

She looked back at the book. "Dear Elilah." She had seen that book before. Where had she seen it? She couldn't have seen it.

She stared at it in shock for a minute before a clinking sound distracted her. Jesse was chipping at the statue with one of his knives. "Jesse, what are you doing?"

"There's a coin stuck in here, I'm trying to get it out."

"Jesse, stop!" The coin suddenly pulled free and a bright light instantly replaced it. Their eyes widened in surprise. Sheik ran her hand along the back of the statue. "It's not connected to the cave wall." The light couldn't be coming from outside.

He tried to pull at the small hole but it did no good. Picking up a stone he smashed it against the statue. "Jesse! What do you think you're doing?" Sheik yelled, shocked at his blasphemously improper treatment of the statue.

"I wanna see what it is!" With another strike of the rock, part of the statue began to crumble. The light shined brighter. "My hands are too big, can you get it?"

Sheik sighed but bent down to peer inside the hole in the statue's side. Her jaw dropped.

It was the Sword of Elilah.

⸻❖⸻

Auni strapped a sheath onto one of his crutches. "What are you doing?" Tara asked, walking over to where he sat.

"Kazzak left some knives in his pack," he explained, "I'm attaching them to my crutches."

She laughed. "Yes, but why?"

"So we can go help."

Her eyes lit up with excitement. "Really? Are you serious?"

"Of course," he replied with a nod. "You wanted to, didn't you? Fang!" The wolf instantly arrived by his side. "Come on." Tara helped him to his feet and he wrapped his arms around the crutches to make sure the knives were easily accessible.

"How are we going to find our way in?"

"Main entrance. We aren't elves, they aren't gonna hurt us."

"But the castle?"

Auni shrugged. "We'll come up with something."

And so they discussed as they walked towards the city gates. It wasn't far, but of course because of Auni's limp it took them some time. Fang followed them obediently, refusing to break Sheik's orders of guarding them.

They got a few strange looks inside the city, between Auni's broken leg and a wolf following behind them. But no one questioned them. Until, of course, they got to the palace.

"Can't let you past, too late for visitors," a guard stepped in front of them.

"I am just going to see my father," Tara stated simply, pushing past him.

The soldier didn't budge. "Sorry, kid."

"Kid?" she gasped. "I would have you know my father is one of the best soldiers under the general's command! He dines with General Grathios himself—and I am sure he outranks you," she added with a sneer, glancing the man up and down. "Now if you do not mind, my idiot gardener here has hurt his leg and is demanding my father pay for medical expenses. We need to get it sorted out right away."

He glared at them for a moment. Auni worried he would call their bluff. "And what's with the wolf?"

"It's their damn wolf's fault that I broke my leg," Auni piped in immediately. "They shouldn't keep a wild beast like that as a house pet. I want it killed."

Tara turned to him with an expression of fake shock on her face. "Don't you dare say that again, you ungrateful little—"

"Shut up the both of you," the guard cut her off. "Fine, fine. I will have someone escort you to your father if you know where he's posted tonight."

Her face went blank. "How am I supposed to know where he is posted?" she retorted in a hostile tone.

The man sighed and signaled for several guards. "Take them to the residence halls so they can look up where her father is posted."

Great. Auni tossed Tara a look of a concern. She remained quiet. They'd have to come up with a plan somewhere between now and when they arrived at the residence halls.

<hr>

"Well?" Jesse asked anxiously.

Sheik remained in awe. There was the sword from her dreams. The sword she was destined to find. How could it have been true? Perhaps this, too, was a dream. No, it was real. She had really found the sword. Atarius had been right all along. He couldn't be right. She wouldn't let him be right.

She wouldn't take the sword.

No, that was ridiculous. She had to take it. But why? Because it was her destiny? No. It was her destiny to find the sword; to take the sword was of her own accord. It was her choice.

Life was a balance between fate and free will.

Destiny had done its part, now she had to do hers. She took the rock Jesse had been using to widen the hole. Unraveling Kazzak's wet cloak, she protected her hand from making contact with the sword as she slowly worked it out. She didn't know the power of the sword or what it might do to her if she touched it with her bare skin.

"Whoa!" Jesse exclaimed once the sword was free. It was exactly as she had seen it in her dream, years ago. Silver in color, the blade covered in runes, the light green vine wrapped around the hilt. The only difference was the bright light the sword hadn't stopped emitting. She wrapped it up carefully in the wet cloak so the only visible part was the hilt—the only part that wasn't shining.

"Hello?" Kazzak's voice echoed through the caves.

"We're here!" Sheik called back.

"I found something," he replied, his shadow slowly coming into view.

"Yeah so did we," Sheik and Jesse said at once, though Jesse's response was far louder and full of excitement.

Kazzak, stepping close enough they could see his face, raised his eyebrows. "Yeah? What?"

Sheik held up the wrapped sword. "A sword!" Jesse shouted out before she could say something. "In the statue—it's really bright, too, like the sun!"

He laughed. "What are you talking about?"

Sheik bit her lip and stared at him for a long moment. "It's the Sword of Elilah."

Jesse gave her a confused look but Kazzak merely laughed again. "Sheik, the Sword of Elilah isn't real. Those weapons are just an ancient legend. It's probably just a gold sword. Maybe we can sell it."

"No, I'm serious. I know what it looks like. I've dreamed about it before."

Kazzak rolled his eyes. "I thought only the descendants of the original owners could dream about them?"

"That's what Atarius said. Only people in the bloodlines. He was convinced that I was."

He shook his head and chuckled. "Sheik, the bloodlines aren't real! There are no weapons, it's just a tale!"

"Fine," she replied. Being sure to only touch Kazzak's cloak and not the metal, she slowly unraveled the sword to show him. The silvery light illuminated the entire chamber. Kazzak's jaw dropped, but he said nothing. After a quick second, he reached out to touch it. Sheik pulled it away. "Don't!"

"Why not?"

"We don't know anything about it or how powerful it could be. For all I know it could kill whoever touches it!" She remembered touching it in her dream and the searing pain it brought every time.

He raised an eyebrow. "If you're the one who is destined to find it though, shouldn't you be wielding it?"

She shook her head uneasily as she rewrapped it and strapped it to her back beside her quiver. "I don't know the first thing about sword fighting. I don't wanna touch it."

A moment went by. "Sheik. We found the Sword of Elilah," Kazzak restated, still processing the shock. "We have one of the divine weapons, we—"

"We?" she retorted with a sly smile. "If anything, it belongs to Jesse."

The young boy, who had been quietly observing their conversation, just shook his head. "You seem to know more about it." He looked over to Kazzak. "Didn't you say you found something?"

"Right! I almost forgot!" He led them through the tunnel, back the way he had come. Before them laid a tall staircase. "Ta-da!" he announced. "Not as grand as the Sword of Elilah, but I'd imagine it goes into the palace." It was difficult to see the top, but, knowing it had to lead somewhere, Sheik began the ascent.

They had to step carefully. While it was obvious there used to be a rock lining to the stairs, it had worn considerably and was easy to trip over with the limited amount of light.

After a painful minute of climbing, they reached the top. It ended abruptly at the natural ceiling of the cave. "Well, that was a waste," Kazzak muttered.

"Wait," Jesse interrupted. "Let me see the torch." Kazzak handed it to him and the small half elven boy snuck past Sheik and held the torch to the ceiling. "There's lines here."

Sure enough, forming a box were four lines colored strangely. Sheik pressed her finger to it. "It's sealant." They were quiet for a moment. "If you get in front, I can try to get rid of what I can of the seal while you push," she suggested, looking back at Kazzak.

He nodded and scrambled around the two. Sheik pulled out her bow and knocked an arrow to it. "Get yours ready, too, Jesse. We may very well run into guards." Then, using her magic, the glue slowly warped away.

Kazzak let out a loud grunt as he struggled to lift the heavy stone. He wasn't able to toss it over as easily as any of them had hoped, but he lifted it just enough to slide it onto the floor of whatever room lay above them. With the glue no longer sealing it down, Sheik allowed it to reform, releasing her magic.

Footsteps could be heard above them and Sheik and Jesse readied their weapons. Kazzak gave the stone another hefty shove, sliding it far enough that he could squeeze through the gap. Pulling himself up, he was surrounded by soldiers before he could even draw a weapon.

One of the men fell to the ground, clutching his ankle. Jesse had released a perfectly aimed arrow, and the distraction gave Kazzak enough time to draw his sword and push the small crowd back a bit. Sheik, too, loosed an arrow while Jesse pulled himself up to join the combat with Kazzak.

Between a couple surprise arrows from Sheik and Jesse and a few swings from Kazzak, the battle was almost over before Sheik had even climbed up to their level. "Leave one!" she exclaimed just before Kazzak swung at the last man standing. Instead of going for a kill, he smashed his blade against the soldier's hand, causing him to drop his weapon, and then pointed his sword towards the man's throat.

"A man came with an army a few days back," Sheik explained as quickly as possible to the anxious guard. "I need you to tell us where we would find him, your general, and the soldiers' barracks. We'll let you live if you can do that."

The guard swallowed nervously and gave a cautious nod. "Royal quarters are in the east wing on the top floor. The residence hall is on this floor, in the west wing," he explained uneasily.

"The leader of the other army will be in the royal quarters?" Sheik asked.

He nodded.

"And Grathios?" Jesse added.

"The east tower."

Kazzak removed his sword from its threatening position. "Alright, down there," he motioned with his blade towards the hole they had crawled out of.

"What?" the soldier exclaimed, but Kazzak's sword pushed against his back. He stopped his complaints and climbed down the stairs as quickly as his armor would allow him.

Kazzak pushed the bodies down after him and, with another painful grunt, slid the stone back to where it had rested. "There," he finally said with a sigh. "He won't be able to draw attention quickly at least."

"I'm going after Spike," Sheik announced, hardly paying attention to Kazzak at all.

"Well, we all are."

"You said we needed to take out as much of his army as we can. You two go to the barracks and start a fire."

Kazzak gave her a look. "A fire?" Sheik knew what he was trying to say. It was a cruel way to die. Far too callous for Sheik, who had once aimed for ankles and calves.

She nodded solemnly. "Yeah. A fire."

They didn't have time for a conversation like this. Sheik didn't have time to consider alternative plans and ways to paralyze rather than kill or kill kindly rather than cruelly. She was here for one reason and one reason only: to kill Spike. She would not leave this palace without killing.

Kazzak, realizing her mind was made up, said, "Take Jesse with you. I can take care of a little arson on my own."

She accepted the compromise and whispered, "Get out as soon as you're done. Don't come looking for us. We'll all regroup back in the forest." He nodded. "Good luck."

"You too," he whispered. And then he left towards the west wing. She watched him disappear before she turned in the opposite direction.

Jesse took the lead. He had better vision than her, which she needed to guide them around the occasional soldier standing watch. It wasn't long before he spotted a spiraling staircase. It climbed endlessly and was beginning to make Sheik sick by the time they reached the fourth floor. It seemed to be the last floor, other than, of course, the many towers.

"Well great," Sheik whispered, "how do we find where Spike is?"

"I'm not looking for Spike," Jesse replied, suddenly taking off.

"Jesse!" Sheik called after him, though trying not to be loud enough to alert any guards.

"I'll find you when I've dealt with Grathios," he called back over his shoulder as he ran into a large chamber and bounded up another flight of stairs. Sheik chased after him into the chamber but stopped at the staircase.

She contemplated following him but before she had a chance to take the first step, a voice echoed through the hall.

"It seems we are alone again."

⸻ ⸰ ⸻

Kazzak walked around the hallways with ease at first. But he soon began to run into soldiers and had to stay hidden, his back pushed up against shadowy walls until the patrolling guards had passed. It was a slow process, and he still had no plan on how he would actually burn the quarters down.

He spotted a torch on a wall and it was then that he noticed hanging below it was a small jar. Oil. All of the torches had an additional jar of oil by them. Between avoiding passing soldiers and collecting the jars, he didn't have time to figure out where, exactly, the residence hall was. Perhaps the whole area he was in was the residence hall?

Deciding that that was the case, he realized he needed to start lighting the area on fire. But with the number of soldiers he had been spotting in the area, he wasn't sure how to do so safely. Maybe there was no "safely," though. Maybe it just needed to be done, whether it meant he got hurt or not. Whether he died or not.

Finally he built up the courage and opened a door to a crowd full of soldiers half dressed in armor. None of them looked up. He had been prepared for them to all instantly charge him, but now that he thought about it, he looked like one of them, just off duty.

Of course, when he started pouring the oil, he could only assume they would begin to notice him. He took in a deep breath, emptying the contents of one of the jars onto the floor. "What are you doing?" one of the soldiers asked.

Kazzak stayed silent, deciding to try to empty as many as possible casually, and then make a run for it when the first soldier drew a weapon. He kept his eyes on the ground, dribbling the oil across the room and into the next. Soldiers stared at him in complete confusion.

Finally one of them stood up. "What do you think you're doing?" he demanded, not letting Kazzak past him. He tried to walk around the soldier but felt the sharp sting of the man's fist hit his jaw. Kazzak stumbled back for a moment, trying not to drop the oil. "Answer me!"

He didn't. He merely reached for a torch off the wall and dropped it onto the ground. It instantly caught fire across the long trail of oil. Everyone leapt to their feet, stamping at the fire, trying to put it out.

Kazzak ran. He tried to spill more oil as he ran, but his mind was focused on the running. Zigzagging in and out of rooms, he hoped to cause the most possible damage. It was obvious at this point that he was their enemy. Soldiers had weapons drawn and were shouting to catch him. A large, strong door stood in front of him.

The end of the residence halls.

If he could make it there and prop the door shut, maybe he could not only save his own skin, but also lock the soldiers in with the fire. It was his only hope. He sprinted as fast as he could, no longer caring about spreading the oil evenly. His last few jars dropped and exploded as they caught fire.

A soldier swung. He dodged. Another soldier pierced. He jumped out of the way. An unarmed soldier planted a fist into his shoulder, which stunned him for just a second. Another sword. He pushed it off, taking the brunt of the blow with his other shoulder. A mace landed against his back, knocking him to the ground.

Kazzak reached up, feeling the metal of the door handle. He used it to pick himself up while, in the same swift motion, he pushed the massive door open. His strength was failing him, his shoulder bloody and his back aching. Another weapon stabbed into his side.

Blood poured out. He thought he might vomit and collapse, but before he did so, he managed to squeeze through the narrow opening in the door.

At least he had been right. There were no more soldiers as far as he could see. He had lit the entire residence hall on fire.

Holding his wound together, he fell against the door, trying to keep it closed with the last of his strength. His mind raced. He tried to think of the last time he'd had a wound that bled this much.

He hadn't.

The blood spilled past his fingers. He could already feel the color draining from his face, his head growing light. Soldiers pushed against the door like a battering ram. With each thud, Kazzak felt his wound tear further and further open. The pain echoed through him, but at the same time a peace called to him. As much as the pain made him want to vomit, it also made him want to pass out. And once he passed out, he knew he wouldn't feel the pain anymore.

He wouldn't feel pain ever again.

<hr>

Spike paced around Sheik.

Her bow was drawn, an arrow nocked. She raised it and took aim. At his heart. Not his knees, not his ankles. She would kill him, and she would not hesitate.

He laughed. "Are you going to shoot me?"

No.

She wanted to kill him. She wanted so desperately to watch him die. To know he could not haunt her anymore. But she knew she was doing it for the wrong reasons.

Sheik had promised herself she wouldn't hesitate. That when she needed to kill, she would take the shot. But she didn't need to kill Spike. He could stand trial for his crimes. She only wanted to kill him because she wanted revenge. She wanted him dead for what he had done to her. Was that a good enough reason to kill?

Sheik lowered her bow.

"Spike, I'm asking you to surrender." He chuckled again. "I know why you did what you did," she began, ignoring his laughter. "I know you raised the New Prosper Army for the northern plains people. You conquered Isandas because the royal family was corrupt, and evil, and treating you unfairly. But you've gone too far. You've become the monster you sought to kill."

The man stepped closer into the light. "Is that so?" He smirked. "A monster, hmm? Tell me, what would you do if it were your people being killed?"

"It's over, Spike. Now surrender."

"What would you do?" he screamed, taking a step closer. She lifted her bow back up, ready to draw it back should he make an offensive move. But he didn't. He merely smiled again, his voice quieter. "We'll see soon enough. When I've burned down this forest, killed all your little elf friends. We'll see what kind of monster you become." With that, he turned to leave.

"Don't you move!" It was like he had a death wish. She pulled back ever so slightly on her bowstring, taking aim. "I will shoot you if you do not surrender!"

Finally he froze. He turned back towards her. "I'll tell you what kind of monster you'll become. The kind of monster who sits idly by as you watch your people burn. You aren't like me," he shook his head slowly. "You aren't capable of doing what I did for my people."

"You're right. I'm not like you!" she spat out. "I would not slaughter cities for my people." My people? Where had she heard that before?

Then it hit her: Asroth's journal.

For my people are a superstitious people.

It had not been Asroth's journal. It had been Spike's. And Sheik remembered the next sentence: My sister's hair would be a perfect match.

Her stomach dropped with the realization. And her resolve doubled. "I'm not like you. I would not hurt innocents. I would not defile my own sister."

Spike's expression changed. His mouth hung open as her words hit him. And then he snapped. "You!" he screamed. And in an instant, he was rushing towards her. "You helped her escape!" Before he could reach her, Sheik loosed her arrow.

It fell to the ground. The tip was warped into a right angle. And as she watched it, shocked, it slowly bent back.

Spike was a sorcerer.

And now he was upon her, his fist swinging. She ducked and dropped the bow, drawing one of Farin's knives instead. It grew unbearably hot, and she was forced to drop it, too. "Fine," Sheik mumbled, now taking a swing at him herself. He couldn't alter her fists, and so that's what she would have to kill him with.

A stone rose up from the floor, causing her to trip and fall. Then a stone from the ceiling came loose. She rolled away just in time. Fragments shattered against the ground.

But she had magic of her own.

Mimicking his strategy, Sheik used her magic to loosen a stone in the ceiling. Spike threw it back at her with his mind. She blocked it with a magical shield as she pulled herself to her feet.

Then she froze his clothing so he could not move. It took all the magic she could muster to hold him in place, to keep him from taking another step. But he merely willed it away. His magic was stronger.

Her head throbbed. Before she could regain her senses, smoke began to bellow around her. Sheik coughed and swung her hand wildly, trying to see through it. For a second there was silence. Just the pulsing in her head and the stinging of her lungs as she struggled to breathe through the haze.

Spike struck like lightning, knocking her to the ground.

He wasn't walking, he was flying.

By merely controlling the stones below his feet, he soared above her. She shot pieces of rock, ice, fire, everything she could think of, but he simply maneuvered around it. He was too fast, and she could not reach him. And her head was aching. How much longer could she go on?

Overwhelming heat poured over her. He had created fire. Fire, slowly encircling her. It came from all edges of the room, growing closer, hotter. She tried desperately to will it away but found herself unable.

Thinking of no better escape, she mimicked Spike's magic and raised the stones she was standing on. And now she chased after him through the air.

It was difficult to balance and impossible to keep up with him. When she finally thought he was slowing, when she finally had hope she might reach him, there was a deafening crack.

The outer wall was caving in.

She wasn't sure if it was his magic or the wall simply giving out after they had torn away so many stones. But it cascaded towards her, and she found herself focusing all her attention on staying ahead of the collapsing wall.

Before she was aware of what he was doing, he had warped away the stones beneath her feet. Sheik tumbled to the ground with an audible thud. Her face hit the floor at the same time as her arms and knees. And though it pained her, she twisted her body and threw up her hands, forcing a magical shield around her as the wall collapsed on her.

It took a second for the rubble to settle. As her shield wavered away, dust descended upon her. She blinked several times. The room was bright now, illuminated by moonlight. Spike landed gracefully and she was reminded of the first time she had seen his face. Angelic.

Sheik knew it was over.

Coppery blood dripped into her mouth. Her body ached in several spots. Worse, her head throbbed. Her weapons were useless, she couldn't get close enough to hit him, and he was more talented at magic than her. There was no way to beat him.

But she would not give up.

Spike walked to her, taking his time as she pulled herself to her feet. When he came within reach, she threw a punch as hard as she could. He caught her fist and twisted it back painfully. Her left arm swung next. He instantly created a chunk of metal, and Sheik's knuckles split as they crashed against it.

Spike's fist smashed into her stomach, knocking the wind out of her. She drew another of Farin's knives but dropped it as Spike delivered a swift kick to her gut. Sheik fell to the floor. She gasped for air but found only pain.

The fallen knife was almost in reach, but Spike pushed it away with his foot. He bent over and picked up her bow, snapping it in half over his knee.

"No!"

The small, whispered cry split her lungs. The bow Atarius had made for her. The bow that had once meant nothing to her. Now it meant everything. It clattered against the ground, the two pieces attached only by the bowstring.

"You stole her from me!" Spike screamed. Delivering a kick to her face, her nose sprayed blood. He bent down next to her, yanking her head up by her hair and spitting in her bloody face. "You will pay," he spoke slowly as he let her head fall back to the ground. "You have no idea the power I control. Are you ready to meet your destiny?"

Destiny.

Of course. She had been destined to find the Sword of Elilah. Atarius had told her she belonged to a bloodline that was meant to retrieve the sword and to use the sword. That was her destiny.

But Spike seemed to know what she was doing as she reached for it, trying to find the hilt of the sword strapped to her back. He caught her hand with his foot, pinning it down against the ground.

She tried to push back against him but suddenly found her wrists tightened against the stone floor. Spike had created metal cuffs which now shackled her down. She tried to use her magic to will them away, but he was just as focused as she. No matter how much she thrashed about, her wrists were secured. She was unable to reach the Sword of Elilah.

His right hand lowered to her chin, lifting it ever so slightly. His left hand did not reach towards her. It reached towards his own head. His fingers wrapped tightly around his long hair. With an effortful pull, it ripped away.

Spike was completely bald.

He let the hair fall away—a wig.

She stared up at him, up at his exposed head. It was the sign. The sign that he had taken the Oath of Evil. The sign that he had sold his soul to Carve for power. The sign that he could use dark magic. "I want you to watch what I do to you," he whispered.

A tear escaped her eyes, remembering the last time he had said that to her.

CHAPTER 26

Auni and Tara exchanged another glance. What were they going to do? Somehow Auni had thought their plan would go much smoother. Now, though, they were surrounded by four guards and were being escorted to a residence hall which would be full of many more guards.

"Alright," one of the men spoke up as they turned the corner, expecting to show them the list of guards on duty. To their surprise, a man sat slumped on the ground in front of the main residence hall doors, a loud commotion going on inside.

"Kazzak?" Tara blurted out. Fang, too, let out a bark.

Auni seized the opportunity. In one swift, fluid motion he pulled the knives attached to his crutches free and slammed them into the two guards next to him. The crutches fell to the floor, but Auni stayed standing, using the knives and soldiers' bodies to hold up his weight.

Tara let out a shocked scream. Fang reacted quickly. The wolf tackled one of the four guards to the ground, ripping at his throat.

The last guard drew a sword and swung at Auni, who dropped to the ground. He pulled the knife loose from one of the slumped over soldiers and used it to block the soldier's next attack. He couldn't get himself back on his feet, but grabbed at the man's ankle, trying to throw him off balance.

Fang came to his rescue, forcing the man to the ground and tearing at him.

"Help Kazzak!" Auni shouted as he stabbed the man a final time and checked to ensure all four soldiers were dead.

She did as she was told. "Tara?" Kazzak asked weakly.

"Don't worry, move your hand," she instructed. Auni glanced over at them. He hated watching Tara heal, but he couldn't look away. Taking in a deep breath she placed her hand over Kazzak's bloody wound. The healing began almost immediately. She screamed out in pain.

Auni winced. He watched the sweat drip from her face. The tears well in her eyes. "Tara," he whispered. She continued to scream. "Tara, you need to rest!" He scooted himself over to her and grabbed her by the shoulder. "Tara!"

She relented and fell back. What started as a relieved sigh turned into a sob. "That's all I can do," she muttered again and again. The skin had pulled together and healed over the wound, but Auni knew she couldn't do anything about his blood loss or any internal organ damage. Kazzak stayed where he was, slumped against the door, trying to hold it in place against the people ramming into it.

"We need to get out of here," Auni said quickly, giving Tara's hand a squeeze. It seemed to bring her back to reality, and she nodded several times. "Here, put this in the door." He slid one of his crutches over to them. Men began breaking out of other doors further down the hallway. "Now!" he added forcefully.

Tara slid the crutch inside the double door handles, blocking it from being opened. Kazzak weakly pulled himself to his feet.

"Hurry," Auni reminded them both.

Kazzak pointed to one of the torches nearby. "Tara, start a fire with the oil." His voice was slow and quiet. It took him several breaths to talk at all, and a bit of blood bubbled out of his mouth as he did so. Auni winced again. Kazzak's face was deathly white. "Fang," he spoke softly. The wolf came to his side, recognizing his name.

Fang trusted Kazzak. Twice they had worked together to save Sheik's life. And now Fang would have to help save theirs. "Easy, easy," Kazzak repeated. "Auni, you need to climb on Fang." He was down a crutch and wouldn't make it out alive on his own. Kazzak gave him a steady hand and he let his body relax across Fang's back. The wolf seemed to understand and stayed still and calm.

Tara poured the oil, then dipped the torch to it. Suddenly they were surrounded by flames. "Let's go," Auni insisted.

"Tara!" Kazzak turned to her. "I need you to help me walk." More blood gurgled from his mouth. She ran to his side and let him lean against her. "Get us out of here," he whispered quietly. Auni and

Tara exchanged another glance. Even though his wound was healed, they both knew something was wrong.

Kazzak was still dying.

※

Spike placed his hand around Sheik's neck. Somehow she knew it would be the most painful thing she had ever experienced.

But the pain didn't come.

His body froze, his eyes wide.

"Let go of her!" a voice screamed. It was Jesse. Spike turned around, an arrow jutting out of his back. Relief washed over Sheik. Spike rose to his feet carefully. "I'll kill you," Jesse yelled, aiming the arrow at Spike's heart.

"You cannot kill me," Spike scoffed. "I am a god compared to you." Jesse took his shot, but Spike warped the arrow in the same manner he had Sheik's, rendering it ineffective.

Spike loosed several stones from the ceiling with his magic. They tumbled on top of Jesse, and he crumpled to the ground in a pile of rubble.

But in that instant, Spike lost his concentration on the metal cuffs bolting Sheik's wrists to the ground. And before he had realized his mistake, Sheik had seized the opportunity and reached back for the Sword of Elilah, grabbing it by the hilt.

The power ruptured within her. The energy she had felt in her dream so long ago. Like a thunderous clap of lightning reverberating through every fiber of her being. Like the most intense flame and the most frigid cold. Her blood beat with a painful adrenaline.

Pulling the sword free, it no longer shined bright. It had no more need to—it had been found and was resting in the hands of its rightful owner.

This was her destiny.

Wrapping both hands around the hilt, she discovered that she was not controlling the power of the sword, but that it was controlling her. It pulled her to her feet. It told her to strike. Spike smirked, assuming she was using just another ordinary weapon. But as he focused on it with his magic, trying to disarm her, he found he could not.

His confidence gave way to fear.

The blade cut into his face, marring one of the only parts of his body that had no scars. It split his skin, his lip, his nose, his eye. He fell to the ground, clutching his cheek, trying to hold the skin together as the blood poured out.

With the last of his strength, he focused his magic on the ceiling, letting loose as many stones as he could. As several rocks rained down on her, the sword lent her the strength to shatter them with several mighty blows.

Then the sword delivered to her its last command.

In one swift and powerful blow, Sheik planted the blade through Spike's skull.

It smashed through his bone and echoed as it struck the solid stone floor.

When she released the hilt she fell backwards, stumbling from the sudden loss of the sword's power. The godly strength had felt natural in the moment, but now she felt terribly weak. Drained. Slowly her senses came back to her. The beast-like brutality of the sword drifted out of her mind.

"Jesse!"

He was her first thought. She rushed to his side, abandoning the sword, and cleared the stones and debris off him. "Jesse," she whispered, placing her head on his chest. Several impatient moments passed before she heard what she had hoped so dearly to hear.

Breathing.

"Jesse, Jesse!" she shook him desperately, hoping to wake him.

His eyes flickered. "Sheik?"

"Oh thank Elilah!" She hugged him tightly. "Are you alright?"

He nodded, rubbing his head. "I don't know. My head hurts. It's a little hard to see. Is that man—?"

"He's dead." Then it hit her.

Spike was dead.

She had killed him. Relief washed over her. She was free. Free of all the nightmares. Free of all the thoughts of people he would hurt. Free. "He's dead," she repeated again, a small smile forming on her face. It was over. She had really triumphed. Part of her wanted to scream out right then and there, to announce it for everyone to hear.

Jesse let out a sigh, rubbing his head again. "Sorry I wasn't able to help much. Help me up?"

She stood up herself, then stuck out her hand for him. "What are you talking about? You saved my life!" She paused. "Did you kill Grathios?"

He shook his head, accepting her hand and using her to pull himself to his feet. "Nope. By the time I reached the top of the stairs he was awake from all the commotion. He was running. I was gonna chase after him but I thought, why? Do I want him dead to actually help people or do I just want revenge? 'Cause if I really wanted to help someone, I should've stayed to help you. So I turned back."

"Really?" She was glad he had. But part of her wanted him to get his revenge. She wanted him to feel the relief she was feeling now.

Picking up Kazzak's damp cloak that had fallen when she drew the Sword of Elilah, she pulled the sword free from Spike's body and rewrapped it without touching it. She didn't want to touch it with her bare skin again. Not unless she absolutely needed to. As much as the power made her feel indestructible, it was a terrifying feeling being out of control. "Well thank you for coming back for me," she added, strapping the sword onto her quiver. "You really did save my life."

He smiled as they continued their walk back the way they had come. "Anytime. I know it seems strange since we've only known each other for a few days, but you feel almost like family." For some reason, it didn't seem strange at all to her. "Maybe it's just because I've never met another elf before."

"Actually," she paused, "I kind of feel the same way." Jesse gave her a great big smile. "I lost my memory a few years back. So who knows, maybe we are family. Anything is possible."

He let out a small laugh. "Really? Hmm." He was skeptical, but quietly added, "Who knows."

An awkward silence passed by. "I'm sorry you weren't able to kill him."

Jesse merely shrugged. "There was part of me that just wanted him dead to have my revenge, and I don't like that part. I'm glad it's gone. Then there's another part of me that wanted him off the throne. I think that part got what it wanted." Sheik raised an eyebrow. "When I saw him, he was running. He knows someone's trying to kill him, and he's obviously afraid he's not strong enough to fight back. He won't stay here as the general anymore."

Maybe. It was certainly possible, especially if Kazzak was able to wipe out many of his soldiers. But it left countless questions unanswered. Where would he run to? Who would take over the city next? But as long as Jesse found solace in knowing Grathios had lost his power, she was satisfied, too.

"It's weird," he continued. "Now that I'm not bent on revenge, I don't really know what to do, where to go."

The anxiety hit her. "Me either." Now that Spike was dead, what would any of them do? "But wherever I go, you're more than welcome to come."

Jesse smiled back. "I may just take you up on that. Oh yeah," he added suddenly, after a long silence. "Here." He pulled a small book out of his satchel. "You forgot it, back by the statue. I wasn't sure if you meant to or not."

"Oh! Yeah, it's weird, see—" she began explaining until they spotted some guards and she instantly stopped talking. Jesse tucked the book back away as they cautiously approached the commotion.

Fighting. Jesse readied his bow, but Sheik's had been rendered useless. Turning a few corners, following the sound, they spotted Kazzak, Auni, Tara, and Fang, fighting several guards.

Jesse immediately released an arrow while Sheik manipulated the soldiers' weapons with her magic. With the surprise assault from behind, the battle ended in a matter of seconds. "Auni, Tara, Fang!" Sheik cried. "What are you guys doing here?" Then she noticed Kazzak, covered in blood. "Kazzak! Are you okay?" She rushed to his side, taking Tara's place in helping him walk.

"We need to get out of here, half of the castle is on fire," Tara quickly explained. She helped Auni back onto Fang. "Come on, we know the way out."

<hr>

Sheik placed her hand over Kazzak's shirtless side. "He's not getting better. It's not just blood loss." Several hours had passed since their siege on the castle. They had wanted to keep moving in case the soldiers were tracking them. But now, deciding they were plenty far away, they finally stopped for Jesse and Kazzak's injuries. Jesse insisted his head would be fine and he just needed to sleep and let his eyes rest. Kazzak, though, continued to grow worse.

Tara was sobbing. "What am I supposed to do? You cannot heal things on the inside!"

"You can't?"

"Well I could not heal the inside of Auni's leg."

Auni chimed in, "Because my leg is broken all the way. It might as well not be attached."

"And since Kazzak's organs aren't separate from his body," Sheik finished the thought, "well theoretically you should be able to heal them if there's a simple puncture."

Tara threw her hands up in the air. "I don't know how! How am I supposed to heal what I cannot see?" She had been trying for half an hour to no avail and Sheik could tell it was weighing on her. Not only had the healing exhausted her, but so had the guilt of making no progress.

Sheik rubbed her temples, trying to think of a solution. How could one heal what they couldn't see? Could you use magic on things you couldn't see?

Yes. Of course you could—she had done it herself.

The night they had assassinated King Garret. She had picked the lock with her magic to get into King Garret's room. She couldn't see the pins on the inside of the lock, but she had manipulated them all the same. "I know how. Tara, you can do this."

She grabbed Tara's hand and placed it where hers had been. "Feel his organs. Imagine them. It's going to hurt him, but you need to find out where he's wounded. Use your mind to reach inside. If you can get a clear image of what it looks like, where the wound is specifically, you may be able to help him." That was how Sheik had managed to pick the lock.

Tara winced and pressed into Kazzak's side. The man, who had been unconscious moments ago, awoke with a yell. "What are you doing?"

"Hold on," Tara swallowed. Sheik watched the tears stream from her eyes, feeling the man's pain. Kazzak's screaming continued as Tara pressed down on different areas. "There! I felt the blood!"

It was another moment longer before Tara shrieked and Kazzak's screaming finally stopped. "There," she announced, "I did it!" Her face was wet from sweat and tears, but she beamed with pride.

Kazzak tried to sit up only for Sheik to push him back down. "You still need to rest. You lost a lot of blood." He sighed, but gave in, closing his eyes as he lay back down, whispering a quiet thank you to Tara.

———◆———

Waiting for wounds to heal, the group stayed where they were, merely trading off on keeping watch. Jesse was feeling better in no time, his vision completely back to normal by the first day. Sheik insisted he take it easy, but he disobeyed her when her back was turned, sneaking off to go hunting or bring over some water or firewood.

Kazzak healed a bit slower. His face remained pale and his body weak for several days. Jesse made him various teas and hunted lots of meat, reassuring everyone that it would help him get to feeling better in no time. Sheik questioned how he seemed to know so much, but he merely shrugged, saying his mom taught him everything he knew. "Well how did she know so much then?" Sheik asked.

"My mom knew she had to give birth to me by herself. She did a lot of research in nine months," he said with a chuckle.

And she had taught him well. The boy knew how to hunt and fish, knew which fruits and vegetables were edible, and how to cook and prepare them all. He could tan deer hide, fashion his own clothes, mix medicinal herbs, get a fire going, build a shelter, and knew how to read. He impressed her more and more with every day she spent with him.

"Jesse!" she called out, needing help with the fishing line he had set up. The sound of Kazzak's pan flute caught her off guard and she braced herself to begin wincing at any moment. The man had a knack for hitting the wrong note, even on such a simple instrument.

To her surprise, the sound came across smoothly and she followed it a few steps further.

"Jesse?"

He was comfortably positioned on a tree branch, the pan flute in one hand and a book in the other. "Hey Sheik," he called down to her before returning to his music.

"How come you've got Kazzak's pan flute?" she asked, pulling herself onto an adjacent branch.

"He gave it to me." Sheik's eyes made him tell the rest of the story. "Well, I saw it in his pack and was curious. He played it for me and I blurted out that it sounded atrocious," he admitted sheepishly. "I thought that's how it was supposed to sound! That maybe it was a bird whistle or something."

Sheik laughed. "Some bird that would be."

"Well, he threw it at me and told me to see if I could make a better sound on it. And I did," he chuckled, playing a quick line. "See? So he said I could keep it."

She laughed again. "It's better in your hands than his, I suppose. What are you reading?" she asked next, pointing to the book in his other hand.

He set down the pan flute to hold up the book. It was the journal they had found in the cave. She had completely forgotten about it once again.

"What does it say?"

He shrugged. "I told you, I can't read elven. I'm just looking at the pictures of the sword." He climbed down and handed the book up to her.

"It's not in elven, though," she explained. She recognized it, though she couldn't fathom how. How could she have memories of some book, long lost in a cave? A book written neither in human nor elven tongue. She thumbed through its pages. Unexpectedly, she came across a word she knew. "That's strange."

"What?"

She climbed down from the branch to show him the book. Pointing at the word, she explained, "That says 'war.'"

"So?"

"So? So it's not in elven. I shouldn't be able to read this—I don't even know what language it's in."

He gave her another casual shrug. "Your name isn't elven, either."

"My name? What?"

"Sheik. It's not an elven name." She had never even thought about it before. "So maybe you weren't raised by elves and that's why you can read another language."

"What?" she asked again in complete surprise. "No, Atarius named me Sheik, it's not my real name." He wouldn't know who Atarius was, but she didn't bother explaining. Wait—why did Atarius name her a name that wasn't elven? Did Jesse really know what he was talking about? "You're messing with me, right? How would you even know, you don't speak elven."

He shook his head. "My mom knew a bit. She taught me their alphabet. The sounds of your name aren't in it."

Sheik stared at him a long time. It was partially true. The modern alphabet didn't have those sounds. But there were still ways to write her name with older characters. Jesse just didn't fully understand the language. She didn't bother explaining the complexities to him, so instead she turned back to the book.

Flipping open to the first page, she began reading, somehow knowing the language. It was like the first time she had spoken in human tongue without realizing she had been fluent all along. "All that is known of the Sword of Elilah through history and prophecy is recorded here. The language of this book has been taught only to me and my brother's descendants. The most recent prophecy states that our descendants will find the sword. By reading this, you have proven yourselves to be the ones destined to recover the Sword of Elilah," Sheik read aloud.

She was about to continue when Jesse interrupted her. "Read that again."

"The most recent prophecy states that our descendants will find the sword. By reading this, you have proven yourselves to be the ones destined to recover the Sword of Elilah," she repeated, enunciating it slowly and trying to consider what it meant.

"We're the ones that found the sword," Jesse explained. "The destined through prophecy ones."

"So?"

"You can read the language," he continued. "Taught only to whoever and his brother's descendants. Don't you get it? Either the author or his brother is your father! And if I'm the other one that was destined to find the sword, then we're related!"

"But you can't read the book."

"Because I never knew my father. Maybe he was supposed to teach me though."

She rubbed her forehead in disbelief. Since the fire, she had always assumed her entire family was dead. Now, her relative stood before her. A smile spread across her face. "That would make us cousins!"

Sheik heard the crunch of twigs. "Jesse?"

"Nope, it's me." Kazzak stepped out into the open.

"Kazzak!" she exclaimed. "What are you doing out here?" She was rather far from where they had set up camp, mostly so she could get some peace and quiet while she was trying to read the mysterious book.

He grinned. "I'm fine." She had to admit, he was looking better. His skin was back to its normal color and he no longer seemed sickly. "I actually wanted to make sure you were fine."

"Me?"

"Yes you," he chuckled. "Can I sit?"

"Of course." She turned to move the core of an apple she had been nibbling on as she read.

"What's this?" he asked, taking it from her as he sat. "Real food? Not magic?" His eyebrows rose with curiosity. "Since when?"

"A few days," she said proudly. "Elilah is about living like we were created to." Taking a final bite of the apple, she finished, "Humans and elves were both created to eat, just like any other animal. It took watching Jesse gathering all the countless fruits he knows about for me to realize Elilah has provided us with all the food we need. Atarius can make all the rules he wants, but Elilah is about being free."

"Atarius," he repeated, glancing off towards nothing in particular. "He's what I wanted to talk to you about."

She averted her eyes. Atarius? It wasn't a conversation she wanted to have with anyone, let alone Kazzak.

"What are you going to do? Spend the rest of your life avoiding the person you love?"

She took a long pause. "I don't know."

"Go home," he said softly.

"What?"

"Go home. Talk to him. Find out how he feels about you. That's where you belong."

Sheik's stomach turned. "What's that supposed to mean?" Kazzak stumbled over his words, but Sheik continued, "What—I'm not one of you? I don't get to stay? The war's over now, so you all stay together and I have to go back to the forest?"

His eyebrows furrowed defensively, like he might shout back at her. But he said nothing. His face went calm. "I know it's where you want to be." He paused for a second, letting his words soak in. "You belong here. In the forest. I know how happy you've been. Even before we killed Spike. It's like you're... at peace. Right where you want to be."

Her eyes started to water. He was right. And she hated it. But he was right about all of it. She missed Atarius. And the second she felt the shade of the forest, inhaled the scent of pine in the air, heard the chatter of birds and chipmunks, it had all felt right. She was home.

"So, what? We just part ways, never see each other again? Just pretend this past year never happened?" She tried to look at him, but he was a watery blur.

He put his arm around her. "Of course not. Sheik, I'm never going to forget you." She leaned into him and he buried her in a hug. "Not in a hundred million years."

"I don't want to leave you." She tried to regain control of herself, pulling away and wiping her eyes. "You're like family to me."

"We are family. But it's okay to have more than one family." He hooked a loose strand of her hair behind her ear. "We'll still see each other. We'll visit. I promise." He gave her a smile. His warm, carefree smile. "I love you, Sheik. But," he hesitated, drawing out a pause. She knew what he was going to say. *But you don't love me back.* It wasn't entirely true—she did love him. She just loved Atarius more. And that wasn't fair to Kazzak. "I just want you to be happy," he finally concluded.

She stared back at him. He was smiling at her, but the crinkles in his eyes held terrible sadness. And for perhaps the first time in their relationship, Sheik stopped thinking about herself. "Will you be okay?"

"Yeah," he nodded. "I will."

Sheik sighed and gave him a half hug, melting into him. They held each other for a moment, lost in emotion. Sad, but full of love. When he let go, she tried her best to release everything she was feeling. "So what will you do? Spike is dead, his army has fallen, Isandas will soon have another monarch. So what now?"

He laughed. "Well, I'm a war hero now, aren't I?" he joked, stroking his chin lightly, as if pondering his endless opportunities.

"No, I don't know, really." He shrugged. "I think just go back to Calert."

"Really?" She tossed him a teasing smile. "That's it?"

"Why not? It's going home, same as you. Besides, we'll be nice and close that way."

She nodded, trying to remember how long it had taken her to travel from Atarius' village to the Great River. "I'd like that. I can come visit. And you will too?"

He gave her his smile. "Of course. I'll always be there for you."

CHAPTER 27

I t was a tearful goodbye.

Sheik didn't imagine it could be any other way. She had spent the past year with these people. She had come to love all of them like family. They had all been to the abyss and back with each other.

Sheik and Kazzak broke the news to Tara and Auni together. She needed to go back to her old village. And they understood. But they were still heartbroken.

They all agreed to make a habit of meeting every so often at the southernmost bridge. The summer solstice would be their first meeting. It was nearing late spring and so the solstice was not far off.

She tried to keep that in mind as she said her goodbyes. They would see each other again in only a couple short months. With a final hug to Auni, Tara, and Kazzak, she turned and waved goodbye.

Jesse had happily agreed to go with Sheik to her old village. He was eager to live among elves, but she warned him that they may not stay long if Atarius did not return her feelings. He continuously assured

Sheik with a lighthearted chuckle that Atarius was probably "madly in love" with her.

And so the young half elven boy urged her to teach him the language in preparation for living with elves. In return, Jesse taught her about some of the edible and medicinal plants that she had never even heard of. Between their lessons, practicing archery, and running around with Fang, the two never seemed to stop talking and getting to know each other.

He told her all about his mother and how much she had taught him and how deeply he missed her since she had passed. Sheik told him about all the adventures she'd had with Kazzak and Tara and Auni. Where they had traveled, who they had met, what they had accomplished. She also confided in him how much she had missed her village, the simple life.

She was not certain where precisely the hidden town was, only knowing its general whereabouts. They had found and stuck to a path that had been frequently traversed, made obvious by the way the underbrush had been pushed down by countless feet. But soon, they came to a fork in the road.

"South or west?" Jesse asked

She wasn't sure. They were getting close. They were probably only a few more days' travel from the village. "Fang?" Maybe he knew.

But she looked down at him to find his fur was standing on edge. "What is it?" she whispered. His growl grew louder as he wandered a few paces off, sniffing the ground.

Suddenly she felt the small poke of a knife pressed against her back. "State your name and your business."

Her eyes snapped shut in disbelief. How could she have let her guard down? No one ever snuck up on her! The only person who ever could was— "Farin?"

He lowered the knife away from her back. "Sheik?" His weapon fell to the ground as he wrapped his arms around her, knocking the wind out of her with his unexpected hug. "Dear Elilah, are you okay? Where have you been? I've missed you so much!" he exclaimed all at once as he released her. Fang almost knocked Farin to the ground as he leapt on him, licking him with excitement.

She laughed. "I've missed you, too. I've been all over the place. It's quite the tale, really." Clearing her throat, she introduced Jesse. "This is my cousin, Jesse. He doesn't speak elven very well yet. Jesse, this is my friend Farin."

"Cousin?" Farin asked, watching the half elf extend his hand. "What are you talking about?"

Sheik chuckled and lowered Jesse's hand for him. "Elves don't shake hands," she explained in human tongue before turning back to Farin. "It's a long story."

He nodded at the boy with a smile. "Pleased to meet you. Well come on!" he grabbed Sheik and began pulling her. "If we run fast we can make it back to the village in a day or so! Everyone will be so excited to see you again!"

She laughed and pried his hand off her. "I'm quite content walking, really. Why are you even so far away from the village?" They had to be far away; nothing seemed familiar yet.

"Oh, I was looking for Atarius," he explained quite simply.

"What do you mean? Where's he gone?"

He smiled his classic Farin grin. "Looking for you. He's been gone nearly three weeks, so I came looking for him." The sachem was never supposed to stray more than one week's distance from the village.

Her jaw dropped. "You're joking."

"Not at all." His voice was serious, but he couldn't stop smiling. "He's gone all the time. Ever since you left. At first it was just one-week trips, but the past few months? He's been gone more than he's been here. Come on, I'll help you get settled back in while he's gone. Your friend—er, cousin—too!"

⸻◆⸻

Atarius sighed as he continued towards the village. He had been visiting neighboring elven villages for the past eighteen days. He had hoped that one of the many nearby towns might have at least heard of Sheik. But alas, no luck again. He nodded hellos to some of the villagers as he spotted them here and there, but none of them approached him. He supposed they could read the expression of sorrow on his face.

Farin leapt down from a tree branch just in front of him. "Hey there!"

"Hey Farin," he replied easily. Farin was one of the only people he didn't mind seeing him sad. "Anything happen in my absence?"

The scrawny elf shrugged. "Not a lot, really. I have a surprise for you though!"

Atarius raised an eyebrow. "Oh really?" He gave a slight smile. Though he couldn't imagine any present cheering him up, it was kind of Farin to go out of his way to try. "And what might that be?" he asked, forcing his voice to sound enthusiastic for Farin's sake.

"You'll have to go find out!" Farin replied in an enunciated sing-songy voice. "It's in your throne room!"

⁕

Sheik waited impatiently on Atarius' throne. Farin had spotted him coming and had run back to tell her to wait there. She couldn't help but be nervous. As much as Farin had built it up like Atarius had missed her, she found it hard to believe him. And as much as she had missed Atarius, she didn't want her life to go back to the way it had been.

The way he kept his feelings for her secret. She could never read his emotions. It seemed something was always holding him back from telling her what he thought of her. The way he had kept her in the dark. How he had treated her like a warrior preparing for battle rather than someone he loved. As much as she respected his decorum and his devotion to Elilah, still part of her just wanted him to sweep her off her feet with affection.

She felt her hair for about the tenth time, making sure it wasn't messy. Jesse had rolled his eyes at her the second time she had asked him if she looked okay. By the third time, he merely laughed and walked away, tired of reassuring her.

They had only just arrived the day before. Jesse had been introduced to everyone but had quickly forgotten the many names. She remembered how difficult it was to meet everyone at once, and imagined it was even harder not knowing the language very well. But, with what a quick learner he was, she was certain he would be practically fluent in a month.

"I'm going, I'm going," Atarius laughed, just outside. Farin was urging him to move faster. Sheik's heart pounded, listening to him climb the trunk of the tree.

Questions flooded through her mind. How would he react? Did he really miss her? Would he want her to stay? She stood up. Or should she be sitting? But before she had time to sit back down, his head came into view.

Their eyes locked and his mouth hung open with shock. "Sheik?"

She bit down on her lip nervously. "Atarius," she replied simply.

"Sheik, dear Elilah it's really you!" He pulled himself into the room and cleared the short distance between them in an instant. His arms wrapped around her and for once his voice held no secrets as he choked back tears. "I'm so sorry. For everything. I've missed you so much."

"Really?" she replied weakly.

She leaned her head against his shoulder, but he pulled away, ending the embrace. Moving his hand from her waist to her chin, he lifted her head up lightly. "The second after you left, I realized. Sheik, I'm in love with you. And I've been searching for you ever since to let you know."

Sheik savored his breath on her lips, awestruck by his romantic words. "I'm in love with you, too."

Atarius leaned forward, his lips pressing softly against hers as his arms wrapped around her once again. As she returned the kiss and relished in the pure rapture of his embrace, she decided the news of traveling the continent, defeating a tyrant, finding her cousin, and retrieving the Sword of Elilah could wait.

Everything could wait.

◆

Tara slammed the book down. "Clause one hundred and nineteen. You do not have to be a Mainlander to own property. My legal consultant here has read the entire document," she explained, "if you have any questions regarding the specific clause, you may direct them to him."

"But he's a slave!"

"Wrong!" she shouted back. "He *was* a slave. I purchased his freedom a month ago, the documents are right here." She pushed forward a folder full of papers.

"How do we even know he's the man's son? Mr. Dubose is dead!"

An older woman stepped forward. "I will testify to that," she muttered. "My name is Mrs. Liadan Eileen Dubose. The boy is my husband's son. I would not ruin my name and accept an Islander child as my husband's blood if it were a lie."

As insulting as it was, Tara could not help but smile. "Any further questions?" she asked, raising an eyebrow. The man stammered for a moment before shaking his head and sitting back down. Tara, too, took a seat, along with her mother.

"Auni, please rise." The boy stood up, leaning on a new pair of crutches Kazzak had bought for him.

They had stayed with Kazzak for a while in Calert, continuing their life as it had been before. But everything changed on the summer solstice; the day they met Sheik on the southernmost bridge. Once again, Sheik inspired them to do something that completely altered the course of their life.

She had encouraged Tara to write to her family.

At first, it had seemed an absurd suggestion. Tara had no desire to ever see her father again. He was a rapist. He owned slaves. He was a cruel, selfish, hollow man. And Tara's mother was no better. The day she left with Auni had been the day she had sworn to never see them again.

But Sheik reminded her of the great things that Auni and Tara had accomplished from the edge of Vesdar all the way to the Tasvran Mountains. If they could change the course of history, maybe they could change things back in their homeland, too. At the very least, they could attempt to free the rest of the slaves on her father's plantation.

After exchanging letters, Tara learned that her father had passed away. Having had no sons, and with women being unable to own property in Omris, her mother had lost their land and slaves to the district, or, in reality, the district's governor.

But Auni was the rightful heir.

Traveling back into the peninsula of Omris, where slavery was legal, Tara purchased Auni's freedom. The two spoke to the governor, the new owner of their property, explaining the situation. He refused to return the land, and Tara immediately contacted a magistrate to hear their case.

"I have decided the plantation be placed in your hands," the magistrate announced, "along with all of the servants—"

Auni cleared his throat. "Actually, your Honor," he interjected nervously. "I wish for the slaves to be freed."

Everyone gasped but Tara. She beamed with pride.

The magistrate looked at him carefully. "You may want to consult with a legal representative, first, to understand the financial implications—"

Auni shook his head. "No, I'm positive in my decision, your Honor. I would rather live in poverty than in wealth earned by slaves. The workers may continue as paid laborers, but they will never serve me as a slave."

The magistrate studied him for a moment before responding. "Very well, I will have the proper documents forwarded to you. Dismissed."

Tara nearly knocked Auni to the ground with her hug. "We won! We won! Come now, let's go celebrate!" Auni struggled to hug her back while holding onto his crutches.

They went directly to the plantation, Tara inquiring about his plans for his new property. He shrugged. "For the property? No plans, really. For the nation, though, I've got some ideas."

She laughed. "Oh really? What might that be?"

"I plan to make Omris just as free as the rest of the northern lands."

She smirked at the thought. But honestly, she believed it was possible. Together they could rid the country of slavery. After all they had done with Sheik and Kazzak, anything was possible. Auni swung open the door to the main house.

To their surprise, a cloaked man was standing inside.

"About time I found you two," he said as he lowered his hood, revealing his face. They gasped. Taking a step forward, he pulled out a letter and extended it towards Tara. "An invitation."

⸻ ⬥ ⸻

"And the winner is the Blinding Rogue!"

Kazzak pulled off his helmet and hopped out of the arena. He had grown famous in Calert. Sheik's countless war tactics had given him an idea for a new fighting style. Instead of relying on strength, like the other fighters, he used speed and every ounce of trickery to his advantage.

He kicked up dirt, stole opponents' weapons. The tactic that had earned him his nickname, though, was a large shield made with reflective, mirrored glass. As light reflected off the shield, his opponents were temporarily blinded.

He hadn't had to surrender from a battle yet. Soon, he had made his way to the top in several championships and people were tossing out nicknames. Blinding Rogue seemed to have stuck. He went and collected his money from the table.

"Fifty more to go," he mumbled to himself, counting out the money. Despite the wealth and fame he had acquired, he led a fairly simple life. He had moved out of the ratty, abandoned houses and bought himself a nice cottage on the outskirts of the city, close to the Great River and the forest beyond.

It was a peaceful escape from children wanting his autograph, beggars wanting his money, women wanting his attention, and burly warriors wanting a duel. Rumors swirled around about him and how he had liberated Etmos and killed the tyrant Spike. His humble yet mysterious response was always, "I may have had a thing or two to do with it."

When he wasn't carrying his distinguishable mirrored shield, few recognized him. He could pass through the city easily, like any other citizen. And that was how he had managed to meet the lovely lady Mariel. It had been refreshing for someone to be interested in him without him wearing the mask of the Blinding Rogue, to be fond of him without having ulterior motives of money or glamorized ideas of fame.

The couple had fallen for each other quite fast. He had met her just before Tara and Auni had left for the peninsula, and only recently had he revealed his other, more well-known identity to her. Upon discovering that he was the Blinding Rogue, she had insisted they continue a low-key lifestyle. And that was when he knew that she was the one.

He began saving for a wedding ring the very next day. "Fifty more," he mumbled again with a smile, winding through the crowds, giving a quick nod to those who recognized him.

The leaves on the trees around his house were beginning to change color, a rusty green. Autumn was just around the corner. "I'm home!" he called out, opening the door.

Mariel had just moved in and was still unpacking. "Hi Honey," she said with a smile, giving him a quick peck on the lips. He unbuckled the straps of his armor and pulled it off, putting it away in a chest near the door along with his shield.

Following her into the kitchen, he wrapped his arms around her waist, holding her close to him and kissing her neck. "I have to make dinner, Kazzak," she said after a moment of savoring his kisses.

"Make it later," he joked.

She turned around in his arms and gave him a long kiss. But in a flash he pulled away. A floorboard creaked. "Did you hear that?" he whispered, grabbing a knife from the kitchen counter.

Sure enough, a cloaked figure was in the entrance way of their house. Seeing Kazzak, he lowered his hood. Mariel gasped, but Kazzak let out a sigh of relief. "Jesse! You almost gave us a heart attack!"

The half elven boy laughed. "Sorry, didn't mean to. You left your door wide open, though, you know."

Kazzak chuckled, realizing he had indeed. "What in Ziad's name are you even doing here?" Jesse pulled a letter out of his cloak and handed it to him. "What's this?"

"Your invitation."

"Invitation?" Kazzak asked, raising an eyebrow as he examined it. "Invitation to what?"

"To the wedding."

EPILOGUE

Sheik began to stir as Atarius' hand ran softly through her hair. "Good morning," he whispered in her ear.

She moved her head to face him and put her hand on his cheek. "Good morning." He leaned his head against hers and closed his eyes. Sheik laid her arm across his bare chest, snuggling closer to him for a moment. It was cold, late autumn.

Though she preferred warmer weather, she didn't mind the season. It represented change. Things had certainly been changing. In fact, that was why she had wanted her wedding to be during the season.

The wedding had been towards the beginning of autumn, before the cold had set in. It was done up beautifully. All the elves had gathered the remaining summer flowers and decorated the woods with them, ornately hanging them from the trees and along the meadow floor. Atarius had worn his finest suit and mantle, while Sheik had designed and dyed, with Jesse's help, a beautiful wedding dress. Everyone had attended, including Tara, Auni, Kazzak, and Kazzak's fiancée Mariel.

Everything had been perfect. The forest had been lit up with the decorative flowers and the naturally bright yellow and orange trees. All her friends were together, the simple ceremony composed of their short speeches wishing the couple well. Even Fang had participated, carrying the jar of purification, a crucial piece of the wedding where they washed their hands to symbolically cleanse themselves.

It had been the most perfect day of her life.

Atarius interrupted her thoughts, climbing out of bed and pulling on a shirt. "I'm going to go get something to eat, you want anything?"

Get.

While the elves still frequently created their food with their magic, they now ate natural food as well. Sheik had convinced Atarius. Justar was about creating laws and rules to govern society, but Elilah just wanted people to live as they were created to live. Elilah had presented all animals with food, and it was not wrong to accept her gift.

To Sheik's surprise, Atarius was open minded. He listened, took the input of the entire village, and declared the old rule obsolete.

"Sure, just an apple or something." He nodded and scrambled out of the hollowed-out room, climbing down the ladder etched into the side of the trunk. In only a moment he was back, a woven bag full of food wrapped around his neck.

"Here you are," he smiled, handing her the apple as he settled back into bed with her. She curled up next to him once again, using his body to warm her.

"Thanks." She took several bites of the apple before setting it on the small table to the side of the bed. "Any plans for the day?"

"Still working on your new bow." Her old one had been broken above the grip, leaving only the carving of her name still intact. And so she had cut out the grip with the word "Sheik" and hung it on the wall of their tree. The most important piece of the bow that Atarius had once given her. That stupid, beautiful, infuriating, thoughtful bow. "And yourself?"

"I'll probably do some more translating." She had been reading the book she and Jesse had found alongside the Sword of Elilah and copying it word for word from the mysterious language to elven.

Suddenly she was reminded of something Jesse had said to her, quite a few months ago. He had told her the name Sheik was not elven. She had been meaning to ask Atarius about this, but with everything going on she had completely forgotten. "Can I ask you something?"

He sat up a bit, looking at her. His face displayed concern, worried the question would be serious. "Of course."

"Why did you name me Sheik?"

His eyebrow raised, confused. "I told you, it means lord."

"But," she trailed off for a moment, "Jesse said it wasn't an elven name. So what language is it?"

"Oh," he said, suddenly relaxing as if he understood. "It's very old elven. That's why it doesn't sound like it. It's so ancient. It's been forgotten."

"Well why name me a name of such an ancient language?"

He smiled slightly. "The word 'Sheik' came to mean lord because there was once a very important lord named Sheik. The one Elilah gave her sword to. Like Elilah entrusted it to him, I knew she would entrust it to you. I thought it only fitting to name you after him."

It made sense. Sheik was awed to share her name with such a person. Then it hit her. "Wait, I'm named after a man? You gave me a male name?"

Atarius couldn't help but laugh out loud. "Does that bother you?"

"It's like saying you think of me like a man," she retorted, teasing him. "Is that how you think of me?"

He laughed again as he wrapped an arm around her, pulling their bodies closer together and giving her a long kiss. "I think I've made it pretty obvious what I think of you. What with marrying you and all," he added with a smirk.

Sheik couldn't help but smile back as he leaned in to kiss her just behind her ear. Her arms wrapped around his back, feeling his strong muscles flexing as he adjusted his position. His kisses grew more intense as they trickled down her neck, towards her chest. Her heartbeat quickened as his breathing grew heavier, his hand wrapping gently around the back of her right thigh.

"Atarius."

He stopped. "Yes?"

"There's um," she whispered, unsure how to get the words out. She had been trying to figure out a way to tell him for the past several days now. "There's another name you've given me. A slightly more feminine one," she hinted, hoping he would understand.

He didn't. "And what's that?" he asked, raising an eyebrow.

She paused for a moment, pressing her lips together nervously. "Mother."

His jaw dropped ever so slightly. "What?" There was a long pause. "You're pregnant? I'm a father?" She said nothing but nodded slowly. He moved away from her suddenly, as if afraid she might be as fragile as glass. Then, carefully, he pulled her blanket down and lifted her shirt just high enough to expose her stomach. It wasn't any larger. His hand reached out and rested on it, waiting patiently. "I don't feel anything."

She laughed. "Of course not. It's hardly been two months."

"Oh." He pulled his hand away and returned his gaze to her eyes instead of her stomach. "You're sure?"

"I think so. I should have bled by now," she explained. "What, um, what do you think?"

"What do I think? Sheik, we're having a baby!" he exclaimed. "Dear Elilah, we're having a baby!" His arms wrapped around her, hugging her, before he instantly pulled back. "Am I okay?" he asked, worried he was not being gentle enough.

She laughed, wrapping her arms around his neck. "You're very okay," she replied with a smile, pulling him onto her. His body was tense at first, but as she gave him a long kiss, he slowly relaxed. She ended the passionate kiss softly and he pressed his lips against her forehead before laying down next to her as he had been before.

His hand reached out and found hers. Her hand felt small when it was wrapped in his. She was safe, comforted. At home.

She had found her home.

Atarius smiled and his arms draped around her. His lips moved to her ear, and he softly whispered, "We're having a baby."

She smiled and placed her hands over his, repeating the words.

"We're having a baby."

ACKNOWLEDGEMENTS

I want to thank everyone who supported my dreams and helped bring the Sword of Elilah to life! Most importantly, thank you to my brilliant wife, Liz, who has always supported me and my creativity. My deepest thanks to everyone who read and helped edit my book, including my parents Dana and Julie, my brother Jordan and sister-in-law Rachel, and my good friends Dean and Mari. Thank you also to my sensitivity readers, Maggie Jones, Gloria Botbyl, and Nikki Davenport. And thank you to everyone who brought my visions into reality through their gorgeous art: my brother-in-law David who designed the Sword of Elilah, my cover artist J. Caleb, and my Gods and Map artist Shepengul. The Sword of Elilah would not be the book it is without each and every one of you!